Around The Way Girls 2

KaShamba Williams

Thomas Long

La Jill Hunt

Around The Way Girls 2

Urban Books
6 Vanderbilt Parkway
Dix Hills, NY 11746

*This is a work of fiction. Any references or similarities to actual
events, real people, living, or dead, or to real locals are intended to
give the novel a sense of reality. Any similarity in other names,
characters, places, and incidents is entirely coincidental.*

KaShamba Williams

The Life of
Juicy
Brown

Acknowledgments
KaShamba Williams

All praise due to the Higher Being above that continues to bestow HIS mercy and grace upon me.

Much love to my family members for bearing with me during my 'underground' moments – Lamotte, Jahmya, Mecca, Mehki, Mom, Kenyatta, Mom-Mom, Angie and Pete. It's coming to pass as predicted. Thank you for your patience.

To all of my family and friends – thank you for continuing to believe in my vision – Bundy's, Prince's, Williams', Johnson's, Hairston's, Foster's, Haskin's. Gray's, Smoke's, Russ', Lammer's, Moore's, King's, Gibbs', Armstead's, Baker's, Stovall's, Wiggins', Leatherbury's, Wisher's, Wright's, Flower's, Thomas', Furrowhs', Tolson's, Steven's, White's, Chase's, Stansbury's, Carrington's, Booker's, Anderson's – the family and friend tree. You know who you are.

Thank you to all of the literary heads that have embraced me with open arms – Joanie Smith for your dedication and services, Carl Weber, Robilyn, Al-Saadiq Banks, K'wan, Trustice Gentles, Tracy Brown, T.N. Baker, Joylynn Jossel, Nikki Turner, Shannon Holmes, Brandon McCalla, Earl Cox, Reginald Hall, Vickie Stringer, Thomas Long, Shamora Renee, Victor Martin, Hickson, Lenaise Meyeil, J. Unique Shannon, Azarel, Tony Rose, Eric Gray, Marc Anthony, Relentless Aaron, Crystal Winslow, Ralph Johnson, Kalico Jones, Moody Holiday, Shawna Grundy, Karen E. Quinones Miller, Cho Woods, Angie Henderson, Lou Price, Nishwanda, Kevin Carr, Emlyn, Diane, Jewel, Dawn, Carmen, Marilyn, Shaheeda Fennell, Leondre Prince, Heather Covington, Jessica Tilles, and many more to name.

To the readers and bookclubs that keep me on my job to skillfully hone this craft – Thank you!

Please visit me at www.kashambawilliams.com or email me at precioustymesent@aol.com.

Other titles by KaShamba Williams – Blinded, Grimey, and DRIVEN.

Note To The Reader

We all have our own perception of what an Around The Way Girl is. Whether we depict her in a positive or negative demeanor, we know where to find her – around the way. What way you ask? Anyway, you turn. It may be the woman you see in the projects, the chick at club, the woman working in Corporate America, the girl from the grocery store, the girl on the block or even your grandmother, mother, aunt or sister. Whatever you deem her to be, she will always be an Around The Way Girl…

When I was approached with this venture to participate in Around The Ways Girls II, I thought, "Yes, I'd love to." It was an honor to be selected in an Urban Books project. Then, after giving it some thought, I wondered if there was really an Around The Way Girl story in me to share and not even a second after I had that thought, I quickly responded to myself, "I am an Around The Way Girl."

I pray that you enjoy this story.

Until next time,

Precioustymes

One Love, One Spirit,

KaShamba

The Life of Juicy Brown

"Earleon and Earl, what did I tell you about leaving my got-damn house like this?" I disturbed them, stepping into the house.

I could do without coming home after a hard day of work—slaving for a motel owner that didn't give two shits about me, cleaning rooms all day—to my own place that was in need of cleaning.

"Juicy, I told Earleon's lazy ass to help me clean up this mess," Earl said, dragging blankets off of the living room floor. He was making a pallet to sleep on directly in front of the television. "But she was too busy talking on the phone to Liz." He cleared the area, held the front door, spit outside and checked to see who was out on the block.

Out of my five kids—Earleon, Earl, Icelene, Elgin and Gaynelle—my twins, Earleon and Earl, were my favorite. We were damn near on the same level. I wasn't but twelve years older than they were. I couldn't do nothin' *but* keep it real with them.

I had insisted upon Earleon months ago to stop fuckin' with Liz, a.k.a Casper, the poor, white, trailer park trash chick that seemed to always come in between the tight bond that I'd developed with my daughter. She won't no good for her as a friend, but a hard head makes a soft behind, ya know. Liz would have Earleon up in rock clubs, girly bars and shit. I even thought I overheard Earleon during a telephone conversation saying that they had been to a swinger's club recently . . . Let me find out.

I was too young to be called Mom or Mommy, so I told my kids to call me on a first name basis . . . Juicy. They were cool with it, and so was I. It was more fitting for them to do so because of our slight age difference.

I wasn't born with the name Juicy. This was a name I thought I was deserving of, so I changed my government name, Deidra Brown, that I was given by my mother, to Juicy Brown. That name had more sex appeal than Deidra did. I would attract men on the strength of my name, okay. The problem I had was keepin' the men interested in my ghetto fabulous ass.

Most of the people from my old neighborhood called me Dee-Dee, a spin-off from Deidra, but I absolutely hated the name and had to check people when they addressed me by that. That's why I changed my name in the first place. I wanted to rid myself of the Deidra omen. All the Deidras I knew had fucked-up lives.

I talked with my kids openly, dealing with problems in the hood, relationships, family matters, and most importantly, getting money. Well, me, Earl and Earleon did. My other kids, sometimes they held shit in and tried to deal with their issues alone. Later they'd realize that they couldn't handle it by themselves, and let it all come out during the family meeting that we had once a month. Oh well. I loved them, but I had my own issues to deal with. I could wait to hear their tad bit of trials and tribulations. When they wanted to talk, they would. Besides, I had more serious shit on my mind, like how in the hell we were going to get out of the projects.

I got pregnant with the twins when I was 12 years old. Yes, I was young, and so was the twins' father, Juney. Both of us were virgins, experimenting and shit. We didn't know what the hell we were doing. All we knew is that we both were curious, and that desire to find out what it was like to have sex took us there.

Having the twins devastated both of us, so much so that the mothafucka Juney turned gay on my ass. I should have known he was a little too happy-acting from the start. At 13 years old, he was five-foot-four with his church shoes on. Back then, he was a cute little brown-skin sharpie with nice, sandy brown curly hair. He used to bring over his tambourine after church on Sundays to sing a church melody for me.

I got tired of it when he started bringing the tambourine over every time he came to see me, beating to the same old songs. I told him to get rid of it or stop coming to see me. Well, it must have meant more to him than me because his bitch ass stopped coming over, though his mother maintained contact with my mom regarding the twins until his mother died.

When Juney broke it off from me, I was angry for a week. But you know at that age don't much faze you, and neither did the fact that Juney paraded out of my life. I didn't see him again until I turned 18 and moved back around the way.

Nowadays, Juney wouldn't be caught with an instrument in his mouth unless it was a slab of meat from a man. His days of tambourine playing had long gone. He eventually told me after we became friends that the choir director was the one who turned him on

2

to men in a physical way, although he credited me for turning him to men emotionally when we were younger. He conveyed often that I was much too bossy *and* vulgar to be a woman and that I needed to tone it down if I wanted to get and keep a man.

He had a fuckin' nerve to be giving me advice when for many years he had been a deadbeat father to my kids. The twins didn't really know him. They knew of him and didn't care to become acquainted with him when I told them that he was gay. And he wasn't the calm, in-the-closet gay man. He was the flamboyant, girlie type. They certainly didn't want anything to do with him or connect with him at all knowing that. But could you charge that to them? They didn't have any characteristics of him . . . not to my knowledge. What would they chitchat about, the niggas that's giving their father some pipe? I mean, he could gossip with me about it and me not be biased toward him, but my kids damn sure didn't want to hear it. To tell the truth, Earl wanted to put a slug up in his ass, and from time to time, Earleon felt the same way.

On another note, though, Juney did have me occasionally wondering. Was my shit that bad to turn a mothafucka gay? Or was it always in him? It had to be him. My shit was *too juicy,* and that's a fuckin' understatement!

I met Elgin's father, Wishbone, during my pregnancy with the twins. He was a high school student that crept after the young girls. I was in middle school at the time, but was considered one of the fast girls, so I guess he figured I was wit' it. It was evident that he was after one thing—pussy—from the way he used to beg me to have sex with him. Talking 'bout he heard pregnant pussy was the best, and since I wasn't a virgin, he could at least be the first boy that gave me some "big wood" while I was pregnant.

I'd overheard a girl in school say that the most common thing a girl could do was to have sex with another boy while she was pregnant and he wasn't the baby's daddy. That's the only reason I didn't do it. However, it seemed like the further I was in my pregnancy, the hornier I became. I came close to giving it up to him several times.

One time, I let him put the head in me, but the little voice in my head kept telling me it was wrong, so I made him stop. I didn't fuck him . . . well, not until I had my six-week checkup.

3

I'm still mad as hell I did that. Not only did I get pregnant again, but also the young pussy hounder gave me the crabs and told everybody in North Philly that I gave him those shits! Lying-ass bastard! He gave the crabs to me. To top that off, he told them that my pussy was stretched out of shape for a girl 13 years old and that I must've been getting dick for a long time. How was I to know that I was still wide open after having the twins? That shit tarnished my reputation from that day forward. Wishbone got ghost on my ass, as did Juney, but he moved out of state to live with his father. I ain't even sure if the nigga knew he left a son behind.

After having the twins and Elgin, my mother, Gayle, sent me off to live with my Aunt Angie and my Uncle Saint in Crown Heights in Brooklyn, New York. I didn't know it at the time, but Gayle had Lupus in the body that caused her extreme discomforting pains and excessive swelling in her body. All those nights I heard her cry, I thought she was crying about me and how out of control I was, the great letdown I was to her. But her cries were for dual reasons: out of concern for me, and out of pain, knowing she wasn't far from meeting her Maker.

I didn't find out about Gayle's illness until the day of her funeral, on the ride there. My Uncle Saint was the one to break the ill news to me.

"Listen, gal," he gasped, driving down the highway with bloodshot eyes. I could tell he had been either drinking or crying.

"What is it, Uncle Saint?" I thought he was giving me a break from Albany Projects and taking me and the kids home to spend some time with Gayle.

"Your mother went on home last week."

"That's good," I replied. They had informed me the day she went into the hospital for "flu-like" symptoms.

"No, gal." He looked in the rearview mirror at the kids and I in the backseat of his squared black Lincoln Towncar. "That's not what I meant. Your mother was ill."

"Uh-huh, I know. That's what you told me last week," I said, oblivious to the matter.

"Deidra, Gayle had Lupus, a disease that deteriorated her health. She fought this disease for five agonizing years until it ultimately claimed her life. Baby, she couldn't fight no mo'."

If my ears were deceiving me, my heart wasn't. I felt an emptiness that pitted the bottom of my stomach. "Are you saying that Gayle died?" I began to shake, and goose bumps popped up all over my arms.

"I'm sorry, but yes, I am."

My ears burned, and I temporarily lost my hearing. It felt like I was left in this world alone to face life without a helping hand. I remember sitting in the funeral on the first wooden pew, with all my babies crying from seeing me cry. It was then my ears finally popped from all the screamin' that we were doing. Losing my mother was like taking a piece of me. I never fully recovered the piece I lost, either.

Brooklyn was miles away from Philly. It was a fast-paced city filled with too much activity for me to get into. There were boys, boys and more boys for me to select from. This was the best decision Gayle could have made on my behalf. She didn't know I was in heaven.

Aunt Angie and Uncle Saint lived in Albany Projects. I'll never forget living there. Uncle Saint was employed as a truck driver for a warehouse company that distributed electronics to businesses all over the United States. He was on the road the majority of the time. We had more electronics than we bargained for, so the surpluses were sold at cheap prices to families in our high-rise. Uncle Saint made plenty of extra money for the family on that hustle. That was simply one of his many ways of getting paid.

On the road, he would purchase cartons of cigarettes to resell per pack to people in New York, undercutting the bodega's high-ass prices. The hood loved Uncle Saint and so did I. He treated me significantly well, as if I was his own. If I had been into electronic games, my days would have been occupied. I had every new game and previous versions of the games at my fingertips before they hit the stores, but I wasn't into them. What Uncle Saint gave me, I'd give to Ice or Donnell, my other babies' daddies, as gifts or to resell if they already had one.

When my uncle was off of the road, he usually maxed out with my aunt, wasting time away with each other. If I'd come home late

5

after he'd have a beer or two, he'd start telling me that I should get my shit together.

"Deidra? Is that you?" he'd say, stern in his attempt to guide me in the right direction.

"Yes, it's me, Uncle Saint," I replied, high or feeling good from a beer.

"Let me talk to you for a moment."

Right then, I knew my ears would be filled with his "do's and don'ts" of life.

"You living wrong, young gal. I'd like for once to come home and not hear about a new rumor that these boys are spreading about you."

"Well, Uncle Saint," I'd say, "I really don't care what they're saying about me. They lie on me anyways, and you can't believe every rumor someone throws your way, either."

"I'd beg to differ," he'd say, sitting upright. "When it comes from four or five sources, there is *some* truth in it, young gal. I'm not going to tell you how to live your life. You have to experience it on your own. I *will* provide you with Uncle Saint's valuable knowledge, though, and hope that you put it in your reserves for your future."

"I'll do my best," I'd respond sarcastically.

"Hey," he'd mulled over, "Gayle loved you, girl."

"How do you know? And if she did, why did she send me here knowing she was going to die? You would think she'd keep me closer to her knowing that!"

Uncle Saint always leaned his chair back and lit up a cigar anytime we spoke of my mother, like the smoke was his way of exhaling.

"Some things are not to be discussed." He'd end the conversation.

Many days, that would be my escape from further communication. Aunt Angie and Uncle Saint seldom wanted to talk about Gayle and her passing because they knew how strongly it affected me.

Crown Heights, Albany Projects

Crown Heights, Albany Projects, twelfth floor of the first building is where we lived. When the elevators were down, which was nearly all the time, I got plenty of exercise walking up and down the steps. Most of the girls hated me because I was the new girl in the building and all the boys sought after me. I tried forming friendships with a few of the chicks, but it always ended in an argument or a fight about a nigga that was feelin' me.

The chicks my age in Brooklyn were just as experienced as I was. If they didn't have a kid, they'd had an abortion or two by the time they were 14 years old. They could do that in New York because Medicaid paid for abortions, but not in Philly. If you happened to get knocked up, you had to come out your pockets. The older girls in Crown Heights would even sell you their Medicaid card for the day to get an abortion. All you had to do was impersonate like you were them to get the procedure taken care of. Chicks did it all the time. I heard now that Medicaid keeps a record of how many abortions you had that they've paid for, and after a certain number of abortions, you couldn't get no more. Well, you could, but not at their expense anymore.

I gave my body a break for a year after giving birth to Elgin before getting pregnant with my fourth child, Icelene, at fifteen. Aunt Angie helped out a great deal with the kids and still allowed me to be a teenager. This was good in a sense, but bad in another. I went to all the house parties by myself, searching. I was always on a prowl for the hottest dude in the hood. That's where I connected with Ice, with his fine Brooklynite ass.

I vividly remember going to a party that his cousin's father threw for him on his eighteenth birthday. I was on my way to take my stroll around the projects that I did often. I wasn't going nowhere but to the corner bodega, just to get out the house, away from the kids and my aunt and uncle. His uncle stopped me in my travels and invited me to the party. I wasn't impressed with older men, but this one was finer than Clifton Powell, the man that played the role as a pimp in *Dead Presidents*.

I followed him to the party, where twenty to thirty peeps were piled in the three-bedroom apartment. The lights were off and the weed and beer bottles were being passed around generously. I was trying to kick game to his uncle, but my advances went unnoticed. I guess he wasn't into young North Phillies. That didn't ruin my mission to hook up with another, okay. I was a bold bitch. I took rejection as fuel to ignite my fire to make it happen.

In the corner of the room, I spotted the dude that I knew I was going to make my main man. I had a beer in one hand, trying to down it before I approached him. One boy grabbed my hand, and I gave him my empty beer bottle to hold without giving him the time of day. He was hot when I did that. I didn't give a damn. I was on assignment. We were all too young to drink or smoke, but I take it his uncle didn't mind since it was in the house, so neither did we. At the party is where I made my love connection with Ice.

"What up, shortie doo-wop?" he asked me with his legs propped up on the windowsill ledge. I wanted him, and that's what my intended plan was—to get him.

"What's your name?" I responded, breath smelling of Old English beer.

"Ice," he said. "Where you from with that accent?"

"North Philly, baby, representing to the fullest!" I said, making sure each word came out with a strong Philly accent. "You ever been with a chick from North Philly?" The two *L*'s rolled off of my tongue.

He pulled me closer to him, responding, "No."

I whispered in his ear, "Well, you will tonight."

"Word," he stated, taking me into the back room, past all the other peeps dancing or coupled up.

I had never French kissed before, but that night Ice taught me how. I was so used to pulling my pants down and spreading my legs, I didn't know anything about foreplay. He was different. Ice took his time with me. He rubbed on my head, pulling my hair—not to hurt me, but enough to turn me the fuck on—while he bit down on my neck and slid his tongue in my ear, French kissing it. That shit felt *sooo* good! I never had that done to me, ever! I fell in love with him the first night we had sex. Whenever I seen him after that, I wanted him to do the same thing . . . make me feel like he did that night all over again.

Ice was 18; years older than I was at 15 years old. He was a little possessive at times, but I didn't care. He made me melt on the inside. It wasn't one place in my aunt's building that we didn't get our freak on—on the roof, in the stairwells, in the elevator, or the bench outside in front of the building. Anywhere we could fuck, we did.

My aunt and uncle were raising my kids and felt indebted to Gayle. Aunt Angie had stuck her foot in her mouth when she told Gayle to send me to live with her. She bragged she would straighten me out, talking 'bout she'd make sure I never had another baby while in her care. Did her plan backfire? Hell yeah! I had two more babies while living with them.

Uncle Saint barely said two words to me after I had the last two. I guess he was tired of kicking his knowledge to me. Before, he rarely let an opportunity go by where he wouldn't inform me that I continued to make a bad name for the family by putting myself out there like that. Now, he ain't say shit.

Aunt Angie had given up the notion that I would start practicing abstinence as she so preached to me daily. She knew I wasn't listening to that bullshit, especially when I'd eavesdrop on her and Uncle Saint bumpin' and grindin', banging the headboard against the wall. Married or not, I had a sexual side that was on overkill, and I needed a fix.

I trust that if Aunt Angie wasn't Gayle's sister, a distant cousin maybe, she'd never have taken the responsibility of trying to raise my kids and me. Their only daughter, Kendra, was in prison for life for a vehicular homicide. I think that may be part of the reason why she took me in. She was guilt-trippin'.

Growing up, Aunt Angie didn't set but one example for Kendra—how to down a liquor bottle. Although she got herself together, becoming more stabilized, Kendra followed in her path of becoming an alcoholic. I guess Aunt Angie felt she could change the situation with me by early intervention. However, for me it was much too late.

When I was a young buck, Kendra was attending college at Cheney University. She would come to visit Gayle and me, most times on the weekend or during the week to grab a bite to eat. She had a gang of girlfriends that always swarmed her, like she was Janet Jackson or someone famous of that stature. Kendra was most popular in Cheney for organizing the new initiations for her sorority organization that she represented. They'd hit the clubs mostly every weekend. They had some really wild parties, from what she told Gayle.

During her four years in college, she grew very close to Gayle, considering her like a mother away from her mother. Her and Gayle would lounge for hours, talking about her sorority sistahs and the events that occurred. Gayle would always tell me that Kendra was the older cousin I needed to model my life after because she knew in her heart Kendra was going places in life. That may have been true had she not got drunk and passed out on the highway, killing a woman and severely injuring the woman's child. For that, she wasn't going no damn where.

Gayle was sick with heartache when Aunt Angie explained to her in detail about the accident. What had happened was Kendra had thrown a big party for the girls on the line that crossed over. They had liquor by the barrels donated by their frat brothas. One of her sorors challenged Kendra to tequila shots. Well, Kendra was all for it, winning hands down, downing seven shots and beating out her competition by two. Normally, she had a designated driver for such an activity as this, but her driver had dipped out with her new male friend. So, when Kendra was ready to go, she grabbed her keys and hit the road . . . literally.

She never made it back to her off campus apartment, but she did make it to central booking. Aunt Angie didn't have the money to post bail, so Kendra sat until her sentencing date. She was slapped a life sentence for vehicular homicide while under the influence of alcohol. Her sentence was true to her case, since she had previously been arrested for driving under the influence twice before, and her license was previously revoked.

I knew the real reason Aunt Angie sent for me was to try to make me a positive example like she tried to do for her daughter after she came to grips and was on the road to recovery. However, I wasn't Kendra. She couldn't make it right with me for the mistakes she'd made with her. She should have never promised Gayle that I'd change. In my heart, Gayle died thinking that I would, because I was in her sister's care. That's what I choose to think. Aunt Angie may have believed it for a moment, but when she came to the conclusion that I wasn't changing, it was time for me to go.

I didn't stick to any of the rules in their confines. I would pretend to go to school in the mornings but end up at Ice's crib. Who needed an education when I had Ice? I loved me some Ice, and he truly loved me. I know that now. We were an inseparable pair when we were together, right from the day we conceived our daughter, Icelene, to the day she turned two years old.

Every moment we had outside the house, we spent it together. I was too young to understand true love then. Had I never fucked up . . . maybe he would have married me. Who knows? That's when my cute ass decided that Ice's cousin, Donnell, was too irresistible and I started sneaking around with him. It was at Donnell's party that I met Ice, and the guy that grabbed me that I gave my beer to, that was Donnell. He kept secretly telling me that he wanted me to be his main girl. I never knew him and Ice competed with females. They had cousin rivalry, like who could get the prettiest chicks and who would be the first to hit. Dumb shit like that.

Naturally, girls flocked to Ice because he was so damn cute, but financially, they leached to Donnell, 'cause he had a little paper from selling rocks. He was flashy with his shit, too—oversized gold chains, outrageous gold rings—anything to make him stand out. Nigga was sick with it. All the dumb girls, including myself, fell for him.

When Ice found out, he beat my ass and spit in my face. He said he was hurt that I'd do him like that, and how could I go behind his back and do his cousin? He thought that our relationship was special. So did I until Donnell kept flashing his money and treating me to hero sandwiches. The panties came off without regard to Ice after that. Call me Fertile Gertle, Loosey Goosey, what the fuck ever.

I got pregnant with Donnell's child and named her Gaynelle after him and Gayle, who passed away the same year Gaynelle was born, just a few months before my eighteenth birthday. Who would know that at eighteen years old, I would be the mother to five damn kids? Unbelievable, right? I know.

Donnell had me out on the block selling rocks with him. I made some real money, too, while I was out there with him. Ice would kick my ass whenever he seen me with Donnell. That turned me on to him even more. Behind Donnell's back, I started letting Ice hit it again, but it wasn't like it used to be. Those times felt like I was just a convenient fuck. He didn't like to do it any other style but doggy style. He said he didn't want to look me in my face anymore, that I was poison in his mind, so he'd rather hit from the back. Talkin' 'bout he wanted to fantasize that he was having sex with someone else than actually having it with me. Can you believe that nigga?

Neither Ice nor Donnell gave a shit about their kids. They were only concerned with being able to fuck me at will. Free pussy, that's what they all want. An easy lay, right? That's all I was to them.

Aunt Angie and Uncle Saint had honored Gayle's request by taking me in and caring for their great nieces and nephews, but said I was grown now and they'd done their part. I had to go. Aunt Angie had me and the kids' shit packed and at the front door a few months after my eighteenth birthday, with a one-way ticket back to Philadelphia. She said that Brooklyn turned me out worse than I was when I was living in Philly. I knew the day was coming with the tension that was in that house. Aunt Angie had sat me down and told me frankly that I wasn't the woman she anticipated for me to be.

"Deidra, you haven't the least bit of common sense. I feel sorry for these kids. God knows your mother is turning in her grave," she speculated with the calmest demeanor.

"What's there to be sorry about?" I objected to her judgment of me.

"Put it like this—I'm not witnessing another child of mine, and I consider you one of mines, throw their life away. I gave you a break that most wouldn't. Your uncle and I took care of your kids while you went to school *and* while you ran the streets. What did you do in turn? You had more kids instead of trying to better yourself. We sacrificed our lives for you. Did you pay attention to your cousin at all? Did you learn anything from her mistakes?"

I slouched my shoulders, allowing her to beat me in the head again with the same lecture.

"We gave you free will, but you used yours to have sex. Girl, you will be trying to play catch-up the rest of your life, and when you look up, your kids will be grown and you'll realize you are far behind. You'd been then passed along your burdens and issues down to them."

"No, I won't either," I flatly denied. "Did you when you were a drunk?" I spit out in disrespect.

"Honey, hell yes! That's what happened to Kendra. She followed my footsteps. You may not be in the same predicament as Kendra. Well, at this point, you *are* equivalent to her. She's in jail, and so are you, mentally. You are young and have yet to experience what life is about. You haven't traveled but from North Philly to Brooklyn, and though you might think that you've been somewhere, you ain't been nowhere."

"I've been to Maryland before," I said disputing her statement.

Aunt Gayle pulled her lips in rigidly. "Your cousin had it made, but her reckless behaviors and uncaring attitude caused her to make a conscious decision to continue to drink and drive. I thought she'd learn after the first charge. We vowed to stay clean together. I kept my end of the bargain, but she didn't. I'd learned that after the second charge came, three months before the third one came—this one with hardhearted penalties. You know, you only get a number of chances to get your life straight, and before I watch another tragic ending for a loved one, I'd rather loose myself from it. I pray that your kids will follow another path, other than the one you taken."

I tried to understand what Aunt Angie was saying to me about my life, but most of it went way over my head. She cried on Uncle Saint's shoulders when we left out of Albany Projects, heading to the bus station. Uncle Saint was willing to drive us there, but my feelings were so hurt, I told him, "No, me and the kids will be a'ight." I'd overheard Aunt Angie tell him that I was doomed to fail and I'd never make it with all those babies. I had to show them I didn't need them to survive. Whatever difficulties came our way, we'd handle them without asking for help.

You should have seen me and my five stair-steps trying to get comfortable on the Peter Pan bus en route to Philly. I held that shit down, though, leaving behind the love of my life, Ice. Fuck Donnell! He ruined shit for me, with my only possibility of a husband. I regret fucking with him 'til this very day.

North Philly

When we got to North Philly, I got on Welfare, got me a three-bedroom project house and had been living there ever since. It might have been a high crime area, shootouts every other night, robberies, burglaries, all that shit, but we were living as a family. Some people would die to have a tight-knit family like I had. I was 30 years young, though I'd have to admit that my dark, aged skin made me look about 40. My kids were damn near grown. The twins were 18, Elgin was 17, Icelene was 15 and Gaynelle was 13 years old.

Shit was good for us until Welfare started fuckin' with me. Since I hadn't earned enough credits to graduate, I received a certificate of participation for the effort of attending. Welfare thought it was best if I continued my education and got prepared for the workforce. Those bitches made me enroll in classes. If I didn't, my benefits would be terminated. Before, you didn't have to do shit to get a check. Some corporate sons of bitches, somewhere in an office, done gone and changed the fuckin' rules and guidelines. That's why I went behind their backs and got a job to supplement my check.

They had me attending some bullshit workshops twice a month to receive that little bitty check that still didn't amount to shit. Earl could make that amount in less than ten minutes selling his own shit. Most mothers would have a problem with a child selling drugs, but shit, I didn't. I did it. What made him any different? His ass won't too good to hustle. I made him help me clothe, feed and keep a roof over our heads. Not another mothafucka had ever done that for us. They daddies didn't give a fuck! My kids knew that shit. None of them but Juney kept in contact with us, and he was more of a girlfriend to me. Our relationship strengthened due to the loss of both our mothers. We had something in common, like Bobby and Whitney.

Somebody had to stand the fuck up and be the man of the house. Earl took that role proudly. My son was "that" nigga. What the fuck you thought? I knew he was going to be the one to get us up out of this slump.

Now Earleon, she was my girl, no doubt. She had a fancy job as a clerk on Baltimore Street at the check-cashing joint. I ain't never report her income to housing either. For what? So they could raise my rent? Hell naw! Not on Juicy, they wouldn't. For every penny that came into our household, they wanted two of them bitches.

I sat my severely worn-out workbag down on the black metal futon and hurried to get the bug spray to kill a flying roach. I'd encountered many of bugs and rodents in Albany Projects—rats, mice, roaches—but never a flying roach, though. I could deal with dem roaches. They'd scatter when the lights came on. But those damn flying roaches weren't scared of shit! Seemed like the house bred them bitches. I hated to bring a man over, fearing one of them would embarrass me by flying around.

Most of the time, I met my dates at their crib. Besides, what man my age wanted to be involved with a woman 30 years old with five kids, especially teenagers? Elgin, Icelene and Gaynelle would run a mothafucka away anyways! Earl didn't bother my friends, and Earleon was so into her little world she could care less who I fucked with. My other kids were nosey and asked too many fuckin' questions.

I tried spraying the roach, but the fucker flew higher out of my reach. Earleon ignored me while Earl sat up there and watched me make a fool of myself, shifting around furniture trying to get it.

"Juicy, call the bug man. This shit is trife! Tell them niggas to get out here today. Here's two hundred dollars. Handle that," Earl demanded. Finally, I gave up and walked over to the closet to hang up my beige raincoat.

"Did you go to the meat market?" Earl asked, ready for me to get in the kitchen and hook him up a meal. Aunt Angie taught me well. I could fry up the chicken and make a hella pot of chicken and dumplings, but I couldn't keep a man to save my damn life. Trust what I tell you!

"You know they cut my damn food stamps off. Why you think I'm going to those stupid-ass classes and working part-time to get extra money?"

"Fuck 'em! As long as I got, you got, Juicy! I'll send Earleon over there to get a meat bag. That bitch Liz live near the market. She'll go."

"I don't care who goes. The cabinets are bare," I signified.

"Juicy, what I tell you? I got dis." He frowned like he was uptight. "Chill the fuck out!" My kids spoke candidly and foully. I taught those mothafuckas well, didn't I?

The front door of our house came flying open. Elgin was trying to speak, but his words stumbled. "Juicy, Icelene down the street getting her ass whooped by some nigga!"

Earleon and Earl flew out the house before I did to find out what the hell was going on. By the time Elgin and me made it to them, Icelene's face was bloody and swollen. She had two black eyes, and blood was coming from her busted lip.

Earl chased the boy down until he caught him. Once he did, we opened a can of whip-dat-ass on him. The nigga was try'na tell us that Icelene gave him the herpes. I knew that shit had to be true because Earleon had told me Icelene had to go to the clinic for a female problem. I thought she had a yeast infection, got burned even, but I didn't know my daughter was tainted with herpes. I guess that's why she had reoccurring cold sores on her lips. That bitch better not ever use the bathroom before me, unless she was disinfecting it real good! She won't gon' have the whole house with dat shit.

When we heard the siren sound we all scattered, making way to the house. Stupid-ass Elgin left the door open. When we got inside, the fucking 27-inch TV and DVD player was gone! I bet it was that crack head ass Chan that stole our shit. We took a seat, observing the empty spot where the T.V. once was.

Icelene injuries were bad. That nigga beat her ass good.

"Damn, he fucked you up!" Earleon said, fixing the bobby pins in her ponytail piece, which was barely holding on to her bald-ass head.

"Yo, dat nigga is dead!" Earl yelled, pacing back and forth.

I tried to calm Earl down. "Hold on before you do some dumb shit. If he come back on some rah-rah, lullaby his ass, but if he don't, he's in the wind. Let that shit die down. Icelene is just at fault for giving him a lifetime disease."

My kids were like my crew. We got down for ours, together . . . all except Gaynelle. She was the only one of my kids that attended Bible study and went to church on Sundays. Let me find out the church members were talkin' bad about me to her. They could get it too!

Most of the time we did shit together or had family meetings, Gaynelle was away. You know her snitching ass almost caused the state to take my kids away before? Uh-huh, several times she was up there telling her teachers that I smoked weed with her brothers and sisters, telling them that her brother sold drugs and I knew about it. She gave up all the tapes to her teachers and guidance counselors. We had to clean up our shit for months, until those mothafuckas left us alone. We couldn't even smoke our shit in the house no more. We had to smoke outside. Now ain't that some shit! I beat her ass for a month. They had me all paranoid in my own damn house. I wanted to fuck her up for all the times I had to go outside and smoke my shit. Who the fuck she think she is telling our business? What happens in the Brown's family, stays in the Brown's family—that was my number one rule!

"Earl, light somethin'." I knew he was ready to smoke just as well as I was. He pulled out a baggie full of weed and placed the stogies on the stained wood table.

"Here, crack this," I said to Elgin, handing him the cigar. Icelene took it upon herself to pick up another one.

"Oh, no the fuck you ain't! Didn't you get your ass beat for giving someone the herpes? You won't give it to us. You can smoke your shit solo!" I may have hurt her feelings, but I had to keep it tight, not real.

"Let's get this clear right now. From now on, Icelene, you are to scrub the bathroom down with bleach every time your ass use it."

"Juicy, I ain't got no AIDS. It's only herpes. I don't even have break-outs that often," she said with blood in the crevices of her gums.

"How the fuck we supposed to know when you have a break-out?" I had to ask her 'cause I knew she didn't think she was gonna get off that easy.

Icelene smacked her big-ass swollen lips.

Earl thumped Elgin in his head. "Why your dumb ass leave the front door open?"

"I didn't." He flinched. "Juicy was the last one to leave. She forgot, up there blaming me for that."

"Earl, leave that boy alone. The streets talk. We'll find out who stole our shit. Don't even worry. Meantime, you need to hustle up another TV and DVD player. It's bad enough the cable is disconnected."

"What you mean it's disconnected? I gave you the money to pay it. What you do with it?" Earl asked, posted up in my face.

"I paid the mothafuckin' electric bill. That's what I did with it! Now either you gon' step your game up, or you gon' shut the fuck up, 'cause if you was really making paper, we wouldn't have to be like this. You told me you were getting us out the projects. How many years has it been since you said that? Nigga, you hustlin' backwards or some shit?"

Elgin had finished rolling, picking up the stogie and placing it in and out of his mouth to keep it sealed.

"You lickin' that like a bitch," Earleon stated, directing our attention to him.

"Ain't no homothug shit happenin' over here. You can cut that shit out!" I announced to them. Wasn't no punk bitches coming out the Brown's residence.

"Juicy, where Gaynelle? Is she here?" Icelene asked with those big-ass jigga soup coolers for lips. I wanted to whack her for being so fuckin' stupid.

"She ain't here."

On an average day, our household was jumpin'; music blaring, weed smoking freely and munchies scattered about. We kept plenty of snacks—fruit bars, Twinkies, potato chips, candy bars, and Tastykake Butterscotch Krimpets—anything to cure our case of the munchies after getting our smoke on. We'd sit around watching movies or comedy shows together just having good times. This is how we got down.

Meet the mothafuckin' *hood* Brown family! Welcome to the life of Juicy Brown.

Earl

"Two for one! Two for one! I ain't giving this deal out all day. Y'all betta jump on this sale while you can." That was Earl's favorite sales pitch. He was known as the two for one man.

Earl reminded me so much of myself when I was younger. He had those starry coal eyes with a stubby nose, just like I did. Earleon was blessed not to have a nose like ours. It didn't stop him from getting girls, though. Shit, all the hoodrats loved my son. I never got close to not nary one of them. That was a no-no. Earl's rule was he didn't love dem hoes. "Bitches ain't shit but hoes and tricks," he'd say, so won't no need for me to get close to them. If he ain't deal with them, neither did I. I had to make sure I got my cut from him. Didn't need to mess it up by forming a relationship with dem chicks. They weren't the ones giving up the dough, Earl was.

Earl weighed in at 165 pounds, only five feet eleven inches in height. He wasn't that thick at all. I told him if he started to lift weights, he'd be all good. My son was good-looking, but not as cute as Elgin. But of the twins, he was the one with the looks. He must've stole all the essential nutrients from Earleon while they were in the sack. If she wasn't dolled up, she'd make a mothafucka frown their nose up at her.

I turned my son out at the age of 14. He had never been with a woman. Hell, at 14, I had three kids, which meant my son was too far behind. We went down on South Street and found him a pretty, big-bone chocolate girl named Hershey. She was older than me. Juney turned me on to her when I told him Earl needed his first shot of pussy. He said all the niggas talked about how good Hershey was in bed, and he was sure that she'd handle her business.

I asked him, "How do *you* know?" He said one of his lovers that goes both ways told him.

I made sure Earl got fucked, sucked and some extra shit. I told him after that night, he better not ever pay for pussy again. That situation was only to give him the experience he needed to mack other hoes.

He came out the motel room a man. That's when I put him on to Sterling, a hustla from the block that tried to get in my panties much too often. I told him to teach my son the game. Shit, times where hard. Fuck what you heard! Who gave a fuck about keeping up with the Combses?

Our electric had been cut off again, but this time for a month. My kids had to take cold baths because our water heater operated off of electricity. I'm glad it was in the summer when it happened. I can't lie; it had been cut off previously for two months. I swore that as soon as I got money to pay a portion of the bill, here came another one. I was always playing catch-up with the bill collectors. The only time we were really secure was in the winter. Peco wouldn't disconnect us in the winter, but recently them bastards were getting slick. They would cut your shit off December 20, a day before winter, if they had to then leave your shit off until you paid the balance in full! That wasn't happening to us again, not while Earl was out there in the streets doing his thing.

I'd sat Earl and Earleon down and was like, "Which one of you are gonna help me get this money?" Earleon acted like a real bitch at first, crying and all. She wised up quick. I ain't make her sell her ass, nothin' like that. I taught her how to do braids, cornrows and micros. She even learned to get fancy with zigzags and other designs. She made good side money . . . tax-free! Like I said before, I sent Earl to the block.

I done heard all kind of rumors about me and my kids. The craziest was when they said I was sleepin' with my own son. They done said all kinds of shit. They didn't know a damn thing about us. What happened in our family, stayed in our family! They could kiss my big, black, ashy ass. I was not that hard up for no dick that I would sex my own son. Come on now, that's some ill shit. That's big down South, not in the North. Ya heard me.

For Earl to really make money, we thought it was best that he drop out of school. He was always getting suspended for fighting or disrupting the class anyway. His grades each semester read: *F, F, F, F.* Why torture the school with a student that didn't want to learn? So, he came out and became full-time in his profession. I always felt if you were going to do it, do it right.

I was mad because he wasn't bringing in as much money as he should, which told me something won't right. He been hustlin' for four years and we still hadn't seen $50,000 at one time. Let me find out he got some extracurricular activities going on! I would call that nigga out.

Earleon

For some reason, ever since Earleon accepted that job at the check-cashing place she'd been acting all conceited, like she was better than me. Somebody needed to tell her that the owners didn't care anything about her. She'd learn the hard way. Watch what I tell you.

Her best friend in high school was a dirty blonde white girl named Liz, that I called Casper. She wasn't but a second away from being clear with her pale white trailer park trash-looking ass. She had the hook-up with the job and put Earleon on. You know how white folks stick together. Liz was the senior clerk, and Earleon was a clerk in training. I bet Liz made it to the top by fucking the boss. She seemed to me to be that type. She had big, fake silicone titties and a small waistline, with an ass too fat for a white girl. Her mother must have fucked a black man or Liz specialized in ass crunches, somethin'. Her ass was fatter than Earleon's.

Liz didn't have one particular choice in men. She like them all rough, raw and thugged out. White, Hispanic or black—it didn't matter with ho-ass Liz. When she drank, she'd overdo it. That's why I didn't like to go out with her and Earleon together. It was always some shit going down.

Earleon had the nerve to keep bringing her over. I told Earleon to keep Casper away from our house. That went in one ear and out the other. She still invited her over anyway. When she'd come over, I'd catch her ugly white ass winking at Earl. I told her in front of all the kids the best she could do for my son is give him a professional. You should have seen how humiliated Earleon was. She knew I ain't hold my tongue. I'd be damned if Earl brought a mixed child up in my house. Mixed children had added concerns of being accepted by either race. Casper hadn't come back to the house since I made that remark. That was fine with me.

I had to remind Earleon constantly that we were still black, strugglin' and poor. I told her, "Don't let the job make you think nothing different." She better be glad I ain't make her ass drop out of high school too. She wouldn't have that job today if I had.

I loved my daughter, but I hated it when I went to her job to cash my check. She'd be in there talking all proper, sounding all white at her job, frontin' for her boss. Then soon as she hit the hood, it was slang 'til she die. I told her it's okay to be black and professional. It's not necessary to put on this façade for no man.

Them bitches knew on my job I said what the fuck I want. I wanted them bastards to fire me anyway. I hated seeing the same faces every day, all perky and shit in the morning from drinking a pot of coffee, breath smelling like shit.

"How are we this morning, Juicy?" they'd ask me knowing the obvious.

I said the same goddamn thing every time they asked me that shit. "Mothafuckas really don't want to know. They just nosey as hell," I'd say and continue on with my daily routine.

I didn't hear shit else from them all day after I made my comments. You would think they'd learn, but Whitey will ask you the same question again, hoping to get a different response. The Blacks on my job would be like, "I ain't got time for her ignorant black ass." Not Whitey, though. They loved trying to act like they cared.

They got Earleon brainwashed in that bitch, telling her she needed to find a place of her own. She could listen to them if she wanted to. Without a Section 8 voucher or a project house, she won't gonna make it.

I told her to sign up on the housing list. She said, "No, I'm not trying to be in the system." Somebody should have told her she was already in that bitch! She done forgot where she came from, but let me be the first to remind her that she was the same little girl that wore holes in her shirts, high-watered pants and too-small shoes from the Goodwill. Hello! What the fuck she thought? Things changed because now she can finally afford knock-off name brands? Get the hell outta here! She better get off her high horse and come back down with the people on reality row . . . like Juicy Brown.

I had reason to believe she'd been fucking Day-Day, a friend of Earl's, in my house. Look, I already knew my kids were having sex, but we made a pact that as long as they screwin' elsewhere, meaning out of my house, they'd be cool. The minute I found out they'd been disrespecting the rule, we were going toe to toe. I know you can feel that. All I needed to do was catch her one time and her ass would be mine. Bitch thought we was best friends anyway. She kept forgetting . . . I am *her* mother.

Maybe I crossed the boundaries when we started club and bar hopping together. I introduced her to the fake ID, strip clubs, mixed drinks and all. Earleon's ass loved to have dick slangin' in her face. That was probably where half her money went, to the strippers. She fell in love with sexy-ass Tank. I know he bent her over a couple times in his dressing room. Those times she would leave to "rub him down with oil," she thought I didn't know what she was really doing. I ain't no fool. If he'd have asked me, I'da went too. He could holla at this woman. Fuck what you heard!

I was fortunate after having five kids not to have kept all the weight on me. I didn't have an excessive bulging stomach. My skin did sag a little, but what the fuck? I still was up to par. Not a dime, though. I was about even with a nickel piece. I was cool with that. Gayle didn't leave me with much in the looks department. I could still pull a date, though. Don't get it fucked up.

Earleon's dark skin was firm and tight. She had one of those plump asses and titties that sat upright. Yeah, her body was like that! Hate to admit this, though, and this is my child, but she was a little unique when it came down to facial appearance. She took after her mother. You know all dark skin folks aren't cute. My daughter and I might fit in the category. Her hair wasn't but a minute long. Our nickname for her was small-head-baldhead, and that was complimenting her. Thank you dearly to the person who created tracks, ponytails pieces and braid hair. They surely enhanced the area that we lacked.

Earleon almost didn't make it to see the age of eighteen. On the twins' seventeenth birthday, I treated them to a night out at the Boots and Bonnets club in Chester, PA. It was another hole in the wall spot, but it was always live. They never carded, and even if they did, I had fucked the doorman and he would let the kids slide on the strength of getting some more of this juicy pussy.

Earl was sharp that night, wearing Wu-Tang wear, a blue jean outfit with a spankin' brand new pair of Timberlands. Earleon had on a silver ensemble—silver jacket, silver skirt and a pair of thigh-high silver stiletto boots with straps down the back of those bitches. They were sharp! She was wrapped up and shining like aluminum foil. You couldn't tell her she wasn't cute, either. Her micros were pulled up into a Chinese ponytail. I was in a V-neck blue jean jacket with a blue jean mini-skirt to match—nothing fancy.

My shit was passable to get in the club. All of us were fucked up that night. I barely remember what happened after we got to drinking. I was in the middle of the dance floor, singing out, "It's your birthday. It's your birthday." We were having a ball, but you know how niggas get with a little juicy-juice up in them. They get right niggafied.

The freak nasty came out of Earleon, who was wedged between some girl's man, who had excused herself to go to the ladies' room. Earleon was running her fingers up and down this woman's man's shaped-to-perfection sideburns. You know how Philly dudes do. Their cuts are on point. When Earleon slithered her way up to him like a snake, it got buck wild in the Bonnet. The girl came stumbling from drunkenness to the table where Earleon was entertaining her man.

"Bitch, what's good?" is what she said to her.

"Your man," Earleon snickered.

The girl threw a couple of punches, making Earleon stumble back to the bar, ripping her silver jacket. It was on then. Earl and I had to come to her rescue. We tag-teamed the chick, but when shots rang, all started running. Her man was packin' deep in his waistline. I yelled for Earleon to hurry up and get out of dodge, but she had dropped to the ground.

"Get up, Earleon, before you get popped."

"Juicy, I think I *have* been hit," she said slowly.

"Stop playin'. Girl, that's not funny," I said with quick anticipation to get up out that spot.

Earl was out of the club waiting for us. I reached down to help Earleon and noticed her silver jacket was stained with blood. She had been shot in the upper right shoulder. All I could think about was how in the hell I was gonna get her out of this club before the cops arrived and found out she was under age.

I ran outside and yelled to Earl that I needed his strength to get Earleon up because she had been shot. He rushed back inside and we dragged her to the car, driving her straight to Chester Crozier

Medical Center. When they asked me about the gun wound, I told them it was a drive-by shooting—anything to protect me from the law. They always had a shooting in Chester, so it wasn't too far-fetched. They called Chester the "pop-a-lot city." Niggas would cap your ass in a second there, no lie. They bought into the lie when Earleon sided with me. She left with twenty-four stitches and a bullet still lodged in her body. It's still floating inside of her.

Elgin

What the fuck can I say in favor of my son, Elgin? He was the pretty boy of the family. He could pass to be in the same bloodline of Nelly. He was built like him too. In the back of the house, he done made himself a hood gym with cinder blocks and metal clothes poles to workout with. The feature that set him and Nelly apart was his nappy-ass head. He ain't ever comb that shit. Won't no convincing needed – he ain't have no good hair. When Earleon or me braided it up, he was good to go. Other than that, he was a hot-ass mess.

Elgin was the fun dummy of the family. He was 17 in the eleventh grade, failing terribly. I dared not consider him dropping out. If I did, there would be no hope for him. It was bad enough he had trouble reading. What kind of job could he get? I was too scared to put him on the block. Somebody would've killed his stupid ass by now for fucking up.

I did discover he was artistic. Nigga was freaky with it, but he had talent. He knew how to sketch an image to perfection, although he mainly sketched half-naked or nude women from the *Black Tail* magazine. Most of his drawings were hanging up all over the walls in him and Earl's room. He even had them taped to the wooden frame of his twin bed. Them big wigs that came to inspect once a year from housing be all uptight when they came out of their room, like they ain't seen ass before. Those upper corporate folks done seen it all. They started the porn business. What, you didn't know?

Elgin basically came and went as he pleased. I didn't put a lot of pressure on him. He was either high when home or high when he wasn't home. He was so fucked up one night from taking E and smoking that hydro weed, he slept out in the back where his hood equipment was located. He claimed he thought he was in his bed, but he hadn't even made it in the house.

Little girls chased behind him, but he would never bring them to the house 'cause of those damn bugs in the house. It's the same reason I didn't invite my friends over. He was embarrassed as hell.

Elgin was asshole tight with Icelene. They bonded together like the twins, and were always together. They attended the same school, went to house parties, down to South Street, to the Gallery Mall and all that together. Icelene done probably screwed all his friends—nasty tramp. I'd been informed that she gave it up on the first night. That's why she hung around him, I bet, to have a first-hand pick on his friends.

I done been to the school so many times on the strength of Elgin it was sickening. The principal kept trying to convince me that he may need professional help. I didn't give a fuck what they said. They better not expel him is all. I knew he was a menace, but he needed a good education. Knowing my son, he done stole half they shit, so expulsion was coming, I knew.

Elgin always had sticky fingers. He would steal a penny if you left it out, damn kleptomaniac. One time, his thieving ass broke into a barbershop and stole all of the owner's shit. Well, the next day, do you believe Elgin's dumb ass went in there and tried to sell the owner his own clippers? He deserved that beat-down the owner gave him. We didn't do shit about it. Elgin had that one coming to him.

You had to sleep with your pocketbook underneath your arm for him not to steal what was inside. I caught him one time hiding underneath Earleon's bed, digging inside her pocketbook like a crackhead searching for crumbs. Earleon didn't even feel him underneath of her. Either he was that damn good or she was in a deep sleep.

Aunt Angie had taught me to check the house before I laid down to rest. While making my rounds to check the house, I spotted these flaked-up athlete's feet with toe jam in between his toes, stickin' out from underneath of Earleon's bed. I thought it was Day-Day trying to hide. I reached for his feet and with my strength, slid his body from under there.

This boy was trying his best to hold onto the wooden legs to the frame of the bed, so I started kicking his ass all in his side. I had caught him red-handed with the pocketbook in his possession. When he came out from under there, I was dazed that Elgin would go that far for a buck. That's when I authorized the kids to put locks on their valued possessions 'cause we had a thief amongst us.

I was worried about him. Nigga had those dope fiend tendencies. If I didn't stop him, we'd be visiting him in jail or at an all-night Narcotics Anonymous marathon.

Icelene

Out of my kids, Icelene was the one that acted the most like me. I foreseen Icelene's outcome when she was a little girl. She was the only child I knew who went crazy over clean clothes. She was obsessed with them shits. She'd smell them, roll in them, get dressed in them, fall asleep on top of them, and do that shit over and over again. She was bizarre then, and her ass was still hot-blooded.

Oh, she was a hot little mama. She got that cherry popped at eight years old. She even beat my record. How 'bout that? I had to give it to her on that. She was always too big for her age. She could easily pass for a 21-year-old and she was only 15. Big-ass breasts, wide hips with an apple bottom sound good, but that shit isn't cute with herpes blisters all up under there. Eew! That's what happens when you've had over twenty-five partners unprotected. I told her after the first five, be sure to use a condom, but she never took my advice. Her risks of getting a disease would be slimmer. Her smutty butt didn't listen, and now look at her, all diseased up. A hard dick can make an infested behind. Young girls need to take heed to this shit!

Most thought I was the blind leading the blind. You haven't heard it from me, though. I did wonder how long she had it. I hoped that was all she got. I wasn't ready to take care of no HIV blistered-up patient. I guess it didn't matter if she was steady passing it on to others. It was inevitable that she'd catch a worse disease than she already had.

Like Earleon, I taught Icelene how to get her hustle on braiding, but who wanted to sit between her corroded ass? Her shit most certainly had to stank. Shame, too, 'cause Icelene was a very pretty girl. She had that exotic look like her daddy, Ice, with that Caribbean appeal. She didn't need to wear a weave, although she did. Her hair was silky and straight after a Soft & Beautiful relaxer.

She was passing in school, but she did ditch a lot. I knew that might be her downfall. She'd be laid up over some dude's house, thinking she grown. Shit, she was the youngest girl on the block giving blowjobs, so laying up goes hand in hand with that.

I asked her, "How could you be so young giving brain to men?" Guess what her response was?

"If I suck them off, I won't have to worry about getting pregnant."

That was then, when she was on that kick. She done had two abortions in the past. She could get pregnant again if she wanted to. I wasn't accepting any got-damn grandkids. I was too fuckin' young. Besides, I wasn't babysitting. Ain't nobody baby-sit for me since we came back to Philly. I was always stuck with my kids. She was gon' feel that shit once more if she did get pregnant . . . the suction, that is.

Don't know why I was trippin' about it anyway. Her insides were rotting more and more every day. Now, I may have been a fast-ass, but we wasn't sucking no dick when I came up. As a matter of fact, my daughters started sucking dick way before I did. Imagine the school contacting you to come immediately because there was "a situation" that had to be dealt with, only to find out your daughter was caught in the boys' locker room giving brain to two (not one) boys!

Sitting inside the principal's office, I was trying hard not to black out and kill her ass. I had to concentrate on all the plaques he had on his wall from colleges, organizations, even the Mayor's office. This man was well connected, and here I was trying to plead to him to let Icelene remain in school, promising him that she wouldn't suck dick in school no more.

Icelene wasn't even ashamed. She held her head up high like she was the number one dancer for Uncle Luke of the Two Live Crew. Pretty soon she'd be pulling apples, oranges and beads from her pussy like his dancers did.

What kind of conversation do you have with your child after an incident like that? Do you ask her, "Why did you have to suck two dicks?" Well, that's what I asked. I didn't know what else to say to her. She was frisky—too damn frisky, if you ask me, 'specially when her reply to me was, "It turned me on to suck two dicks at once."

How do you stop a child at 15 who loves to have sex . . . vaginally, anally and orally? If you have the answer, please do share because my daughter was not "off the meter," that bitch shattered the mothafucka!

31

Gaynelle

Mmm, Gaynelle . . . it's hard to explain her. This was my "I need to save the world" child. All the kids loved her, even though she told all of our business. They sympathized with her. She stayed sick a lot, always weak, you know. My neighbors, Deacon Wright and his wife Laverne, they looked after her when she was ill, even taking her to all her doctor's appointments. That freed up my time. By them taking her, I didn't have to go. Besides, Laverne knew to better understand the doctor's lingo. They'd expressed interest in adopting her more than once. I wouldn't let them, though. She was my baby. Won't nobody else gonna be her mammy but me!

Gaynelle was the mirror image of my mother. She was short and chubby with high cheekbones, just like Gayle. She wasn't grown like other girls her age. She prayed a lot and mostly stayed to herself when she was home. Most times she was with the deacon and his family.

Aunt Angie pointed out to me that Lupus is hereditary and I needed to have all my kids checked for it. So far, all of them were okay. The last time I took Gaynelle to the doctors, they pulled blood to test her. They said it was a strong possibility that she had the disease, but it takes many tests to be properly diagnosed. She was experiencing all the symptoms of it: skin rashes, extreme fatigue, body aches, and bad swelling in her body. Lately, I'd been feeling real sorry for her. She done missed over a month of school because she couldn't even get out of bed. I hated to see her when she was in that condition.

She was staying over the Wright's all the time. They'd been taking care of her. They knew more about Systemic Lupus Enythematosus or SLE, like I call it 'cause I can't pronounce it correctly, than I do. Laverne said it run in her side of the family too. She had two sisters who passed on from it.

What's crazy is nine out of ten people who have Lupus are women between the ages of 15 and 45 years old. That's a damn shame. My baby wasn't but 13 years old. What percentile did she fall in, .001%?

They put her on precautionary medications to ease her swelling and joint pains, but Laverne done told me that while the medicine made her more comfortable, it could also lead to stomach ulcers and kidney damage if she had to take them over a period time. She'd been on the same medications for two years now. My baby couldn't win for losing.

When Gaynelle started getting rashes, I scrubbed her body with an oatmeal bar, assuming she had rashes from eczema. What? I ain't know! I thought she won't washing properly and had a "D.R.", a dirty rash. She'd cry when I'd do that to her.

I hadn't taken her health that serious at first and felt bad because I had beat her time after time for running her mouth to people about us. If her body was ridden with Lupus, her bones already ached, which meant I added to her pain. God was going to punish me for that one, I knew.

Gaynelle held a special place in my heart, but I hated it when she told our business, putting the house under surveillance. That shit wasn't cool. She was gon' get us all locked up and put out. Shit, we needed our housing . . . wasn't nowhere else for us to go. She could live with the Wrights, we couldn't!

The Deacon and his wife believed in holistic medicine remedies. They'd asked me if I would let them try alternative herbs. I agreed. Anything to help my baby get better. They needed me to sign a release paper for them to do that in case it backfired, so I did willingly. They had it notarized, stating that I agreed with them giving her holistic treatments while she was in their custody.

In God We Trust

The dingy, flat-painted walls with peeling linoleum on the floors decorated the check-cashing joint that Earleon was employed at. It sort of reminded me of the corner bodega in Crown Heights that I used to frequent when I lived with Aunt Angie and Uncle Saint. I hadn't heard from them ever since Gaynelle told them about me beatin' her half to death for running off at the mouth. Aunt Angie said she was so dissatisfied in me and my behaviors with my kids. She said I, without a doubt, needed parenting classes. She should have told that to Gayle. She was the reason I turned out this way. Nobody told her to go get sick and die on me. Being sick, she never had time for me, so I turned to other things, mainly males, for the attention I needed.

I was scanning over the employees in the place and couldn't believe my eyes. How in the hell T.C. got a job as a security guard, I don't know. I remembered him as a juvenile delinquent, and I was sure that followed him to his adulthood. Most times it does. Once a criminal, always a criminal—that's what most people think. Then again, I guess people do change.

I had on my powder blue linens, my work uniform. I didn't have a chance to change into my street clothes. I was ready to cash in on my chump change for the weekend. A nice cold Cobra beer would feel good traveling down my throat. Mmm, it sure would. I wanted Earleon to service me because I didn't have a valid ID card. The only other ID I possessed was the one Welfare issued to me.

"May I help the next customer please?"

It was the damn po' white trailer park trash Liz asking. I tried to get the gray-headed, elderly white lady in the back of me to go, but she had to be hard of hearing. She just stood there, slumped over on her walker like she had a bad case of osteoporosis.

"Here, Juicy. I'm available," Liz personally informed me.

Walking to the counter, I noticed only three tellers were working, and one security guard, T.C. That was odd for a busy cash center such as this. Earleon had spilled out to me that the owners had problems with their security cameras and they weren't scheduled to get them fixed for a couple of weeks. You would think that being the

34

case, they would up the numbers in security, right? Wrong! Those sons of bitches are tight as hell with the money. The less money they had to spend, the better.

I knew my daughter was nervous about getting robbed since the cameras were down. She shoulda been. I remember her telling me that on any given day before the armored truck arrived, they housed over a million dollars in cash. That's a lot of damn money for security cameras to be out of order!

"What can I do for you today, Juicy?" Liz asked, with her stringy, greasy hair that needed a good Clairol wash.

"What the fuck you think I'm here for? It ain't to visit yo' ass!"

"Oh, Juicy, do you have to always be so modest?" she said cynically, flipping her hair behind her ears.

"Look, I'm here to cash my check, and I ain't got my state ID. The only ID I got is from Welfare," I said, bobbin' and noddin'.

"Sign the back of your check and I'll take care of you," she said, glancing over to Earleon, who was cracking up laughing.

I passed the check to her through the glass and looked over to my daughter.

"Good day, Juicy," she greeted me.

I stuck my middle finger up at her. Liz shook her head, counting out my money, placing it in a white envelope.

"You have a good day, Juicy," Casper said pleasantly.

I put my money into my pocketbook, along with the nickel and dimes that I had in there, waved at T.C. and slipped him my number.
✦

I waited on the corner of 52nd and Baltimore Street for the bus to arrive. There were about five other people standing out there with me, waiting patiently for the bus to come. One girl had three kids holding on tight to her, and to top it off, she was expecting another. Kind of reminded me of myself. Her face with ridden with distress. I wanted to embrace her and tell her that she could make it, but a mothafucka never did that to me. So, I got my ass on the bus and sat far in the back, away from her and those whiney-ass children. I had to pay my dues, and so should she. Maybe by the time her fourth child arrived, she'd realize that her life was over, that her struggle was just beginning. I never said I was a mentor, and never considered being one. I needed a mentor my damn self.

"Juicy Brown, how and the hell are you? I haven't seen you in a month of Sundays." Tianna and I grew up in the same neighborhood before Gayle sent me to live in Brooklyn. I hated this girl—well, woman—with a passion. Why did my past have to continue to haunt me?

When I moved back to Philly, I'd bumped into her before. I remember all the snide remarks she'd made about me having five kids and about me living back in the projects when she had graduated from college and she was now a reporter for the Philadelphia branch of *Don Diva* magazine. She was trying to get information about my hood since she had been promoted to feature stories of fallen dons in the magazine. She wanted to use my hood resources. I'd be damned if she was going to use me.

I told the bitch, "Don't be scared to come back. This is where you originated. What good is it to make good money and can't go back to your old stomping grounds?" Now all of a sudden she scared that somebody gonna rob her bougie ass. She must have forgot that she used to plot on niggas the same way.

She was all slicked out with her black pinstripe Dolce & Gabana suit, wearing a pair of authentic black patent Gucci boots. Her hair was jet black and smooth like she'd paid a trip to the see Dominicans. Her shit looked shiny and beautiful. I was hatin' on her ass dearly! Tianna was the type of bitch that made you realize how fucked up your life was. Bitch was carefree—no kids, no man, nice crib, pushing a luxury car.

"Hey, Tianna, what's your too-good ass doing on the bus?"

"Oh," she said, sweeping her hair from in front of her eyes, "I had to drop my CLK Mercedes off for service. I decided not to take a loaner car. By taking public transportation, I can keep my ear to the streets. And you? Still don't have a car?" she asked, trying to intimidate me with what she had.

My eyes darted like fire. "My son has my car," I said to clear her curiosity.

"You mean that green minivan I see him driving in with his ho? You know what? That would be right. It would be appropriate for your family size. You got like six or seven kids, don't you?"

This bitch was getting ready to feel it! "Actually, I have five. However, you already know that. You ask me the same questions

36

every time we bump into each other. And my van is blue, bitch, not green. Oh, and for the record, my son don't fuck wit' hoes, only high-class bitches."

"I was close, though, wasn't I?" she guessed. "Anyway, I know you heard about Juney. He's made it big in the fag world. He snagged up a rich Italian man that's taking care of him something *real* nice. He drives a sharp-ass, wine-color Chrysler 300E. Have you seen him lately?"

My heart fluttered, not off some boyfriend-girlfriend jealousy, but on some "no his happy ass didn't come up like that!" Juney and I were still cool. I hadn't seen him in a few weeks, but generally we didn't miss a week of conversation with each other. Normally, he would call me and tell me about all of his affairs. His punk-ass must have slowed down on the convo because he had a little paper now. Shit, he owed me over $30,000 in back support for the twins. I didn't care if they were 40 years old. I wanted my damn back child support!

Tianna was talking all loud, pissing me off. I guess so others could hear, trying to downplay me.

"I haven't seen Juney's gay ass," I replied.

"He is the father of your twins, right?"

"Bitch, you know they his kids."

The young girl sitting next to me with a burgundy-streaked, feathered wig and big bamboo name earrings tuned her ear to our conversation, ready for me to bring the drama.

"No need to get hostile, Juicy. I was just making sure. You know how you do. Daddy here, daddy there . . ."

My hands reacted before my thoughts. I had her ass pinned up against the tinted glass, banging her head against it.

"Unh-uh, bitch! You don't know me like that," I gritted through my teeth.

The SEPTA driver stopped the bus, calling for police assistance. Tianna yelled to him that she was okay and she didn't need him to call for help. I released my hands and exited the bus, cussin' out everybody that stared in my direction.

"Mothafuckas ain't gon' keep downplaying me and my kids 'cause we live in the projects and don't drive a big boy toy!" I screamed out. "Or these mothafuckas will really meet the Brown family," I stressed.

37

Tianna yelled out to me before the bus door closed. "Juicy Brown, to what extent will you go for your kids?"

I didn't respond to the siddity bitch.

Where Dem Dollars At?

I had to relieve some stress after seeing Tianna the day before. It was the first Saturday of the month, which meant . . . *stripper time*! Hey! Where dem dollars at?

Earleon and I were hanging out that night. I told her she better not bring Casper and if she did, I was going to embarrass the hell out of her. Every time she went to the strip club, she ended up sucking of a couple of dicks, making the situation bad for us. All the other strippers thought they could get the "Liz special" on the house.

Now, I would sex one or two once in a while, but I wasn't into sucking like that. That was in Earleon and Icelene's department. Them whores read too many of my Zane books and watched too much of Janet Jacme and Heather Hunter with me when they were coming up. I didn't know if they were both fighting for the title of Superhead or not, but somebody needed to tell them somebody already held that title. And from what I heard, she held that title to the fullest. No need to fight for that spot. The original Superhead was holding the crown with a forceful grip and wasn't trying to let that bitch go.

The line to get in the hole in the wall strip spot was ridiculous. Those bitches acted like they ain't never seen dicks before. Half of them had on little skirts that exposed the paw print. Shit, I don't blame them. I had on mines too!

Before we left the house, Earleon told me I looked right stank, showing ass cheeks and all. She was only mad because I told her it was my turn with Tank tonight. She had him the last time when we where here. Oh, we were regulars. They depended on our cash flow. Earl had given us both $100 worth of ones to put in their G-strings. I had an extra $200, just in case . . . for a little extra.

Pistol Pete was supposed to be a special guest. I couldn't wait to see his fine Cuban ass. I was never into the exotic featured men, but Pistol Pete had a golden tan and thick broad shoulders, not to mention the thickness that swung between his thighs. He reminded me of the rapper Cuban Links. Tank didn't have anything on him, but I loved me some Tank!

39

I spotted Sneed, one of the bouncers of the club. I knew he had a crush on Earleon. I told her to flirt with him a bit so we could cut the line because my legs were getting cold standing outside in that long-ass procession. Earleon had on a pair of black wide-leg Capri pants that hugged her ass, and a low-cut draped black nylon top with a broach that dropped between her breasts. Icelene had glued in a 12-inch jet-black weave for her. It looked damn good on her, hanging down her back. She had fixed up her own makeup, surprising the hell out of me. The only problem was that damn bright-ass red lipstick that she had plastered on her lips. I hated when dark-skinned women wore red lipstick. That shit just don't work for us.

When Sneed took a glimpse at Earleon, I knew we had it in the smash. We were in that bitch! I was either fucking Tank or Pistol Pete. Sneed wasn't going to let Earleon out his sight. That didn't mean she wouldn't dip on him. She wasn't going to let him stop her flow. For me, that meant I had the man of my choice.

"Hey, baby," Sneed said, sucking and licking his lips and teeth at the same time, with his big, black, 350-pound lard ass. "You rolling with daddy tonight?"

Earleon didn't have to respond because I answered for her. "Damn sure is! Now, let us cut the line." She wasn't down for that, but he thought she was.

"Come on, baby. Follow me," he said, yearning to fuck.

Earleon rose on her toes to hug him, purring, "Thank you Sneed."

Texas Massacre was slingin' that pipe to Tupac's throwback song. *I won't deny it, I'm a straight rider; You don't wanna fuck me . . . His* ass was poppin' to the melody. He had a li'l redbone on all fours, legs spread-eagle. I bet her panties were moist with cream. The air was sweet and smelly from the scent of perfume and ass. The round, brown ass on Texas Massacre humped back and forth as he aimed to please the li'l red female. Her tongue was out her mouth, dangling like a thirsty dog.

"You betta pop that pussy on him, girl," I hollered to get her attention. I wanted to put my dollars right in the crack of his ass, just like them bi-sexual dancers like it. I could tell he was into that by his wandering eyes.

The male bartender serving tables stopped to get our order. I was drinking clear rum and orange juice. Earleon ordered a Henney on the rocks. We were getting toasted because next up was our man, Tank. Now I was debating if I should wait for Pistol Pete or say, "fuck it" and spend all my money with Tank. Neither was a bad choice.

The instrumentals of "Tell Me Again" by Usher, Ludacris and Li'l Jon commenced to play. "Awww shit!" was the sound heard throughout the club. Hands were up in the air, fingers poppin'. When Usher's lead part chimed in, so did Tank, in a red leather suit, body waving on the dimly lit stage. Colorful lights flashed off and on his body. Damn, he was a hella-man! Earleon's nasty ass was licking her lips like she was tasting him. The crowd was going bananas. Tank knew he had the fans tonight. He done probably had every one of us in the club with his big, curved hammer dick!

"This way, daddy," a well-proportioned female screamed. Oh, it was competition in that bitch tonight!

"No, ova here, chocolate," another chick yelled, shaking her droopy titties at him.

He began the tease, coming out his leather, revealing his custom-made red leather thong with devil ears. One pull of the ears on that thong and the lights would have went out. One big orgy was going down.

I raised my ones, all three hundred of them, and told him, "This is all yours, baby!" He gave me that naughty nod and danced in my direction. Those young girls were mad as hell, including Earleon.

He picked me up, and my little skirt rose to my stomach, showing my deep purple thong. Dimples were poppin' from everywhere. He laid me on the stage floor and raised one of my legs then motioned for me to pull the ears of his thong for them to come off. Once I did that, he forcefully gripped my ass and grinded his way in me. I swear we were getting our freak in front of everyone on the stage. The bitches were lusting, wishing it were them. The lights went out, which signaled to us that we had gone overboard.

Tank pulled me up and took me off stage to his dressing room. It was on when we got up in that piece. That was one hella night! Next month, though, I was gonna concentrate on Pistol Pete. Tank put a hurtin' on my hot ass.

Show and Prove

Two days later, Icelene was in the kitchen fixing hot dogs and baked beans. Earleon had finally purchased the meat bag. We had a freezer full of food, and Icelene was reaping the benefits of it. I had to recoup from Saturday night's workout with Tank. He worked the hell out of this beat-down pussy.

"What's up, Juicy? How was your day at work?" Icelene asked. My thought was on if her nasty ass had washed her hands before going into my refrigerator. Apparently, she read my body language and knew I had a problem with her.

"Why you all frowned up? I'm only cooking for me, nobody else," she tried to convince me.

"I hope you washed your hands. And how come you're not dressed?" I said, observing the gear she had on.

"I am dressed, Juicy, in my pajamas. I can't go out looking like this. Look at my face," she pointed out. "I'm still a mess from dude beatin' on me."

"I'll second that," I agreed, passing her off. "Did the mail come yet?"

"Yeah, it's on the dining room table," she said, devouring half the hot dog with one bite.

I went to retrieve the mail, and the first envelope I picked up was from Social Services. They'd finally reinstated my food stamps. Good! That meant I could pocket the grocery money that Earl gave me.

I began reading it then called Icelene to finish because they were speaking in legal terminology. Icelene was good at dissecting and putting words into common terms.

"What do they mean?" I watched her.

She smoothed out the crease in the paper and began reading slowly. "Juicy, it means that they're gonna have you prosecuted for frauding the government!"

"Get the fuck outta here," I replied, shocked.

"They say you didn't report your household income while you were receiving a Welfare check for the last five years."

42

Part of their complaint was true. I couldn't disagree. "How much them bastards say I owe? I guess they finally caught up to my ass, huh?"

"They went back five years. You owe them over twenty-three thousand."

"Bullshit! They must be out of their got-damn minds! I don't owe them bastards a damn dime," I said, trying to play hard. "What income they talking 'bout anyway that I didn't report?" I wondered if they really did their research or they were just probing to get me to tell on myself.

"Earleon's income and your income from the motel, Juicy. You in big trouble," she said, more upset than I was. "How come you didn't report it?"

"What the fuck you think? Same reason you didn't tell me you was getting paid for giving blowjobs in school and to the neighborhood hustlers. You wanted some extra money for ya'self, and so did I!"

"Oh, Juicy. You always trying to take the focus off of you," she said, furious.

"So, what they gonna do?" I asked, passing off her comment.

Icelene scanned over the letter. "They're giving you a chance to respond to their allegations. You have ten days to contact them for an appeal. If they don't hear from you, you're admitting that their claim is true."

"Well, them bastards gon' have to do what they gotta do. I ain't reportin' shit. They can cut all my shit off. My son gonna take care of me and mines."

Icelene cut her eyes under her swollen lids at me. "Earl ain't big-time, so don't count on it. You the only one gassin' him up to be a big time hustla."

I always knew Icelene was envious of the twins, but I won't gon' let her talk bad about them. "If he's so petty, why you always beggin' him for shit?"

"You know what, Juicy? It's not that serious, but what is, though, is the charges they gonna slap on dat ass."

"I ain't even worried. What I gotta do, thirty days? I can do that with my eyes closed," I said, snatching the letter from her. "Go put that long dong in your mouth. You're used to it, you triflin' bitch."

Icelene grinned at me with her deformed lips. "Juicy, you ain't got one day up in you. Stop frontin'."

"I sure don't," I confessed, opening the letter from the oncologist that recently tested Gaynelle.

"Here, Icelene. This is about Gaynelle. I don't want to know if it's bad news. You read it."

Icelene lowered her face, placing her right hand on the tip of her chin. "Damn, this is not good. Look, Juicy," she said, pushing the letter my way. "After all these years of testing, Gaynelle finally tested positive for Lupus, it say."

I raised my glass of grape Kool-Aid to drink it. "Didn't I say if it was bad news to keep it to ya'self? Hardhead-ass kids." I sighed.

"Juicy, they say to call them as soon as you get this letter. They want to discuss her treatment plan."

"I'll call them tomorrow. For now, call the deacon and Laverne. Tell them the outcome of Gaynelle's test. Maybe they got another holistic remedy over there."

"All right. I'll stop by there in a little while," she confirmed.

Honey, Hush!

Elgin stood at the front door, opening it for Juney. I hadn't expected him to visit, but since he had, I would drill him about my back support. Juney glided his happy ass to the futon and demanded his presence to be known. I saw why he was given the nickname Lollipop, from the way his oval lips twisted.

"Hey, family! Juney's in the house. Y'all already know what I'm about!" he sang, sounding like RuPaul during a live concert in Las Vegas.

I slouched back in the chair opposite him, crossed my legs and contemplated on if I should bitch-slap him now or after I finished what I had to say. What the hell was I thinking when I fucked him? Twelve years old or not, how come I didn't recognize his gay tendencies? You know they show them signs well before they come out the closet. He had to be this happy back then.

"What's up, Dee-Dee?" He knew I hated to be called that.

"How many times I have to tell you, Lollipop? It's Juicy. The nickname Dee-Dee has been dead for years." I watched as Juney reared his body to the side.

"Didn't come to fuss, Miss Thang, okay," he said, putting his hand in the air as if to say, "Don't go there."

Elgin was tickled by the way Juney was talking. He always teased Earl and Earleon about him.

Icelene was back in her room, trying to heal still, and Earleon hadn't been home since we left the stripper club. I think she got mad at me that night and left with Pistol Pete. He was probably keeping her hostage, putting "the D" up in her all kind of ways. I wasn't mad at her if he was.

Earl was out doing his thing. I hoped he didn't come home while Juney was there.

"Excuse me, you're not going to offer me something to drink? How rude," he said, batting his cosmetic lashes.

Elgin mumbled, "I don't want his dick breath on our shit." He thought I didn't hear his ignorant ass, but I did.

"We don't have nothin' to drink but grape Kool-Aid and good old-fashioned tap water. Take your pick."

"I'll take grape Kool-Aid, thank you."

I asked Elgin to get Juney a disposable plastic cup. This was the perfect time for me to bring up what Tianna blabbed her mouth about.

"What's this I hear about you got a rich new Italian lover?"

"Oooh, who told you, girl?" He blushed, covering his mouth with his neatly trimmed nails, trying to shield his glow.

"All I want to know is when are you gonna pay your back support, bitch? Fuck the rest!"

"Juicy, you definitely know how to spoil a moment, don't you?"

I thought back to the night I lost my virginity to Juney. We were in his mom's basement playing house. I was the dad and he was the mom. Juney called it reverse role-playing. That shit is really funny, right? I was acting like I was mad because Juney, my wife, didn't make dinner. Juney was trying to make it up to me by giving me a shoulder massage. It started out at that, but before we both knew it, we were naked on the carpeted basement floor, experimenting.

Juney found my tight, virgin canal and worked his way in. I remember it feeling like someone was pulling off layers of my skin from an open wound. It stung like a bee had stuck his stinger in me. It was the most uncomfortable feeling I'd ever had. Nine weeks later, I found out that I was pregnant.

I remember Gayle was so embarrassed when they told her the results of my pregnancy test. When I think about it, I don't remember ever seeing Gayle smile. She was always so sad, just like Gaynelle was now.

Juney later told me that I was the first woman and the only woman he'd ever been with. He said he didn't like the way pussy felt when he was inside of it, that it felt too gritty. He said he knew back then that he had an attraction for boys. Ain't that some shit! Why did he do that to me if he knew he had an attraction to boys? I lost my virginity to a gay man. What a waste of a tight pussy! Thinking of that made me vexed.

"Juicy, you know I don't have no job. Why do you keep pestering me? Child, them kids grown up now. What you need my

46

few pennies for?" He was straight trippin'. Didn't he have a nerve? With his happy lollipop ass!

"I wouldn't care if they were sixty years old plus some years and I was eighty about to croak over. I want the paper owed to me, bitch. I raised them by my damn self while you ran around with Tom, Dick and Harry, slut. Let's not forget that. You owe me."

"Hold on, Miss Thang. What about all your other baby daddies? I'm not the only man you had kids with."

"No, bitch, you the only woman I got kids by," I reacted with animosity.

"You need to try and track the others down. It shouldn't be hard to track down the cousins that you fucked. They're in the same family."

"Put a dick in it, Juney. Way up there, too."

"Dee-Dee you were always good at hatin' on the next because you can't keep a man, bay-bee doll. Humph, I see you finally gave up."

My left arm bent as my hand grasped onto my hip. Icelene had come into the living room with us to watch the Riker's Island documentary that Elgin put in. That documentary was enough to scare anyone from going to prison. Those niggas on there would slice ya face open in the flip of a wrist. That's where the *real* thugs are . . . in Rikers Island.

"Suck a limp dick, Lollipop," I said with a hellfire grit on my face.

"You ain't never lied, Juicy. That's all gay men do," Icelene tagged on.

"Well, I see I'm not welcome here," Juney said, slightly offended.

"Oh, please," I stated. "Turn your bitch sensor off, getting all mushy!"

"You should know, Dee-Dee. You're the one turned me out. One shot of your shit ruined me for the rest of my life."

"That shit may be true, but you earned the nickname Lollipop well after our session. Don't even try it."

"That's all well and good, but let me ask you . . . what name do you think you earned?"

"Who gives a fuck? People will never stop talking about me. I'm a mothafuckin' hood legend, nigga!"

On that note, Juney reached for his keys and left. Oh well. He'd get over it. He always did.

Loose Strings

I was up at the crack of dawn with Elgin and Icelene, who were preparing for school. I reminded them that we had a family meeting later on that evening, and I didn't want to hear any excuses about them being late. Icelene's eyes were still a bit dark, but she was carrying her ass up out of here. She had already missed a few days of school.

Elgin had let me put a cute Allen Iverson braid design in his hair. He was looking like a topnotch teen with his big brother's clothes on. They weren't too conservative to share. What one had, they all shared. If Earleon wanted to wear the shirt or jeans, Earl would let her. They wouldn't front on each other. I told Elgin to watch over his sister, and if something were to go down, he better ride it out with her.

When they were on their way out the door, I screamed to Icelene, "Stay out those damn bathrooms, too. I know that's where you been fuckin' at in the place of the boys' locker room." A couple of girls from our projects laughed at her for a split second, then stopped because they knew I would call their little triflin' asses out too . . . down in the janitor's closet by the recreational center, bent over, with a train of boys waiting for their turn. My sons were two of them. These little girls were openly sluttish. Shoot, coming up, we were in-the-closet hoes.

I put on a fresh brewed pot of coffee. The smell filled the air, arising Earl, who had not too long ago come in the house. He had on a pair of dark gray cotton boxer briefs, exposing his barely visible peach-fuzzed chest, rubbing his nose and making that horrible grunting noise like something was caught in his throat.

"Let me get a cup of that." His voice sounded husky. I reached to get the "Boss Man" ceramic mug to fill it with mud, just the way he liked it. He loved his coffee black without the extras.

"So, what we working with?" I assumed he was ready to talk money.

"Last night I killed 'em out that bitch. I made like fifteen hundred in record time," he said complacently.

49

You know when I first put my son down with the game, I had high expectations of him, but the nigga kept proving me wrong. On an average night, a petty hustler could make fifteen hundred, and here he was bragging that he killed them by making that little bit of paper.

"Earl, that's not what's up! That ain't shit to brag about. Had you said you made three thousand, *that* would have been a good night for you, since you nickel and dime'n it. I told you if you gonna be in the game, make some real money. Now, where is my cut?"

"Juicy, that's all I got," he replied hesitantly, not wanting to give the money up.

"Yeah well, I need that," I countered back to him.

"Everything?" He sat back, sipping his muck.

"That's what the fuck I said, didn't I?"

"Damn, Juicy!"

"I'll tell you what," I negotiated. "You get your ass out there tonight and make some real money and I'll let you keep every dime. Is that cool?"

"Yeah, that's what's up, na'mean?" he agreed.

"Don't forget the family meeting is this evening. I'll stop to the deacon's to get Gaynelle, so don't worry about her."

"But don't they have prayer at the church tonight?"

"They ain't got to stop praying 'cause she ain't there. Now, I gotta go get ready for work," I said, taking out some frozen hamburger meat to thaw out. Earleon was fixing her sausage spaghetti special for us later.

Contrary to what I told Earl, I had taken off of work to go down on South Street to get my hair braided by the Africans. I had seen this bad-ass style that would do me justice. My supervisor sounded like he was mad when I called in. I didn't care. Let his ass fire me! Shit, I was already in trouble with Welfare behind that petty penny-pinching company.

When I was dressed and ready to go handle my business, Earleon halted me. "You off to work, Juicy?" Her weave was a mess. Track pieces were coming unglued, making them lopsided. Now, I hadn't seen her in a few days, and she was acting like everything was everything.

"Where the fuck you been at? You ain't call or nothin'. How was I to know you were doing okay?"

She had guilty eyes that let me know she did some shit she didn't have no business doing. "I need to talk to you, Juicy, when you get back, okay?" She had a trembling in her vocals that made me shiver inside.

"You're not pregnant, are you? You know how the fuck I feel about that. Don't make this your sixth abortion."

I had fucked up my life early. I wasn't about to let my sons or my daughters do the same. Another rule of my house was no babies. If my daughters got pregnant, termination was the only option. Fuck what you heard! If my sons got a girl pregnant and she acted like she wanted to keep it, we'd find a way for her to miscarry . . . hint, hint. I wasn't playing that shit. It was hard enough for us now. We didn't need any extra heads in the house.

"We can talk later at the family meeting," I suggested.

"Maybe afterwards?"

"All right," I said, knowing she had an issue she wanted to discuss. "I got a bus to catch. I'll see you later."

➤

I hated when I got on a bus and everybody stared at me like they were trying to read my thoughts. Sometimes I would make a loud outburst for people to think I was crazy. You know when a mothafucka think you psycho, they limit the amount of times they look at your ass. I'd do shit like talk to myself, laugh out loud, keep nodding my head and rocking my legs to make people tighten up—anything to take the attention off of me.

I was diagnosed with a social anxiety disorder after Gaynelle was born, which made me somewhat 'noid in the company of a lot of people. My condition stemmed from the after-effects of Gayle's death. I was put on Paxil, a medication to help calm my bipolar-like jumpiness, but for a woman my age, I still didn't have any friends. Perhaps it was because of all the kids I had. People parents probably thought I would be a bad influence. My own mother did.

Once upon a time, I did have a close friend before Gayle made me move up north. Her name was Marchand. When the twins were born, she helped out with them because Gayle sure didn't. Marchand would help feed them, bathe them and even sing to them. She had a voice like Denise Williams. She would sing the song "Black Butterfly" like she was Denise Williams herself. She did a damn good rendition of her—even Gayle thought so. She often told Marchand how she was proud of her and her accomplishments in school, while I, on the other hand, barely made low D's.

I was a little envious of how she gave Marchand her props, but never raved a positive word about me. She probably was the one who told Marchand that it wasn't a good decision to be hanging around a girl her age that had kids. Later, that's what I learned someone told her. She let me know then that she wasn't allowed to be friends with me anymore. I cried hard that day. I had grown to love Marchand like my sister. What's even sadder is the fact that when I came back to Philly to find her, I was told that she died from breast cancer. That damn Gayle ruined that. I know she did. Marchand was my only friend, and she took her away from me too.

I didn't have a man, but I was content with that. All I had was my kids. That's all I needed. If I wanted to go out, I went out with my son or my daughter. When I needed to get shit off my chest, I talked it over with my kids. My kids were my world. It's always been about us—fuck everybody else. With the exception of Aunt Angie and Uncle Saint, nobody even did a damn thing for us.

Well, it was that one time when Power 99FM granted us a Christmas wish. They came through with a boatload of gifts, groceries and hit me off with some cash. They did look out lovely. I have much respect for the radio station for that, especially Q-deezy, Uncle O, Mikey Dread and that chick with the whip, Golden Girl, who delivered the packages. That was the first time my kids seen me cry. I had to be the chief to lead my Indians. Some may think I've indulged in unthinkable practices as a parent, but if I didn't teach my children, who would have? I wasn't giving anybody the opportunity to turn them out. What they learned, they would learn from home.

I sat in Uma's chair—the African that ran the shop—listening to her speak in French to the other Africans working in there. This was the time I wished I could speak another language. Them damn Africans and Dominicans always talked shit in front of your face because they knew most of us couldn't understand a word they were saying.

All the paper these damn Africans made from braiding, how come they never had centralized heat? They always had a kerosene heater centered in the middle of the room to heat the shabby-looking place. We wasn't in no fuckin' Kunta Kente village. I'm quite sure they could afford it. They was getting like $140 per head, and I know they had at least three or four customers a day, with three or four workers working in the spot. They were making some money up in that spot. Why didn't they try to make it more comfortable? Buy some new chairs, even. After all, we sit for the minimum of five hours, right? A damn comfy chair might make up where they lack— stingy bitches!

Uma handed me a bunch of magazines and even turned on the bootleg version of *Soul Plane*. I sat there all day, entertained by movies, magazines and Africans talking shit. It took six hours for Uma to finish.

While I was on South Street, I stopped at Ishkabibbles to enjoy a chicken cheese steak. Fuck the Philly cheese steak. Yeah, they good and melted in your mouth, but so did the chicken cheese steak. Ishkabibbles mighta been small in size, but I know the owners' pockets were on swollen from all the business they got.

The line was halfway down the block with people trying to place an order. He had over a hundred framed pictures of entertainers on the wall. It ranged from Usher to Phyllis Hyman, from athletes to exotic dancers. Tank's picture was one of them. I flashed back to my latest encounter with him.

"How you want this dick?" he asked, stroking it until it became hard as a piece of sheet metal. There was only a small love seat in the room, in front of four square mirrors that were singly nailed to the wall.

"I want it doggy style, so I can watch you go to work on this fat ass. And make sure you keep the light turned on."

I spread-eagle, placing both hands in grip mode as if I were riding a motorcycle. I watched Tank getting a plastic tube out his duffel bag to prepare for our episode. He also unwrapped his black magnum condom wrapper.

"What's that?" I asked with curiosity.

"What you ordered." He smiled, squeezing the tube for the ointment to fill the tip of his fingers.

53

"I don't need lubricant," I told him, offended if that's what he was insinuating. "My shit is wet enough."

He smacked me on my ass and stroked his dick across my clit. "I know, but your ass ain't."

"Huh!" I screamed in surprise. By the time my head turned, he had applied the Anal Ease in the crack of my ass and was putting the head in. I know everybody in the club heard my wailing as he broke in my ass virginity. That shit hurt like hell.

"Whew," I said to myself, coming out of that flash. I didn't have a problem with bowel movements ever since he did that.

I knew Earleon was cooking gourmet tonight, but I couldn't resist purchasing a chicken cheese steak. I didn't have any plans of sharing it, so I dined in. I talked shit with Walter, the handsome black cook with the dreads, until I finished. I promised him I would come through and holla at him next time I came down. I knew I wouldn't, but saying it made it seem like I would.

All the shoppers walking the beat on South Street—young, old, straight, gay, black, white—didn't bother me for once. I didn't even need to take my medicine to calm my nerves. I smoked a blunt in the place of it, like I normally did.

My braids were fly and my gear—well, it was average. I never lied to myself. I had on a basic pair of Jou-Jou blue jeans, a white cotton V-neck shirt with my Fila sneakers and Earl's black North Face goose down coat. What? Wasn't nothin' wrong with that. I told you, I'm no fashion queen. I'll leave that for the young girls who got it like that. Me, I don't. Ain't no future in frontin'.

I thought about how worried Icelene was about that Welfare issue I had to address. What would happen to me if I were prosecuted? I wasn't going to let that stress me out. I was too blessed to be stressed, okay! They were gonna do what they wanted to anyway when it came down to my case. I wasn't even responding to that bullshit. When they asked me to take a class, I did. When they asked me to bring in required paperwork, I did. Maybe not the income stubs, but hell, how do they expect us to get ahead? For every dime we make, they take away two from our checks. I couldn't keep ahead for them trying to make me take steps backwards. And what about the added responsibility we had with Gaynelle? Social Services wouldn't pay for childcare when kids are over twelve. I had to pay the deacon and Laverne. Yeah, they said they did it from the goodness of their hearts, but they accept the $700 a month I gave them for caring for her. They didn't ever turn the money down. One time, on some bonus shit, I would hand over my EBT, Electronic Benefit Transfer card to them.

If Earl wasn't hustlin' and Earleon and me weren't working, the six of us wouldn't be able to survive. I mighta dressed like a damn 'Bama, but my clothes were clean and my kids were always looking jiggy. As long as they had, I was all right. So, if I had to go down for fraud, all the mothafuckas that illegally benefited should go down too, right? Nah, I wasn't a snitch bitch. I did my dirt all by my lonely, just like that sexy chocolate-ass Treach from Naughty by Nature does.

I would discuss this issue with my kids that night at the meeting. I didn't want any of them to be in the dark about what might happen to me.

A Family That Balls Together, Falls Together

The aroma of cooked sausage mixed with Italian tomato sauce filled the house. Earleon was in the kitchen dicing up onions and bell peppers. Elgin and Earl were watching *A Time To Kill*, commenting if they were Samuel Jackson's character and a man raped their daughter, they'd have done the same thing—killed him. Icelene was trying hard to primp and prim. Don't know why. Who was she trying to get cute for? Gaynelle was walking turtle-like slow behind me with a cane to aid her stability. Her skin was pale and she had lost weight dreadfully. She had dark rings around her eyes, which scared the hell out of me. I knew her health was deteriorating, fading from her body quickly. It happened so rapidly. The deacon hadn't a choice but to start her back on the medication that the doctor put her on. That holistic shit apparently wasn't working.

"Icelene, bring a blanket in here for Gaynelle. Her fingers are ice cold."

"Sure, Juicy. Your micros look cute," she complimented me. Her comment led to a few necks turning to see my new 'do.

"Juicy, when did you have time to get your hair done? Didn't you have to work today?" Earl asked suggestively, trying to catch me in a lie. There he went with that questioning shit. I thought I had no reason to lie to him. He was no man of mine.

"I didn't go to work today. I called out," I replied coldly.

"To get your hair done?"

"No, to get my hair and nails done, to be exact," I said, flashing my acrylic-filled nails in his face. They were airbrushed over two coats of bright orange polish.

"Damn, Juicy, don't hurt 'em, girl," Icelene teased.

"You know I do my thang-thang," I teased back, doing my best version of The Whop, an old school dance we used to do in Brooklyn. Everybody in the house laughed. Even Gaynelle attempted to grin. I always knew how to entertain my kids. When I wouldn't, we'd get together and pop in a Tyler Perry "Madea" tape and laugh our asses off at the play.

Icelene curled up on the futon with Gaynelle and allowed her to use her arm as a pillow. She went above and beyond for Gaynelle. All the kids loved their baby sister, but Icelene was the one connected to her hip. She visited Gaynelle more than any of us when she was away from home. She would feed her when she was weak, bathe her and even read the Precioustymes Youth Series books for teens to her. She may have been a hot ass, but she had a heart that pumped golden red blood.

Elgin picked up the phone after the first ring, knowing the rule when we had family discussions was not to answer it. I was back in my bedroom putting on my orange Chinese slippers to match my nails. When I hit the talk button, I heard T.C. on the other end having small talk with Elgin.

"What's up, T.C.? What you know no good?" I cut in.

"Dee-Dee, I've been thinking about you since I seen you at my job, girl. You still look the same, all good and juicy and shit." I accepted his compliment, but left it at that. I couldn't tell if he was bullshitting me or not. He was easy with the compliments, but he was always like that when he was younger.

"T.C. I don't go by Dee-Dee no mo'. Everybody calls me Juicy. You can too," I said with a slight edge in my voice. I didn't want to flip out on him like I did to Juney, because I hadn't seen him in a minute and figured he just didn't know.

"Juicy, huh? That's fittin' for you." He laughed, making me muse as well at my persistence in being called Juicy. When I was coming up, mostly all the teachers mispronounced my name calling me Deh-dra, so to stop it, I told them to call me Dee-Dee. I didn't start to have a dilemma with it until I got grown. Dee-Dee wasn't cute no more. I wanted a jazzier name.

"I don't want to cut you short, T.C., but I'm in the middle of a family meeting with my kids. Can you call me later?"

"Oh, okay, but before I let you go, let me run something pass you."

What T.C. was talking rang sweet tunes in my ears. After the meeting, I set a time to discuss my plan with him.

Earleon had finished everybody's plates, even hooking us up a Caesar salad. You know, for a long time I told my kids that salads were for white people. That was because I never had one. I wasn't introduced to salads until I became an adult. Earl was the first man to take me out to dinner. We ate at the Olive Garden restaurant and the first dish was a huge bowl of fresh Caesar salad with croutons and a blazin' in-house salad dressing. Since then, I made sure we had plenty of vegetables in the fridge to make a salad when we had a taste for one.

Icelene made a request that threw us all back. She wanted to bless the food and put up a special prayer for Gaynelle. I was devilish, but who would turn down a request like that? Only a fool, and I sure wasn't one of them. I never played when it came down to the Lord.

Our bellies were full; however, none of us denied a slice of pineapple upside-down cake that Earleon had hidden from us as a dessert surprise. Earl turned off the TV and we sat round robin, all together for our family discussion. The eldest of the kids always went first. Each of them had a turn to discuss an issue or situations they needed help with. It was sorta like Bible study without the Bible, though we didn't discuss God, we discussed hood issues.

Earl began telling us about the growing rise in corner beef on the block where he was hustlin' at. "Niggas ridin' my dick out there. They want a piece of the action."

"Do you know dem niggas?" Elgin asked.

"I mean, they come through once in a while, na'mean. Yo, niggas go by the names of Brownsville, Nap, Hank and Scoot. You heard of 'em?"

"Puh-leeze. I know Brownsville and dem niggas," Icelene bragged. "They makin' *real* loot. If I was you, I'd get down wit' 'em."

"Hot ass would know," Earleon added.

"Mm-hmm. Which one of the niggas you fucked?" I questioned her.

"Only Brownsville and Scoot. My girl did Nap and Hank," she replied with no remorse.

"Whatever man, she's fuckin' me up with dis ho shit," Elgin responded, speaking of Icelene.

"Fuck that. I'm trying to steer clear from beef, but niggas trying to take my block. I may have to bring the heat to these cats if I choose not to get with 'em."

I asked him, "How much paper they holding? Are they real moneymakers?"

"True dat," he spit. Icelene seconded that motion.

When he said they were, I told him to join them if they were going to front him shit—case closed! Now, his second issue, none of us were ready for. When the money started to get short, I had a feeling something was going down. Then he dropped the bomb on my ass. This mothafucka had a family on the side and said he was moving out to live with them if I didn't accept them. You should have heard his bitch ass sounding like his father.

"Juicy, I know how you are. You don't accept grandkids, but I needed to tell you because I've been holding this shit in. I have one-year-old twin daughters, Deidra and Dionne. That's were most of my money goes."

"What the fuck you mean?" I bounced up in his face.

"I know you told me not to fall in love with hoes, but I love my ho. She holds me down out there. I've made up my mind if you can't deal with it . . . " he breathed deep, "I'll just move in with her."

None of the other kids hummed a word. This nigga was shorting our family for a money-hungry whore and her kids, which probably wasn't even his.

"Who is the fuckin' girl?" I screamed. "What happen to the nigga that said bitches ain't shit but hoes and tricks, huh? 'I don't love dem hoes'," I reminded him. My son fit right along with the group of niggas that always talked bad about hoes then ended up with their tongues inside the legs of one.

"It better not be one of these around the way girls!" Icelene yelled, wanting to know who it was right along with me.

"Juicy, it don't matter. What matters are my little shorties. I love them like you love us. I want them to be a part of this family, if you'll accept them." He hoped desperately that I'd say yes. "If not, I have no choice *but* to go be with them."

"Fuck that!" I yelled. "Who is the fuckin' girl?"

He hesitated briefly. "Remember the chocolate girl you hooked me up with when I was fourteen?"

I heaved to clear my throat, which was itchy from hollering at him. "Your dumb ass fell in love with that hooker bitch? To top it off, you made babies with her. Don't you know every man in the inner city done ran up in that?"

How vexed I was at this bitch-ass nigga. I took him to meet Hershey for her to teach him how to screw, not to make him her man. She was thirteen years older than him, and a year older than I was, and much more experienced than my son. She knew better! I guess by him naming the girls after me he thought I would be easy with it.

I was so mad with him I turned away to face the opposite direction and went on the next child, Earleon. I'd deal with his bitch, Hershey, in my own way later. I knew from earlier that Earleon had some shit to get off her chest, so I needed her to let that shit loose.

"Your turn, Earleon. What bullshit you gonna hit us with?" I could tell she was busting her brains, thinking hard on saying it after what Earl informed us of.

"Juicy," she said, burning a hole in the floor from staring at it so hard, "that night you stayed at the club with Tank . . ." My sons' eyes opened wide with alert. They all knew about Tank, the stripper from North Philly, but they didn't know that I slid out with him on occasion to the back room. "I ended up leaving with Pistol Pete. We hooked up with Liz at her apartment and had a threesome." Icelene covered Gaynelle's ears to protect her innocence.

"What?" I game-faced like most of the niggas did in Albany Projects. "You did what?"

"I'm not even trippin' off the threesome," she said without stiffening. "My dilemma is I enjoyed the sex with Liz better than I did with Pistol Pete. If lightning didn't strike me twice over when Liz put that tongue on me, I'd be lying."

"Juicy, you know that gay shit run in her family. Look at her punk-ass pops," Elgin commented, displeased with his older sister.

I knew it was highly likely that one of the twins had Juney's gay tendencies. I guess I was relieved that it wasn't my son that liked dick. A lesbian was easy to deal with.

"To be real with you, Elgin, I thought you'd be the homo thug, so shut the fuck up," I stated. "Earleon has the floor. Wait your mothafuckin' turn."

Earl, Earleon and Icelene hollered. This shit was serious, though. It won't a damn joke. My kids were losing their got-damn minds.

"You a lesbo now, Earleon? *What?* Then you picked the ugliest damn white tramp you could find to be gay with? You know I don't like Casper, and that's probably why. Damn chomp monster."

Earleon and Earl looked as though they'd taken a load off their shoulders.

"Don't knock it until you try it, Juicy. Liz can eat a—"

"Please! Save us from the fuckin' details. We don't need to hear all that." I motioned to Earl to pass me a cigarette. I only smoked them when my nerves bothered me, and they were jumpin' from every muscle.

"Elgin, go ahead. What are you hiding from us? Before you tell us, one of you mothafuckas betta light up some strawberry haze, because I feel a panic attack coming on," I said, inhaling the cigarette with force, making O-rings while heavily tapping my feet.

All of them except Gaynelle whipped out a blunt with the quickness. I needed to be high to deal with this shit tonight. We took a twenty-minute intermission. I taught them to be open, but I didn't expect them to be this wide open. Dayum! The shit they were telling was straight-up primetime for a *Jerry Springer* show.

During the break, I called T.C. back to find out what he was hittin' for. I knew he wanted another shot to get my goodies. The last time we tried, we were young. It was around the same time I got pregnant with Elgin. He wanted me bad, too, but I kept getting sick, throwing up and all. In turn, it turned him off, so we never had a chance to do the nasty. He tried after I had Elgin; almost succeeded too, but Gayle had in her mind it was time for me to exit Philly. I had caused enough gossip for the neighborhood to talk about. I still remember his tear-stricken face when I told him I had to move away. I don't know if he was crying because he didn't get no pussy or he was just sad to see me go.

As fate would have it, though, here we were a second time around. When I came back in town, I'd heard T.C. was in and out of juvenile homes, cased up. I had yet to figure out how he dodged criminal charges as an adult, but I was going to find out.

"T.C.? You there?" The line was full of static from the cheap-ass cordless phone.

"Yeah, Dee-Dee, hit the channel button to clear the line." I hit the button a few times until there weren't any distracting sounds to interrupt our call.

"Didn't I tell you to call me Juicy? Make that the last fuckin' time you call me Dee-Dee, a'ight?"

"You know it's gonna take me some time for me to get used to calling you *Juicy*," he said with much exaggeration.

"You heard what I said. Now, what's up? I only have a few moments to talk," I said, drawlin' in the weed smoke.

"I wanna holla at you," he tried to mack.

"You are," I said, annoyed by the small talk. I wanted him to get to the point.

"I want to start off where we left off as kids," he confessed.

I sucked my teeth. Here this grown-ass man was scared to say he wanted to fuck, feeding me a bullshit line. I had five fuckin' kids. What, he didn't know?

"T.C., just ask me when we gon' get our fuck on."

He snickered at my comment through the phone. "You were never a person to hold your tongue. Straight to the point, as always."

"That's the only way I know how to be. Now, is that all?"

"No. What I was saying earlier, I was serious."

I knew exactly what he wanted. "So, you wanna jeopardize your job, huh?"

"We're not gonna get caught. That damn security system is still malfunctioned. But if we're gonna do it, we have to move on it this week."

I blew smoke in the air, puckering my lips, feeling real nice. "Let me see what I can work up."

"Don't play with me, Juicy. This is on some real shit," he said, agreeing with my wicked thoughts about him. I knew this nigga was still scheming. Criminal minds think alike.

"Look, T.C., I never been a bullshitter, and I ain't about to start being one. I'm about my business. I need to pull a team together is all for this job. I'll call you after I round them up. How much paper you think we gon' get?"

"I know about five hundred thousand or more, without the blue dye packs in the bag."

"And how you figuring we divvy up the money once we execute this plan?" I needed to know this beforehand. If he was going to do some shiesty shit, I'd be able to read into it by his choice of words.

"Uh . . . uh," he struggled for the answer. "I figured sixty/forty"

"What? And who's getting the sixty percent?" I knew he wasn't thinking me. "Nigga, you must be out yo' mind. My daughter works there too! I'd be endangering her livelihood as well. You might wanna come betta, like sixty-five/thirty-five, with me getting the higher percentage. I got extra heads to pay off."

"Damn," he mouthed. "All right, you got that. Call me when you're ready. I got things to take care of."

See how the situation changes when money is involved? Nigga wasn't even pressin' over the pussy anymore. It was about business.

All the years in the game, I just knew Earl would be the one to get us out of the projects. My vision of that was getting blurrier by the day. I had taken it upon myself to muscle my way out this bitch for me and my kids. If things went smoothly, we would be able to buy a house—not on the hills, but in the Wynnfield section of town. I would even settle for a townhouse off of Ellsworth Street in Southwest Philly.

I had to lure Earl and Elgin into the hustle. Wouldn't be hard. We couldn't tell Earleon about it, and we damn sure had to keep it private eye secret from snitching-ass Gaynelle. Yeah, I know she was sick and all, but we couldn't take any chances of getting caught.

I came out my room feeling agreeable. My kids had been waiting on me to return. Gaynelle was choking off the weed and shit. I bet the contact relieved her of some joint pain, though.

This meeting had turned into some straight hood opera like the book *Diamond Drought* by Brandon McCalla. Secrets were seeping out the woodworks. After smoking another blunt with the kids and drinking a chilling cold Cobra beer, I was calmer and ready to continue on with our conversation.

"Okay, Elgin. It's your turn." I had regained their attention.

"I just have a confession to make. The TV and DVD weren't stolen. I had one of my friends take it out the house, so I could sell them to make a few dollars. I was broker than a mothafucka." That was about the stupidest stunt he'd ever pulled. I guess he figured his news wasn't so bad as the twins. Wrong!

Earl got up and punched him in the back of the head real hard. "Nigga, I could have gave you cash if you was that hard-up," he said like he was the boss playa.

"I needed money to help my shortie get an abortion," he said, ducking his head to avoid getting hit again.

"What you sell them for, fifty a piece? Nigga, that wouldn't even put a dent in the cost for an abortion."

"If I knew you let your bitch keep hers, I would've done the same with mines."

"See what kind of example you're setting, Earl?" I directed my attention in Elgin's direction. "Nigga stealin' from his own family 'cause he too scared to ask for help in that situation."

"That ain't my fault, Juicy. You the one who sets all the fuckin' rules of the house," Earl said with ease.

"Earl, please. Earleon done had five abortions already. I ain't never had a problem with giving up money for that shit and you know that. Your stupid ass shoulda given money up for one. Don't even go there with me."

Icelene rose to tell her tale. What bullshit did she have to tell, I wondered.

"Besides the fact that dude is trying to ruin my rep at school, I'm good," she said, as if her reputation hadn't been scarred already. "Y'all have enough drama for all of us," she said, pointing in Earl and Earleon's way. "My real concern is about Gaynelle and Juicy, but I'll let Juicy tell y'all what's going on."

Gaynelle never complained or said a word. Normally, she would laugh at her ghetto fabulous family members. Today, she barely grinned and hardly gave us any eye contact. While my life seemed to be closing in from general bullshit, my kids' situations were beginning to worsen.

What kind of pleasure did Earleon get off of letting a woman bump bushes instead of lettin' a man make her kitty purr? What difference was it? She'd rather have a woman's head moving up and down, licking her clit? And what the hell was Earl thinking by impregnating a street prostitute? What made Elgin steal from the only family that gave to him? Why did my 15-year-old daughter

64

seem real confident having a serious disease and giving a boy her age the same disease that would stay with the both of them for life? Gaynelle was the only sane member of the family, and she was evaporating in front of us all from Lupus. Why? Just why? I had to continuously ask myself. I'd had enough.

The weed made me analyze each issue that each child brought forth. Each one of them shared a fundamental nature of who I was. With that being the case, who was I to question? They were being the only way they knew how to be . . . like their guardian.

"Listen, all of you." I gestured to my kids. "Icelene, lift Gaynelle up some so I can see her face."

"Ayah, ayah," Gaynelle moaned when Icelene repositioned her. Earleon went over to aid her as the looks on all our faces changed to worry.

"We have bad news on top of bad news. First, let me iron out some wrinkles. Earl, you can forget about moving in with Hollyhood. That ain't happening. You can do what you want as far as the kids are concerned, but you still have a responsibility to *this* household, which means you have to hustle *twice* as hard to make enough money to support both houses. You got that?"

"I got that, Juicy. Does this mean you'll accept the twins?" he asked, trying to alleviate all his added weight. I knew if I told him yes in front of the other kids, that would open the door for more grandkids, so I stood my ground. As much as I wanted to see if my grandbabies favored me and what they felt like if I were to hold them, I couldn't let the kids see me break.

"Hell to the capital N-O," I responded very rudely.

Earl put his head down in disappointment, an obvious signal that all he wanted was my support.

"Now, Earleon, you sit here in front of us all with your lesbian stories and expect us to agree with your sudden change?"

"I am who the fuck I am," she interrupted with arrogance.

"Bitch, don't get cute. If you wanna keep your nose filled with fish, go ahead, but your ass won't do it here. I'll give you a free pass to move out. That way housing won't be on my back about you anyway."

Earleon nodded and rocked back and forth.

"I guess I need a new partner to hang out with. Icelene, are you down?" I asked her in all seriousness.

Earleon smacked her lips and let out a loud sigh. "She's *way* too young, Juicy, and you know that. Isn't it bad enough that you took me along when I was sixteen and turned me out? Damn! You're turning your kids out in record numbers. We don't have to worry about a mothafucka from the streets to do it."

"Hell yeah, I'm down, Juicy," Icelene shouted. "I've been waiting for this day. Hey! Mix a li'l Cris with li'l Dom Perignon. Heading to the strip club, you know we fit'na carry on," Icelene sang, creating her own version of a line from 50 Cent's "Disco Inferno" rap.

"You don't like girls, do you?" I had to ask her to be certain.

"No, baby. Strictly dickly, okay!"

"She's a dumb ho, man," Elgin uttered, expressing how he felt.

"No dumber than your dumb ass," I countered in Icelene's defense, even though he wasn't lying. Those two were stupid and stupider.

"Elgin, I'm not but seconds off of your ass now. If I were you, I'd keep it simple, stupid."

My babies, though most I had forced to mature early, understood our circumstances and the struggle. We fought the system together and were weathering the storm right here in our project house together. We would get through all of our issues together. Fuck the outside world. It could have been World War III inside our crib and our neighbors wouldn't know it. That's how secretive we were at times.

"I found out that Gaynelle has Lupus. It's been confirmed by her oncologist."

"What's that?" Elgin asked for clarity.

"That's what grandma Gayle died from," Earleon declared.

"Is Gaynelle going to die?" Earl wanted to know, with tears filling in his eyes.

"Men don't cry," I said with a black stare, tuning out the possibility of Gaynelle passing away. If there were tears getting ready to drop, they wouldn't now.

"No, she's not gonna die. We won't let her. The deacon and Laverne been giving her medicine to make her better."

"She sure don't seem like she's getting better." Earleon was telling the truth.

"She's going to get better. We'll see to that. The doctor wants to run some more tests next week. I'll know more then."

"What's the other bad news?" Elgin probed.

The mood had changed. I had them right where I needed them. My eyes peered to the plastic-framed picture of Gayle on the living room family portrait wall. I wanted to throw the beer can in my hand at it for all the trials and tribulations I went through when I lived without her. She left me in the hands of somebody else to give up the fight for her life. If she had tried harder, she'd have made it, but she copped out like a coward, leaving the responsibility she had—me—for the next man to deal with. She never taught me anything. The one valuable lesson I learned from her death was to never turn my back on my babies. Gayle turned her back on me and caused me to search for love in the streets. While out there, I ended up with five kids at a mere age of eighteen. My life hadn't even started, and it was already ruined. I hated Gayle for that. She left me with nothing—no rules, no words of encouragement, no tools to survive—nothing! She let me do whatever the fuck I wanted to, and look at my final result. Why, Gayle? Why'd you have to let the disease win?

I had to take T.C. up on that offer, not for me but for my kids. If I didn't do anything else with the money we were planning to steal *but* buy a house, I was going to buy a home for them to always have a place to lay their heads. Who really wanted to live in the projects forever? Nobody. We were made to because we didn't have any other alternatives for housing, but my family damn sure would soon.

"Juicy, tell them about the situation with Welfare," Icelene kept nagging me. I was totally lost in my vague memories of Gayle and our prosperous future.

"Oh, I was cut off of Welfare, Medicaid and food stamps because I frauded the system," I said without regret.

"Didn't they cut you off before?" Earleon questioned.

"Yeah, but that was for failing to attend job readiness classes. Remember when I started going? Had I known they were going to terminate my benefits altogether, I'd of never attended. Wasting my time . . . bastards!"

"Why they cut you off?" Elgin asked me.

"I didn't report the petty income I made from the temp agencies and from the motel I work for now. Oh yeah, and I failed to tell them about Earleon's job at the check-cashing place. They're going back five years on my ass, talkin' 'bout I owe them over twenty-three thousand."

"Damn, Juicy!" Elgin yelled. "What you gonna do?"

"No, mothafucka, it's what *we* gonna do. We're in this together. The money I made went into this household. If I'm found guilty, so are you," I retaliated, waving my hand at all of them. "Meeting adjourned," I said with frustration. I had to piece together the heist.

A Dose of Reality

Normally, I'd walk around the projects as I did in Brooklyn, looking at all the trash stuck along the side of the curbs, shaking my head at the trash build-up. The sewage drains were filled with all kind of stuff, mostly street garbage. I'm certain that's why when it rained, the still water always flooded our area. The trash men stayed on strike. It was bad enough that SEPTA cut back on some of the driving routes, now we had to be subjected to stinking-ass waste piled up in front of our houses, making us represent the image that most media reported 'bout us. We weren't animals and didn't want to live like this, so why couldn't we get fuckin' trash service? I bet you those bitches sitting in high places living in their suburban residential communities were gettin' service.

Around our projects, it was the night of the living dead every night, and people were try'na snatch the life up out of any mothafucka they could. I knew I had to get my kids away from the hellhole we were living in. The aura of hopelessness had been sucking the life out of all us for years, living in these unhealthy conditions. It just won't right, livin' in this bitch like this. We live in a boxed-in community with boarded-up houses scattered around us, and they wondered why it was a high-crime area. Who cares when people think we are less than *they* are? When a nigga starvin', they're bound to do anything. That's what happened in my hood.

The recreational center used to have topnotch programs for the kids to attend. Now, they didn't have shit for the kids, unless they were getting money from the state or private organizations to pay for them to attend. It was all about the almighty dolla now. I remember when basketball leagues at the rec were free. Now, you definitely had to come off some cash if you wanted to participate. Why they continued to advertise all the programs they offered, I don't know. When the fuck was open enrollment and whose kids were they enrolling? My kids never had a chance to benefit from them. The way I saw it, if the programs were for the kids around the way, then they should have first preference, right?

69

They used to have art classes at the center, but when Elgin tried to sign up, they told him all the spots had been filled. It was only five kids in the class, and they were white. They had subcontracted out to get money from those they thought had it. They didn't think us poor folks had the money, so they started cutting back the free programs for us.

It was a time when my kids would go away for a week with the Salvation Army to a camp in the Poconos. It was only twenty dollars per child and less if they siblings were going. That was very reasonable, and it gave me a break from the kids. I had no problem paying that, and the kids had a good time. However, the next year, I guess after they seen the number of kids participating, they made it one hundred dollars per kid without a family discount. I didn't have that kind of cash to send them away again. That broke my babies' hearts. To make it better for them, I pushed the furniture close to the walls in the house and made a tent with the help of mop sticks, broom sticks and some good old sheets, improvising. The homemade tent kept falling down, but the kids loved it. We made popcorn, hot dogs and ate marshmallows like we were on campgrounds. It was so much fun and they were pleased. It didn't take much to please them when they were younger.

I would get a broom and a dustpan sometimes to try and sweep up some of the trash. If I didn't give a fuck about the outside appearance of my home, nobody else would. It had to start with Juicy Brown. I knew most people had the perception that I was low-class and wayward about my life, but I was a woman from around the way that got caught up early with five kids. I didn't have a baller for a man to create a false picture to everyone that my shit was sweet. In fact, most of my male friends were only fucking partners that I didn't get a damn dime from. Did I desire a soul mate? Hell yeah. What woman doesn't? However, it didn't bother me that I didn't have one. My life had to move on. Fuck being depressed and shit about a man.

Time To Execute

I had thought about the nerve of Welfare making a big issue about me working. That's what the mothafuckas started Welfare to Work for, right? Well, that's what the fuck I was doing, going from Welfare to getting a fuckin' check from work. What was the mothafuckin' problem? Those bullshit-ass, low paying, entry-level jobs that they offered to Welfare recipients wasn't shit but minimum wages. How could we survive off of $5.75 with a household of six? Yet people wanted to fault me for making my kids find other hustles. Shit, without them, we'd starve. I'd face the consequences, whatever they were, that were coming my way. Sink or swim, I wasn't scared of those mothafuckas.

Juney came through my front door looking like Tina Turner did when she came running out the limo into the hotel lobby, after Ike beat dat ass in *What's Love Got To Do With It.* His lover must have put a serious bitch slap across that left eye. It was blue-black.

"Damn, Lollipop! You look like Icelene did last week," I fucked with him.

"Dee-Dee, this shit ain't no joke! Sweet Cheeks gon' pay for this here," he said nursing his eye like a sissy bitch.

I knew Juney was upset, because he knew how I felt about being called Dee-Dee, but who gave a fuck about his eye? Not me!

"Bitch, it's Juicy. Stop gettin' it confused before that right eye match up with the left."

"Not today, Juicy." Juney clammed up, bawling worse than an abused woman. "I need your help. Sweet Cheeks put all my shit in his driveway. I need a place to stay for a couple of days. Can I stay here until he cools down and let me come back home?" he sniffled. "By then things would be smoothed out between us. And I don't have no money, so don't ask," he stated firmly, switching his tone.

Oh, Lord! I thought. "You know how the twins feel about you."

"Come on, Juicy. I need you," he pleaded. "Just this once, until Sweet Cheeks is levelheaded."

"Okay, just this once. But you gonna have to sleep in my room."

71

Juney curled up his thin, duck-shaped lips like he was appalled by my request. "Juicy, you know I'm not into women."

"And I'm not into tucked dicks, either. Look, I'm try'na to help your sweet ass. You ain't doin' me no favors by staying here," I snapped.

"Okay, okay," he said, aggravated.

"Go ahead, tell me what happened. I know you're dyin' to tell me anyway."

Juney got comfortable on the futon, crossing his legs like they was cute, and gently caressed his black eye. Elgin and Icelene were in school. Earl was probably stuck under Hershey. Gaynelle was with her second family, and Earleon was at work. They were all safe from hearing about his spat with his lover. I was still buggin' that Juney felt comfortable calling his lover Sweet Cheeks to me. I guess that was his pet name for him.

"Where do I begin?" He panted like a bitch, wiping his fallen tears from his face.

"From the beginning, Juney," I said, giving him my approval nod. After Juney finished telling me about his drama, I wanted to slap my momma for not teaching me the birds and the bees. Why did I ever have sex with this he/she? Was I that much in denial?

First off, his crazy ass met Sweet Cheeks, government name Antonio Wyield, over the Internet on Gaysingles.com. They went out for drinks, and the same weekend Antonio introduced him to a group of elite, upper-class gay men. They weren't a secret society. These were openly gay men, out-the-closet type. All of them held high positions in the corporate world, most of them stockbrokers. They all made a substantial amount of money. Every month, "the group" would get together on a yacht owned by one of the members and have an all-out orgy.

"Gay men have orgies?" I asked in disbelief.

From what Juney told me, dicks be slangin' everywhere. When the lights went out, any ass could get poked. "A toe is a toe," Juney stated. Go figure!

Since they'd met, they had been going to this outing, never having a problem until Juney and Antonio decided that they wanted to swap partners with another couple. Well, Sweet Cheeks couldn't take the way Lollipop was downing the other man's joint and went off. See, I knew that Juney was a male whore. That's where Earleon gets that freaky shit from, mm-hmm.

I told Juney not to tell anyone else that story. He had me gagging, showing me how he damn near swallowed 10 inches of manhood. That's why they called him Lollipop—he sucked a mean dick to death!

While Juney was still whining, T.C. called. "So, did you get your team in order?"

"Not yet," I responded.

"Come on, Juicy. We don't have much time. Get your people together tonight and be ready to get this shit done by tomorrow evening. It's that simple," he responded in a deep baritone before bangin' the phone on me.

I hung up the phone and figured since Juney was here, he could be of some use. I'd put him down with us. It would be me, Earl, Elgin and Juney. I'd be the money grabber, Earl and Elgin the gunmen and Juney the so-called lookout. All I had to do now was to let the boys in on this.

I had Juney call up to the school for Elgin for an early dismissal, perpetrating like he was me. I had called Earl and spoken to him briefly, so he was on his way. If it were sweet like T.C. said it was, it would go down without any problems.

He'd told us the best time of the day to come was right before the check-cashing place closed. Earleon and Liz were working that shift. The other employees would have been relieved of their duties an hour and a half before closing, which meant there would only be three people working during that time, T.C., Earleon and Liz.

Earl came inside the house, cussin' up a storm about Juney being there. "What the fuck do his punk ass want?" he said in obvious discontentment.

Juney immediately bucked up. "I'm still ya daddy, no matter how you think of me," he said, switching his tense.

"I don't have a father. He's dead in my eyes." Earl heaved.

"Easy, Earl," I commented. "We have business to discuss. Sit down, please, and no more comments like that to Juney, a'ight? He *is* still your father."

Earl pulled a blunt from his pocket. "Fuck that," he said, sucking in his haze.

Juney glanced as if he wanted to ask Earl for a pull. I shook my head at him. That blunt was for Earl and me to share.

Elgin finally arrived and the plotting began. I didn't want to slick-talk any of them. I wanted to be real honest.

"Look, we have an opportunity to make some quick cash," I began.

"Why is this nigga here then?" Elgin questioned with grave intent. "He ain't family."

I knew I had to be on point to tactically get them to work together. "Let me finish before you start interrupting," I whispered on some top-secret mission type shit. Elgin leaned back. Earl and Juney were attentive. As crooked as we all were, I knew when I started mentioning the money that was involved nobody would have beef. It was strictly business. Earl was gritty. Elgin was a cold-blooded thief, and Juney was a gold-diggin' homo. Me, I was just trying to eat. Difference was, I wasn't doing it for selfish intentions. It was for my family.

I made sure everyone knew their position.

"Okay, Elgin, you and I will take the clerks. Earl, you hold down security, and Juney, you just watch our backs. Got that?"

I explained to them that one simple mistake could land us all in jail. I made our motto "If we fail, don't tell," meaning "Shut the fuck up!" Just because you got busted don't mean you have to bring everyone down with the operation. I guaranteed them they would still get their cut of the money if they got caught.

Earl and Elgin were with it. Juney was kind of hesitant.

"I don't know, Juicy," he doubted. "This is not my forte. Usually I'm on the receiving end. I'm usually not the guy positioned in the back watching everything."

"Don't we know it," Elgin hunched.

"You know, for a young boy that happens to be a little too close to his li'l sister, I wouldn't talk too much."

"Juney!" I yelled. "That's enough and cut that out. My kids do not get down like that. Remember, Elgin is still a minor."

"But I'm man enough to beat his faggot ass," Elgin replied.

"I wouldn't try that if I were you, youngin'," Juney said in his manly voice.

I had to laugh. "Make up your mind, bitch. You want to be man or a woman?"

"I want the best of both worlds."

"Nigga, didn't Jay Z and R. Kelly teach you anything? Bringing both worlds together, that shit don't work. You can only have the best of one world."

Turn For The Worse

I stopped past the deacon's house to visit Gaynelle. They were a modest family, God-fearing. I guess their faith was what kept them grounded. I know they felt like I was less than a mother to let my sickly child stay with strangers. They weren't completely strangers, though. Gaynelle started going to church with them when she was 8 years old. We met them when they were out evangelizing door to door. I never sat and listened to that shit, and neither did the rest of my kids, except Gaynelle. They peaked her interest, not mine. She would stand at the door, listening to every word they had to say. When they invited her to church the first time, I told them no, she couldn't go. But when Gaynelle started to cry, I said, "Go on then." That's how they formed a bond with her.

I guess the more they got to know her, the more they found out about my family. Gaynelle told them every damn thing. I got to the point where I had to tell them to mind they fuckin' business. I didn't have any problem with their relationship with Gaynelle, but the rest of my family was none of their concern. That's how people do. They find a way to leak into your household and then want to tell you how fucked up you living before they clean around their own front door. Would mothafuckas just leave me and mines alone? I never asked anyone to do for us. The deacon and his wife volunteered.

I pressed the doorbell and Laverne came wobbling to the door with her sanctified, holier-than-thou ass.

"Come on in, Juicy. We were just about to call you."

I stepped into the dimly lit pastel-colored living room, and the smell of sickness filled my nostrils.

"Gaynelle's not doing so well. I think we need to have her admitted to St. Joseph's Children's Hospital."

When I walked into the bedroom, I wondered what Laverne was talking about. Gaynelle was resting peacefully.

"Get up, Gaynelle. Juicy is here." I massaged her arm. Gaynelle moaned loudly from my touch.

"Juicy, don't do that," Laverne stated, pushing my arm away like I was a little child. "The girl is hurting. We need to call an ambulance to come get her to be checked out."

The deacon stood in the doorway, watching us, waiting for me to make the call. Laverne had the phone in the palm of her hands, waiting for me to dial the number since I was Gaynelle's guardian. I reached for the telephone, but instead of dialing 911, I called home. Icelene answered the phone.

"Icelene, is Earl and Elgin home?"

"Yeah, they here, Juicy," she answered.

My eyes filled with tears. "Okay, you tell them to meet me at the deacon's house. We need to carry Gaynelle home."

Laverne grabbed the phone from me. "Icelene, don't you listen to your mother. We need to get Gaynelle to the hospital or she's going to die."

Gaynelle hadn't moved since I'd been there, though she continued to moan.

"You can't carry her out of here like this, Juicy. We can't let you do that," the deacon stated in a stern, ministering pitch.

"She's my fuckin' daughter, and if I say she's going with me then that's what the fuck it is!"

Laverne leaned toward me, clutching my shoulder. Her hands were gripping me tightly. "Have you lost your mind, Juicy?"

"Yes," I honestly answered. "Years ago. Now, get your hands the fuck off me!"

"This little girl needs help. If you take her home and not to the hospital, she won't live through the night. Her blood pressure is at sixty-four over forty-six, which is close to the borderline of death. I just took it minutes ago." If Laverne hadn't worked as a certified nurse's assistant years ago, I wouldn't have believed her, but she kept most of her medical supplies, such as her blood pressure cuff.

"We need to get her to the hospital immediately," Laverne demanded.

The deacon tried calling for help, but I kept smacking the phone out his hands, even pulling the cord from the wall. Icelene, Earl and Elgin were at the front door. I rushed to the door and let them in.

"Come, look what they've done to your sister!" I cried.

Elgin looked like he was fresh out a "get high" house. He reeked of weed, and his hair had lint balls in it. One side of his head was braided and the other side was flying wild. Earl and Icelene were both decent.

I knew the deacon and his wife meant well for Gaynelle, but every time they took her, she got worse. It seemed like they helped to spread the disease throughout her body. I had made up my mind that they weren't going to use my daughter as a guinea pig no more. She'd been on so many medications that some of it was working against her like Laverne had once told me.

I knew when they informed me she had Lupus there was a strong likelihood that she was going to die. I wasn't going to do like Aunt Angie and Uncle Saint did to me. I didn't see Gayle until the day of her funeral. They hadn't even taken me to see her in her last days. If my daughter were going to die, it would be in the arms of her family, not with a bunch of strangers or outsiders.

"Come on Earl. Help me get her up."

"Juicy, no!" Laverne screamed, shedding tears. "Please!"

Earl had a sympathetic look on his face. "Juicy, are you sure of this?"

My kids never second-guessed my word. They usually followed through with any request I made to them. Icelene and Elgin were in a stupor, waiting on my response.

"Do I sound like I'm jokin'? Now come on, boy. You grab her upper body and I'll get her bottom half. Icelene, when we get her up, you put the blanket over her, hear me?"

She nodded. "Yes."

The deacon and his wife embraced, comforting each other like I was doing something very wrong. I had allowed them to take her off of the prescribed medicines, praying that the holistic health remedies were going to work in her favor. They failed me, and now my baby was paying for it. They were to blame, not me! I'd never depended on anybody when it came to my kids, and the first time I did, the consequences could be fatal.

Gaynelle's body was weak and limp. Her limbs dangled like a rag doll when we positioned her body in our arms. The pain she felt in her joints must've been excruciating. Her moans turned into loud shrieks. I knew she was hurting to the high heavens, but I wasn't gonna let her die like Gayle, in the hands of someone else. I had to get her out of there fast.

I knew we had to execute the plan sooner than we bargained for, all in the name of Gaynelle.

Let's Get It On!

We settled Gaynelle in my bedroom, kicking Juney's ass out to the living room. Icelene ran to the medicine cabinet and placed each brown pill bottle ever prescribed for Gaynelle on the bed. She knelt down on the floor, a much too favorable position for her, at the side of the bed to read what each prescription was for. Earl and Elgin remained in position as we tried to make Gaynelle as snug as we could.

"Here, Juicy. She needs to take these." Icelene handed me the pills and Earl ran to get me a glass of water. Gaynelle was not good at swallowing pills. She always feared that she would choke off of them, but I was going to make her swallow them today, somehow. Earl came back in the room with a glass of orange juice, hoping that it would ease her fear of choking. If it didn't work this way, I would crush them shits up and put them in her drink.

"Come on, baby. Wake up." I tapped her on the face. "You have to take this medicine so you can get better." This was my hope that she would.

She moved up and down just slightly. Her head tilted back as she tried hard to part her lips. Her tongue hung from her mouth like she had been the victim of a stroke.

"Open wider for Juicy, Gaynelle."

She opened her mouth just enough for the pills and a sip of juice to pass through it. "Now close and swallow," I instructed too impatiently. Gaynelle tried, but the orange juice ran from the sides of her mouth while the pills started to dissolve on her tongue.

"Swallow, Gaynelle, swallow!" Icelene and I hollered.

"Why don't you crush the rest of them, Juicy?" Earl suggested rashly.

I had that in mind to begin with. I should have done it that way as I planned. A straw would have been better, if I had some. Icelene started grinding each pill as finely as she could, putting the powder-like substance into the glass of orange juice. Gaynelle's eyes rolled to the back of her head scaring us shitless!

I panicked. "Gaynelle, come on, baby," I tried to encourage her. "Drink this and you'll get better, I promise."

This time, she gained just enough strength to sip down the orange juice gorged in medicine. My kid's facial expression read death. I wasn't accepting the grim reaper's call for her life. I was rebuking that shit.

"She's gonna be fine. Now go on 'bout your business. Let her get some rest. Stop acting like this is the first time you've seen her like this. We got through it those times, and we'll get through it again. Now, go!" I said, hoping to give an ounce of peace.

We all went into the living room, keeping the door to my bedroom open. I could hear Gaynelle call out to me, but vaguely.

I rushed back inside the room. "Juicy's here, baby."

"Mommy," Gaynelle said in an angelic voice, "I love you."

I couldn't stop the tears from coming. This was the first time I'd ever heard any of my kids call me Mommy. I was always equivalent to their level. Gaynelle was the first to make me realize that I was the mother and not the sister that I made them *let* me be.

"Oh, and I love you too, baby girl." I wrapped my arms around her in a way a mother should, not giving her a pound or a hood handshake that I normally would.

I called for Icelene and asked her to sit with Gaynelle while we—Earl, Elgin and Juney and me—handled some business. I told her if Gaynelle got any worse to call 911.

I knew I was wrong for leaving her in that condition, but I had to maximize the moment. This may have been the last chance I had at knocking this place off.

"Should I call Earleon?" Icelene asked, unknowing of our plan.

"No, I'll handle that. You just make sure Gaynelle stays alive."

➤

We had gone over the plan four times when we finally got up the nerve to follow through with it. I know we smoked about eight blunts before we left. It took away the nervousness that each of us was feeling. None of us had any idea what the outcome would be.

I called T.C. and gave him the code that we were en route. He excused himself from his post to unlock the back security door for us to gain access. We parked the minivan a few blocks way, all of us dressed in black. Elgin had stolen black winter hats that pulled over our heads to expose only our eyes, nose and lips. We were to put them on seconds before hittin' up the check-cashing place.

Earleon had no knowledge we were going to do this. I made sure that we didn't use actual guns. Pellet guns served the purpose. We had four of them, courtesy of Elgin. They looked identical to .45 automatic guns. We could get away with that.

Our time to shine had come. As bitchy as Juney could be, he acted "all man" to get this money. I could tell this wasn't the first stick-up Elgin had been on. He was much too calm, even before the weed. Besides, why the hell else would he have pellet guns in stock? He was keen to detail, and showed outstanding leadership qualities during the whole ordeal. Earl was the clammy one. I just hoped he didn't freeze up once we got inside. I taught my kids better than that, and I had to rely on that once we got in there.

With our masks on, we had four minutes to get in and get the fuck out.

"Go, go!" Elgin screamed as he timed us with his Timex stopwatch after peeking in to see if the store was empty of customers. We ran inside the cash-checking spot and Elgin yelled to T.C., "Lock the mothafuckin' door! This is a mothafuckin' stick-up. Run it, nigga."

Earleon immediately threw her hands in the air. Casper tried to reach for the silent alarm button to scare us off, but we knew it didn't work.

"Hands in the air, bitch!" Elgin hollered. Liz looked to Earleon in fear. Juney's eyes kept searching the threshold. I threw two pillowcases on the counter and told them to fill them shits with cash, no blue packs. Earl had T.C. at pellet point to make the heist appear to be real, not a set-up.

When Earleon reached for the one pillowcase, I noticed a hint of hesitation.

"Put the money in the bag, bitch," I warned her. Yes, she was my daughter, but I couldn't show my hand.

Casper had filled her bag, even trying to put a die pack inside of it. Elgin noticed quickly and butt-slapped her with his pellet gun, putting a gash in her forehead. He wasn't supposed to do that. We had agreed this stick-up would be non-violent.

Earleon stacked the money in the pillowcase and handed it to me, shaking her head in shame. I don't know why I didn't buy new pillowcases to take with us. These were the same pillowcases from the house. Earleon knew it was us. We did a good job muffling our voices, but the pillowcases were a dead giveaway.

Earl led T.C. to the back as Elgin, Juney and I backed out the door quickly but cautiously. He made T.C. lay down on the ground as we made our getaway. Believe it if you want, we go off scot-free! That was so easy, I would have tried it again.

Meeting Adjourned

We were fast approaching the house when we seen the flashing light, not from the police, but from the paramedics. Gaynelle's condition had to have changed. They were wheeling her into the back of the ambulance with Icelene by her side.

"Slow down," I mouthed to Earl in caution. "Let them take her to the hospital first. We can go there later." I wanted to make sure no extras were at the house.

All of us started to peel our clothing to discard any evidence. As I was pulling off my shirt, I had a fucked-up feeling to cover over me. Here we both were, Juney and I, with our son together, after robbing a spot. What kind of parents were we?

Fuck that feeling, I thought, to convince myself I'd done nothing wrong. We were the fuckin' victims here. I was the best parent I knew how to be. I had to respect the hustle. We had a family full of hustle. Jay Z said it best—you can't knock the hustle—so neither was I. We were getting money together. Shit, I taught them all from the opening of the gate to the closing of it. Stack your paper, whatever you do.

When the flashes and sirens trailed out of the projects, we went back into our safe haven. Who gave a fuck what Casper, Earleon and T.C. were doing? Probably talking to the cops by now, giving details to the cops about the robbery. I dragged one of the filled pillowcases to my bedroom and Elgin followed suit with his in grip. Juney finally spoke. He hadn't peeped a word since we left the house the first time.

"You's a gangsta bitch, Juicy. I gotta give it to you."

Earl laughed at his father's joke, for the first time agreeing with what his sissy daddy said. "Juicy is the truth, ain't she?" he also acknowledged, which made me feel damn good.

I had done it. Though I had relied on my kids to make it happen, the day had come, and *I'd* done it for them.

"Come, come," I signaled. "Sit around the bed. Let's count this money." Once we counted it all, I remembered to put T.C.'s portion to the side. I divided the money up in stacks of $10,000. Altogether, we'd lucked up with $600,000. I set aside $200,000, a little under the 35 percent that I promised T.C. Fuck him. We put in most of the work. I tucked $200,000 for myself, and evenly split the remaining $200,000 with Earl, Juney and Elgin, which was a little over $66,000 a piece. Juney took his cash gracefully, even giving me back the child support he owed me.

"Take this before I change my mind," he said in a diva-ish way. "This is for my back child support. Now, can you go to family court and drop the open case on me?"

"Ain't this a bitch?" I laughed. "You gonna give me back what I helped you to get. And I'll think about droppin' the case." I smiled.

"Yes, bitty!" he said, right back to his bitch tendencies.

I split the amount Juney gave me for Hershey and Earl's twins.

"Take this money and put it in an account for my grandbabies, but don't deposit it until this shit blows over. The police are going to be tracking and sniffing out anything suspicious from the staff down to their family members."

Elgin clutched his cash and went into his room to stash away his share of money. Earl rose from the bed with his portion and got up to leave. Juney had called Sweet Cheeks to patch things back up, begging him to let him come back home. He must have agreed from the elated look Juney had on his face.

"My baby said I could come home. I am outta here! Thanks, Dee-Dee, for everything. You know I still love you, girl."

In one nod, I believe Juney did, maybe not physically, but emotionally, as a friend. We never let the fact that he was gay or a deadbeat father interfere with our friendship.

➤

I smelled the money. Some of it was funky and wrinkled, some fresh and crisp. Gaynelle's scent kept overpowering the scent of it all. I smelled her essence all in my covers. Going over to my closet to my hidden safe, I secured the money, not once fearing Elgin would try to cheat me out of any of it.

I went outside to find Earl to take me to the hospital to check on my baby girl. Ever since my cousin was arrested for vehicular homicide, it made me nervous to drive. That's why I had no problem catching the bus or letting Earl chauffer me around.

The streets were dark 'cause the pole lights were busted out. This was the hundredth time this occurred. The hustlers always busted them out to keep the area dark while they hustled. I wouldn't have to worry about that no more. We were moving on up—right out of the projects, that is.

The money took a burden off me. I could pay Welfare back and tell them to go to hell. I was still going to slave for the motel, at least for the next six months. I didn't want to be that cocky. I did have a little bit of sense—maybe not much, but a little. I had thought about taking a trip to Crown Heights to see old-ass Uncle Saint and Aunt Angie to thank them for what they'd done for me. I was even thinking about throwing a little cash their way. I'd even check up on Ice and Donnell . . . well, maybe.

I wondered if Ice still hated me for what I'd done or if he'd forgiven me. He probably moved on by now, married with kids. Who knows? Nah, that nigga probably doing a life bid. Murder was all in his eyes. Donnell, he was almost certainly up to his old tricks, doing the same shit he did when I was out there.

Albany Projects had a lasting impression in my heart. While I was there, I learned the hustle of life, putting me years ahead of my peers when I went back to Philly. I may not have been a true-bred Brooklynite, but I damned sure felt like one.

Earl was loungin' out front at the entrance of the projects, talking with Hershey. He must have called her soon as he got back. Trick-ass nigga!

"You know you wrong. Right, bitch?" I wanted to punch her dead in the face.

"Juicy..."

I put my hand in front of Earl's face. "This is not about you. Stay the fuck out of this, a'ight?"

Hershey's face was worn with hardness from the years of being on the stroll. She was once pretty underneath those hard layers of skin.

"Who is it about then, Dee-Dee?" Hershey asked, squaring with me toe to toe. "You came to me and told me," she said, aiming to her chest, "to turn him out, and you want to guilt trip on me. I did the job you paid me for. Is it my fault he fell in love with the Hershey?"

The bitch was right, and I didn't intend to contest that. Against my better judgment to punch that bitch in the throat, I just looked to my son as if to say *You dumb mothafucka*! But he only followed my lead, so I couldn't be mad at him.

I gripped my chin, stroking it hard like I had a beard, as I routinely did when I had ill feelings. It was like a camera was stuck on flash, lighted in front of my face, and I couldn't see past the blinding light.

"Where are my grandkids, bitch?"

Earl's shoulders slouched down in relief from being so stiff, awaiting my comeback.

"Inside the car, *Grandmom*," she said, guiding me to the minivan identical to mine, but in another color—green. This was the van Tianna was talking about.

I walked over to the minivan, and through the window I seen the most stunning round faces in the image of me. No wonder they named them after me. Earl opened the door for me and I sat in between the car seats, kissing each of them on the forehead.

"Bring them to the house tomorrow," I told Earl, emotionless. I saw the happiness in his eyes. "But let me get the keys to the van for now. I need to check on Gaynelle." I had to get over my fear of not driving.

Earl reached in his pocket to hand me the keys, but decided it was best if he came along with me. He sent ho-ass Hershey home with the twins.

Game Over

Gaynelle was in the pediatric intensive care unit. I was pointed over to an isolated meeting room where Icelene, the deacon, Laverne and a hospital social worker were in discussion. I felt an ill suspicion that matters were shady. The social worker was filling out paperwork, asking the deacon a thousand questions. I broke into the conversation.

"What the fuck is going on in here and why are we not with Gaynelle?"

Icelene blurted out, "They're going to take Gaynelle from you, Juicy. That's what this is about." She began to cry. "They sent the paramedics over to the house and had the police here waiting. The social worker is assisting them in filling out the paperwork for abandonment and neglect."

"No, the fuck they not!" This hit a few nerves in my body. I needed a cigarette quick.

"Miss Brown, the condition that Gaynelle is in is a clear indication of abuse and neglect." The young, white blonde stated, reminding me of Liz. "Due to the severity of this case, which is a bit thick, Miss Brown," she said, lifting up Gaynelle's medical records, "we are asking for the courts to step in."

Shit, Gaynelle had been coming back and forth from the hospital for years. Most times, the deacon and Laverne would bring her, before they'd even diagnosed her with Lupus. They were the ones who couldn't find out what the fuck was wrong with her. It wasn't my fault that her file was thick with paperwork. The deacon and his wife couldn't even look me in the eyes with their deceitful asses.

"Did they tell you she was in this condition when I picked her up from their house?" I asked the young woman who was trying to do her job. "Did they also tell you that they were the ones who took her off of her medications?"

"Yes," she replied, "*but* with your consent. In fact, Ms. Brown, *everything* is with your consent. Had you never given them authorization to act as her temporary guardians, maybe this wouldn't be happening, but it was you who signed the paper. Here they are, right here. I have a photocopy of the notarized statement," she said, flashing them at me.

I banged hard on the table, shaking it on both ends.

"You two are supposed to be good Christian folks. I trusted my child in your hands and you turn this on me, like I didn't give a fuck if she got better or not. My question to both of you is, was this all a set-up to gain custody of her because I told you a number of times before that I wasn't giving you permanent guardianship? If it's for the money, Welfare ain't gon' pay you nearly as much as I pay you per month. You fucked up if that's what y'all are thinking."

They couldn't say a thing. They had set me up! They knew I would never consent to such a thing if it were going to hurt Gaynelle. Laverne also knew I had trouble understanding medical terminology. She used that against me.

An officer walked in the meeting room with paperwork in his hands. After Icelene read it, she told me it was an affidavit stating that the deacon and his wife were granted to oversee Gaynelle until we went to family court. This meant that they had a right to make decisions on her behalf.

The deacon and Laverne had gathered all the information they needed from Gaynelle when she was well, to document how unfit of a mother I was. They already had the records from Social Services from the many times we were investigated. There was nothing I could do to change the outcome. I told Icelene to come on, and stormed out the room to see my baby.

Gaynelle was plugged up to every piece of equipment that was in her room. Shit really didn't look good. I pulled Icelene close to me and we cried together.

When I Look Into Your Eyes

When I got home, I was so mad and frustrated that I trashed the place, breaking plates, cups—anything ceramic. Icelene was crying from the heart.

"How can they do this?" she questioned, wanting me to reply. "You think I'm to blame, Juicy? I know I shouldn't have let them take her to the hospital."

I comforted her, explaining it was nothing she could do and not to worry because Gaynelle was in the best place. We were consoling one another once more when Earleon came through the doors ready to fight me. With the way I was feeling, she picked the wrong got-damn time.

"You bitch," she said in a voice I'd never heard her use before, like I was her enemy.

"Who the fuck you calling a bitch, Earleon?" Icelene jumped in to protect me.

"No, Icelene," I said, pushing her out the way. "I've been waiting for this day. Bitch thinks she's better than me anyway. Let's see what's really good!" I rolled up my sleeves and knuckled up.

Earleon tried to charge me, but I dodged to the side. She went tumbling on top of the futon and it flipped over from her weight. Once she got up and tried to rush me again, I hit her dead in her weak zone, her stomach. She knotted up quick, after which I dropkicked her ass in the face. Icelene kept screaming for us to stop. I don't know where Elgin or Earl came from, because once we came from the hospital, Earl separated from us and Elgin had been gone to do his own thing. But now they pulled me off of Earleon and tried to get her to leave.

"Fuck you, Juicy! You don't give a fuck about nobody but ya'self. When you said you'd do anything for us, you meant that literally, didn't you? Even involve us in the middle of your bullshit. You better hope I don't call the cops on your ass."

I wasn't worried about that. She would never do such a thing.

"Earl and Elgin, I can't believe you were in on this. How could y'all do that to me?"

"What are you talkin' about? Do what to you?" Icelene was absolutely confused.

Earl slammed Earleon to the floor without warning. "Bitch, don't you ever disrespect Juicy like that! We did that shit for *us*. You gonna get your cut. That money don't belong to you. It belongs to those shifty dicks that owned that mothafucka. They got insurance on it. They'll recoup their loss. Dumb-ass bitch!"

"Don't tell me that dyke been in your ear and you listenin' to her. You feel committed to that trick and not us? We are the only mothafuckas that really love you." I knew Liz would eventually be the one that cut off my relationship with Earleon. She had too much influence over her.

Icelene pried Earl off of Earleon. "While you're trying to fight on Juicy, Earleon; Gaynelle is at the hospital fighting for her life. What's crazy is we stick together for everything else. How come we never come together for Gaynelle?" She expected answers, but none of us said anything. "And we wonder why the deacon and Mrs. Laverne did what they did. They seen we didn't give a fuck! What the fuck is up with that, Juicy? Gaynelle is our blood." Icelene boiled in venom.

I really didn't know what to say. Gaynelle reminded me so much of Gayle that I didn't mind her being out of my company. Out of sight, out of mind. Watching and overseeing Gaynelle meant dealing with the pain I felt about Gayle, and I didn't want to deal with it. So, I let Gaynelle go. I latched onto my other kids because they didn't remind me of Gayle at all, but that damn Gaynelle did, and now she was trying to make me lose the little bit of sense I had by dying on me just like Gayle did.

I couldn't take it. I just broke down and cried in front of them all. They didn't know what to do.

A Trip To The Pen

A week after our family crisis, I'd decided to pay my cousin Kendra a surprise visit and give her the largest care package that the institution would accept. Kendra was a stand-up citizen in her best days as a college student. Her life had changed in a matter of seconds, rapidly destroying her future. I hadn't visited or checked up on her since I'd left Aunt Angie's. I used to correspond with her through mail when I was younger, but stopped when I began my extra activities. She seemed to be a real-type chick from her letters. I understood why Gayle took a special liking to her.

Once on the prison grounds, the secured, gated community made me feel claustrophobic. It had me thinking I should've taken my Paxil. I knew this was not a place for me. The visit itself was enough to scare my 30-year-old ass straight.

"ID please," the black male guard stated. "If you have anything in your pockets, remove it now. Otherwise, it will be considered as contraband."

I emptied out my Doublemint chewing gum and placed it on the counter.

"What about this?" I asked.

"There," he pointed. "The trash can is where you can put that."

"Gum is considered contraband?"

He slid me a visitor's form. "Here. Fill this out and get your badge from the other officer at station number two." His job was routine for him, and he scarcely made eye contact with me or the other visitors.

I handed my form over to the officer in station two and she passed me a visitor's badge, but not without searching me first. I sat down in a room with visitors young and old, all waiting to see their loved ones. I knew jail was not a place I wanted to be and that stunt, although I got off with some cash, could have landed my sons and I a hefty prison sentence. Even Welfare fraud could have done the same. I realized I was fortunate. I dare not try it again, even though I said I would. Jail wasn't in me to risk my life again.

We were sent back into the bright, cemented, divided wall barrier visiting room. Female prisoners sat on the inside of the dividing wall, and visitors sat on the opposite side. The room was so crammed, voices bounced from the walls. The sounds couldn't land anywhere *but* from wall to wall. People in conversation were hollering at one another, trying to over-talk other voices just so they could hear. It was too much confusion and yakking going on for me. I vaguely caught the words Kendra was throwing my way.

"Cousin Dee-Dee, are you with me?" She waved. She wasn't the pretty soror woman that she used to be. Yeah, she had the shape still, but her permanent lines and ripples in her face showed the physical features of a worrywart.

I was there physically, but emotionally I was on another ride. Here I was, visiting her while throwing bricks at the penitentiary at the same time. Aunt Angie's saying was, "Visitors make prisoners." That's why she never came to see her own daughter. She'd send her plenty of money and care packages, but that was it.

Uncle Saint was the one that came to see her every month. He was the one who stressed the importance of family meetings. He said that family should get together on the minimum of once a month to eat together, talk and enjoy each other's company. He was so right. I took heed to that and put it in my reserve for when my kids got of age, and that's when I began our monthly meetings.

"I'm sorry," she apologized. "My dad told me you changed your name to Juicy Brown," she reasoned.

"Huh?"

She hollered to me again for me to hear her.

"Oh girl," I laughed, "you so crazy."

"You better not come in here with a name like Juicy Brown. You'll have all the women on you."

Only for a second that was funny. I'd never thought of it in that way. Kendra had her hair braided, going straight back to the cusp of her neckline with hangtime. I reminisced about when she had the latest hairstyles. She was penciled in on the books at the hairdresser's every two weeks, faithfully.

"What's it like in here?" Her body language told me I didn't want to know.

"Whatever you do, don't come here. That's the best advice I can offer you. No need in asking if you're not doing anything to get here."

I shifted my eyes around the room at all the female prisoners' faces that smiled and hung low with depression at the same time.

"Do you wish you could rewind the time?"

"Don't all prisoners?" she replied with a dumbfounded expression. "I had the life. I mean, even though my mom did some foul shit to Aunt Gayle, we had a decent family. I had no reason to destroy my life like I did to get drunk off alcohol. I had an addiction that I didn't address long before I started getting arrested. I enjoyed drinking and even tried to plead to the judge during my sentencing that the liquor made me do it. You know what his response was? 'The liquor is what caused you to get this life sentence. What kind of fulfillment will you get from that?' I couldn't even come back after he said that."

I felt bad that she was in this situation, but my mind wondered what foul shit had Aunt Angie done to my mother. That's where my head was.

"What did Aunt Angie do to Gayle?"

"She didn't tell you?"

I guess she thought I knew. "No, but you can," I coached her.

"I don't know if it's my place, but I'll tell you anyway, because you should have been told by now. The Browns know they can hide some shit."

I dug into my itching ear, lining my gut up to hear what she had to say. I knew Aunt Angie was holding out on something. I couldn't pinpoint what it was, though.

She commenced to explain. "My mom moved to Brooklyn when her and Aunt Gayle had a falling out. My mom was the wild child, and your mom was the calm and collected one. See, way before you were born and she got sick, she had a job as a supervisor at the Wal-Mart department store. She overseen three sections and was responsible for incoming merchandise.

"My dad, your uncle, well . . . He met your mom first. He came there often to re-stock the electronic merchandise for one of her sections. You know how sharp your mom was wit' her two gold-trimmed teeth in her mouth and her jazzy Philly style. My dad fell right for her. To make a long story short, he started dating your mom. They had a long distance relationship for a while.

"My mom didn't have a man with her carefree ways. Therefore, when she seen how happy Aunt Gayle was, she wanted in on it—well, on my dad, that is. Once when my dad came to visit, Aunt Gayle was at work, but my mom was there. She seduced him into the bed, and I was the result of her seduction. Granted, my dad was amiss, but so was my mom."

I had a mangle on my face that was hard to straighten out.

"Uncle Saint was my mom's man *first*?"

"Yep!"

As loud as the other visitors were, I could only hear Kendra at the moment.

"Your mom backed off of him when my mom rubbed it in her face that they had an affair. She was always jealous of Aunt Gayle. Your mom was so hurt that my mom carried on this way. Meanwhile, my mom moved us to Brooklyn for a change, and my dad moved in with us, but his heart was still with Aunt Gayle. He continued to deliver to Wal-Mart doing his best to befriend your mom again. Aunt Gayle was stern, but even the strong have a weakness for love. So, behind my mother's back, they started seeing each other again. Hence, here you are."

"What!" I remember asking Gayle about my father, and she would always tell me he was on the road. I never imagined in my wildest dreams that she was talking about Uncle Saint.

"You realize they should've been the ones telling you this, but my mom was always good at handling her scandality," she professed.

"That would make you my sister *and* my cousin, my uncle is my dad and my aunt, my step-mom."

"Uh-huh, but one small detail was left out. My dad never married my mother because he told her that his wife should have been Aunt Gayle, and he owed that to her for stepping out there with her sister. So, technically she's not your step-mom."

Ain't that a bitch! All these years of lies untold. Aunt Angie talked all that shit to me and she was just as frisky as I was in her time. I didn't get it from my momma; I got it from her. No wonder we clashed. We were too much alike.

"Why didn't Gayle or Uncle Saint ever tell me?"

"You were Aunt Gayle's life. She wanted to protect you from the humiliation. She didn't want her last days to be filled with disorder. She was a woman of peace."

"I don't get it," I stated, feeling totally betrayed.

"Listen, your mom found out after you gave birth to the twins that she was in the advanced stages of Lupus. The family knew she was going to die, and so did she. That's why I spent so much time with her. What's more is she told me all of this. I confronted my mom about it, and she cursed me out. She didn't deny it, but she didn't co-sign it either. That's when I took my first sip of liquor, after that conversation. I realized my mother was living my aunt's life and that *her* life was a lie."

My head tilted to the side in heaviness.

"Don't worry," she acknowledged. "I felt the same way you're feeling right now—betrayed. I felt my mom was so desperate for love that she snatched it from your mom in hopes that my dad would love her as he did her sister. It was only right that my mom send for you when your mom was in her downtime. Aunt Gayle wasn't in any condition to chase after you and tend to her grandkids while she was sick. Really, my dad was the one who suggested that you come, not my mom. Now, don't think ill of Daddy, because he always took care of you. He sent money to Aunt Gayle faithfully every month."

"How could he be fine with me calling him Uncle, knowing that I was his daughter?"

"Aunt Gayle wanted it that way. She didn't want it to be known because had you known, she would've had to explain, and she wasn't try'na go there with you. Daddy honored her request."

"My life," I said, shaking my head.

"Don't go blabbing your mouth to them, telling them that I told you, either. Some matters aren't to be discussed. They're better left untouched." All of a sudden, she wanted to guilt trip, sounding like Uncle Saint, but in my heart, I thought it was better that way too. I had issues behind them, and my kids had enough for me to be bringing more issues home. They never asked about him anyway. I had told them years ago the same thing Gayle told me—he was on the road.

"Were you there when Gayle died?"

"No, I was in prison by then, but my dad was with her, holding her hand as she faded out. My mom was home with you and the kids."

A deep breath came from my bosom. I had always wondered if she died alone. It was glad to hear that she didn't. This information shed new light on me about Gayle.

"Why wasn't Aunt Angie with them? I could care for my kids. That was her sister dying."

"She couldn't face her. It took her forever to accept that Daddy had backtracked with Aunt Gayle. Ain't that some stuff? She was mad at her, and she *stole* him from her. Hey! You reap what you sow. That's why I'm here now."

The whistle blew, informing us that the visit was over. It was just what the doctor ordered for me. I needed to find peace with Gayle. I was so glad that I came to see Kendra. She answered many of my questions that had lingered for years.

I wasn't even going to address Aunt Angie or Uncle Saint about this newfound information. That made things very clear. No wonder Uncle Saint didn't have a problem raising my kids . . . his grandkids. I had to leave this issue the way it was, for I didn't want my kids to know about it. Why kick up dust when it was settled? If Aunt Angie and Uncle Saint wanted to go to the grave with this, I was okay with it, because I would too. I did want to ask Aunt Angie this one question. Did she learn anything from her mistakes? She had to have made a mistake. Her daughter was in jail and not me.

"Come back and see me again, *sister*, okay?" Kendra smiled.

I gave her a bear hug, letting her know I would. She didn't know, though, that if I didn't stop doing what I was doing, I'd be in a cell next to her and she would see me more than she asked for.

Nothing Changes If Nothing Changes

It had been over a year since the check-cashing heist and the stunt that was pulled by the deacon and his wife. I was angry for months about them being so shiesty, but what really mattered to me was Gaynelle getting better. They managed to stabilize her Lupus, making sure it was regulated daily. She still had her days, but most were very good days.

Instead of me going to their house to visit her, they allowed Gaynelle to visit us once a month in our new home on Columbia Avenue in the Wynnfield section of town. Yes, Juicy did get a house as promised. I don't think Gaynelle could stand much more of me than I did of her *but* once a month. She treasured spending time with her two nieces the most when she was over.

I had forgiven the deacon and Laverne and had no choice but to give them custody because Gaynelle begged me to say yes to her living with them. When the judge talked to Gaynelle about whom she wanted to live with, she didn't hesitate to say the Wright family, crushing me entirely. Though this didn't influence his decision, I did. It was really in her best interest. She never fit in with us crazy folk. She was still my daughter and I was still her mammy, though. Laverne could never take my place.

The Wrights did some real conniving, fucked-up shit, but it was all in the best interest of my daughter. I knew I would never care for her like they would, and I had come to that conclusion and accepted it. What I didn't want to accept was that from my actions, I had lost a daughter. Was it all worth it? Afraid not.

I had also accepted the fact that Earleon didn't really love me for the person I was. That's why she bucked a lot, trying to make me not like her. But whatever she did, I was always cool with it. That's what made it so fucked-up for her. She wanted me to discipline her, but I never found it necessary for any of my kids.

She had moved all her belongings out of the house and had completely moved in with Liz. It wasn't nothin' I could do but deal with fact that she was gay, bi-sexual or whatever you wanna call it.

It took some time, but she forgave us for the robbery. She told me that everyone was fired except for Liz. They blamed her and T.C. for not adhering to the procedures when the robbery took place. Liz was the only one who did by pressing the alarm button, as the police reports indicated from their interviews immediately following the robbery.

I told her, "Whitey don't give a damn about you. Only for his own kind. That's why they didn't fire Liz." Somebody had to take the fall. It sure wasn't going to be the manager for failing to have their cameras repaired in a timely manner. That's what those lazy mothafuckas get, I still say.

I still didn't like Casper, mainly with the fact that she turned my daughter out. She still wasn't allowed in my house. I know all kind of wild, kinky shit happened in their apartment—nasty asses! Earleon still came to the house frequently and had yet to miss a family meeting. Ain't shit changed. She still had shit to get off her chest, this time about her and Liz's catfights.

Contrary to what I told him, Earl moved out anyway. I fought against it, but Hershey put that good thang on him. With his money from hustling and his side change (robbery money), he bought them a house in North Philly, just a block or two away from the projects we used to live in. I'd never been invited over, so I didn't know where exactly they lived. Hershey was satisfied with that as long as they were together. She knew no other man would do for her like my son, so she had to dig her claws in deep. Too bad my son fell for it.

I saw the twins all the time. I loved them like they were my own. Thought I wouldn't be able to, but how couldn't I? They were my blood.

Elgin trickin' ass still lived with me. Since he got that money, he'd been spreadin' love to all his girls. You know it's always one or two children who just don't want to leave home. That's Elgin and Icelene. They had a chance to move in like their brother and sister, but didn't want to. Both of them would be with me forever. They loved my swagger! We sat and got high together, watched football, basketball and boxing matches together—shit like that. We wore the same Donovan McNabb football jerseys when we hosted a football party for the Eagles the day of the Superbowl XXXIX, in which they lost against New England. Oh well, better luck next year!

Elgin did graduate. Barely, though, with a line of *D*'s, but his dumb ass made it with a diploma, unlike the certificate of participation I received. You should have seen us at his graduation. Ghetto fabulous, horns sounding and all!

Icelene, well let's just say herpes don't stop the show. Hello! We be at the strip clubs tossin' it up! Icelene loved that shit. I let her get it in. Hell, you only live once. She was the one to help me set up a payment plan to pay Welfare back. I wanted to pay them in one lump sum, but I didn't want to play myself.

I didn't get away as scot-free as I thought. Welfare did prosecute me for fraud, and I received a hefty court fine in addition to the amount that I owed them. All in all, though, I made out like a fat rat.

T.C. was thankful that I followed through with his proposal. He said he had tried many others, but all of them were scared to take the risk. His only reason for working at that spot *was* to rob it.

I stand correct when I said I knew he had an adult record. Uh-huh, *yeah* long. He got the job using a fictitious identification card and Social Security number that he paid a dude fifteen hundred dollars for. That gave him a new start, and so did the money he made off the deal.

I finally treated him to some of this good punany. He wasn't but a minuteman with a little-ass dick. I had wasted my time once again. After he was given the opportunity to fuck me and get his paper, the nigga vanished from my life.

Juney was back having his problems with Sweet Cheeks, and still called on me for advice . . . me, of all people. My ears are still burning for his drama. I don't know why I loved to hear about it, but I did. Maybe it was to help balance out all the fucked-up shit I did, because listening to another mothafucka's problems will have you believing you ain't got none, or yours ain't all that bad. I must say, I do consider Juney my best friend, in spite of it all.

Out of it all, at least I have a spot to leave my kids when the grim reaper makes his way for Juicy Brown.

Fuck it. Nothing changes if nothing changes. I had changed my situation. It may have been fucked-up the way I did things, but in my mind, we were hood rich.

I was once asked this question: "Juicy Brown, to what extent would you go for your kids?" At that time I knew, but I didn't want to reveal it. If they'd ask me again, I'd tell them, "I was dealt this hand I was given in life, and will forever continue to play it until I lose. As long as my kids are alive and breathing, I would go to any extent they need me to go. They are all that I got in this life."

Even though in my life I moved from North Philly to Brooklyn, back to North Philly then advancing to the Wynnfield section of town, I'm still that around the way girl you will see . . . around the way! Holla at me when you come through Wynnfield— Columbia Avenue. Just ask for Juicy. They know me. You know it don't take me long to wreck shop! Stop by when you come through. We can go out and you can have a beer on me, just for listening to *The Life of Juicy Brown*.

Thomas Long
Diamond
N
Da Rough

Dedication

This story is dedicated to every young girl searching to find her true self in the midst of her own personal tribulations. I hope you take this story as a source of inspiration and a voice of hope. I know that some of you have to take the hard road alone to find your way through the darkness. No matter what obstacles life may throw ya way, what roadblocks that impede ya path, what heartaches you endure, when it may seem like there is no way out, know that the strength to overcome it all lies within You.

1 In Da Beginning

Roxanne Paine awoke to the chirping sound of her alarm. It was 6:00 in the morning and time for her to wake Precious for school. Her head had just touched down on her pillow not more than an hour before the alarm clock on her dust-filled dresser went off. She had been out all night doing her usual routine of smoking crack 'til the wee hours of the morning in some filthy apartment.

Her life had taken a dramatic twist from her days as a schoolteacher. In just a few short years, she had gone from a college graduate and third grade teacher to a full-fledged crack head with only one mission in life—to chase that ultimate high. Her only saving grace was her little girl. With all of the insanity that her life brought, Precious' innocent little smile glistened bright like a diamond every morning when she woke her for school. The sight of her 9-year-old's face gave Roxanne a brief respite from her life of insanity out in the streets. She reminded Roxanne of the naïve youth that she too possessed many years ago.

Roxanne and her two older sisters were raised in a two-parent family in northeast Baltimore, near Morgan State University. Her father was a truck driver, and her mother worked as a secretary at Northern High School. The Paine family always managed to make ends meet, and there was even a little extra at times. Roxanne and her sisters always had the latest fashions and never wanted for anything.

Being the youngest child, Roxanne received the most attention. She usually got whatever she wanted if she threw a loud enough tantrum. This caused her two older sisters to resent her. Being spoiled so much by her parents would later prove to be part of her downfall.

Roxanne's sisters, Michelle and Janine, both went on to earn PhD's. One became a college professor, the other an architect. They were nerdy, straight-A students who never partied or drank alcohol. As far as Roxanne was concerned, they were squares, and she avoided them as much as possible.

Roxanne was the rebel of the family. From the moment she entered school, she was a frequent visitor to the principal's office. She was well known for mouthing off to her teachers or getting into fights with other girls in her class. Nevertheless, in her parents' eyes, their baby girl could do no wrong. Whenever they were called to the school for a conference about her behavior, they would just make up irrational excuses for her. If a teacher complained about Roxanne acting out in school, Mr. and Mrs. Paine would claim it was the teacher's fault that Roxanne didn't feel the need to follow directions in class. They never disciplined her when she got suspended from school. No matter how much they yelled at her, in the end, she would always find some way to make herself look like the victim. They fell for it hook, line and sinker every time

Roxanne fell in with the fast crowd when she entered Mervo High School. She wanted to go to Mervo because her sisters were at a different school. She did not intend to follow in the footsteps of her boring, do-right sisters. Roxanne was smart enough to pass all of her classes without studying, but she was more concerned with hanging out with the 'in crowd' who got all of the attention.

The allure of the older cats in school that hustled and drove the BMWs and Mercedes Benzes intrigued Roxanne. One guy in particular, Rafael, caught her eye. He would later prove to be a negative force that led her down the path of self-destruction.

Rafael Parker was a senior when Roxanne was a sophomore. He was considered a pretty boy with his flashy clothing and pretty, white teeth complementing his sexy smile. He was tall and slim, with a coal-colored skin tone. The fact that he was a big-time drug dealer with pockets that ran deep made him even more attractive. He drove a black convertible BMW with BBS rims, which only further symbolized his status as a ghetto celebrity.

Out of all of the girls that chased behind him, Roxanne seemed to be the one who fascinated him the most. She wasn't the most beautiful girl he had ever seen, but there was something about her sassy demeanor that attracted him. Her long, almond-colored legs and full-sized chest also had his nose wide open. Soon after they met, they became high school sweethearts and were virtually inseparable.

Roxanne's parents did not approve of her relationship with Rafael. They wanted to see their daughter with someone better than a lowlife drug dealer. Mr. Paine had Rafael pegged as no good from the first time he met him. His expensive clothing and jewels didn't appeal to a hardworking blue-collar man such as Mr. Paine. He knew that Rafael was into something illegal because he was too young to have so many lavish things. Nonetheless, with time, Roxanne managed to convince him and her mother to accept their relationship.

When Roxanne became pregnant with Precious in her first year of college, her parents were furious. They put her out of the house and banished her from attending family gatherings after she refused to have an abortion. They tolerated all the trouble she got into as a kid, but her pregnancy was totally unacceptable. They took it as an insult for Roxanne to have a baby out of wedlock. In reality, her parents shared part of the blame for creating the irresponsible, spoiled person she had become, since they never disciplined her. But they didn't want to deal with that guilt, so instead they turned all their emotions into anger at their daughter.

This was something new for Roxanne. It was the first time she could not manipulate them into seeing things her way. Their rejection of her and her unborn seed pushed her further into Rafael's arms, and they wound up moving in together.

After giving birth to her daughter, Roxanne went back to school and managed to keep her grades up to a B+ average. She graduated a year behind schedule because of the time she took off, but earned a bachelor's degree in elementary education. After graduation, she started teaching at Grove Park Elementary School in northwest Baltimore. She loved her job as a teacher because she always wanted to work with kids.

Up until Precious was a little more than four years old, she and Roxanne had a normal mother-daughter relationship. Roxanne would go to work, pick Precious up from daycare when she got off, then spend the rest of the evening doing all of the things that a mother should do in teaching her daughter how to become a respectable young lady. She looked forward to the quality time they spent together. She seemed to welcome motherhood, and responsibly accepted the challenges.

Rafael showered her and his daughter with expensive gifts and a phat-ass crib out in Baltimore County. He was ecstatic to be a father.

Over time, Roxanne started to miss her partying days, especially when her girlfriends would call and ask her to hang out at the club. She started to feel like an old maid, and wanted some excitement in her life. When Precious turned five, Roxanne felt comfortable leaving her with a babysitter while she went out with her girls for drinks after work and then to the club on Fridays. She was trying to recapture the part of her youth she felt was taken away from her when she became a mother so young.

It was also during this time that she began to dabble in hard drugs with Rafael. She used to smoke weed and drink with her girls back in high school and college, but that stopped when she became pregnant with Precious. Rafael never let her hang out with his crew from the streets because he tried to shield her from that life. He was into drugs, but he loved Roxanne and his daughter. However, her persistence wore him down. She had seen him smoke crack on numerous occasions and wanted to know what it felt like because he seemed to enjoy the high so much.

Roxanne had always been adventurous, eager to try new things, until she became a mother. She wanted that feeling back. After her first pull on the crack pipe, Roxanne was hooked. She began the most passionate love affair with the drug. Rafael loved the high just as much, and this became a very serious problem between them. There were never enough drugs to satisfy both of their insatiable appetites.

Rafael started to fall quickly as his tolerance and craving for the drug increased. He was no longer the baller with the fancy cars, or the slick playa all the ladies sweated for attention. Crack became his be all, end all. He had to have it 24/7. About twenty pounds lighter than he was in back in the day, he had become the typical smoked-out crack fiend always looking for his next hit. He walked around wearing clothes that were two sizes too big and sneakers with multiple holes. All the money that he had saved from hustling was gone. He smoked up product and profit.

Roxanne also began to unravel. She lost her job as a schoolteacher because she was late for work one too many days. Without her income, they weren't able to keep up the payments on the house, and lost it when the bank foreclosed on the property. They were forced to move into a run-down two-bedroom house on Bartlett Avenue back in northeast Baltimore. All of the trappings of drug addiction had begun to take its toll on both of them.

Their struggles with addiction made young Precious' life a living nightmare. Even though Precious prayed for things to change, they just got worse year after year. She was subjected to endless arguments between Roxanne and Rafael about drug bullshit that had no relevance to her. She just wanted to be a regular little girl who played with dolls and didn't have a care in the world. However, she saw her father violently strike her mother on numerous occasions when he claimed she took the last hit off of the crack pipe and didn't share it with him. Precious would always comfort her mother after these attacks or when Rafael disappeared for days on drug binges. Many times, Precious watched her mother crawl on the floor, looking for more rocks when she geeked out from smoking too much. In her short childhood, she had seen more than any child should ever see. Crack stole her parents and her childhood from her.

Roxanne hit rock bottom when Rafael finally ran out on them for good. He became involved with another neighborhood smoker named Sadie, who lived around the corner from them. When Precious was seven years old, her father moved in with Sadie, and what little family life she had known was gone. Rafael and Roxanne fooled around on occasion, but their relationship was never the same. He began to neglect his daughter, often treating her as though she didn't exist. All he wanted to do was get high.

Roxanne was left to fend for Precious and herself by any means necessary. Her drug habit had taken total control of her life as well. For a while, her father would bring food whenever she called and said that she had nothing for Precious to eat. They wanted to take Precious, but she would not leave her mother.

After a while, food wasn't the only thing Roxanne tried to get from her family. She would make up ridiculous lies to tell her parents and her sisters to con them out of money to get her next blast. When they discovered what she was doing, her parents put her in treatment several times, but she always left before she completed the program.

Finally, they had come to her rescue one too many times. They stopped taking her calls and refused to answer the door if she came to their homes. Her family would not help her anymore. If Roxanne ever planned to beat her addiction, she would have to do it on her own.

Since she had no financial assistance other than her measly Welfare check, Roxanne resorted to turning tricks and boosting to supplement her habit. She took a different man into her bedroom every night. They were willing to pay thirty or forty dollars to fuck her for a couple of hours, and Roxanne was willing to take their money.

Precious saw so many men come and go out of her mother's room that it confused her. Part of her wished her daddy would come and rescue them so they could be a family again, but whenever she saw Rafael on the streets, he acted as though he didn't even know her.

One day, she saw him as she was walking home from school with her friends, and she ran over to him to hug him. He pushed her away, told her to leave him alone, and said that he wasn't her father. This not only broke her heart but left her even more confused. She was embarrassed because her friends saw the whole scene. Whenever she saw him after that day, she just kept walking, her eyes filled with tears.

Her grandparents wouldn't see her because of her mother's addiction. She felt alone in her own little hell, with no one to turn to. Her family now consisted only of her and Roxanne, who was high almost all the time. Roxanne did have one friend, named Patty, who took a liking to Precious and tried to be like a second mother to her. Patty had problems of her own, though, so there wasn't much true mothering going on.

Patty had auburn hair, and her teeth were stained yellow from getting high. She always smelled like a lethal dose of cheap liquor and Newport cigarettes. It was easy to tell that she used to be fine before the drugs took a hold of her soul. Patty was the best booster in the game, known throughout East Baltimore for being able to steal the flyest high-end clothing from any department store. She sold her merchandise dirt cheap in the hood. She had been busted a few times, but it never stopped her hustle.

Roxanne was a quick study, and Patty taught her how to boost like a pro. In no time, she and Patty were partners in crime. Trickin', boostin', and gettin' high became Roxanne's full time jobs. Being a mother to Precious was what she did in between.

Precious spent a lot of time alone and learned to take care of herself. At the age of nine, she was cooking her own meals and ironing her own clothes. She often helped her mother into bed when she passed out in the living room from one of her drug episodes. She kept the house as clean as possible with all of the traffic that her mother had coming in and out. Precious was getting an education from her mother's activities that would shape her life in the coming years. She started to believe selling her body and boostin' were normal ways for a woman to make it in the world.

"Precious, are you up, sweetie?" Roxanne asked from her open bedroom door. The bags under her eyes were so big that it would have taken toothpicks the size of salt and pepper shakers to lift her eyelids.

"Yeah, Ma. I've been up. I'm straight. I want you to get some rest. Don't worry about me. I'm fine," Precious responded.

"That's my li'l angel. Mommy loves you. I swear things are gonna get better for us real soon. I'ma make you proud of me. I swear to you, baby girl," Roxanne promised like she had a million times before.

"I know you will, Ma. I know you will. Now get some rest," Precious responded. She continued getting ready for school as Roxanne drifted back into unconsciousness.

Precious watched daily as the ability to live left her mother's body at a pace much too quick for a young woman. She hated her father for leaving her mother with the burden of raising her alone. He never even came back once to see how she was doing or to bring money to help with the bills.

Her mother never mentioned Rafael around her, especially after Precious told her about the incident when he claimed he wasn't her father. Precious prayed that her father would burn in hell for abandoning them. She was too young to understand that he was just as sick as her mother was from the disease of addiction.

After she was dressed, Precious made her usual breakfast of scrambled eggs and bacon with oatmeal on the side. She drank a glass of cherry Kool Aid to rinse it down. When she finished eating, she went to the bathroom to brush her teeth. Once that task was complete, she grabbed her book bag, went into her mother's room to kiss her on the cheek, and headed to the front door.

When she opened the door, two mean-looking black men greeted her with angry scowls on their faces. She didn't recognize them, but could sense that they meant nothing but trouble. She tried to shut the door on them, but one of the men grabbed her arm and lifted her little body off the ground, dragging her back into the house.

"Where you goin', you li'l bitch? Where is your slut of a mother?" he asked. Precious shuddered at the sight of a distinctive scorpion tattoo on his neck.

"My mother ain't here. You need to leave. My daddy's on his way over here." Precious hoped her lie would scare the men away.

"Li'l girl, please. Your daddy don't live here anymore. We know, because he the one that told us ya momma got the best pussy in da hood. We're tryin'a find out if it's true. He the one that sent us over here," the other man responded.

Precious was angry about what the man said about her mother, so she kicked him in the leg. She was no match for him as he restrained her. Precious started to yell in fear, hoping someone would come to her rescue.

The sound of Precious scuffling with the two men woke Roxanne from her sleep. She came down the stairs with a baseball bat in her hand. As long as there was life in her body, nobody would harm her baby girl. A mother's love was the closest thing that one could find to God's love, even in the craziest situations. Precious was the only reason that Roxanne had to live, and she would die before she saw harm come to her child.

"I don't know who y'all niggas is or why the fuck you in my house, but you better get ya funky hands off of my baby right now!" Roxanne yelled. She gripped the bat in her hands, ready to step up to the plate and send one out the park like Barry Bonds. She made her way down the stairs into the living room.

"Roxanne, ain't no need to be hostile, sweetie. We came here to see you. Rafael told us about you. He ain't never lied. You is a fine motherfucka. Let's talk. Put that bat down, baby," the taller man said.

The stockier of the two loosened his hold on Precious, dropping her to the ground. Precious ran toward her mother with tears in her eyes. She was visibly shaken up by the rough treatment she had received.

"Ain't shit for us to talk about. Get the hell outta here or I'm calling da cops. I don't know what that no-good Rafael told you, but this my house, and you in my space right now. Get ta steppin'!" Roxanne barked.

"That's right!" Precious yelled. She poked out her chest in a show of solitude, as if to cosign her mother's demand. She had faith that her mother would handle her business and get rid of these two clowns, but they didn't move. They stayed put, both wearing devilish smirks on their faces.

"We ain't going nowhere. My man just got outta the joint. We done paid Rafael. He said he was ya pimp and he gave us ya address to come over here to have a good time, so that's what we gonna do. In fact, your daughter looks about ripe to get her cherry popped too. We can do this the hard way or the easy way. Which way do you want it, bitch?" the shorter man said.

A feeling of rage came over Roxanne at the mention of someone threatening her daughter's innocence. She was also pissed that Rafael had tried to pimp her out. "I'ma kill that motherfucka the next time that I see his ass for doin' this shit! He better put his bitch Sadie out on the block to work for him," Roxanne said angrily.

Roxanne thought Rafael had probably sent the two goons over there for two reasons. First and foremost, he was probably looking to get some money out of them to get a fix. And second, he probably wanted to get back at her for not kickin' out the ass. She hadn't messed around with him in a few months because she was tired of his bullshit. He would pay for this, she thought. In the meantime, she had to get these two men out of her house and away from her baby girl.

Almost out of sheer instinct, she swung the bat and connected with the side of the shorter man's head. He fell to the ground and grabbed his face. Blood ran rapidly down his cheek. When she raised the bat to strike the taller man, his large, mitt-like hand grabbed the bat in mid-swing. He took it from Roxanne and threw her frail frame to the ground. Precious tried to jump on his back, but he quickly tossed her to the side.

"A'ight, pretty lady, I see we gotta do this the hard way. You hurt my man here. Now, we gotta return the favor. Let the games begin," he said.

The taller man pounced on top of Roxanne and began pulling her clothes off. She wanted to fight back, but she knew it was a losing battle. Her mind was fixed on how to save her little girl from any physical harm, and from the sight of her pending assault.

"You can do whatchu want with me, but please don't hurt my baby. I'll fuck both of you however you want," Roxanne pleaded.

"Now, that's what I'm talking about!" the shorter man said. He had gathered his faculties back somewhat from his injury.

The taller man had totally undressed himself and Roxanne in the middle of the living room floor. He climbed on top of her and inserted his dick in her unlubricated pussy. Every thrust of his penis sent sheer agony through Roxanne's body. The shorter man held Precious down as she screamed for his partner to stop hurting her mother. When the taller man came inside of Roxanne, he exchanged positions with his accomplice. Precious was forced to watch him assault her mother until he busted a nut. When they were done, Roxanne lay on the floor, her eyes open and her legs shaking.

"What you wanna do with the bitch now?" the taller man asked.

"Let's kill the ho. She might go to the police," the shorter man responded.

"Don't kill my mommy! Please don't kill my mommy!" Precious yelled.

"Shut up, you li'l bitch. You better hope we don't kill you," the taller man said.

The shorter man walked over to Roxanne's traumatized body and pounded on her with relentless force with his rough hands. In between the blows, Roxanne screamed to her daughter, "Run, baby, run! Get the hell outta here!"

"No, Mommy. I don't wanna leave you!"

"Go, Precious. Get outta here, I said!"

Roxanne began to choke on her own blood. The taller man joined in on the attack, kicking and stomping on her weakened frame. He bent down to check her pulse, and that was when they realized that she was dead.

In the midst of the assault on Roxanne, Precious had managed to escape the house. They had no clue where she had run off to.

"Man, that li'l bitch might finger us. What the hell are we gonna do?" the shorter man asked.

"Don't even sweat that shit. She's so fucked up in the head that she won't be able to tell nobody shit. Let's get the fuck outta here." the taller man replied. They gathered their belongings and crept out the back door.

Precious had run to Patty's house around the corner. After she calmed down, Precious told her what happened, and Patty called 911. Precious had locked the faces of her mother's murderers in her memory. That knowledge would serve her well at a later date. She planned to send them both straight to hell for taking away her mother. At nine years old, she was scarred for life, and only more hell awaited her.

2 Eight Years Later

"Precious, how many times do I have to tell you to clean up this junky room? This don't make no sense at all. You act just like your hardheaded mother," Mrs. Paine said to her wayward grandchild when she peeked into her room and saw that it was in shambles. Clothes lay everywhere, and empty CD cases were scattered across the floor. Her room was the typical 17-year-old's paradise and represented her carefree lifestyle, but it irritated the distinguished-looking Mrs. Paine. She was an elderly woman with stunning gray streaks running through her hair, which she wore in a bun. She walked with the grace of an accomplished ballerina, and she could not tolerate the chaos of this teenager's room.

Precious was sprawled across her bed, watching Rap City as she did her homework. After her mother's death, Precious moved in with her grandparents. Patty did make an attempt to get custody of Precious, but Child Protective Services wouldn't allow that. The caseworker took one look at Patty and knew that she was a drug addict. There was no way in the world that she planned to give Patty custody of a child, given her unstable lifestyle, especially since the child did have blood relatives.

Precious was angry that she couldn't go to live with her Aunt Patty. She was more like family to her than her grandparents were, because they never took a personal interest in her while her mother was alive. She felt no connection to them whatsoever.

The Paines, distraught over Roxanne's death, wanted to take Precious to soothe their own guilty consciences. Despite all the trouble they went through with Roxanne, Precious was family, and they thought they could do better by Precious than they had with Roxanne.

However, having Precious living with them wasn't easy. Before Roxanne's death, they had both retired, and were happy that they would finally have the house to themselves. Precious' presence delayed their plans for a few more years. On top of that, she was a difficult child because of everything she had seen in her early years.

It had been eight years since her mother's tragic death, but Precious remembered every detail like it was yesterday. She cried herself to sleep many nights, and she still missed her mother dearly. Her killers were never apprehended, so Roxanne's death went down as just another unsolved murder of a drug-addicted hooker in the hood. Precious was haunted regularly by nightmares of the murder, and she saw the faces of the two killers in her dreams. She kept the dreams to herself, vowing that those two bastards would pay for her mother's death if it took her whole life to find them. The same held true for her no-good-ass junkie father. In the meantime, she just had to deal with her grandmother, who always seemed to be on her case.

"I'm gonna clean up my room, Grandma. Why you always on my case? You don't complain like that when Corinne comes over and leaves a mess in the other room. In fact, you make me clean up her mess!" Precious protested.

Corinne was her Aunt Michelle's daughter, who went to private school and was spoiled to death by both her parents and her grandparents. She constantly reminded Precious of how pampered she was, regularly showing off all of the expensive gifts that she got. Precious hated when Corinne came over to stay with them for the weekend. Corinne would make attempts to hang out with her, but Precious wanted no parts of her conceited ass.

"You better shut your mouth, Miss Thang," her grandmother scolded. "Corinne ain't here every day to get on my nerves. She's with her mother. If your momma were here to raise you, you wouldn't have to hear my mouth every day. Instead, she had to hook up with that no-good father of yours. He ruined her life."

Precious had to hear the same negative shit about her mother and father ever since she moved in with her grandparents. Mrs. Paine always accused Precious of acting just like her no-good mother, telling her that she wouldn't amount to anything if she didn't do as she was told. This hurt Precious deeply and only increased the inner anger and turmoil that she battled with on a daily basis. She began to hate her grandmother and everything she stood for.

Mrs. Paine wouldn't allow Precious to go out to parties with her girlfriends or to hang out at the mall on weekends. This didn't stop Precious, however, who would sneak out of the house anyway when her grandmother was sleeping. Whenever she got caught creeping back in, she just accepted whatever punishment her grandmother saw fit to give her. The fun she had hanging with her girls was a welcome break from her grandmother's constant nagging.

Precious' relationship with her grandfather, on the other hand, was much better. He was more understanding than his wife, and was sensitive to the difficult life Precious had experienced, having lost her mother so violently. He felt deep regret for the years that he and his wife hadn't allowed Precious to be a part of their lives while her mother was lost in the streets. He loved and missed his daughter, and tried to make Precious' stay as comfortable as he could in the face of his wife's constant yelling.

"Martha, leave that girl alone. Stop picking on her. She said she was gonna clean up her room. She don't need to hear you going on and on about her mother's mistakes. She's just a child," Mr. Paine called from the living room, where he had been listening to his collection of jazz CDs.

To Mr. Paine, Precious was still a child, but she was quickly approaching adulthood. Precious was now in the twelfth grade at Mervo High School, the same school her mother had attended. In spite of the turmoil at home, she was a straight-A student with perfect attendance. This didn't mean she was a nerd, though, not by any means.

Even though she did exceptionally well in her classes, going to college was the furthest thing from her mind. She was naturally smart and didn't have to study to pass her tests in school. Math was her favorite subject. She was blessed with her mother's ability to add and subtract figures in her head faster than the average person could on a calculator. Her second favorite subject was English because she loved to write. Her teachers would always tell her how smart she was and how she could become anything she wanted in life if she stayed focused on her studies, but that just went in one ear and out the other. Precious felt as though she couldn't fit into mainstream society because she was the child of two drug addicts. In her eyes, she was a social outcast. Her grandmother's verbal abuse didn't help boost her self-esteem either. It just pushed her out into the streets to seek love from her friends.

Her full breasts and hips attracted attention everywhere she went. Her hair was shoulder length, and she kept it done in various styles. She inherited her mother's soft, almond-colored skin and captivating dark brown eyes, as well as her spirited personality. Precious didn't take shit from anybody. The other girls in school knew not to cross her, or an ass whipping would soon follow. She loved the attention that she received from all the boys in school, as well as from the cats she met when she hit the clubs with her girls.

Precious' two best friends were Trish and Tina. They had been friends since the ninth grade. Trish lived in West Baltimore, off of Monroe Street. She wasn't the prettiest girl in the world, with a large overbite and a face full of acne. Her saving grace was her large ghetto booty and perky titties. Even though her face screamed "mutt," her body was like that of a thoroughbred stallion. Tina lived by John Hopkins Hospital, off of Castle Street. She was cuter than Precious, with plumper thighs and a rounder ass. The three of them were called the Butt Sisters because whenever they went out, all eyes were on their asses. Precious loved her girls, and she also still felt a special connection to Patty.

Even after she moved in with her grandparents, Precious stayed in contact with Patty. She loved to hear Patty talk about her mother, about all the plans Roxanne had for her little angel. Unlike Mrs. Paine, who only had negative things to say about Roxanne, Patty kept her mother's memory alive. Whenever Precious was feeling down, she would listen to Patty's stories and feel her mother's love surrounding her.

Patty also helped Precious in other ways. When her grandparents refused to buy her the newest in-style clothes for school, Precious turned to Patty to get her the things she wanted. After a while, Patty taught Precious the rules of the game to become a good thief and boost her own things. Precious, in turn, put Trish and Tina on with the hustle, and the rest was history. They all became experts at boosting and sold at a discount any items they didn't keep for themselves.

Most of the clothes strewn about Precious' room now were things she had stolen, and the CDs were bought with money from selling boosted items in the hood. When her grandmother stormed away from the entrance to her room, she went about the business of cleaning up her room. As she worked, she grumbled Fuck you to herself in response to her grandmother's constant nagging. She called her Grandma to her face, but Queen Bitch behind her back, and often fantasized about pushing her old ass down a flight of stairs for plucking her last nerve.

Her grandfather, who she called Poppa Paine, was a different story. Her grandmother was a controlling person, but he did the best he could to ward off some of her negativity energy. He had a good sense of humor and made her laugh when he knew that she felt like slapping the shit outta her grandmother.

As she was putting her clothes away, the telephone rang.

"Yeah. Who dis?" she asked.

"It's me, girl, Marco. What other nigga you got calling ya house?"

Marco was the dude that Precious was talkin' to for the moment. She met him one day while he was posted up outside the school with his boy, Chet, who happened to date Trish. Marco was 21 years old, drove a silver Hummer, and had his own tight crib out in PG County. He ran with a crew of stickup boys that called themselves the Night Ryders because that was what they did—when the night fell on the city streets, they went riding on a rampage to stick up any drug strip they could find that took down major chips. Marco was a young balla on the move and Precious was at work to make him come up off of some of that loot.

"Shut up, fool. Don't ask me no silly questions. What's crackin' today? What we getting' into?" she asked.

"It's all about you, ma. I'm tryin'a come by and get you around ten tonight. Let's go get somethin' to eat at Micah's, and then go to Blockbuster and get some videos. Then we can go back to my crib and blaze up a coupla Phillies and do whatever comes natural," Marco replied.

Precious knew that he wanted some pussy, and she wanted to fuck him as well, but she couldn't make it that easy. He had to put in some work and trick a little on the shopping tip if he wanted to taste her kitten. Nothing came in her life without a price. When she was finished with him, he would pay through the nose for a sample of that sweet, nasty, gushy stuff she had between her thighs.

"Nigga, please. What I look like, a five dollar ho to you? You think I'ma just come back to ya crib and fuck you on a humble? Nah, sweetie, it ain't even going down like that. And I don't smoke no weed. I ain't one of them broads that fuck for a dime bag and a forty. Recognize my game, nigga. When you step ya game up, holla back at ya girl." Before he could respond, Marco had a talk with Mr. Click as she hung up the phone rudely in his ear. She knew that he would call back, if not tonight, another day.

The one thing that she learned from her mother was never to get high. Her girls smoked weed on a regular, but she wouldn't touch the stuff. She only drank liquor on special occasions. Her mind usually stayed on her money and nothing else.

Precious had no need for a man in her life unless he was kickin' out some paper. She learned that from her father. The memories of the horrible way he treated her mother were always fresh in her mind. She viewed all men as worthless beyond what they could give her materially. Getting married and having a family was not in her plans. She wanted fast money and the best of everything that money could buy. She had stopped believing in love long ago.

The one guy she chose to give her heart to in the ninth grade broke it. His name was Alex, and he was her first lover. He waited almost three months to get some ass. Precious was reluctant to kick it out, but finally gave in when he said the "L" word. She allowed Alex to take her virginity because she thought that he really did love her, but he wound up breaking her heart when he stopped calling her after they had sex five or six more times. From that point on, she built a wall around her heart that no man could break down. She got all the love she needed from her girls.

After she was finished cleaning up her room, she made a few calls to Aunt Patty, Trish, and Tina, to ask about the next caper they planned to pull. Tomorrow was Saturday, which was a busy day at the mall. That meant they had a lot of work to do because the best time to boost was during crowded shopping hours. She talked to her crew and they decided to go to Norfolk, Virginia to hit up the stores at Military Circle Mall. They would meet up the next morning, pile into Tina's hooptie and hit the highway for the road trip. Visions of dollar signs danced around in Precious' head that night.

3 Independence Day

Precious graduated from high school with honors in June of the same year. There was no need for her to think about going to college to get a good job, because the streets showed her mad love. Business had been good for her and her crew. A lot of girls from school put in orders for the latest Gucci, Prada, Fendi, and any other high-end European fashion that they could get their hands on. They were able to get the latest Baby Phat, Parasuco and Rocawear jeans, baby Ts, and sweatsuits that the stores had on the shelves. They also managed to get their hands on the hottest handbags and purses requested by their customers. If you named it and wanted it, they would find a way to steal it. With discounts of over 60 percent off the retail price, Precious and her crew made a killing. They were the talk of the town. Every beauty salon and barbershop across the city placed orders with them. Every hustler in B'more came to them to cop some gear to keep his girl dipped in the latest fashions without hurtin' his flow.

On the average, Precious and her crew brought in anywhere between five and ten grand a week from the proceeds of their capers at the malls. They boosted merchandise from all of the high-end stores in Baltimore, Philly, New York, Virginia, and Washington, D.C. They split the proceeds of their sales four ways, and each of them had enough money to live comfortably in the lap of luxury, except for Patty. Her drug use took up most of her funds.

None of them had ever been arrested or even questioned by the police due to their tight teamwork. Patty, Precious, and Trish did the stealing while Tina waited in the car. She was the get-away driver. By the time any of the store's security team's figured out that they had been hit, the four of them were long gone. They ran their scheme so smoothly that they believed that they could do this for the rest of their lives.

Living high off their successes, Precious and her girls cruised about town in their brand-new matching candy apple red Toyota Solaras. Everybody knew who they were when they pulled up somewhere with their personalized license plates and custom chrome rims. They got much respect everywhere they went. They had each saved up a nice-sized stash of cash over the last two years. They didn't have to worry about how the bills were gonna get paid for a good minute. As long as everybody stayed loyal to the team and stuck together, they couldn't fail.

Patty started trying to battle her drug addiction. Her appearance was improving some since she would get her hair and nails done on occasion. The girls made sure that Patty's rent was always paid so she had a place to rest her head. She didn't use as much as she had in the past, even going several weeks at a time without using, but then it was off to the races. She would be missing in action for days before the girls found her in some crack house having wasted all of her "hard-earned" money making some drug dealer rich. She tried to beat her habit, but the monkey on her back planned to ride her hard until the end. Despite her disappearing acts, Patty could always be counted on to show up when it was time to put in work.

It was June 27, 2003, Precious' birthday, and she was now officially eighteen years old. She made enough money from boosting to afford to live on her own, so it was time for her to move out of her grandparents' house. She couldn't wait to escape from the grips of her wicked grandmother.

Before graduation, she had broken the news to them. Her grandmother merely grumbled when she told her that she planned to move out, telling Precious she would never amount to anything with her fast lifestyle. In spite of her tragic childhood, Precious had managed to graduate from high school as a straight-A student, but her grandmother still refused to give her any words of encouragement. She didn't even try to act like she gave a damn about her. Nothing Precious did would ever be good enough in her eyes.

Her grandfather told her that he was proud of her for finishing school and wished her well in whatever she did with her life. He knew that she wasn't living right, and he prayed that she would eventually get her life together. He told her to keep in touch with him and come and visit him. Precious said that she would, but only when her grandmother wasn't around.

Precious and her girls planned to move in together in a newly renovated brownstone off Eutaw Place in the city. The brownstone was big enough with its three spacious bedrooms for each of them to have privacy whenever needed. They created fake paystubs to make it appear as though they had legitimate jobs at a fictitious company, Mitchell Brothers Remodelers, as telemarketers. Patty's home number was listed as the supervisor to contact for references. The landlord bought their scam hook, line and sinker, and gave them a move-in date for the beginning of the following month.

Precious was in her room, counting the days until she could move out of her grandmother's house, and thinking about how she was going to celebrate her birthday. As she flipped through the countless outfits in her closet, trying to find the right one to wear that night, she heard a knock at her door. It was her grandmother.

Mrs. Paine turned the knob before Precious had a chance to throw on a robe over her black thong and bra. Her grandmother entered the room and gave her an evil stare up and down. Precious was prepared for the same old bullshit, reminding herself that this would all be over soon. She wouldn't have to see her grandmother's old ass once she moved out.

"So, Miss Thang, where are you and your criminal friends going tonight? I see you're looking for something to wear outta that trashy wardrobe of yours. In my day, a woman wouldn't be caught dead dressed the way you hot heifers do."

"Well, times have changed, Grandma. That's why you're you and I'm me. Why you always riding me? What did I ever do to you? I finished school, got good grades, and you still ride my back all the time. Do you hate me that much? I'll be glad when I never have to see your fucking face again!" Precious said angrily.

She wished she hadn't made that last comment, but all of the nagging and verbal abuse she received from her grandmother over the years had finally come to a head. She was tired of hearing her bitchin' all of the time. They said that pressure burst pipes and, at this point, Precious' pressure had reached a boiling point. She was ready to burn her grandmother's old ass.

"You better watch ya mouth as long as you live under my roof!" Mrs. Paine threatened.

"Well, come next week, I'll have my own place. I'll be outta ya hair for good. Your charity work will be over. What else smart you got to say? I'm sick of you!" Precious yelled.

"The feeling is mutual. Now I see that you are truly your mother's child. She was smart just like you, but wasted it all away chasing that fast money. You think that the money you make out there stealing clothes is gonna last forever? Yeah, I know what you and your li'l hoodlum friends are into. I wasn't born yesterday. I see you wearing all of those expensive clothes and you ain't worked nowhere to earn a dime to pay for them. All of that no-good behavior is gonna catch up with you."

"Yeah, well when it does, you'll be the last person that I call. You can bank on that. If you don't mind, I would like to finish getting dressed so that I can celebrate my birthday," Precious barked back in a sassy tone.

"God, please remove this evil child from my house. I done did the best I can with her. She's yours now. Her burden is too heavy for me to carry." Her grandmother spoke with her eyes pointed up toward Heaven as she made her way out of the room and closed the door.

Precious finished getting dressed. Now she was in a foul mood, but she refused to let that stop her from gettin' her party on tonight. She only had one eighteenth birthday, and she planned to enjoy it to the limit. And of course, she planned to look sexy as hell as she did it. She put on a strapless black dress that came down to the middle of her thigh. It hugged her curvy hips so tightly that if she bent over in front of a man, he was sure to get a delightful eyeful of her ass cheeks. Her hair flowed down to her shoulders. Her nails and feet were done to perfection, and she set the whole outfit off with Happy by Clinique perfume. There was nothing more effective than a sweet-smelling woman to catch the right man's eye.

She and her girls had decided to go to D.C. to go club hoppin'. They rented a limo equipped with several bottles of Moet on ice to get them so tipsy that they didn't give a fuck. Tina and Trish had smoked three nicely rolled blunts at Tina's house before the limo driver came to pick them up. "Anything goes" was their motto for the night.

"Happy birthday, Precious. We need to make a toast," Tina said as Precious climbed into the limo. "This glass right here is for my girl. She's legal now. The world is yours!" Tina said.

"Hell, yeah! Nobody can't tell me shit. I also wanna toast to the fact that next week I'ma be free of my evil grandmother's ass. I wanna toast to that shit, for real!" Precious said.

"Friends for life. Can't nobody stop us. Let nothing tear our bond apart. No niggas, no money, no success. Let nothing come between our friendship," Trish said.

They all tipped their glasses and shared the first of many toasts for the night. By the time the limo reached Zanzibar nightclub in D.C., they were all high as hell. They partied there for a few hours before they left to see what was poppin' at Dreams. It was pretty much the same thing there, with bangin' music, strong but sweet mixed drinks, and fine niggas for them to flirt with all night long. At about 6:00 in the morning, they left D.C. and headed back to B'more to get some rest. They all had a good time helping Precious celebrate her Independence Day.

Precious had lived to be eighteen, in spite of growing up the hard way, without once having gone to jail. She did whatever the hell she wanted, when she wanted. As far as she was concerned, she had the world by the balls.

4 Dem Crazy Nightmares

Marco was outside Precious' house, dressed in a brown Azzure long-sleeved T-shirt, a pair of blue denim Azzure jeans, and a pair of Nike Airs that were fresh outta the box. His hair was freshly cut in a low style, sideburns curved around to meet with his neatly trimmed beard. He wore a diamond-encrusted pendant with the image of two .45s crisscrossed on a platinum chain. The ice on his wrist consisted of more than five carats of princess cut stones that gave off a blinding glare.

As he stepped from his ride, he walked around to the passenger side to open the door for Precious. They were on their way out for a night on the town. She stepped up into his Hummer, which was a house on wheels.

"So, where you wanna go at, ma?" Marco asked.

"You treatin', so it really don't matter to me. Cancel that. Let's go to Della Notte downtown. I got a taste for some Italian food," Precious said.

Precious was young, but way beyond her years in intellect. She knew everything there was to know about the finer things in life. She educated herself on what were the most expensive restaurants in town with the best food. She knew about the most expensive clothes. If a guy wanted her to give him the time of day, then he had better be ready to come up off of some cheese to make it worth her while. Marco was no different. She liked him a little, but only because it was easy for her to get him to do whatever she wanted him to do, which was to spend his money. However, once she got all she wanted from him, he too would be just like all of the other niggas that crossed her path.

Marco's face grimaced a little when she said that she wanted to go to such an expensive restaurant. He knew the entrées there cost some grip, but he also knew that he had to spend some loot if he wanted to keep Precious' attention. She pulled his card a few months ago when he tried to carry her like a chicken head. Marco thought that he could get the pussy without puttin' in some work and spending some cash. Oh, how wrong he was. Now, he had committed himself to getting with Precious, so he had to see his mission through to the end. She straight up turned him on like that. He was down to do whatever needed to be done to get her.

Marco saw Precious as sure 'nuff wifey material, if he could just find a way to get her to control her smart-ass mouth. He also liked the fact that she wasn't like most broads he came across who were quick to kick the pussy out. She made him wait to hit it, and this only made him more intrigued with her. Of course, while he waited for her to give in to him, he still kept his stable of young stallions around for when he needed to bust a nut.

"You got that. Anything for you, sexy," Marco said.

He ran his right hand up Precious' thigh, exposed by the revealing slit in her skirt. She wore a shirt so tight that it fit like a body glove. Her nipples peeked out at him and quickly caught his attention.

Precious knew that she had Marco's nose wide open, and she was ready to dig her claws into him for whatever she could get out of him. That was why she no longer resisted his sexual advances. It was time for her to turn up the heat and seal the deal. Four months was long enough for him to wait. She had teased his dick enough.

"You better stop playing, boy. You might get me so hot that we won't make it to dinner," Precious said playfully. Marco's face revealed his thoughts as he flossed a big grin.

They made it to the restaurant and enjoyed a splendid meal. Precious ordered lasagna with garlic bread. Marco had the veal cutlets covered with marinara sauce and parmesan cheese, and a side of spaghetti. After they ate, he suggested that they go back to his place. Precious agreed, and they hopped in his truck en route to their final destination. Marco felt lucky tonight.

When they pulled up at his crib, Marco got out and opened the door for Precious so that she could step down from the truck. He eyed her body up and down as lust began to consume him. Precious cracked a smile because she read his thoughts and knew she had him right where she wanted him. They made their way through the front door and into the living room area.

Marco's house was decorated with the flyest, most expensive furniture, but of course he was able to get a lot of his stuff hot and at a discount from his street connections. When she saw how he lived,

Marco could tell that she was impressed. Her facial expression spoke volumes.

"Damn, this a hot-ass crib, Marco!"

"No doubt, ma. Go ahead and take a look around," Marco said. He took Precious' jacket from around her shoulders and hung it in the closet.

Precious made her way through his immaculate crib, awed by how neat the place was kept. She knew Marco was paid, but had no idea that he lived this large. This nigga could get it tonight, fa sho'!, she thought.

Marco read what she thought as he came up behind her and placed his warm tongue in the nape of her neck. Chills went through Precious' body and her knees buckled from his passionate kisses. Marco turned her around and began to repeat his oral exploration of her body as his mouth engulfed her nipples through her shirt.

Precious was on fire. She grabbed Marco by the hand and led him over to the couch. All the while, her other hand was wrapped around his dick. It was ready to escape from inside his pants.

Precious leaned over the couch and boosted her ass up in the air. Marco bent down on one knee and slid her thong to the floor. He hoisted up her skirt, and her beautiful backside was a sight to behold. He licked her silky smooth ass and made his way between her thighs to taste her wetness, teasing her with his in and out motion until she begged him to eat her pussy with more intensity.

While Precious grabbed a tighter hold of the couch, Marco slid his pants off and threw them to the side. He massaged his penis with one hand and used the other to part Precious' lips as he sucked her clit. When he reached a full erection, he inserted himself inside of her without a condom. He usually wore one, but her pussy was so wet that he just had to feel her juices up against his raw manhood.

Precious screamed in approval of how Marco was fucking her. She came several times to show her gratitude. He did the same. They switched into multiple positions as they explored uncharted levels of arousal with each other. They made their way up to the master bedroom to rest from a night of hardcore sexin'. They both enjoyed the episode and fell asleep peacefully for several hours.

"Run, baby, run. Get the hell outta here!"

"No, Mommy! I don't wanna leave you!"

"Go, Precious. Get outta here, I said!"

Precious' mother's voice became more and more faint with each blow landed by the two men. Those were the last words Precious heard before she awoke from the nightmare. The image of so much blood and her mother's torn flesh left her feeling shell-shocked, like a Vietnam vet who regularly relived the horrors of fighting in the war. She had revisited that agonizing moment in her life more times than she cared to remember.

She was drenched in her own sweat as her body shook violently. Tears flowed from the outer edges of her closed eyelids. Before she became fully awake, she was throwing blows at an invisible opponent like she was in the ring with Floyd Mayweather, Jr. Marco tried to grab her but was met with a right cross to his jaw.

Precious' eyes slowly opened to the darkness that covered the room. That was when she realized that she had been caught up in another one of her nightmares.

"Damn, Precious, what the hell is wrong with you?" Marco said. His hand covered his jaw, sore from the blow she had landed. He never saw any shit like this before in his life.

"I was having a nightmare. My bad. I ain't mean to wake you up." Precious said.

"What the hell was you dreaming about? You was acting like you was fighting demons in ya sleep. Is Freddy Krueger or Jason up in this motherfucka? Let me know so I can get my gat." Marco said jokingly yet still in pain.

"That shit ain't even funny. I don't even wanna talk about it. Whatever I was dreaming about is my fucking business!"

Precious' response suggested to Marco that she was pissed about something. He knew he hadn't done anything to her, so he wanted to know what was up with her coming off at him like that.

"Slow ya roll, P. You ain't gotta be coming outta ya mouth like that to a nigga. I was just concerned about ya ass," he said.

"Well, I'm a'ight. I always have handled my own. I don't need anybody to worry about me," she said angrily.

"Well, maybe you do need somebody up in ya life to be concerned about you, ma. Everybody ain't ya enemy, ya know? You should try to lighten up," Marco suggested. That was his worst mistake.

"Mind ya business, nigga. I ain't uptight. I just had a fucking dream. That's it. What's on my mind is my fucking business."

Marco had enough of her salty mouth. He clenched his fists in anger. The main vein in his neck tensed up. If she were a dude, he would've gone straight to her dome for her blatant disrespect of his genuine concern. Instead, he knew how to handle a bitch like Precious, and how to hit her where it would hurt.

"I hear you. You don't have to worry about a nigga asking or giving a fuck about you again. In fact, I got the pussy now, so you can get the fuck out!" Marco said.

Marco didn't mean what he said to her, but the damage was done. There was no turning back once those words had come out of his mouth. Besides, he was pissed because he had shown Precious mad love and looked out for her a lot, yet she still talked to him greasy. He had violated his own rules by letting his guard down with her. He usually just fucked women and forgot about them. That was just how it went in his line of work. To have feelings and emotions for someone was a sign of weakness to him, but he had thought something about Precious was different, that she was worth breaking the rules. Now he was at the end of his rope with her. No pussy was worth her disrespect or nasty-ass attitude.

"You ain't said nothing but a word, nigga. I'm gone. The dick wasn't that good anyway. I done tricked enough with your tired ass. Let me get my shit and I'm gone." Precious got up from the bed and retrieved her clothes off the floor. Marco watched at her Coke bottle figure as she moved about the room, wishing that her attitude matched her heavenly body. When she was fully dressed in her clothes from the night before, she reached over to the nightstand next to the bed to grab the diamond-covered bracelet, one of the many tokens of affection Marco had given her. Before she got a chance to pick it up, Marco's large hand grabbed her wrist.

"Nah, bitch, you can leave that right there. Sincc you wanna show ya ass, I'm taking that back. I can give it to one of my other hoes that knows how to come outta her mouth the right way to a nigga like me. As a matter of fact, you can give me that necklace that's around ya neck too." Before she could respond, his other hand snatched the platinum chain from around her neck. It broke into two pieces.

"You're a bitch-ass nigga. You give a bitch something and take it back. That's some sorry-ass shit. You're a poor excuse for a man. All y'all niggas is the same. Keep ya shit. I can find another nigga to do the same, if not more, for me. Fuck you! Don't ever call my ass again!" Precious said.

"Ya number is already erased, ho. Outta sight, outta mind!" Marco yelled.

Precious slammed his front door shut, hearing the echo of Marco's loud laughter in the background. She made it away from Marco's house and down the street to the strip mall, where she used her cell phone to call a cab. As she waited for the cab to come, tears leaked from her eyes. She cursed to herself. All men were no-good dogs.

She was in disarray partially because of the way Marco acted with her, but also because of her inability to make the nightmares of her mother's death disappear from her psyche. She suffered migraine headaches on a regular basis because of them. They were so bad that they rendered her bedridden for days when an attack occurred. She felt a headache about to come on. Either that or she was about to lose her mind.

Her life appeared to be a never-ending cycle of mental turmoil from which there was no escape. Her mother wasn't there to comfort her the way that a mother should. Her grandmother hated her guts for no apparent reason. Her aunts treated her as if she didn't exist. They never took the time to teach her all the things a girl should know about growing up to become a woman. She had to learn all of that on her own, the hard way. That hurt her the most. It's one thing not to receive love out in the streets, but not to receive any at home, it made her heart harden.

Now, she just didn't give a fuck about living or dying. She just wanted what she wanted, and didn't give a fuck about tomorrow. She had made no legitimate plans for her future, like going to college or getting a job. That world was for squares, in her eyes. She would never fit in with the "normal" people of the world. All she had were the streets and her ability to hustle to make a dollar, which gave her a sense of power when she had so little power in so many other aspects of her dim reality. She was good at boosting, and no one could take that away from her.

Fuck Marco and his bitch ass! She finally said to herself.

When her cab came, she told the driver her destination and reclined in the seat to relax for the ride.

5 Revelations of the Past

Patty sat in her messy bedroom and reached for the picture of her, Roxanne and an 8-year-old Precious. As she looked at the photo, she felt a sharp pain in her chest and tears began to run from her eyes. She missed her best friend and wished that she could see her again. However, that just wasn't gonna happen. Roxanne was gone forever.

To get away from feeling so down, she thought about Precious and what a beautiful young woman she had become. She knew her mother would be proud of her. Patty was angry that Roxanne was taken away from Precious so violently and she, too, swore revenge for her death. She planned to make due on that promise very soon with the new information she had come across recently. That was why she had called Precious earlier that morning. She wanted her to come over so they could talk. Precious would be there shortly, and Patty anxiously awaited her arrival.

As she waited, Patty rummaged through her belongings in her filthy East Side apartment. There were clothes scattered everywhere about her house, and half- empty containers of Chinese food and greasy pizza boxes on top of her broken-down dining room table. Her living room furniture was so old that it would fit right in with the furniture in an episode of Good Times. The stench of funky socks, alcohol, and cigarettes permeated the place. This was definitely a good place for a Stick-Up air freshener. Any decent living human being would consider Patty's place would a pigsty. And even though Patty knew that, she was still an addict, so this dump was home sweet home for her. As long as there was somewhere for her to get high in peace, all of the trash and foul odors didn't matter.

On any given day there might be a dozen people at Patty's place. All of her junkie and crack-smoking friends would come by to get high and shoot the shit with her. They knew she was making good money from boosting and that she was too generous in sharing her wealth with her friends. Whenever Patty sold all of her hot goods and got a hold of some cold, hard cash, she invited her friends over to celebrate. Their celebration included an abundance of cocaine,

ohol, and whatever other drugs they desired. Since
.c bill, they were all too eager to get a free high.
once all the drugs were gone, the party was over.
.yoody had to leave. Patty was left with an empty house, feeling
depressed because all of her money and drugs were gone.

That was Patty's regular routine in her drug-centered, lonely
life. Outside of Precious, she had no one she could call a true friend
that cared about her. She only had drug associates who sucked away
what they could from her.

Patty didn't have any family in Baltimore. Her parents died in
an automobile accident when she was ten years old. Her older sister,
Eileen, who was eighteen at the time, raised her with the help of
public assistance. Life for the two of them was a constant struggle to
make ends meet. Eileen worked several odd jobs under the table to
supplement the money she got from Welfare, but it was never
enough.

Things got even worse for them when Eileen was diagnosed
with breast cancer. She passed away when Patty was sixteen years
old, leaving Patty on her own. She left school and learned all she
knew from the mean streets of Baltimore.

Patty fell in with the wrong crowd as she sought to fill the
emptiness left by the loss of her parents and her sister. She ran with
drug dealers and pimps who sold her a dream and made her feel
special. They saw her pretty smile and bodacious ass and told her
whatever she wanted to hear to get between her legs. To them, she
was an easy victim, prime for the picking. All of the hustlers she
dealt with got her high, paid her bills, and gave her a sense of
belonging. They also laid the foundation for her to become the
confused crack addict that she now was. Once they got her strung out
on the pipe, she was down for whatever they wanted her to do for
another blast.

When her looks started to fade, they all disappeared. This
depressed her, and her drug use rapidly increased. Without her
benefactors around, she had to support her habit. The first time she
tried to steal something from a store, she got away with it with ease.
When she found out how much money she could make from selling
stolen clothes, she hooked into the game. Boosting became her
means of getting high. However, she was still alone. When she met

Roxanne, she thought that she had finally found a friend. They became like sisters and were regular companions in the nighttime hunt for that next fix. After Roxanne died, Patty felt the need to get closer to Precious as a way to replace the loss of her best friend. In time, her relationship with Precious changed, and rather than Patty being like a mother to Precious, it was the other way around.

Patty wasted most of her money on drugs, barely managing to keep food in her house. If it came down to a choice between getting high or eating, food always took second place. If it weren't for Precious and her girls, her rent, electric and phone bills would never get paid. They proved to be the lifeline that kept her afloat and made her appear to be what the streets called a "functional" addict, one who had a roof over her head and was able to pay some bills in spite of her rampant drug use. What the streets didn't know was that without her enablers, Patty would be just another addict, strung out and homeless. Patty realized this, and had mad loyalty to Precious because of it.

Tired from another night out smoking crack, Patty attempted to make herself something to eat while she waited for Precious. She reached inside the refrigerator, past the carton of spoiled milk and three-week old spaghetti to get out eggs and butter. She scrambled herself some eggs to put something in her stomach so she wouldn't get a headache. She would've made some toast to go along with the eggs, but the bread on top of the counter had green mold on it.

Patty prepared her eggs and ate them quickly, washing them down with a can of cheap beer. She rarely drank orange juice or water because that would've been too much like right. It was as if all of the alcohol and drugs from the night before weren't enough. She had to start the next day off with a can of beer. This was the life that she lived, day in and day out. Right now, however, she needed some kind of substance in her body to be able to face the news she had for Precious.

After she finished eating, she went into the living room to lay across the couch and wait. First she brushed off the roaches that ran along the couch and moved about the house as though they paid rent. She was getting a headache anyway, but not because she was hungry. She was troubled by the information that had recently fallen into her lap. Consumed by her thoughts, she was startled by the sound of a key in her front door. Precious walked in seconds later with a concerned look on her face.

"What's up, Aunt Patty? What's so important that you needed me to rush over here? Is everything all right?" One look at Patty and Precious could see that she had been crying. She sat down on the dirty couch and gave her a warm hug.

"Everything is gonna be all right, Precious. Aunt Patty is okay. I was just thinking about your mother and how much I miss her," Patty replied.

"Yeah, I miss her too. But that's not all that's bothering you. What else is on your mind?" Precious asked.

"Well, honey, I've got some information to tell you that I know you've been waiting so long to hear. I just want you to promise that you won't fly off the handle when I tell what I have to tell you."

"I promise you, Auntie. Now, what is it?" Precious had no clue what Patty was about to tell her, or else she wouldn't have been so calm right now.

"Well, I found out who those motherfuckas were that killed your mother," Patty said bluntly.

Precious' eyes almost popped outta her head. She didn't expect such shocking news. She thought that Patty had called her over to tell her about feeling alone and depressed. This information threw her for a serious loop. She had to find out more.

"Who the hell are they? Where the hell are they? Tell me, Patty! Tell me, goddammit!"

"Calm down, child. I want those motherfuckas just as much as you do. They took my best friend away from me. I'ma tell you everything, and then you gotta promise that we're gonna take care of this my way," Patty said.

Precious was anxious, but she knew that Patty wouldn't tell her everything if she didn't agree. "A'ight, I promise you. Now, tell me the whole story."

Patty broke down the whole story. She was out the night before, smoking crack in West Baltimore, where she overheard a conversation between two men named Trip and Black Phil, who ran the crack house.

She described the men to Precious, and told what she knew about them. Trip was tall and lanky, with a head full of waves. His cheeks were sunk in from hours of sucking on the glass dick. He was a dealer, but he was also his own best customer. Black Phil was short, with a mug that looked like a Pit Bull with his puffy cheeks and big nose. He had a thing for the IV. Shooting heroin was his claim to fame.

They were two old school hustlers who had done several stints in the penitentiary for various drug and assault charges. Black Phil also had a thing for young girls. He had been arrested on child molestation charges several times but was never convicted. There were never any witnesses when it was time to go to court. Once he threatened her family, the young victim would usually change her story at the last minute to say that she had lied. The two of them had a reputation on the streets for having itchy trigger fingers. They were known as two cats not to fuck with.

Their problem was they talked too much. They talked about all of the bodies they caught, money they made, and the bitches they fucked. They reminisced about the old days. They figured none of the heads were listening, and even if they did listen, they wouldn't remember.

The night that Patty was there was no different. She had heard them talk trash many times before and just shrugged them off as being full of shit. She was only concerned with one thing—getting high—and their shit was good. However, on this particular night, they talked about one murder that caught her attention.

They were discussing a murder they had committed almost ten years ago on the East Side, when they killed a woman in front of her child. The murder took place in a house near where Patty used to live, but she wasn't really paying attention to their talk until she heard Rafael's name mentioned. She put her ear to the wall to hear clearer. As she listened to the details, she became sure that the woman they were talking about was Roxanne and the little girl was Precious. The more she heard them talk, the angrier she became. They blew her high, and she sobered up instantly.

Black Phil talked about how Rafael had sent them over to his baby mama's house to get some pussy as a way to work off a debt he owed them for a package he smoked up. They burst into laughter as they agreed that the woman had some good pussy, then continued describing in graphic detail how they beat Roxanne to death. They revealed no shame, no emotion other than pride, over what they had done. In fact, Black Phil was mad that he didn't get a chance to fuck Precious.

It made Patty sick to hear him describe how he would have loved to break her in. Patty wanted to throw up, but she kept her cool. They talked about going to see Rafael recently about another "payment," and mentioned where he was staying. They said that he still copped from them on occasion.

When Patty finished telling the story, Precious was silent. Her palms were sweaty and she breathed heavily as though she was about to hyperventilate. They cried together for a few minutes before Precious composed herself enough to speak.

"So, what do you propose that we do? Those motherfuckas gotta die!" Precious said. She had never killed anyone before, but that was about to change.

"Oh, we're gonna get their asses, but we're gonna need some help. You know any gangsta-ass dudes that you can trust enough to put in some work for us? I got a surefire plan that can't lose," Patty said.

Precious thought for a moment before she responded to Patty's question. After she ran threw a list of thugged-out niggas she knew from the streets, she came up with the person who could help carry out whatever Patty had planned. Marco was perfect for the job. He was a stickup boy, which meant that he was crazy enough with them guns to do just about anything if the price was right. Even though she hadn't spoken to him since their falling out, she knew it wouldn't take much to get back into his good graces. She would work her magic on him like she did before. She couldn't stand his ass for the way he treated her, but she was willing to let that go for now since he could be useful to her. As far as she was concerned, the end justified the means.

"Yeah, I know the perfect nigga, and he got a crew that's loyal to him."

"A'ight. Well, this is what we need to do," Patty began. She ran down the details to Precious, who liked what she heard and was ready to set the wheels in motion.

6 The Serpent Rising

"Damn, yo, you a greedy-ass nigga. Why you hoggin' the blunt to yaself?" Tina asked. She and Trish were in the living room, gettin' twisted off of some bangin' Purple Haze. It was the dead of winter, but they had every one of the living room windows wide open, and were burning incense and scented candles to try to filter out the smell of the bud. They knew Precious would be pissed off if she came home and found the apartment smelling like weed.

The girls were engaged in another one of their "smoke out" sessions with Parrish and Donnell, two dudes who had a weed spot up on Park Heights and Woodland Avenues, where they copped on a regular basis. The girls had gotten cool with them, and they got together from time to time to get their smoke on. Parrish and Donnell were also both easy on the eyes, and definite future prospects.

Parrish had a medium brown complexion with hairy eyebrows that connected in the middle of his forehead like Al B. Sure. You couldn't tell him that he wasn't the finest brother on the planet, though. Donnell was short and pudgy in build, but he was a handsome brother who had no problem meeting women despite his excess weight. He was a smaller version of Gerald Levert, with his processed hair and deep voice. He was dressed sharp all the time and could sing a little, but not good enough to get a record deal. However, you couldn't tell him that he wasn't the second coming of Ruben Studdard. In his eyes, he was gonna be the next big R&B superstar out of B'more. They all flirted with each other on a regular, but no one had ever acted on it.

In the midst of all the fun they were having, Tina thought about Precious. If she came home and saw them in the living room smokin' weed and gettin' drunk, it was gonna be on and poppin'. They would never hear the end of this shit. She acted more like their mother than their homegirl. For whatever reason, she felt she could tell them what to do and what not to do, and lately, her controlling personality and mood swings got on their nerves. They continued to put up with her, but the fact that they were smoking in the house was a sign that they were getting sick of her.

What the girls didn't want to recognize was that Precious had other good reasons to warn them about smoking in the house or having niggas over to smoke. It drew too much attention to them and their activities. The last thing they needed was for one of their neighbors to call the police because they smelled weed or heard them and their company making a lot of rowdy noise. That gave the police a legitimate reason to search their crib and stumble upon some other illegal shit. They had avoided arrest up until this point, despite being questioned several times by the law. The police had heard rumors about their activities from snitches on the streets but never had any solid proof. Precious was smart enough to realize how easy it would be to get knocked off on a humble for some bullshit. That was why she tried to keep their hustle on the low.

The police weren't the only ones they had to worry about, either. Having niggas in and out their crib gave too many people the chance to be in their business. The streets talked, and everybody knew that they took down major figures from boosting. They kept a safe in the house, under the king-sized bed in Precious' room, where they stashed emergency money in case they needed it for bail or something. There was over fifty grand in there at all times. Precious always kept ten percent of the take once their sales figures were calculated, and put it in the safe to add to the fund.

All it would take was for one group of niggas to be jealous and come up with a plan to rob them. Three females living alone made for an easy target. For that reason, only Precious knew the combination to the safe. She trusted no one, and for good reason. Trish and Tina were too dumb for their own good sometimes. They brought home different dudes all the time. They never took precautions, and were too open with their home. This pissed Precious off and started to drive a wedge in their friendship.

The three didn't hang out as much as they used to. Trish and Tina began to think that Precious felt she was better than they were, like they weren't on her level. She didn't hit the club with them as much anymore. She never stayed up late at night with them to clown around as they talked about no-good men. When they tried to introduce her to one of their male friends, she just shrugged them off. When she was home, she spent most of her time in her room with the door closed. The only time that she had something to say was when it was time to do a job. It was like the bond they used to have was gone, and they didn't know why. It was no longer about the friendship between them, but strictly business.

"Shut up, fool, and hit this," Parrish told Tina. "After you do, I'ma give you something to keep that big mouth of yours shut," he joked.

"Yeah whatever, nigga. Keep talkin' shit and we're gonna have both of y'all niggas choking on these pussy hairs down here!" Trish said in response.

"Sounds good to me. I'm tryin'a play some strip poker up in this piece!" Donnell said.

"Keep dreamin' and you might make that shit come true," Tina said. Donnell playfully spanked her on her big ass when she walked by him into the kitchen.

They continued to cut up, going back and forth with the jokes. They passed the blunt around as they took turns hittin' that good shit. The new G-Unit CD blasted from the stereo in the living room while an old Cheech and Chong movie played on the TV. The volume was turned down because they were so high that they didn't have to hear what went on in the movie to laugh at the actors' antics. They also didn't hear Precious come in the front door. Her temperature rose as she scanned the room. Something was about to jump off up in here!

"What the fuck are y'all doin'? Why y'all got these niggas up in here? You know the rules. Y'all got the house smelling like one of them Park Heights weed spots. What the fuck is y'all hoes thinking about? Get these fools up outta here!" Precious demanded. She knew Donnell and Parrish from the streets, and knew that they were some shady motherfuckas.

"Hold up, Precious. You ain't gotta be wildin' out on our company like that. We pay bills up in here too," Trish said.

"Hell yeah!" Tina chimed in.

"Whatever. Y'all asses all highed up right now and talking outta the side of y'all necks. I said get these niggas the fuck outta here and I mean that shit!" Precious demanded with even more force.

"And if we don't?" Tina asked. She stumbled off the couch and got up in Precious' face.

"Bitch, please. You better act like you know. You don't want it with me," Precious threatened.

141

"We're gettin' tired of your ass walking around here like you runnin' shit. The only thing you runnin' around here is what goes on in that bedroom of yours. We pay rent up in here, and we can have company whenever the fuck we want!" Trish said. She too was now standing in front of Precious. Parrish and Donnell were enjoying the show as they watched from the sofa.

"A'ight, check this out. I'ma count to five, and the both of y'all bitches better raise the fuck up outta my face. I got shit on my mind, and I ain't in the mood for this shit. One, two, three, four . . . " Precious counted. Before she reached five, Tina swung wildly in her direction. That was the wrong move, and all the motivation Precious needed to let off some of her frustration.

Precious ducked out of the way of Tina's blow and landed a sharp right upper cut to her eye. Tina bent over and grabbed her eye with both hands while Precious stepped back and threw a roundhouse kick that landed in Trish's chest, knocking her onto the couch. She grabbed Tina by the hair and threw her on the couch next to Trish.

When Trish regained her breath, she tried to charge toward Precious, but Precious was too fast for her. She dodged out of the way, and Trish went sailing into the wall head first. Trish fell to the ground and balled up into the fetal position, holding her throbbing head. Precious made her way toward Tina and began pounding on her with both hands.

After the massacre went on for about two minutes, Parrish and Donnell had seen enough. "Yo, baby girl. You proved your point. They ain't got nothing for ya ass," Parrish said as the two of them pulled Precious off of Tina.

"Y'all better get ya hands off of me and get the fuck outta my house!" Precious yelled at Parrish and Donnell.

"You got that, killa. We outta here. Trish, we're gonna holla at y'all later. Ya know, when the scars clear up," Parrish said jokingly as they left.

"This ain't over wit', bitch. We got something for ya ass!" Trish warned Precious.

"Whatever, ho. Whenever y'all ready for round two, you know where to find me." Precious went into her room and slammed the door.

It felt good for her to let off some steam, but Precious felt bad about what just went down. She had never gotten into a physical fight with Trish or Tina before. This let her know that their friendship, as well as business relationship, was all but over. They could never be the same with each other again after this.

Fuck it, she decided, realizing she had much bigger things to worry about now that Patty had located her mother's killers. She drifted off to sleep, hoping she wouldn't have another nightmare.

7 A Chance Encounter

The next morning, Precious walked down the street, thinking about Trish and Tina. She was still angry about what had happened, and she no longer felt bad about whipping their asses. After all, it had been too many nights she had to come home smelling that funky-ass weed throughout the house, or listening to them making all kinds of crazy noise, fucking God knows who. They switched up niggas like Precious changed her thongs—every day!

Parrish and Donnell were some cruddy-ass niggas, she was sure. They meant nothing but trouble, just like all the other niggas she warned them not to have over at the crib. But they didn't want to see that she was just looking out for them.

She was starting to think it was time for her to get her own place. She didn't need to be bothered with anyone else in her life right now—no niggas, no bitches, no nothing. She just wanted to be left alone, especially since Patty told her about the niggas who killed her moms. Right about now, she was not the bitch to be fuckin' with, and Trish and Tina's antics had just put her in an even worse mood. She felt like the next fool that said the wrong thing to her, she would go off. That's when a stranger approached her on the street in front of the nail salon.

"A penny for ya thoughts, pretty lady. You look like you got something serious on ya mind. Do you care to share what's buggin' you? You're too beautiful to look so stressed out," the stranger said.

"Nigga, if you don't know me, don't say shit to me," she snapped, but when Precious turned around and saw the man who spoke to her, she regretted showing him her nasty attitude. This brother was fine. To say that he was tall, dark and handsome was an understatement. He had the sex appeal of Morris Chestnut, the presence of Denzel, and Tupac's thugged-out yet intellectual persona, all rolled into one man. She figured this out from just one glimpse. For the first time in her life, Precious was awestruck, but she tried not to let it show.

"I'm not gonna take what you said personal. I'm gonna assume that you just had a bad day. Also, I wanna apologize for the brother that pissed you off so much. He was a damn fool to mistreat such a queen. Let's start this conversation again," he suggested.

"My name is Talib. It's a pleasure to meet you. And your name is?" Talib extended his arm and took her hand into his without a second thought that she might resist. He felt the power of the chemistry between them when their palms met.

Precious wanted to have a sassy comeback, but his Adonis-like body and smooth, suntanned skin had her speechless. His hair was in dreadlocks, and he wore glasses that made him look like a harmless schoolboy. She came up to the middle of his muscular chest when they stood face to face. His smile was so disarming that she had to crack a smile as well. She was totally out of her element, not being in control of the situation.

"I apologize for being rude. My name is Precious. And you're right. I do have a lot on my mind. I'm sorry for snapping at you. It's just that I'm sick of niggas walking up on me on the streets, tryin' a holla with ignorant shit."

"I understand. A nigga would approach a beautiful sistah like yourself with no respect. However, I come at you like a black man with knowledge of self, as well as knowledge of how to approach a woman as beautiful and elegant as yourself," he responded.

"Is that right? You talk a good game. How old are you, Talib?" Precious asked.

"I just turned twenty-five, but I'm years older in life experience."

"I hear you. What you know about life? You look like one of them good guys. I grew up in the streets. I could probably teach you a few things about life, even though I'm only eighteen," Precious said. All of her problems seemed to disappear for the moment. She found herself enchanted with Talib and curious to find out more.

"Is that right, Miss Thugette? Well, if you're holding class, I might have to enroll to learn a few things. You should never judge a book by its cover, though. I'm from the streets, but I grew outta that lifestyle. I don't have to advertise where I come from in my every action. That was a time in my life when I was lost. Now, by the grace of Allah, I have a new way of thinking, and I choose not to dwell on my past behavior."

"I see. So, what does your name mean?" she asked. "Are you one of them Farrakhan boys out on the corner selling bean pies?"

Talib cracked a smile. He had heard this question before about his Islamic name and his spiritual beliefs. It didn't bother him at all. He liked her spunk and was fascinated with her charm. He saw her confrontational personality as a challenge. He was up for the job, and willing to put in overtime to get Precious.

"Nah, I'm not in the Nation anymore, but I do give a lot of credit to Minister Farrakhan for making me the man that I am today. I am still a Muslim. My name means "seeker of truth" in Arabic. Enough about me, though. Tell me some things about you," he inquired.

"I don't usually tell my business to anyone, let alone a total stranger. I like for that to be a mystery to be unraveled as you get to know me. However, you are kinda fine. Write your number down and I'll call you some time," she replied.

"That's fair enough. I see that you're about to get your nails done. I've seen you come here before. Tell Chanel that I said hello," Talib said.

He wrote his number on a piece of paper he had retrieved from his Ford Excursion, which was parked on the corner. He didn't ask for her number because he was confident that she would call. As he walked to his truck, he peeked over his shoulder and caught Precious eyeballing his gangsta stride.

Talib had also watched her several times, coming and going from the nail salon. Chanel was his friend from high school, and he had inquired about Precious after the first time he noticed her there. He wanted to know if she had a man. When he found that she didn't, he knew it was safe to make his move. He had also heard word from the streets that she was a booster and sold hot clothes. This fact didn't bother him. It only made him want to get to know more about her. Their love of clothing was something they had in common.

Talib owned a clothing store on the next block, up the street from The Nail Den. He sold his own line of designer urban gear, called Urban Legends, the same name he had given his store. He sold jerseys, sweatsuits, shirts, jeans, and baseball jackets adorned with his unique emblems and logos.

Talib's life was a hood success story. He took his money from his days as a drug dealer and converted it into a legitimate, profitable business. Now, he thought, it might seem strange to some that a clothing store owner would have no problem kickin' it with a booster, but street sense and logic in the larger society were two completely different schools of thought. He respected her hustle because he came from the same world that she did. As long as she didn't boost from his store, he didn't give a fuck.

As she watched him leave, Precious could not believe herself. She had never flirted with a man the way she just did. There was something about Talib that had a calming effect on her spirit and made her continue the conversation despite the foul mood she had been in when he first stopped her.

He didn't appear to be like other guys she had met. He spoke to her with respect, not all that ghetto street corner bullshit she heard all the time. He also appeared to be intelligent. She wanted to know more about him. She would definitely get the 411 from Chanel while she got her nails done.

As she got her nails done and gossiped, Precious was caught up in the idea that maybe she had met Mr. Right. However, she wasn't that far gone that she was ready to totally let her guard down. She had unfinished business to handle that required her undivided attention. Love would have to wait for now.

8 Redemption's Song

Everything was exactly how Precious said it would be. Black Phil and Trip's crack spot was packed with fiends who came to cop. That meant there was a lot of money up in there. Judging from the traffic flowin' in and out the house, they probably made between five and ten grand a day on the low end. Profits probably doubled and sometimes tripled when the first of the month came around, so Black Phil and Trip's spot was a prime target for a robbery. Since the two cats that ran the spot got high, it would be a lot easier to catch them slippin' than some cats who didn't indulge. This job would be a piece of cake. Like takin' candy from a baby, Marco thought.

Precious had called Marco to apologize for the way she acted the last time they saw each other three months before At first, Marco tried to play hard to get and brush her off. He wouldn't answer the phone when she called, or if he did answer, he told her he was busy. Eventually, she wore him down and they started to see each other occasionally.

Precious knew how to get under his skin. Marco had accepted the fact that she wasn't the one for him, but he was cool with their new casual arrangement. When she came at him with a business proposal, he couldn't resist it.

She told him about Black Phil and Trip's crack spot, and how easy it would be for Marco and his boys to rob it. At first, Marco was suspicious about why Precious volunteered this information without asking for a cut. He knew her well enough to know that she wouldn't usually look out for somebody else without something to gain from the situation. When she came clean and told him that those two bastards had killed her mother, the picture became clear to him. She was on some get-back shit.

Precious agreed to pay Marco fifteen grand to bring her Black Phil and Trip alive, and also to kidnap Rafael, so she could have her final revenge. The money would come out of the emergency fund she had stashed in her apartment. Marco was down with the plan. He liked this kind of action. He could pull off a quick lick for some cash, and he got a chance to rough up some assholes just for G.P. He got together with Precious and Patty to get the rundown on Black Phil and Trip so he could come up with the perfect strategy to make things happen.

Marco's got his crew together, first calling his two homeboys, Dre and Cooter. He grew up with them in Sandtown, in West Baltimore. Dre was tall and cock diesel, with his mammoth-sized biceps. He looked like the Rock with his intimidating size and light brown skin. He walked with an air about him, like he would knock a nigga out just for thinking the wrong thing about him. He always wore a long, black trench coat and black facemask when they did a job. He kept a mac-10 up under his coat in case things got ugly and somebody needed his chest plate blasted wide open.

Cooter was just as crazy. He was diminutive in stature and suffered from a Napoleon complex. He got into fights constantly because he felt the need to prove he was tough despite being vertically challenged. Cooter's weapons of choice were twin glocks. They worked well with his itchy trigger finger, and gave him more than enough shells to let off in the heat of battle.

Marco also got his brother involved in this job. Darren was five years younger than Marco, the spitting image of him. Marco had raised Darren since he was twelve years old, after their mother got strung out on crack and left them on their own. Darren looked up to Marco, following behind him in whatever devious deeds he was involved.

In observing the crack house, they noticed that Trip usually left early in the morning to re-up on product. Black Phil left around midnight, carrying a knapsack on his shoulder. They surmised that the bag contained the proceeds from the day's sales. Black Phil took the money to their other stash house around the corner whenever they closed up shop. More than likely, they didn't want to get caught with all of their money in one place if they ever did get robbed.

They both lived in the crack house, which was a stupid move. A true dealer never laid his head where he did his dirt because then enemies wouldn't have to look long and hard to find him. That made for an easy target.

Marco sent a fiend, Benny, into the house to cop and to see the layout of the place. Patty already gave them all the information she knew about how Black Phil and Trip's spot ran, but they needed to be sure. Benny was as good as it got when it came to casing a joint. Marco paid him $50 in rock cocaine for his services every time he used him.

When he returned from his mission, Benny told them that the security inside was weak. There were only two armed guards in the spot, one in the front room near the entrance, and the other on the third floor. The cat on the third floor was supposed to be the point man for any trouble that might arise. He observed everything from the front window, but there was no security at the back of the house, which left it vulnerable for attack. Marco envisioned they could creep up the motherfuckas from behind. They wouldn't know what hit they asses.

On the night they decided to put their plan into action, they waited until 11:30. They knew the house would be empty because shop was about to close and all the fiends had to bounce. They were sure there was a lot of money in the house because they watched all the traffic going in and out that day, and Black Phil had yet to make his money drop.

Marco and Darren, dressed in raggedy clothes to play the part, went along with Patty to cop a couple pills from the crack house. Black Phil and Trip knew her and wouldn't suspect that she was up to anything. Marco and Darren just looked like they were two more of Patty's crack-smoking friends who came to get high. The dude in the upstairs window suspected nothing.

When Trip opened the door to let Patty and her companions in, Marco and Darren bum rushed the door with guns cocked. Almost simultaneously, Dre kicked the frail back door in as he and Cooter pulled up the rear. The security guy in the front tried to draw his weapon, but he was too slow. The first round of shots that Marco let off from his .38 revolver hit the dude at point blank range. He fell to the ground and died instantly.

Darren hit Trip across the head with the butt of his nine, and he fell to the ground. Trip tried to get up, but Darren cracked him across the back of his head, knocking him out.

In the heat of the madness, Patty crept back out of the house, lucky to avoid getting hit by the bullets that flew by her head. Her job was done. She went to wait with Precious in the car around the corner, where Marco had no idea she was waiting. She had followed them to make sure everything went right. She wanted to be certain she would have a chance to meet face to face again with her mother's killers.

In the back room where he had been counting money, Black Phil heard the commotion and ran toward the stairs with his pistol in tow. Entering the upstairs hallway, he fired several shots blindly down the stairs, but none of them connected with their intended targets.

Cooter fired several shots, one of them hitting Black Phil in the leg as he made his way down the spiraling stairs. Black Phil was able to crawl back up the stairs out of the range of the gunshots, but that was only a momentary reprieve for him. When he tried to stand up and walk back up to the top of the stairs, his flesh was torn on impact by the two loud blasts from Marco's gun. One bullet hit him in the arm and the other one grazed his shoulder. He tumbled back down the stairs, hit his head, and was knocked unconscious.

The only person they hadn't yet located in the house was the security guy on the top floor. He tried to escape by jumping out the back window. When he jumped, Dre heard the crashing sound of the glass and reacted. He ran to the back door and saw the man as he ran across the yard. Dre let off a multitude of resounding shots, hitting the man in the back as he tried to climb over the fence. He fell out flat on the grass and bled to death. This robbery had turned ugly and everybody knew it.

Marco motioned to Dre and Cooter to go upstairs and retrieve the money and whatever drugs were in the house. They did so without hesitation.

Trip was still unconscious on the ground, but Black Phil had come to. He cursed under his breath at the robbers, vowing that they wouldn't get away with this shit. His threats were empty words, though, because his wounds made him unable to move. All he could do was wait helplessly and hope that the Devil sent one of his helpers to save his sin-sick soul. The chances of that happening were slim to none.

"C, go get the rope and shit so we can tie these motherfuckas up. Then we can carry these fools over to the other spot," Marco instructed.

Dre bound and gagged Black Phil, who tried to resist. Cooter held the now conscious Trip at gunpoint until Dre was finished tying him up. Once they were bound, Dre carried them over his shoulder, one at a time, to the Chevy truck parked out in the alley. He put both of them in the back area of the truck, which was lined with plastic so that the blood didn't stain the interior. They were stacked up like two large heaps of trash that he planned to drop in a Dumpster.

The four exited the scene in haste with the money and drugs in hand. The robbery had a few glitches, but the mission was accomplished. The only other thing left for Marco and his crew to do was to kidnap Rafael. That part would be easy because he was just another druggie in the streets, so no one would even notice he was missing.

Precious followed behind them from a distance, wiping away tears of relief from her eyes. Patty sat silently in the passenger's seat. Justice would be served tonight.

9 A Familiar Place

Precious thought about her life as she drove down the street. It was like a horror show going on inside her head. She saw images of her and her mother when she was a child, before Roxanne's drug use began. She thought about how her father used to spoil her. Life was so fun for her then, and she cherished those moments, regardless of how few of them there were.

She also had memories of the horrible arguments her parents used to have over drugs. She vividly remembered her father cursing and striking her mother in one of his tirades. Her mind wandered back to the day her mother was killed by Black Phil and Trip, then to thoughts of how miserable she was living with her grandmother and her constant verbal abuse. The hell she endured over the last nine years hit her at once, and it was almost overwhelming. All of it was because of the three no-good niggas she was about to deal with, and they would pay dearly for every ounce of her pain.

"Precious, be careful! You almost ran into the back of the car in front of us. We don't wanna attract no attention," Patty said. Consumed with her memories and with what was about to happen, Precious had momentarily lost control of the car. She stopped just before running into the back of another vehicle.

"Sorry about that, Aunt Patty. My mind was somewhere else," she said.

"I know, child. This'll all be over with soon. That heavy burden you've been carrying will finally be lifted off your shoulders," Patty said. She reached across to the driver's side and grabbed a hold of Precious' hand to comfort her. With her other hand, she wiped away the tears from her eyes.

They had finally reached their destination. Precious parked the car a block away from the house on Bartlett Avenue where they were scheduled to meet Marco and his crew. It was the same house where her mother was killed, but now it was abandoned. Most of the houses on the block were condemned, and the few residents who still lived there were nothing more than junkies who could care less about what was about to take place. They were too busy tryin' to get on for that next high. Precious wouldn't have to worry about the police showing up, because no one would care enough to call them. This was the place where her suffering began, and it was the perfect place to bring it to a close.

As they made their way up to the house, Marco greeted them at the front door. "I'm glad you finally made it. We got them all down in the basement, tied up and blindfolded. You got the rest of my loot?" he asked.

"Yeah, I got you. Here you go," Precious said. She reached inside her pocket and gave him an envelope containing the last payment she promised him.

"That's what I'm talking about. Hey yo, Precious, I know my job is done, but can I stay around and watch the show? I live for this kinda shit," Marco said.

"Nigga, you are sick. I don't care. You can watch if you want to."

As they walked toward the basement, she had more flashbacks of her childhood living in the house. She felt a migraine headache coming on. They made it down the stairs, and Precious saw the three bastards responsible for ruining her life, helplessly tied up, lying on the cold floor. The rest of Marco's crew stood watch over them.

She walked over to Rafael and kicked him hard in the groin. He screamed loudly from the pain. One by one, she took the blindfolds off of the three men. Rafael recognized the girl who kicked him, but couldn't remember where he knew her from. When he saw Patty, he knew who she was.

"Who the fuck is this bitch? Patty, what the hell are you doing here? Rafael, what your shady ass got to do with this? Why the fuck y'all bring us here? Y'all got the money!" Black Phil said.

Patty didn't say a word. She just stood to the side with Marco and his crew. This was Precious' time to face her demons.

"This ain't about no money, motherfucka. This is about your ass. You don't remember me, do you?" Precious asked with a menacing tone.

"Should we remember you? Who the hell are you?" Trip asked.

"Think back almost ten years ago. Remember a little girl that lived on Bartlett Avenue with her mother? Y'all caught the little girl coming outta the house in the morning and dragged her back in. This motherfucka right here sent y'all over to her house to trick," Precious said.

She looked directly at Rafael. He didn't say a word because now he knew this was the daughter he had abandoned long ago. He had carried around the guilt of being partially responsible for Roxanne's death all of these years. To hide his guilt, like a good addict, he sunk deeper into his addiction.

"Do you bastards remember how you raped and beat the woman to death in front of her child? That little girl was me, motherfuckas! That was my mother you killed!" Precious screamed in a state of hysteria. It all started to make sense to Black Phil and Trip. They were fucked. Their chickens had come home to roost.

"Precious, I'm sorry, baby. I never meant for things to go down like that. I know I was wrong. Please forgive me," Rafael begged.

"Forgive you? Forgive you for running out on me and my mother? Forgive you for acting like I didn't exist? Forgive you for sending these bastards to our house and me having to watch them rape and murder my mother? Fuck you, you son of a bitch. You better pray that God can forgive you, because you about to leave this fucking earth!"

"Just give me a chance, baby. I swear I can make everything right between us. It was the drugs, baby. They got my mind all fucked up. If you let me go, I'ma get clean and we can be a family again," Rafael pleaded.

There was no way in hell that was gonna happen. Precious stood in front of him, showing no emotion. "I hope that the Devil got a detox center in hell for ya ass, because you're about to be face to face with him. You can be a family with these two goons. Patty, hand me that can over there."

Patty retrieved the can of acid that Marco had brought for her. Precious poured the entire can over the three men then watched with a look of satisfaction on her face while they yelled in sheer agony, the acid eating through their flesh.

"Oooh. Get this shit off of me! It burns like hell, you li'l bitch!" Black Phil yelled. The acid made the pain of his gunshot wounds more intense.

"Fuck you, ya whore. I'm glad we killed ya mother. We shoulda killed ya ass too," Trip said. He knew he was about to die, and didn't give a fuck what he said.

"Yeah, you shoulda killed me, but you didn't, so now the joke's on you, motherfucka. Y'all ready to get outta here?" Precious asked her entourage.

"Precious, you is a gangsta-ass bitch. I like your style, girl. Let's get the fuck up outta here, fellas," Marco said. He loved seeing this wicked side of Precious. It turned him the fuck on watching her put her murder game down. He and his crew bounced to let Precious have her final moment.

"Patty, you wanna do the honors so we can get the hell outta here too?" Precious asked.

"Of course, sweetie. It would be my pleasure." Patty retrieved two cans of gasoline and poured one can all over the basement floor. She poured the second can all over the three men. The remaining gas was emptied in a path leading to the basement steps.

"I hate the fact that we gotta run now, but . . . it's gettin' hot in here," Precious sang. She and Patty shared a moment of laughter. They were standing on the top of the steps when Precious struck a match and threw it down the stairs. It landed on the gasoline and within seconds, the basement was covered in flames. As they made their exit from the house, they could hear the agonized screams coming from the basement. All three men would be dead shortly, their flesh burned to a crisp. She wanted them to suffer a miserable death for the agony they had caused her.

Precious had avenged her mother's death. Maybe now she could finally put this behind her and move on with her life.

10 Fallin' In Love

Two months had passed by since Precious had taken care of her mother's killers. The fire was reported all over the news, but the police did not have any leads. Precious was in the clear. Even though she knew that killing the men wouldn't bring her mother back, she still felt like a load was lifted from her shoulders. She started to at look her life differently. Contributing to this change was Talib.

Talib was everything that he said was. He was everything that Precious thought a man could never be. She was a totally different person when she was around him. He could make her smile when she tried hard not to. He always had words of wisdom that provoked her to think positively about things in her life, especially when she felt they couldn't get any worse.

She had never shared this kind of bond with a man in her life. With the exception of her grandfather, her relationships with men had been about money and sex. Talib, however, was more into stimulating her mind and seeing her become a more complete woman. Amazingly, they had not yet had sex. Because of his strong Muslim faith, he wanted to wait until the time was right. Besides, what unfolded between them was much deeper than the physical. There was no doubt about it. Talib had his hooks dug into her heart. She was crazy about him, and he felt the same.

It took Precious several weeks after their first meeting before she finally broke down and called Talib. It wasn't so much that she was playing hard to get, but she was distracted by other things in her life. Even after she got revenge on her mother's killers, she had to deal with her deteriorating friendship with Trish and Tina.

Things had not been the same since the night of their big fight, and it started to affect business. They argued about the littlest things around the house. Precious would go days without speaking to them, and vice versa. She noticed that they were chummy with each other but gave her the cold shoulder. Precious didn't give a damn. She didn't need their asses any more if they didn't want to be her friends. Besides, she kind of expected them to be different after she kicked their asses, so now she took a "fuck them" attitude.

Precious was even more pissed when she found out that they got jobs as bank tellers. With their new jobs, Trish and Tina started boosting less and less with her and Patty. Pretty soon, it was just Precious and Patty out on the hustle trail. Even though that meant they didn't have to split the money as many ways, it also meant they couldn't boost as much. That fucked with Precious' cash flow, and that was a no-no.

Precious still managed to make good money, but she wanted more. They argued about this issue constantly, but it was a no-win situation. Trish and Tina eventually gave up the game altogether, giving the impression that they were going legit. They had a bigger scam in the works, but their plans did not include Precious, so they just kept their mouths shut around her. There was nothing Precious could do about it but accept it and move on.

Despite their differences, everyone still paid their share of the bills, and that kept a degree of peace in their household. How long that would last was another issue that only time could answer.

Not only did she have to deal with losing the bond with her girls, she also had to deal with Patty's issues. After they handled the situation with Rafael, Black Phil and Trip, Patty gave her some terrible news. The memory of that day still stung Precious like it was yesterday.

Patty and Precious had lunch at TGI Fridays in Owings Mills when she dropped the bomb on her. "Precious, I love you like a daughter. There's nothing in this world that I wouldn't do for you. What I have to tell might shock you, but don't feel sad for me. I did this to myself," Patty said.

"Aunt Patty, what are you talking about? Did you let some fool get you for your money again?" Precious asked. She was used to Patty telling her stories about some dude that she messed around with running off with her loot and/or drugs.

"I wish it was something that simple, baby. Aunt Patty is very sick. I'm HIV positive. They tried putting me on medication, but my T cell is still dropping. My doctor said that my count is under ten and there's nothing they can do. I don't have much longer to live." Those words echoed in Precious' head and rendered her speechless.

Patty said she found out a while ago but didn't want to tell her because she knew Precious would only worry herself crazy. Patty had no idea who she contracted the disease from, but that didn't matter. With all the running she did in the streets, gettin' high and hoein', she felt she was getting what she deserved.

Now Precious was faced with losing the only other person she loved. The feelings of loneliness she had as a child came flooding back. Her boosting crew started out four strong, but now she was about to be on her own. Her resiliency in dealing with adversity began to break down. She needed an escape. That was when she decided to call Talib, the tall, handsome stranger who struck something in her when they first met. Just the touch of his hand made her skin tingle. She had no idea what kind of voodoo he had worked on her, but she wanted to unlock the mystery.

They talked on the phone for about two weeks before Precious agreed to go out with him. In their many conversations, they felt each other out as they discussed their likes and dislikes. They found out that they had a lot in common. Talib had also lost his mother to the streets and drugs. His father was like so many other absentee fathers in the Black community—missing in action. Talib last saw him when he was three years old. For years, he harbored resentment toward his father, just as Precious did toward Rafael.

Talib, who was born Malcolm Atkins, was in foster care from age five until he was ten and his maternal grandmother became his legal guardian. His relationship with her was the exact opposite of Precious' relationship with her grandmother. She was the most important person in his life and his biggest supporter. She loved him as best she could in the face of his grandfather's harsh treatment.

Talib's grandfather beat him constantly as a child. He used extension cords, a hot iron, shoes, just about anything he could get his hands on. There weren't any real reasons for most of the beatings. Talib was a pretty good kid despite his lack of guidance at a young age. When he was told to do something, he generally did as instructed. Still, his grandfather blamed Talib's father for the death of his only daughter, and he released his anger on the boy.

His grandfather always told him that he would be no good, just like his father. Talib developed a serious dose of self-hatred and low self-esteem. He felt out of place with the other kids.

The beatings ceased when he reached the age of fourteen. Not because his grandfather realized the error of his ways, but because

Talib decided that he had enough. One night, his grandfather came home drunk after losing his job. He tried to take his frustration out on Talib, who snapped and wound up stabbing his grandfather ten times with a steak knife.

His grandfather survived the attack, but Talib ran away from home in fear that he would be arrested. He was on the run for nearly two years, and during that time, Talib was homeless. He survived by eating food from trashcans or whatever handouts he could get. He slept on park benches in the warm weather and shelters in the wintertime.

When he was finally apprehended, he wound up serving two years in juvenile hall. Juvie was kind to him. He wasn't a small dude, so no one messed with him. It was there that he was introduced to the drug game. When he was released, he started dealing.

Once he started making big money from selling drugs, he got mad love and respect. All of this newly discovered adulation gave him a natural high. He could buy whatever he wanted. He could have any woman he desired. The way the junkies and crack heads fiended for his product gave him an intoxicating sense of power. He was the man, and nothing could stop him.

That reality changed for him quickly after one of his crew snitched on him. He ended up serving four years on a possession with intent to distribute charge. It was in prison that Talib had a spiritual awakening. He met a Muslim brother by the name of Khalid who befriended him early in his bid.

Khalid was a lifer, serving time for the murder of a police officer back in the early 1970s. He was heavy into the Black Power movement, and a strong advocate for establishing a Black Nation. He considered himself to be a political prisoner much like Geronimo Pratt, claiming that the U.S. government framed him because of his anti-Establishment political views. He worked countless hours with jailhouse lawyers and a human rights advocate group trying to get his conviction overturned.

Khalid introduced Talib to the teachings of the Nation of Islam. He gave him his Arabic name and a new lease on life. He taught him his history as a black man, and told him how to love himself as a black man with a rich heritage. He showed him how selling drugs was a detriment to the black community. He broke down how Talib's family environment contributed to his negative actions later in life. However, he also advised him that it was his duty to accept responsibility for his own actions. Now that he had this knowledge, Talib was challenged to work toward improving himself as a person.

Khalid instilled in him a level of self-awareness and consciousness that made Talib want to become an asset to the community instead of an enemy to the progress of his race. Talib left prison a reformed man, determined to become a productive member of society.

Since coming home from prison, he had established an even stronger relationship with his grandmother. She never held a grudge against Talib for the incident that took place between them. When he came back into her life, she was just happy to have her grandson back and to see that he had made something of himself. She felt that if the Muslims could make a better man out of her grandson, then she was all for them. The fine man that he had become was an indication that they had done what she and her husband were not able to do with Talib—make him a responsible and respectful black man.

His grandfather had died of a heart attack before he went to prison. Though he was never able to tell his grandfather this, Talib had evolved to the point that he forgave him for his abusiveness. He understood that he had lived a hard life himself, and his spirit was broken years ago over his own disappointments. Talib reasoned that the beatings he received were his grandfather's way of taking out his frustration over the loss of his daughter and his inability to hold steady employment or to do more for his family. His new way of thinking didn't make his grandfather's behavior acceptable, but it allowed him to move past that chapter in his life. He knew that holding a grudge would only leave him with a heavy burden that would dampen his newfound spirit.

After Talib told her about his transformation, Precious was even more attracted to him. She admired him for turning his life around. She was attracted to his strength, and wondered if it could possibly rub off on her. He made her open up and share some of the pain that she had hoarded away for so long. Precious, for the first time, opened up about what happened to her and her mother. It felt good to be able to do that. She still kept many of her feelings and thoughts to herself, but she felt like she had finally met someone who could relate to her without judging her. Maybe someday she would even be able to tell him about what she had done to avenge her mother's death. Precious started to feel like there was a brighter tomorrow for her.

Their first date was unlike anything Precious expected. Most guys usually suggested a dinner and the movies, but he was on a different kinda time. Talib was much deeper than that and had a bigger vision of their relationship from the start. Precious was thrown for a loop when he took her out to dinner to meet his grandmother. He told Precious that since she was about to become his woman, she needed to meet the other most important woman in his life.

Precious and his grandmother, whom she called Miss Mabel, hit it off instantly. It was as if his grandmother could read what was in her spirit. She looked past her tough exterior and saw that Precious was really a confused young girl in need of some direction in her life. She knew that Talib could handle her, with a firm hand and unconditional love. That was why she gave their relationship her blessing and wished them well.

From that first date, Precious began to spend more and more time with Talib. They were almost inseparable. If they weren't on the phone, they were back and forth, spending the night at each other's houses. They never made love in all of those nights together. They would just stay up 'til the wee hours of the morning, talking about anything that popped into their heads. Talib wanted her to become his best friend, and to be her best friend as well. He knew she had issues with men, but he was willing to do what he had to do to gain her trust.

Precious started to change in a lot of ways. She didn't spend as much time wondering why God gave her such a rough road. Talib turned her on to several books that dealt with black women's issues as they strove to find a place for themselves in the face of racism, materialism, and a male dominated world. She read the books from cover to cover and learned some important lessons from them, but she wasn't ready to leave all of her old ways behind just yet.

He tried to talk to her about going to college, but she wasn't too open to that idea. She wasn't quite ready to join the regular world. As much as he stimulated her mind and as much as she started to change, Precious still had a lot more of the streets in her. Boosting was still her main source of income. She loved doing what she did. It made her feel powerful, breaking the law and getting away with it. Besides, she still didn't fully trust the relationship, so she wasn't about to change completely. If Talib knew the secret that Precious held, he might just up and leave her, and she felt like she had to hold on to the streets in case he did go.

Precious' secret, which she had just discovered, was that she was pregnant. It was Marco's baby. After he helped her out with Black Phil and Trip, she had slept with him a few times before she started talking to Talib. She had no plans of telling Talib that she was sleeping with Marco, but now she would have no choice. She couldn't hide her pregnancy from forever.

Her only option for avoiding the truth would be to push him away before she started showing, but that thought was something she didn't even want to deal with. The love she felt for Talib had worked its way into her heart, and she didn't want to have to give him up. She had it bad for him.

11 A Bump Along the Road

It was early on a Tuesday morning. Precious moved slowly around her apartment. Her two roommates hadn't been home in three days. She wasn't concerned because they weren't on speaking terms anyway. In fact, as soon as their lease was up, she planned on moving out of the apartment. She figured that they were probably in New York or Jersey somewhere, gettin' high and fuckin' wit' some up-North niggas that they had just met. That was their style—find 'em, fuck 'em, and talk shit about 'em later.

Precious missed Talib badly. He was in New York for a business meeting with some investors. He had plans to take his clothing line national, but needed some major financial support to make it happen. He envisioned seeing his line in all of the major department stores alongside Puffy and Jay Z's clothing lines. He had arranged a meeting with a group of rich, white philanthropists to present his business plan. She was sure that his meeting would be a success because Talib had the charm and wit to sell himself to anybody.

Along the way to the bathroom, Precious stopped to admire herself in the mirror. Her hips were a little wider and her cheeks looked fuller. It wouldn't be long before she looked truly pregnant, but she wasn't prepared to deal with that right now. She made her way to the bathroom and turned on the shower, relaxing a bit as the steaming hot water soaked into her skin.

She was taken away with thoughts of Talib's strong arms holding her. She imagined his tongue doing a slow dance along the outline of her curvaceous figure. Her nipples rose as the water streamed over them. Her soft spot became moist with anticipation of his hardness penetrating her. She fantasized about what it would feel like to have Talib's head between her thighs, engulfed in her juices. She was almost at the point of orgasm when she heard her cell phone ring, snapping her out of her daydream.

She had yet to make love to Talib in reality. He still wanted to wait until the time was right and she was sure that she wanted a committed relationship. In her mind, the time was right now, and she knew she wanted to see if he could make her squirm and squeal in the worst way. To hell with the relationship for now. She wanted to sample his sex.

She decided to let her phone ring. Whoever the hell it was would leave a message if it was something important. Once she finished her shower and dried off, she massaged cocoa butter and aloe vera lotion into her skin, giving it a rich glow to enhance her natural beauty. She went into her dresser drawer and retrieved a cream-colored thong and bra set then sprayed J-Lo's Glow perfume on her neck. Next, she grabbed a pair of skin-tight Guess jeans from her closet and threw on a thin brown sweater with matching brown ankle boots. She was now dressed and ready to go to work.

Precious checked her phone and saw that the missed call was from a new client who wanted to buy some merchandise. They had met through a mutual associate named Rochelle. They all went to the same hair salon, Avanti Hair Studio on Liberty Heights Avenue. Rochelle bought clothes from Precious on the regular, and told her that her girlfriend, Chanice, wanted the same hookup.

Chanice gave Precious a list of the items she wanted, and Precious agreed to get them. She and Patty did their thing, easily getting all the items on the list. If all went well, Precious would make two grand off this one exchange. That meant a grand apiece for her and Patty. You couldn't beat that.

Precious dialed Chanice's number to return her call. "Hello. Can I speak to Chanice?"

"Speaking. Precious, is that you, girl?"

"Yeah, what's up? I got everything you wanted. What time do you want to hook up?"

"Three o'clock is good for me. So, you mean you got the Ferragamo, Prada and Manolo shoes, the Gucci and Coach bags, the five pairs of—"

"Yeah, yeah," Precious interrupted. "I got everything you wanted. You got the money?"

"I know you said two grand, but can I get a discount? I got like around fifteen hundred on me now," Chanice said.

"A discount? You already gettin' a discount. It's two grand in cash for the goods, and nothing less. Do you want this stuff or not? If not, I gotta bounce, because time is money. You wastin' my time right now when I could be makin' money."

"Okay, I'll get the other five hundred from somewhere. Two grand for all of the merchandise is cool. That is cheap considering its worth much more than that. Are the sales tags still on everything?"

"Of course. I run an organized business over here. All of our merchandise is authentic. We ain't into selling the bootleg shit," Precious said.

"Okay, then its set. We're gonna meet at three in the parking lot of Avanti's. Then I can get my hair done when we finish," Chanice said.

"That's fine. I'll holla at you then," Precious replied before she hung up.

It was now noontime, and her stomach growled from hunger. Precious grabbed a bite to eat from Sister Sandra's Place on Reisterstown Road. She had a fried catfish sandwich with a side of mashed potatoes, which she ate in the car because she had moves to make. She had a few stops to make at salons on the East Side before her 3 o'clock appointment.

After she finished filling a few small orders, she decided to pay her grandfather a quick visit. She hadn't seen him in over a month, although she talked to him at least twice a week. Her grandmother's black Nissan Altima wasn't parked in front of the house when Precious pulled up. That meant she wasn't home, a relief to Precious. She rang the bell and her grandfather opened the door.

"Hey, baby girl. How have you been? What, you decided to stop by and pay an old man a visit? Let me look at you. My baby girl is as pretty as the sunshine," her grandfather gushed.

"Thanks, Poppa Paine. I'm fine. How are you?" Precious asked then kissed him on his cheek. He led her into the living room where they could sit down to talk.

"Well, Precious, your grandfather ain't doing too well right now. I went to the doctor the other day. He told me that I need to take it easy. He said that my blood pressure is up and I have high cholesterol, and my heart ain't in the best shape. Mentioned something about me having clogged arteries or something. With all of this going on inside of me, it means I can't eat pork, fried chicken, and macaroni 'n cheese if I wanna stay around a little longer. He also gave me some medicine to take every day. Shit, I told him that I'm almost seventy years old, and I'ma eat what I want. If it's time for me to go, then I'll be ready when the good Lord calls my number," he said, cracking a half-hearted smile.

"Poppa Paine, stop talking like that. You better do what the doctor tells you. I wanna keep you around for a while. You're all the family I got. I guess I ain't the only one around here that's hardheaded, huh?" Precious said.

"Hush ya mouth, child. I ain't ya only family. Your grandmother loves you. So do the rest of your aunts and cousins as well. They just don't know how to express it in the right way is all."

"Anyway, do I have to come by here more often to make sure that you take your medication?" she asked, ignoring his comment about her family. He wouldn't let it go, though.

"No, I'll be all right. I want you to listen to what I have to say right now, and don't interrupt me. You might think that you're all alone in this world, but you're not. When your mother got hooked on drugs, it devastated this whole family. Her death just made it that much harder. She was the baby girl around here. We all spoiled her to death. Nobody ever said no to her whenever she wanted something. She had to have her way. As much as I hate to admit it, we all probably played a role in her bad decisions.

"Her death hurt your grandmother the worst. She always defended your mother when she did bad things as a child, wrong or right. She would never let me, or anybody else, discipline her baby girl. When Roxanne died, she blamed herself for creating the selfish person she had become. She believed it was her fault that Roxanne went down the road she did. The hardest thing for a mother to lose is a child. That's a special love right there. You'll see that yourself one day when you stop running the streets and settle down.

"Every time she sees you, she sees your mother's reflection in your face. It just makes her relive the pain of losing her. The anger she shows toward you is really her anger at herself. She doesn't mean what she does or says to you. She's still grieving inside.

"I talk to her about the way she treats you all the time. She's starting to realize her mistakes, slowly but surely. Keep ya mind open and try to be receptive if she reaches out to you. If anything happens to me, I wanna know that I left this Earth knowing that you two tried to make amends. You have to make me that promise," he said.

"I promise you I'll think about it," Precious said.

Her grandfather's words touched her in a special way. They made her realize that maybe she was being selfish in not recognizing her grandmother's pain. She started to understand how she had adopted some of her mother's bad ways with the choices she made in her life. She never took the time to see things from her grandmother's perspective before, but now her mind was receptive to the idea. Dealing with Talib had made her more able to start seeing things through the eyes of others.

"So, now . . . how is that nice young man with the funny name doing? You know the one that you're always talking about. I was impressed when you brought him by that day," he said.

Precious smiled at the thought of Talib. If her grandfather liked him, that must be a good sign. She made a mental note of that one.

"His name is Talib, and he's doing fine. He' s outta town right now on business," she replied.

"You need to stick with him. He seems to have a good head on his shoulders. You need a strong man in your life to be firm and loving with you. He reminds me of myself when I was younger," he said.

"I hear you. He's a good guy," she said with a smile. "Well, I gotta get ready to run. Now, give me my kiss so I can go."

They exchanged hugs and kisses and she left. He watched her drive down the street and out of sight, thinking everything would be okay for Precious. She just needed some time to find herself.

Precious sped down the road en route to her appointment. It was almost 2:30, and she had to make it across town in less than thirty minutes. She bobbed and weaved through traffic to make it on time, eager to get that cash. She had made almost a grand from her stops earlier in the day, and once she finished with Chanice, she would head to the salon to sell her last few loose items.

It was five minutes before 3:00 when she pulled up in the parking lot of Avanti's. She saw Chanice's Highlander sitting in the back of the lot. She got out of her car and went into her trunk to get the items she planned to sell. Once she had everything she needed, she walked over to Chanice's truck.

Chanice was a heavyset woman with sagging breasts and an oversized rear, but she had a pretty face and kept her hair done. Those two things offset her unshapely body and gave her some appeal that might attract a man. Maybe the designer clothes would help, Precious thought.

"Hey, Precious. I see you're on time. I like that. We can definitely do business again. Let me see what you got in those bags," Chanice said.

Precious gave her the bags. After Chanice scanned over the items and confirmed Precious had come through with everything she requested, she reached into her glove compartment and pulled out a white envelope. She handed it to Precious, who counted the cash inside to make sure it was all there. The money was right, so the transaction was complete. Precious put the money inside her purse.

"It was a pleasure doing business with you. Hit me up when you need something else. You see I'm nice with mine. I can get you whatever you want. The more people you bring to me, the more of a discount I can give you," Precious said. She had confidence in her skills.

"Oh, you know I will," Chanice said, following behind Precious as she walked to her car. "Oh, Precious, there's one thing I forgot to tell you before you go."

Precious stopped and turned around. Chanice was standing too close for comfort. "And what's that?" Precious asked.

"You're under arrest. You have the right to remain silent. Anything you say can and will be used against you in a court of law. You have the right to an attorney. You have . . . " Precious tuned out the rest of Chanice's words as she continued to read her rights.

Chanice and Rochelle turned out to be undercover cops. They got a tip from Trish and Tina about Precious' boosting operation. They swore to her that they would pay her back for that ass whippin' she gave them, and they did. Rochelle and Chanice had Precious under surveillance for quite sometime before they decided to make a move on her.

Customers in the salon came outside to see what the commotion was all about. Several police cars were now in the lot, surrounding the scene. They turned the parking lot into a light show. Anyone driving by would've thought they were about to make a major drug bust with all of that hoopla.

"You ain't got nothing on me. You can't prove shit!" Precious screamed boldly, but her heart raced in fear.

"Think again, you li'l thief. Remember our phone conversation earlier? I got that on tape. Our little transaction we just did was also being recorded. All of the clothes you sold to Rochelle, we got you on video tape making those deals as well. You can thank ya girls, Trish and Tina, for helping us bag ya ass. Your luck has run out, Miss Thing," Chanice said, smiling with the satisfaction of a job well done.

Rochelle stepped out of the police van parked in the lot. She was laughing as she walked toward Precious and Chanice.

"Fuck you, you fat, outta shape bitches. I hope y'all asses choke on a Twinkie, you hefty hoes!" Precious yelled. She knew that she was in hot water.

Precious yelled several more expletives at Chanice as they put her into the back of the police car in handcuffs. How this could have happened to her, Precious wondered. She was always cautious about who she dealt with. She couldn't believe that Trish and Tina had dropped a dime on her.

She was about to make her first trek through the legal system. She closed her eyes and leaned her head against the seat of the police car. The handcuffs were tight around her wrists. Where the hell was Talib when she needed him?

12 The Valley Of Decision

Precious sat in the holding cell, mentally exhausted from the recent turn of events. She looked around at the other females in the cell and wondered how the hell they all wound up in the same place. They weren't on her level in any way, shape, or form. One of the women was an over-the-hill prostitute named Nina, who looked like she had seen better days. Her body looked like she had turned one too many tricks with her sagging tits and all the scratches on her arms and legs.

There was another girl about Precious' age, locked up on a drug charge. Her name was Vonda, and she was dressed like a dude in baggy jeans and an oversized hockey jersey. She had "bull dyke" written all over her. She was checking Precious out on the low, but Precious peeped her game and shot her a look that let her know it wasn't even that kinda party.

The rest of the chicks in there were drug addicts. One of them was suffering heroin withdrawal, throwing up and sweating profusely. Precious couldn't wait to make bail to get the fuck outta this hellhole.

This was her first time in jail, and it wasn't a pleasant experience. She didn't look forward to spending more time there than was necessary. She knew that she was breaking the law when she boosted clothes, but she never thought she would get caught. Being arrested finally made her understand that there were consequences to her actions.

Doing time in jail was a consequence she was just not prepared to face. She thought about how much it would cost her to pay a lawyer and make bail, and she was worried. She had started spending more of her savings lately, so she was down to ten grand in her personal stash. She kept that money hidden separately from the loot she hid for her and Trish and Tina.

After she paid Marco the fifteen grand for the job he did for her, there was only thirty-five grand left in the emergency kitty. She had no choice but to use that money to foot the bill for her legal expenses. After all, she wouldn't be in jail if it weren't for them bitches. However, she had to get to the funds first. She used her one phone call to call Patty, who answered on the third ring.

"Precious, what the hell you doin' calling me from jail?" Patty asked with concern, fearing that the police had found some way to connect the fire and the murders to Precious.

"They got me down here on selling stolen merchandise and theft charges, Aunt Patty. Them bitches, Trish and Tina, set me up," Precious replied.

"Oh, no they didn't set my baby up to take a fall! How much is ya bail?" Patty asked. She was concerned that Precious was locked up, but relieved that it wasn't for the more serious charges.

"It's fifty thousand. I need you to call Talib for me. Tell him I need him to get me outta here. Here's the number." Precious repeated Talib's phone number for Patty, then asked her to make the call right away. She couldn't stand it in that jail too much longer.

"I'ma call him as soon as I get off the phone with you. How are you holding up?" Patty asked.

"I'm maintaining. You know I can handle mine. I ain't sweating none of these broads up in here," Precious replied with false courage.

"I know that's right. I'ma handle this business for you to get you home as soon as possible. Just hold on. I love you, Precious."

"I love you too, Aunt Patty," Precious responded before she hung up.

When they returned her to the cell, Precious looked around the pen where she was being held. It was filthy and smelled of the stench of urine. Add in the smell of all of the body odors from the other prisoners, and it made for one hella funk box. There was graffiti all over the walls, no doubt left by previous inmates during their brief stays there. The toilet in the cell looked like it had mold all around the seat. She didn't plan on using that, no matter how bad she had to go. Her pretty, soft ass would never be contaminated with such nasty germs.

The women in the jail were loud as hell, making all kinds of racket about nothing. Precious had no choice but to listen. Nina talked for an hour about how upset her pimp was gonna be because she wasn't out on the track makin' money. She also talked about the number of police officers she sucked and fucked to avoid arrest. Vonda bent Precious' ear, talkin' about how she would beat her charge and how she couldn't wait to get home to her girl. She also took the time to show all the jailhouse tattoos she got during her many trips to the penitentiary. Other inmates occupied their time telling war stories about their escapades in the streets, spreading bullshit rumors about who was gettin' money and who was fuckin' whose husband or wife.

All of the senseless conversation irked the hell outta Precious. Her prayers were finally answered when the officer came to the cell and called her name. By then she felt like she had been in custody forever.

"Precious Paine, somebody paid ya bail. You're free to go," the officer announced. He unlocked the gate.

Precious had dozed off in the midst of all the confusion and commotion in the cell, but as soon as she heard her name, she bolted off the bench like Flo Jo in her heyday. She had her "get outta jail" card and couldn't wait to get the hell outta there. After all of her paperwork was processed, she retrieved her personal effects and made her way out to the lobby of the police station. When she reached the front door, she looked outside, hoping to see Talib. There he was, seated in his truck, parked right in front. She ran down the steps.

"Damn, baby, I'm glad to see you," Precious said as she closed the door on his truck. She reached across the seat to give him a hug and a kiss. He returned her kiss, but without emotion, giving her only a cold peck on the lips in return.

"I'm glad to see you as well, but not under these circumstances," Talib said with a serious look on his face. She had never seen him look like this before.

"I didn't plan for this to happen. What, you got an attitude with me? You act like you ain't know what I was into," Precious said.

"Did I say that I was upset?" he shot back.

"You know what? I don't need this. I had to be around all of them crazy bitches up in there all that time. I'm really not in the mood to argue with you right now. I just wanna go home, please." Precious folded her arms and pouted in the passenger seat.

"You're a motherfuckin' trip. A brother comes down here and spends his money to bail you out and you act like this. I was worried sick about you. You're so ungrateful. You need to get ya life together. You gettin' to be too old to be going through this bullshit," he said. He had never cursed at Precious before.

"Whatever, man. You didn't even give me a chance to say thank you for bailing me out. Don't worry about your money. I'm gonna give you every penny back. Just get me to my house, if you don't mind." Precious rolled her eyes and laid her head back on the seat.

"Gladly," Talib replied.

The ride from the police station to her house was a long, silent one, each refusing to talk the other. Talib made a few calls on his cell. Precious called Patty to let her know that she was out then closed her eyes and tried to act like she was asleep. She was really in deep thought. She regretted snapping at Talib like that. She wondered if she had finally gotten on his last nerve and he was done with her.

Oh, well. I knew he was too good to be true. He's just like all of the rest, she decided.

They finally reached Precious' house. Before she could step out of the truck, Talib grabbed her arm, seeming uncharacteristically nervous. He swallowed the lump that formed in his throat before he began to speak.

"Wait a minute, Precious. I need to apologize to you. I'm sorry for cursin' at you. It just scared me to think of you in that jail, and I took out my emotions on you." His apology caught her off guard.

"Apology accepted. Let's go back to your place instead," Precious responded. There was no need to say a host of words. They looked into each other's eyes and became engulfed in a long, sensual tongue kiss. When they broke the kiss, Talib made a U-turn and headed to his house.

When they got there, they headed for the door, holding hands tightly like two young lovers caught at a crossroads in their relationship. Talib put his key in the door and led her down the hallway to the living room, where he took a seat on the couch. Precious joined him. It was time for them to have that long awaited conversation. They needed to iron out their differences.

"Precious, we need to talk. Right now, I just want you to listen to me," Talib said.

"I'm listening. What's up?"

"Well, I think by now you know how I feel about you and how special you are to me. I think it's pretty obvious, don't you agree?" Talib asked.

"Yeah, I do. I feel the same way about you," Precious replied.

"You don't know how long I've been waiting to hear you say that. From the first time I saw you, even before we actually met, I felt that there was something special about you. The more I get to know you, the more I see how much potential you have. The only thing holding you back from doing anything you wanna do in life is you. You are your worst enemy—not your grandmother, not Trish and Tina, not society, but you. I know it was hard for you growing up without your mother or father, but we all have obstacles to overcome in life."

"So, what's ya point?" Precious asked, uncomfortable with hearing the truth about herself. After so many years of blaming her life's outcome on other people, she wasn't ready to accept any of that responsibility.

"My point is that you can't continue to use those things as excuses to hold you back from seeking something better for yourself. You don't need to boost and run the streets anymore. I'm asking you now to stop running and put your trust in me. I think that I've proven to you that I'm in ya corner, one hundred percent. Good or bad, I got your back," Talib promised.

"I know you do, Talib. You're the best thing that has ever happened to me," Precious said softly as a lump began to form in her throat and her eyes watered.

"Well, baby, what I'm saying is that I wanna share my future with you. The two of us together, baby . . . The sky is the limit for what we can accomplish as a team. So, what you wanna do, baby?" Talib asked, staring into her eyes and wiping away the tears that had begun to stream down her face. Precious was overwhelmed. Her nerves were so bad that her arms and legs began shaking.

"I don't know what to say. I never thought I would meet a good man, but I guess I was wrong. I think you might be too good for me. Before I can respond to what you just said, there are some things you need to know about me. After I tell you these things, you might change your mind." Precious was determined to finally come clean about everything.

175

"There's nothing you could say to make me change how I feel about you. I promise you that. Tell me whatever is on your mind." He gently wiped away her tears, which were falling more rapidly by this time.

"I don't know where to start. First of all, I told you about how my mother was killed when I was a child, but I didn't tell you the whole story. I found the two motherfuckas who killed her. Patty and I, along with some other cats that I hired, set their asses up and we killed them. I also killed my no-good-ass father right along with them for his involvement in the whole thing."

Talib didn't ask for the details, but she felt the need to get absolutely everything off her chest. "I poured acid all over them then I left them in the basement of an abandoned house and set it on fire. You might've heard about the big fire on Bartlett Avenue a few months ago where they found three bodies in the basement. Well, that was my handiwork," Precious said cautiously.

"Keep going. I know you have more to tell me. I'm still listening," Talib said. He didn't appear to be shaken up by her revelation, so she continued.

"Well, I did these things because I wanted them to suffer for what they did to my mother. I loved every minute of it. It gave me a sense of release like I never felt before. The police didn't give a damn about solving her murder, but she was my mother!

"I know what I just said sounds crazy, but it is what it is. I remember every detail of that day like it was yesterday, especially the scorpion tattoo that one of them assholes had. I could never forget that as long as I live. When I saw those bastards face to face, I just lost it. My rage took over my actions.

"I wanted you to know this because I don't want you to be pulled into my drama, seeing how you've turned your life around. If the police come for me, I don't want you to be involved in my mess," Precious said, now crying uncontrollably. Talib pulled her into his arms and held her as she wept. He rocked her back and forth in an attempt to calm her down.

"Is that it? I know it was hard for you to keep that bottled up inside. You have no reason to feel ashamed of what you did. Shit, if that was my mother, I probably would have done worse things to them than you did. I went through a similar experience with my grandfather and all of the evil things he did to me. At the time, it felt good when I stabbed him. I felt like I had slain the beast that tried to ruin my life.

"I told you when I met you to never judge a book by its cover. Even though I have changed my life, I'm still from the streets. I still believe in holdin' court in the streets when it's needed. You gave those demons what their hands called for."

He waited for a while until her tears subsided a little, then spoke quietly to her. "You were right in saying that the police usually don't give a damn when a black life is lost in the streets. To them, she was another no-good black junkie who deserved to die. But for all of her faults, that woman gave you life, and I am eternally grateful to her for that. Without her, there would be no you in my world. If that is all that was on ya mind, you don't even need to stress over that. We can weather that storm together, no matter what comes along down the road."

"That's not it, Talib." She wiped her tears and gathered the strength to tell him the news she thought would push him out of her life forever. She blurted it out all at once.

"I'm pregnant. The guy that I'm pregnant by is named Marco. He's a stickup boy from over West that helped me get those two bastards that killed my moms. We messed around for a minute before I met you, and once after we started seeing each other. We had sex without condoms. I know that I was foolish, but what can I say? Now, I know that you don't wanna be involved with me given that I'm carrying another man's baby . . ." she said, finally stopping to take a breath.

Talib looked pensive, and she was taken aback by his silence. He usually came at her with a quick, intelligent response. This was the first time she saw him at a loss for words. She hoped it didn't mean his rage was building.

"I know that dude," he finally said, in a voice much more calm than Precious expected. "We had beef years ago when he tried to bring my crew a move. Do you wanna be with that fool? Does he know about the baby?"

"Hell no! Like I said, it was only a fling. I used him to get what I wanted and he used me to get what he wanted," Precious replied with regret in her voice.

"First of all, you need to stop thinking negatively all the time. I know your situation seems extreme in that you're carrying that nigga's baby, but Precious, I'm in love with you, and I'm willing to accept anything that comes along with you. The child in your stomach is a part of you, and that means it's a part of me. I still wanna be with you. As far as the world is concerned, this is our child. That baby is gonna need a strong man in its life. Marco ain't the one for the job."

Precious didn't know how to respond. The fact that he still wanted to be a part of her and the child's life proved how deeply Talib cared for her. Her heart began to beat rapidly.

Talib gently turned her face toward his and they kissed passionately. Precious stood up and grabbed his hand, leading him into the bathroom. He willingly followed her because he knew what was about to take place. Premarital sex went against his religious beliefs, but his love for Precious forced him to respond to a higher calling.

Precious' body language said that she was now ready to be all his. She was his woman. He was her soul mate. It was official. They made love throughout the night. They did it in the shower, in the kitchen, in the living room, and against the wall in the bedroom. They tried every position imaginable. Talib was everything she fantasized he would be and then some.

They fell asleep in each other's arms. Tomorrow would be a new day for the couple. The only problem they had now was to figure out how to handle Precious' legal situation so they could begin a new chapter in their lives.

13 The Day After

Precious loved the idea of waking up in Talib's arms every day. She enjoyed making love to him over and over again even more. He made her feel emotions she never experienced before. The intoxicating effects of his love had her floating on cloud nine, and she wanted the high she was on to last forever She hoped that nothing would come along to tear them apart. If this was a dream, she never wanted to wake up. In reality, she was looking at doing some time in jail very soon, barring a miracle. Her uncertain future had her worried about what was to come of their relationship.

Talib was still asleep as Precious stared at him from the other side of the bed. She noticed how peaceful he looked in his sleep, with a slight smile on his face. She imagined that he was dreaming about her, and it allowed her to forget her legal worries for just a moment.

She turned over to retrieve the remote control from the nightstand to turn on the 42-inch plasma T.V. Her movement woke Talib. He wiped the sleep from his eyes and glanced at his Nubian queen. Her name would soon be Mrs. Talib Muhammad, he thought.

"Hey, pretty woman. What are you doing up so early?" he asked. Precious leaned over to kiss him, but he covered his mouth. He didn't want her to smell his morning breath. She pushed his hand aside and kissed him smack dead on the mouth anyway.

"I couldn't sleep. I had a lot of things on my mind," Precious replied.

"Things like what?"

"I was thinking about how amazing you are. I was thinking about how much you manage to give unselfishly of yourself even though I don't deserve it a lot of the time. This is the first time in my life I've been attracted to a man for his mind and not his money or what he could do for me, and yet you do so much for me. You make me wanna step my game up and meet you on your level. Mr. Talib, you are truly something else," Precious said, surprising even herself with her honesty.

179

"I'm glad that you feel that way. I feel the same way about you, Precious. Sometimes in life it takes a special person to make us realize how special we are as individuals. I hope that I can be that person for you. I wanna help you unlock all of the greatness that I see in your future. You're like a diamond buried under a piece of rough coal that's been waiting to be polished. Once you've been fine-tuned, your light is gonna shine so bright for the world to see."

"Well, I'm willing to learn whatever you wanna teach me, on the real. You know what? My grandfather even likes you. You must got it goin' on," she said, laughing.

"That's what's up. Now we gotta figure out what we're gonna do about this case you got comin' up. I already called my attorney, Warren Lee. We have to meet with him later on today to come up with a defense strategy for you. I can't let them lock my precious flower in a box without a fight. You don't have to worry about how you're gonna pay for an attorney. I got you on that end. You can also forget about paying me back the money for posting ya bail," he said. It was as though he read her mind. She had the questions, and he came up with the answers without being asked.

"Nah, Talib, I can't let you do that. I got money to take care of my own problems. I appreciate ya offer, though. Please, don't argue with me. I know you mean well, but I need to do this on my own," Precious said.

"A'ight, baby," he said, smiling at her. "Let's compromise. I wanna pay for half of everything. If we're a team then let's handle this business together. I wanna have a fifty/fifty love thing with you."

"Fair enough. Let's go back to my crib so I can get some loot," she said.

"That's a bet. Oh, speaking of loot, I was so caught up that I forgot to tell you how well my meeting went with the investors. They loved my idea and agreed to invest the money. Now I can take my clothing line nationwide. We're about to blow up, baby!" Talib made sure to include the word "we" in his statement. They were now a team destined for big things.

"You da man, Talib! You da man!" Precious shouted.

They showered and got dressed then made their way over to Precious' apartment. When they reached the front door, they noticed that it was ajar. Precious didn't see Trish's or Tina's car parked out front and started to worry. Something wasn't right. The door shouldn't be open with neither one of them there. Talib told her to wait a minute while he went back to his truck and retrieved his nine from under the seat. If there was somebody up in the apartment, he wanted to be prepared.

He held the weapon in his hand as he opened the front door. Precious followed closely behind. They crept quietly into the apartment, where all of the lights were on. Looking in Trish's room, they saw that all of her belongings were gone. They went into Tina's room and saw the same thing. Something strange was definitely going on.

When they went into Precious' room, they found the biggest surprise of all. Her room was in shambles. Her dresser drawers were wide open, and clothes were scattered everywhere. Her 32-inch television was smashed into little pieces on the floor. The pictures hanging on the wall were broken up. Worst of all, her mattress and box spring were positioned against the wall, and the safe underneath the bed had been cracked open. All of the emergency money was gone.

Precious looked inside her closet for the personal stash that she kept hidden in a locked steel box. It too had been cracked open and emptied of its contents. Everything was gone. She had been jacked for everything. She was as broke as the first day she started boosting.

"I can't believe this shit. Them bitches done robbed my ass! They skipped the fuck outta here and took all of my loot!" Precious yelled. Talib stood at the door and put his pistol in his jacket after he saw that there was no one else in the house.

"Calm down, baby. Let's try to see this shit through to make some sense outta this. How much money did you have up in here?" he asked.

"About forty-five grand altogether. Now I ain't got shit. Fuck calming down. I gotta find them bitches and deal wit' they asses. First they set me up to go to jail and now this shit! Oh, hell naw! I want my fuckin' money!" Her nostrils flared with rage.

"Shit. How the fuck did this happen? They set you up to take them charges? I know you told me about the fight y'all had, but they took it that far to get back at you?" he asked.

"Yeah, them jealous hoes musta been plottin' this shit for a while. The cop that arrested me told that it was them that put her on me. After this shit I'ma lay them hoes down."

"Nah, it ain't even goin' down like that," Talib said calmly. "You got enough on ya plate right now. You need to let this go. It ain't worth making the situation worse than what it already is. Karma is a motherfucka, and they are gonna get theirs."

"What am I gonna do now that all my money is gone? All of the chances I took to get that dough, and now I ain't got nothing to show for it," she said.

"Don't worry about a thing. I told you I got enough cash coming to take care of both of us. What's mines is yours," Talib said with conviction.

"You always know the right thing to say at the right time. Whenever I feel like all is lost, you come along to save the day," Precious said, her voice full of love for him.

Talib reached out and held her. "That's what I'm here for. Allah put us in each other's lives for a reason. Get all the things that you need from here and let's bounce. You'll be staying with me from now on."

Her husband-to-be had spoken. She collected as much of her clothing and personal belongings as she could. Whatever was left behind, she would get another time. When she was done, she took one last look in both of her ex-friends' rooms. Snake-ass bitches, she though then grabbed Talib's arm and walked out the front door.

She hoped she got better news from the lawyer when they met with him later. She sure could use it.

14 Life On the Other Side

Precious regretted having to make the long walk to the hospital room. She didn't wanna do it, but this might be the last time she got to see Patty alive. Her health had taken a turn for the worse over the past few months. She had lost almost fifty pounds because she was unable to eat. She contracted Hepatitis C and a host of other infectious diseases due to her weakened immune system. The case of the flu that she now had forced her to be hospitalized. Her body was falling apart more and more with each passing day.

Precious had been sitting by her bedside day in and day out to keep her company. She loved Patty with all of her heart. Patty was her last link to her mother's memory, and she wanted to cherish every minute she had left with her.

"Baby, you know, I regret ever turning you onto the boosting game. I shoulda set a better example for you after ya mother was gone," Patty said.

"Aunt Patty, I don't hold you responsible for anything that I ever did in my life. I made the choices that I made, and I have to pay the consequences for what I did. You did more for me than you'll ever know."

"Your mother would be so proud of you and how you turned out. Look at you, all grown up and beautiful, with that fine-ass man by ya side. You better hold on to him. Y'all look good together. If I had found me a man like that, maybe I wouldn't have wound up being the no-good junkie that I am now, laying here with all of these tubes running through me," Patty said sorrowfully.

"You better hush that foolishness up, Aunt Patty. I don't see a no-good junkie up in here. I see a black queen who just made a few wrong choices. I see a loving person who gave me strength when I felt as though my own family didn't love me. I don't give a damn what the world thinks of you. You're somebody special to me." Precious tried to hold back her tears.

"Precious Paine . . . that name sure fits you, girl. You are so precious, because with all of the pain that I'm in, you know how to make me smile," Patty said.

"I love you, Aunt Patty."

"I love you, too, Precious. I ain't got much longer on this here Earth. When I see your mother on the other side, I'ma finally have my best friend to cut up with again. If God'll allow us to . . ." Precious laughed at Patty's silly comment.

"Well, tell my Momma that I love her and I promise to make her proud of me."

The medication Patty was taking started to make her sleepy, so she nodded off to sleep. This would be the last conversation Precious had with Aunt Patty. She died the next day in her sleep.

Patty's funeral was a small but respectable service, with only ten people in attendance. Out of all of the junkies and dope fiends that she treated to free highs on a regular, none of them took the time from their busy schedules of chasin' the dragon to pay their respects. Patty died the same way that she lived her life—alone.

The least Precious could do was to ensure that Patty had a proper burial. If no one else would miss her Aunt Patty, she would. Talib paid for Patty's funeral because he knew how much she meant to Precious. He arranged to have her buried at King Memorial Park, a few plots away from Precious' mother. That way Precious could pay her respects to both of them at the same time.

Patty's burial was an emotional moment for Precious, but she tried to be as strong as she could. Tears welled up in her eyes and she began to hyperventilate. Talib was steadfast in his efforts to console her in her time of grief.

"Child, it's gonna be all right. The Lord is gonna make a way. Just be relieved that she's free from the demons of this world. She's in a much better place."

Precious heard the voice, and was surprised when she turned around to see her grandmother. Mrs. Paine came to the funeral to support her granddaughter. She knew the pain she was in, and felt the need to stand by her in this emotional time. She had experienced the same emotions when she had to bury Roxanne. For the moment, their bitterness toward each other was put aside.

"I know, Grandma. It just hurts so bad. She didn't have to die this way," Precious said. Her belly was now swollen as she neared the end of her final trimester of pregnancy. Mrs. Paine and Talib held her in their arms as Patty's casket was lowered into the ground and she said her final goodbye.

Not long after the funeral, Precious and her grandmother sat down to try to mend their relationship. Her grandfather, with Talib's assistance, had arranged for them to get together and talk things over. They both finally had a chance to get a lot of resentment and anger off their chests.

Her grandmother apologized for the way she treated her for so many years. She admitted that she still grieved over Roxanne and took that hurt out on Precious. Now that she knew Precious was pregnant, she wanted to help her in any way to ensure that her baby had a strong family around her. The healing that took place between Precious and her grandmother made both of them better individuals.

As for her court case, Precious was found guilty of grand larceny and selling stolen goods. She was sentenced to five years of probation, ordered to pay restitution and go to counseling. Her sentence was light given the fact that the prosecution had video and audio tapes of the crimes being committed.

When the judge handed down her sentence, Chanice and Rochelle were pissed. They knew they had done a good job, and went strictly by the book in arresting Precious, so they were sorely disappointed that she got off so easy. They wanted to see her behind bars. The disgust was obvious on their faces as they exited the courtroom.

Precious' attorney, Warren Lee, was brilliant in convincing the judge that even though Precious was guilty of her charges, she too was a victim. He explicitly detailed the tragic loss of her mother at a young age. He brought in experts to testify how this had a negative impact on her psyche and contributed to her delinquent behavior. By the time he was finished speaking, he had the jury and spectators in the courtroom feeling sorry for Precious. Several of the jurors even wept. However, the most compelling statement came from Precious' grandmother. She shocked the entire courtroom with her compelling speech.

"Your Honor, if it's okay with the Court, I would like say something on behalf of my granddaughter before you sentence her," Mrs. Paine pleaded.

"By all means. The court would like to hear what you have to say," replied the judge, a modest-looking black woman with short hair.

'Well, Your Honor, I'm not gonna lie and tell this court that my granddaughter didn't do anything wrong and that she shouldn't be punished. That would be a waste of your time. What I would like to say is that I hold myself partially responsible for some of the bad decisions she made," Mrs. Paine said.

"What do you mean by that?" Judge Brown inquired.

"Well, ever since her mother died and she came to live with me and my husband, I was unjustly hard on her. I took out all the frustration that I had toward her mother for getting involved with drugs. I said and did a lot of mean things toward her that I wish I could take back, but I can't.

"I can honestly say now that I can see how Precious didn't feel loved at home because of me, and why she turned to the streets for attention. Even though her mother's murder was hard on me, I can now only imagine how hard it was on her to have to witness it with her own young, innocent eyes. This child has been through a lot that she didn't deserve. I'm just asking this court to show some mercy and take that into consideration before you decide to send her to jail.

"I believe that she has learned from her mistakes. If you make the decision not send her to jail, with God as my witness, I will do all that I can to make sure that she stays on the right path. I might not have been there for her in the past, but I promise you I will be there for her in any way that I can today, for as long as the good Lord sees fit for me to stay on this Earth," Mrs. Paine stated to the Court.

Precious was overcome with emotion like she'd never felt before. For her grandmother to stand in public before a room full of strangers and pour her heart out on her behalf told Precious that she really did love her.

Judge Brown was so moved by the speech that she had to ask the bailiff to get her a tissue to wipe the tears from her eyes before she handed down her sentence.

"Ms. Paine," she addressed Precious, "I hope you realize that today is your lucky day. I could throw the book at you and give you all of the time that you really deserve for what you did. However, I feel like giving you a break."

Precious breathed a sigh of relief, but the judge wasn't through with her yet.

"Don't be confused into thinking that I'm letting you off easy, because I'm not. I too grew up in a broken home and was raised by my mother alone. I had to struggle through being poor and not having much as a child to get to where I am today. I sympathize with everything that has been said about you in this courtroom today, but that doesn't make it right, what you did.:

Precious nodded her understanding as the judge continued. "You should feel blessed that you have so many people in your corner. I want you to take this experience as a building block for your future. I want you to go out and do something positive with your life. You need to set a better example for that baby you're carrying, so he or she won't go down the same road that you did. You appear to be a very intelligent young lady. You need to take that brain of yours and put it to use in a more constructive manner.

"If I see you in my courtroom again, even if it's for jaywalking, I promise that you will do all five years of your probation behind bars. You can trust me on that," the judge concluded after she read Precious her sentence. Precious could do nothing but nod her head and thank the judge for her mercy.

Two months after her final court appearance, Precious gave birth to a beautiful baby girl. She was the spitting image of her mother. She had Precious' eyes and nose, and nothing that resembled Marco. That would make it easier for Precious to pass her off as Talib's biological daughter.

Talib gave her the name Ameera, which meant "princess" in Arabic and was fitting to describe his newborn daughter. He planned to ensure that Ameera would have a good childhood and not want for anything in life.

As for Marco, he was gunned down in a robbery attempt. His crew was met with a hail of gunfire when they tried to stick up a group of young hustlas on McHenry Street. The youngstas were ready for their asses. Marco's brother, Darren, was also killed. Scooter and Dre managed to escape unharmed. Even though their crew was two men down, the two of them continued their crime spree on the streets of Baltimore.

Trish and Tina got what they deserved for stabbing Precious in the back. As it turned out, they were caught committing a robbery with Parrish and Donnell at the bank where they worked as tellers. They were each sentenced to fifteen years in prison for their involvement in the crime. Karma truly was truly a motherfucka for them.

Talib's clothing line was scheduled to hit all of the major department stores that coming fall. He was excited to see his plan come into full fruition. Precious came on board to work alongside him as a fashion consultant. She had developed a keen eye for quality fashion from her years of boosting. Precious was in the process of evolving into the woman that Talib had envisioned her to be. She planned to attend college to study fashion design once the Urban Legends clothing line was more established in the marketplace.

Talib and Precious planned to get married in July of the following year. Life was truly sweeter for her since she decided to put aside her baggage and give herself a chance to grow into a mature, responsible woman. It took a series of tragedies and the love of a good man to make her appreciate her true value as a black woman. She had opened up Pandora's box and unleashed her true inner self. The sky was the limit.

LA JILL HUNT
Who Got Game?

Acknowledgements

I was told to make this brief, but there was no way I could allow this story to come out without thanking some special folks.
To God, for once again, giving me the opportunity to utilize the talents you bestowed upon me.
To my family, for constant love and encouragement.
To my daughters, for inspiring and providing comic relief when Mommy needs it. I love you!
To Pastor Brown and the Mt Lebanon Missionary Baptist Church family, thanks for your continual love and support.
To Carl and Martha Weber, for your guidance.
To Roy Glenn, Dwayne S. Joseph and K Elliott, my big brothers!
To Robin, Cherie, Yvette, Pam, Mechellene, Chris (Big CTY), and my girl Selena – you know I can't forget you. Thanks!!!
To all the readers who support me and my dream – I appreciate you more than you'll ever know!!

Feel free to email me at MsLajaka@AOL.com

Be on the lookout: Coming November, 2005
Shoulda, Woulda, Coulda

La Jill Hunt

1

"I love Valentine's Day," Alicia commented as she hung the red hearts on the bulletin board. "It has to be my all-time favorite holiday."

"You've gotta be outta your mind," Lyric, her co-worker, replied. "Valentine's Day doesn't come close to Christmas, and it damn sure ain't more important than my birthday."

Alicia smiled and shook her head. "Okay, I can't front. I like Christmas and my birthday, too, but Valentine's Day is a day of love, true love. Pass me those cupids."

"Look, some of us have real work to do while you're around here hanging Valentine's Day shit," Lyric huffed as she got up from her desk and thrust the cutouts into Alicia's hand. She had a lot on her mind, and Alicia's babbling about the upcoming holiday was becoming a distraction.

Lyric had received a letter from the finance company advising her that if she didn't pay her car note in full by next Friday, they were coming to pick it up, something she had no intention of letting them do. That car was her baby. The silver Acura TL with the sleek spinning rims made her feel like a queen when she was behind the wheel. All heads turned when she rolled by, both male and female. That car gave her power, which she loved to have and wasn't about to give up. The note was two months behind, due to her lack of budgeting skills and self-control when it came to shopping. She had come up with part of the money, but she was still about four hundred short. Lyric slumped back down into the chair, trying to come up with a solution.

"What's wrong, Lyric? You've been in a bad mood since you got here this evening," Alicia asked.

The typical fly girl, Lyric dressed like a cross between a fashion model and a video vixen depending on her mood. Her deep almond complexion was flawless, which she highlighted by wearing almost no makeup. She wore her hair short and never had a curl out of place. She was one of the most beautiful girls Alicia had ever seen. It was her attitude that was a problem.

191

Lyric was a true diva. People commented on her quick temper because she would curse people out without a second thought. Her reputation as a real bitch was so well known that Alicia was hesitant when she learned that she had been assigned to work the evening shift with Lyric at the check-cashing stop where they were employed. But over time, Alicia began to see that Lyric's bark was worse than her bite. It was Lyric who picked her up and took her home when the weather was bad so she wouldn't have to walk. Lyric even covered for Alicia when she had to study for mid-terms, even though she was a student herself and could use the study time. It was as if she had taken Alicia under her wings like an older sister. Alicia liked Lyric, and she knew that Lyric liked her.

"They're talking 'bout towing my fuckin' ride, so I gotta find some loot quick." Lyric sighed, opening her cell phone and scrolling through the numbers.

"For real? You can't just ask your parents to help you out?" Alicia offered.

"Yeah, right. My dad works as a security guard at the Crowne Plaza and my mom serves food to high school kids. They have plenty of money laying around." Lyric rolled her eyes.

"Well, what are you gonna do?" Alicia asked, her eyes wide.

"Watch and learn, young buck. Watch and learn." Lyric winked. She found the number she was searching for, picked up the office phone and dialed. She took a deep breath, telling herself that she had to do whatever it took to keep her car. She was relieved when the voicemail picked up and instructed her to leave a message.

"Hey, it's me. I need to talk to you," she said in the most pitiful voice she could fake. "I . . . I just . . . I don't know what to do."

Lyric looked up to see Alicia staring at her, eyes wide with concern. It took everything to hold in the laugh she felt coming on. She decided to use the quiver in her voice to her advantage, and quickly spoke into the phone. "Please, please call me as soon as you get this message. I . . . I need you."

When she hung up the phone, she couldn't contain herself. She laughed so hard that tears came to her eyes.

"Are you okay?" Alicia asked, obviously concerned.

"You should see your face. You're looking at me like I'm an orphaned puppy."

192

"I mean, you're crying into the phone. Here I am concerned, and you're acting like I'm the crazy one." Alicia sat at her desk, sorting through the remaining decorations.

"That's what you get for being nosey. Believe me, I'll come up with the money. That call right there was a guaranteed four hundred. I just need to make one more call and I'll be straight. Watch me work my magic."

Lyric scrolled through her phone again and dialed another number. Alicia watched and listened to her tell someone else that she was desperately in need of help and she needed to see them. This time, Alicia even thought she saw a tear come into Lyric's eye. She had to admit her coworker had a flair for the dramatic, and she was interested in what the game plan was. But before she could even ask, the office phone began ringing.

"Cash and More, Alicia Woods speaking."

"Good afternoon, Ms. Woods. You working hard?" Omar, her boyfriend of the past two years, asked.

"Yeah, I'm hanging up decorations for Valentine's Day. You do know that it's coming up, right?"

"As if you would even let me forget. Of course I know it's coming up. That's my baby's favorite holiday. What time you getting home today?"

"I should be there by six. Are you coming to see me?" Alicia smiled. It was Tuesday, the day her mom worked double shifts at the post office, and Omar knew it. Tuesdays were their "hookup" days. He often picked up dinner, which they almost never ate, and a movie that they never watched past the opening credits. She was sprung, and Tuesdays were her favorite day of the week.

"You know I am, baby. What movie you want me to pick up?"

"Whatever you wanna see. I don't care."

"Then I don't need to pick one up, because the only thing I wanna see is your fine ass laying cross the bed butt naked, waiting on me."

"Omar!" Alicia hissed, feeling herself turning red. "Watch your mouth. Somebody could pick up the phone and hear you."

At that moment, Mr. Grant, their manager walked in and said hello. Alicia looked up and saw that Lyric was clearly listening to her conversation. She smiled with embarrassment.

"Why I gotta shut up? You are the finest thing I've ever been with and I love you. I don't care who knows it. Don't you love me?"

"Yes, I do," Alicia answered.

"You do what?"

"Don't play, Omar," she warned.

"I ain't playing. You scared to say it in front of your little girlfriend?"

"No, I'm trying to be professional on my job, that's all."

"You better say it. I mean it. If you don't say it, I ain't gon' be all up in *that* tonight like I know you want me to be. So, if you want me to tighten you up, you better tell me," Omar growled into the phone. She closed her eyes, trying to maintain her composure, but he knew he had her where he wanted. "You know you want me to taste it, suck it, and then stroke it like only I can. You know how bad you want me to turn you over and hit that ass from the—"

"Alicia," Mr. Grant called, startling her. He was looking at the board she was working hard to decorate. She knew he was about to have something negative to say, because that was him, always complaining. He was somewhat of a grump most of the time, but they were used to his somber moods. Lyric had also proven that his bad moods were mostly an act anyway. She had been late for work several times, and each time he ranted and raved, threatening to fire her, but he never did.

"I gotta go, Omar. I'll see you at six," she muttered hastily.

"Not if you don't tell me. I swear, you'll be home alone faster than that li'l McCauley Caulkin dude was with Michael Jackson."

"I love you," she whispered, hoping he was the only one that heard her.

"And you want me to tear that—"

Alicia hung up before he could say anything else. She glanced over at Lyric, who was obviously amused by the entire situation, then walked over to Mr. Grant.

"Alicia, you put this board up?"

"Yes, Mr. Grant."

"I like it, especially the caption. Good job." He put on his jacket. "I'll be gone the rest of the afternoon. I have to make plans for my wife for Valentine's Day. You two hold down the fort." He waved as he walked out.

"What the hell was that?" Lyric asked, confused by her boss' change of attitude. "That bum complained about his wife all of Christmas and Thanksgiving. Now he's making plans for her?"

"It's Valentine's Day. It brings out the best in people. I told you, it's about love."

"Speaking of love, you have a call on line two."

Alicia slowly returned to her desk. "Don't you have some real work to do? Or at least some fake calls for help to make?" she asked Lyric as she sat down.

"Don't hate the player, hate the game." Lyric winked. "But I will go and get me a soda so you can have some privacy. I'll bring you something back to cool your hot ass off."

"Shut up and get out." Alicia laughed as she picked up the phone. She was glad that Lyric and Mr. Grant left. She was all alone, and there weren't any customers in the store. She could give Omar a taste of his own medicine.

"Oh, so now you wanna hang up on a brother? I see how it is. That's cool," Omar told her.

"I'm sorry Omar, but Mr. Grant was calling me. Where were we, baby? Oh, I remember." Alicia sat back in her chair. "You were about to tell me how you were gonna hit this ass from the back, right?"

"Oh no, forget about that. I ain't hitting nothing since you hung up on me. My feelings are hurt now."

"Baby, I'm sorry. I promise I'll make it up to you," she purred into the phone. It was her turn to get Omar as turned on as she had been earlier, and she knew just what to say. All she had to do was imagine his sexy ass right there in front of her. Just the thought of him could send her imagination into frenzy with scenes of their lovemaking and what she wanted to do with him.

"And how you gon' do that?"

"What if I give you something to look forward to if you come over tonight?"

"Like what?"

"Like me greeting you at the door butt naked, kissing you before you can even get in the door, pulling you into the living room and pushing you onto the couch."

"Interesting. Keep going."

"Taking off your shirt while I suck on your neck and play with your chest, licking further and further until I come to that spot."

"What spot?"

"You know what spot. *Your* spot. That spot right between your chest and your abdomen, where you like for me to kiss. You know what spot, boo," she moaned, knowing she had his attention. "And then I'll take your hand and kiss your palm, sucking your fingers one by one."

"Yeah, I like that. Then what?"

"I guess you'll have to show up at six and see." Alicia giggled. "Are you coming to see me?

"Damn right." Omar laughed. "See you later. Love you."

"Love you too." She sighed, knowing that this was definitely love.

Alicia was singing along with Mary J. Blige and hanging up decorations when Lyric returned.

"You and Romeo finished?" she asked, passing her an orange soda.

"Yes, thank you very much. And don't get mad because I love my man and he loves me."

"Believe me, I ain't mad, girlfriend. Do your thing."

"I can't wait until the day you come in and say, 'Alicia, I have met the one. I have found true love.' And I promise I won't even say I told you so."

"That will never happen. You can count on that. That love thing is not for everyone, especially not for moi."

"Why not? You don't believe in love?"

"Nope, I don't. Never have, never will. Don't get me wrong. If you're happy, then that's cool. But to me, I'm all about getting mine before I get got. Most men only want one thing, and we all know what that is. They say what they think you wanna hear, they do whatever it takes, as long as it's not too much work, of course, to get you to give it up, and it's all good until they find someone else they wanna screw. Then they dog you out so you don't wanna be bothered or they break your heart. Either way, they win. But me, I'm different. I'll play along with your little game and make you think you're winning. I get all I can, and then by the time you figure it out, I'm gone. Simple."

196

"I don't think so. I think that's called using people. And in the end, someone winds up hurt."

"But it won't be me. That's for sure. I don't even let it get to that point," Lyric told her, shrugging.

"Then I feel sorry for you, Lyric. True, you may never feel the pain of true love, but you will never feel the joy of it either."

Lyric looked at Alicia and smiled. They had been working together since August, and she had learned a lot about her. Alicia was a typical good girl. She was smart, honest, wholesome and a genuinely good person. She was a pretty girl who looked a lot like Tisha Campbell. She was an average size, standing about five-foot-three, and she couldn't weigh more than 125 pounds.

Lyric was shocked when she learned that Alicia not only had a boyfriend, but Ms. Goody-Goody got her groove on the regular. She had figured her to be a virgin, saving herself for marriage. She knew the guy must be some geek-type nerd, definitely not one of these hardcore niggas usually up to no good. They were plentiful in Brooklyn.

She often wondered what Omar looked like, since she had never met him. He worked at a warehouse during the day, and she and Alicia didn't really hang out after work. Whoever dude was, Alicia was sprung, and Lyric prayed that Omar wouldn't fuck it up. Funny, though, something in the back of her mind wondered if Alicia was right and maybe, just maybe, she would find her own true love one day.

"God, that was the bomb," Alicia panted, rolling off Omar's stomach. Their lovemaking that night had been as intense as ever, and she was more than satisfied. Not only did Omar fulfill her sexually, the fact that he loved her made it even better. It was like being on an emotional high, and she never wanted to come off it.

"It's always the bomb with you." Omar rolled over and kissed her on the nose.

"With me? What's that supposed to mean?" Alicia pulled away from him.

"You know what I meant, Alicia. Don't go there." He started playing with her nipples.

"Go where? I'm trying to figure out who you coulda been with that it ain't been the bomb with. You fucking around on me, Omar?" She sat up, pulling the sheet over her body.

"Where the hell did that come from? Have I given you a reason to think I'm fucking around on you?" He frowned at her.

She looked into his handsome face. His mocha complexion enhanced his strong facial features. *He could be a model*, she thought, admiring his dark eyes. His trimmed mustache and goatee were set off by the deep waves of his hair, which he wore cut close. Her eyes traveled to his chest, chiseled by the heavy boxes he lifted every day at work. His abdomen was free of flab and led to that portion of his body that she was at first afraid of, but now she loved. She had never been with a man before Omar, and the first time she saw his penis, her eyes grew big and her heart beat with fear. She just knew he would split her in two with it. But he was a gentle lover, and she appreciated his girth. She doubted that any man would ever be able to satisfy her like Omar.

"Answer me, Alicia. What's up with you?" He lifted her chin and she was once again looking into his eyes.

Things between them had turned into a routine, and maybe he was becoming bored with her. She tried to remember the last time they had even gone out. It was a while ago. Was their relationship becoming just about great sex? *Could he be out to get what he can from me until something better comes along? Maybe Lyric knows what she's talking about.*

"I don't know. I'm just tripping off something Lyric told me this evening about guys. And then you made that comment. Forget about it." She pulled his arms around her and nestled into his chest.

"Oh, so now you listening to some chicken head who doesn't even have a man? You know she just wanna mess up your good thang so you can be lonely together, right?"

"That's what you are, my good thing?"

He placed her hand between his legs and she felt his hardness. She immediately got wet, knowing that round two was on its way.

"You feel that? You don't think that's a good thing?"

She kissed him on the mouth, savoring his taste, not answering. He pulled away and she felt his tongue between her legs. "Yes, it's a good thing. A damn good thing," she told him as she closed her eyes, putting all thoughts of Lyric and everyone else out of her head.

2

"I take it you had a good night?" Lyric asked as Alicia walked into the office, humming.

"Yes, I did, no thanks to you," Alicia answered.

"Me? What did I do?"

"You and your talk about men only wanna use women to get what they want. You had me tripping to Omar. I asked him if he was cheating."

"I didn't say that applied to your man. And don't blame me. He must've given you a reason to ask him, not because of me and my beliefs," Lyric told her. She was surprised that Alicia had even confronted her precious Omar. She thought things between them were damn near perfect. Maybe he wasn't so flawless after all. Besides, as much as she thought the relationship between Alicia and Omar was cute, she still felt obligated to school the girl on the realities of men. She didn't want the girl to be suicidal if and when Omar broke her heart.

"No, he didn't," Alicia retorted. She began sorting through the mail, deciding that she wouldn't even get into this discussion with Lyric. She was confident with her relationship and Omar was right, maybe Lyric was jealous because she didn't have a man.

Mr. Grant came out of his office and assigned tasks he needed them to do. Both women worked in silence until Lyric's cell phone rang. She quickly answered it then told Alicia she would be right back. She checked herself in the mirror, grabbed her purse and rushed out.

Alicia glanced out the window and saw Lyric climb into a black Yukon Denali parked out front of the building. Lyric, who had seemed fine before she went out there, now had a distraught look on her face. The guy rubbed Lyric's back then leaned over and hugged her. They had a quick conversation then Lyric nodded and hopped out of the truck. Alicia turned to her computer and pretended to be hard at work when Lyric came back in.

"Did Mr. Grant come out?" Lyric asked, her cheeks rosy from the cold.

"Nope, he didn't even open his door. Who was that?"

"That was pawn number one. He should be back in a minute, so I'll have to run out again." Lyric smiled smugly.

The office door opened, and one of the tallest guys Alicia had ever seen walked in. He wore a varsity jacket, letting everyone who hadn't already figured it out know that he was a basketball player. Lyric walked over to the counter and greeted him with a smile.

"Hi there, handsome. How can I help you?"

"I have a package for you," he answered, returning the smile.

"For little old me? Why, Curtis Taylor, I didn't know you cared." Lyric reached for the envelope he pulled out of his pocket and put it into her purse.

"Have you met Alicia? Alicia, this is Curtis Taylor, future NBA player."

"Nice to meet you," Alicia told him, extending her hand.

"Same here," he replied. He looked over at Lyric and said, "I gotta get to practice. Can I see you in the hall for a minute?"

Lyric looked down at her watch and said, "My break is in thirty minutes, can you come back then?"

"Nope, I got practice."

Alicia could see the wheels turning in Lyric's head. With pawn number one due back soon, Lyric couldn't risk being seen with Curtis.

"Tell you what. Pull around to the back of the building. I'll pretend like I'm going to the bathroom and then sneak out the back door so Mr. Grant won't see me." She gave him a sneaky smile.

"A'ight. I'll meet you in a minute, McGyver," Curtis joked.

Lyric waved at Alicia as she hustled to the back of the building, past Mr. Grant's office. She opened the back door with such precision that Alicia could barely hear the click of the lock.

Lyric had just stepped outside when Alicia turned to see the black Denali pull up in front. Lyric's cell phone began to vibrate on her desk at the same time. Alicia didn't know what to do. As if things couldn't get any worse, Mr. Grant's voice sounded from the intercom, demanding that Lyric come to his office. Alicia grabbed the cell phone and hit the END CALL button, hoping it would go straight to voicemail. She ran to the back door and beckoned for Lyric.

"I'll call you later and check on you," she heard Curtis tell LYRIC.

"Thanks, Curtis," Lyric said, then seeing Alicia, added, "I gotta get back to work."

Alicia made sure he was down the hallway before she hissed, "Lyric! Mr. Grant is calling for you, and you have a visitor out front. Not to mention your cell is blowing up."

"Okay, okay. Tell Mr. Grant I went to the bathroom or something. I'll be right back. Damn!"

"Lyric Crenshaw, I need you ASAP!" Boomed Mr. Grant.

"Toss me my phone," Lyric hissed.

Alicia realized she was still holding the phone. She tossed it to her and rushed over to the desk. She hit the intercom and said sweetly, "Mr. Grant, Lyric went to the restroom. Is there anything I can help you with?"

"I have a meeting downtown in five minutes. I need the reports from last quarter, now!"

"Yes, sir." Alicia wasted no time grabbing the reports from the file cabinet. She knocked before entering Mr. Grant's office and placed them on his desk. Noticing a brochure from a florist, she asked, "You decided to send your wife flowers?"

"What? Oh, yeah. It seems like that's as easy as anything else."

"Why don't you send her a cookie bouquet instead? It's different, and I'm sure she'll like them."

"Hmm, a cookie bouquet? I like that idea. Get me the info so I can send them." He grabbed the folder off the desk and left the office.

"No problem," Alicia told him.

Alicia was distracted by the sound of bass booming from a car stereo. She peeked out the window and saw the familiar black truck pulling off. She didn't see Lyric anywhere, and wondered what was happening. When she picked up the phone and dialed Lyric's cell number, there was no answer. She was about to dial it again when the phone rang.

"Cash and More."

"Do you love me?"

"Excuse me?" She asked, startled by the question.

"I asked if you love me. It's not a test question."

"Yes, Omar, I love you," she answered, realizing it was him playing on the phone.

"What are you doing? You sound distracted."

She kept looking out the window for any signs of Lyric. Ms. Buchanon, one of their regular customers came in. Alicia knew that Ms. Buchanon would have another one of her famous excuses for not being able to pay back the payday loan she had gotten from them. "Uh, nothing. A customer just walked through the door, that's all."

"Okay. Well, I was just calling to see how your day is going. I see that you're busy. I'll call you when I get off."

"Huh? Okay. I love you too, Omar," she said and hung up the phone.

"Hi, Ms. Buchanon, are you here to pay your loan back this afternoon?" Alicia smiled.

"Actually, I need to talk to you all about that," Ms. Buchanon answered.

Alicia stopped her before she could even start one of the outlandish stories she came up with every month. They'd heard it all, from her child support check bouncing to her job messing up her paycheck. The woman always had an excuse for not being able to pay the five hundred dollars she had borrowed over two months ago.

"I'm sorry, Ms. Buchanon. You know that we need a payment or we're going to have to deposit the check you wrote. We can't hold it any longer."

"I understand." She gave Alicia a fake smile and tried to pull down the tight denim skirt she was wearing over her thin body. "Mr. Grant wouldn't happen to be here, would he?"

"Sorry, he had a meeting downtown." Alicia shrugged.

"I'll see if I can catch him before you all deposit the check," Ms. Buchanon told her and turned to leave. "You have a good day, Alicia." She opened the door, and Lyric floated in, carrying a gift box and grinning from ear to ear.

"Hello, Ms. Buchanon."

"Lyric." The woman rolled her eyes and walked out.

Alicia barely let Lyric make it to her desk before she gushed, "What happened? Did either of them catch you?"

203

"Honey, please. I'm a pro at this. I know all about being slick. I never get caught." Lyric made a clicking sound with her mouth. She opened the small box and took out a small gold charm in the shape of a music note, with three diamonds. "Awww, this is so cute. I needed this one, too."

Lyric collected charms and always wore a charm bracelet. She had all kinds: a dog, a ballet shoe, an elephant, a graduation cap. She had been collecting them for years, and they all signified an event in her life. She had so many that Alicia often complained about them jingling when she typed.

"Not another charm." Alicia said with a sigh.

"You're right. Not another charm. Another charm *and* four hundred dollars!" Lyric pulled a wad of money out of the box and did a little dance.

"What? You're kidding." Alicia walked over to her desk.

"And let's see what's in envelope number two," Lyric said, reaching into her purse and opening the envelope Curtis had given her earlier. "Three-fifty. Good job."

"Wow, they both gave you money for your car. That's great. Maybe having two men ain't so bad after all," Alicia teased.

"Girl, they don't know it's for my damn car. They think it's for an abortion."

Alicia was stunned. "Lyric, you're pregnant?"

"Hell naw! I may be a lot of things, but pregnant is not one of them." She laughed.

"I don't get it. You lied to them about being pregnant? Both of them? And they both gave you money for an abortion?"

"It's all about getting them before they get you. I tried to tell you. You see, sweet Curtis, Mr. NBA, he's been after me since the summer. We finally hooked up one night last month. His girlfriend had been acting funny with the cootchie, and brother needed some release. I figured, hell, this motherfucker is six-eleven and wears a size fourteen shoe. Why not? So, we went to one of his boys' apartments and got it on."

Lyric smirked and told Alicia, "Here's a bit of advice: just because a man has a big boat does not mean he knows how to sail it properly. Remember that, okay?"

"I don't have a problem with my man's boat or sailing ability," Alicia announced. "Okay, so what's up with the guy in the truck?"

"That, my dear, is Bed Stuy's finest, Deacon Carver."

"You're lying! That was Deacon Carver? He's like a big-time dealer. You'd better be careful because I heard he can get crazy."

"Please, Deacon is a pussy cat when it comes to me—or shall I say he's a cat when it comes to this pussy? Cuz that brother can lick it like it's fresh milk and he ain't had nothing to drink for days."

"That is definitely too much information."

"Anyway, same situation. See, women think they're doing something by holding out on a brother, but they'd better be careful because there are plenty of sisters like me that see "backed up" men as a window of opportunity and take advantage. Now I have my car payment plus some shopping money." Lyric flashed the cash in front of her.

"Okay, then why lie about being pregnant? Why not just tell them you're in a jam and need the money so the repo man won't snatch your ride?"

"Good questions, both of them. Because number one, they ain't my niggas, so they don't give a shit about my car. But they are obligated to help me get rid of the seed they think I'm carrying. And number two, because if they did give me the money to help me out, then that would make me obligated to them, in a sense. This way, I ain't obligated to do shit.

"All they care about is me getting rid of it and no one finding out. Curtis' girl is still walking around here thinking she's the shit when all along I had him. And Deacon, well, he got enough mouths to feed, dealing with all these hoes that got pregnant by him on purpose. He respects that I ain't trying to cause no drama in his life. Besides, he is so much of an asshole that he deserves to be had every now and then."

"Wow, that is mad crazy."

"It's just part of the game. I just got them before they got me. And no one wound up hurt."

"This time," Alicia commented.

"No time," Lyric corrected her. "I play the game to win, and when I win, there are no hurt players, believe that. Your ego may be

205

a little bruised, but you ain't injured for real. And here's the crazy part: I used condoms with both of them."

The office door opened, and a small guy carrying a large bouquet of roses entered.

"I have a delivery for Lyric Crenshaw," he read off his clipboard.

"That's me," Lyric sang as she walked over to him. He showed her where to sign her name then reached into her pocket and tipped him two dollars. He thanked her and left.

"Are those from one of your fake baby daddies?" Alicia smirked.

"No, they're from my real daddy," Lyric told her, and passing her the small card that was attached to the flowers.

Alicia scanned the message on the card, which read: *To the world's greatest daughter. A father couldn't ask for a better blessing on this day. Have a great birthday.*

"It's your birthday? Why didn't you say anything?" she asked, wondering why Lyric hadn't even mentioned it.

"Yes, I am the big two-three today. Damn, I remember when I thought twenty-five was old." Lyric laughed. "Now it's just around the corner."

"Does your dad live out of town?"

"No. Why do you ask that? Because he sent me flowers?"

"Well, to be honest, I *am* a little shocked. Given your attitude toward men, I thought you didn't grow up with a father figure. No offense. I'm just a little surprised."

"No, my attitude toward men has nothing to do with my father. He's always been there for me. Anthony Crenshaw is the only man in my life who has never disappointed me." Lyric sniffed the flowers. "But he's a different breed. He always has and always will love my mother and would never do anything to disrespect her or their marriage. Guys these days don't know anything about that. First of all, most of them come from homes where nobody taught them any better—hell, most of them grew up without a daddy, so they don't know *anything* about being a man, let alone staying faithful."

"I don't agree," Alicia told her, thinking about her own father and the impact he had on her life. He and her mother were happily married until the day he died. She was grateful that neither she nor her older brother grew up with a warped view of relationships like Lyric seemed to have.

"You're in love. I wouldn't expect you to agree." Lyric said. "But when those blinders come off and you see things for what they really are, you'll understand where I'm coming from."

Alicia just shook her head, thinking that would never happen.

"Let's just say my heart was destroyed a long time ago by a man. That shit won't happen again. I promised myself that a long time ago."

"Sounds to me like you're just going to live a lonely life," Alicia told her, feeling sorry for Lyric.

"You call it lonely. I call it being in control. I call the shots, and what I say goes. No one fucks with me, I fuck with them. That's the way I like it."

Lyric put the flowers on her desk and said, "Let me tell you a story. When I was sixteen, I found out that my boyfriend had been sleeping with my best friend for a year because I wouldn't put out. Then, as soon as I gave up my virginity to him, he left me for her because she was better in bed. The next man I trusted wound up clearing out my back account and having a baby with my first cousin. So you see, I learned a long time ago that you can't trust bitches or niggas."

"So, you don't trust me?"

"There's a difference in trusting someone and liking them. I like you, Alicia. You're my girl. But I don't even trust myself when it comes to dealing with men. You need to stop being so naïve and learn to watch your back."

Alicia took a deep breath and let Lyric's words sink in.

3

"So, what are you saying, Omar?"

Alicia and Omar were sitting in her living room, facing each other. It was April, and they had only seen each other three or four times in the past two months. She had been getting ready for finals and he had been working overtime. Now, he was telling her that he was canceling their plans once again. He had been distant when they talked on the phone. Even their usual passion-filled lovemaking had been blasé the last time they slept together.

Alicia had a strange feeling that Omar was losing interest or worse, that he had found interest in someone else. Lyric had been constantly reminding her of the telltale signs of cheating, and now Omar was demonstrating a lot of them. There were times she called him and he seemed disappointed that it was her on the phone. He made excuses about not wanting to come over. There had to be someone else.

"It's just that some guys from work are going on this trip to Atlantic City and I've decided to go with them," he answered. "What's the big deal?"

"The big deal is that we don't see each other enough as it is, and now you're blowing me off for some bullshit trip to Atlantic City?"

"Look, it's not my fault we've been slammed at work. I figured you would want me to go hang out and relax. You know what? Fuck it. I won't go. Forget I even mentioned it." Omar stood up, frustrated. "What do you want to do this weekend?"

"Oh, hell naw. You're not about to treat me like I'm some secondhand rag. You wanna go on your little trip, fine then . . . "

The sound of the door opening interrupted their argument, and they both looked to see who it was. Alicia let out a scream when she saw her brother, Jeremiah, walk through the door.

"Jeremiah Woods, what are you doing here?" She ran and hugged him, causing him to drop his bags.

"Damn, can't a brother come home every now and then?" He smiled, looking like his younger sister. "What's up, Omar? You still hanging around?"

"I'm trying to, anyway. What's up, Remy? How long you home for?"

Jeremiah was a merchant seaman who stayed gone months at a time. It was nothing for Alicia and her mom to go nine or ten months without seeing him. But he called often and sent money home every month, and there were plenty of gifts on holidays.

"Actually, I'm here until at least September, believe it or not," Jeremiah told them.

"That long? Why?" Alicia asked.

"Don't sound too disappointed. They have to do some work to the ship. It's docked in Jersey, so I have to go to report, but I figured I'd just catch the train back and forth. Where's Mom?"

"Today's Tuesday. She works late. Does she know you're home?"

"Nope. Figured I'd surprise everyone. My room still straight, or you been using it as an extra closet?" He picked up his bags and headed down the hallway.

"You think Mom would let me even go in there? You're her precious son, don't you remember?" Alicia called to him.

She sat down on the sofa and looked at Omar, who was standing with his arms folded.

"Well, I guess I'll go. You and your brother can have some time alone to catch up," he told her.

"You're leaving? But it's Tuesday," she replied.

"Yeah, but I don't even feel up to it," he said as he opened the door to leave. "I'll talk to you later."

"Oh, so since you can't get none you just gon' leave like that?"

He didn't respond, just closed the door behind him. Alicia blinked back the tears that were forming in her eyes. Omar had walked out on her without even a hug. He had never done that before, and now she was filled with hurt and disappointment. She took a deep breath, determined not to let his childish behavior stop her from enjoying her brother's homecoming.

"What was that all about? Did I interrupt something?" Jeremiah asked, putting his things away when Alicia walked into his room.

"Naw, we've been having problems for a minute now anyway. I think we're drifting apart. It's cool, though."

"Well, shit happens. If it's meant to be, it'll be. You know that's what I always say."

Alicia sat in the middle of his bed and asked, "Speaking of meant to be . . . have you talked to Raven?"

"No, I haven't. In case you didn't know, I've been in the middle of the ocean for damn near twelve months. I really haven't talked to anyone."

"You call me and Mom."

"You're my family."

"She was your fiancée. That's almost your family."

"Almost doesn't count," he told her. "And don't go trying to be in my business. If she finds out I'm here that's one thing, but I don't need you yapping your mouth, telling her to come over for old time's sake. You got it?"

"Fine," Alicia agreed. "Wanna go get something to eat?"

"You think I'm gonna say no? Let's roll. A brother's stomach is on *E*."

Alicia was depressed and Lyric knew it. She figured it had something to do with Omar since he hadn't been ringing the phone off the hook, making Alicia blush. Lyric tried to pretend as if she didn't notice, but it had become pitiful in the office. There was no laughter, just the sound of her charm bracelet as she typed, and Alicia didn't even complain.

"Did you deposit Ms. Buchanon's check?" Lyric asked.

"No, I thought you did. Did it come back returned? I figured it would," Alicia looked up.

"No, look in her file and see if it's in there. Her name is still on the open accounts, but I don't see her check in here."

Alicia walked over to the filing cabinet and looked in Ms. Buchanon's file. "It's not here. That check has to be somewhere."

The two women were searching for the missing check when Mr. Grant walked in. "What are you two doing?"

"Mr. Grant, we can't find Sheila Buchanon's check. She's still listed under the open accounts. She hasn't paid her loan back nor has she made a payment since February."

"Uh, you don't worry about her account. It's already taken care of. She's paid in full," he said quickly and rushed into his office, closing the door behind him.

"That dog!" Alicia huffed. She could not believe it. It was obvious that Ms. Buchanon had indeed spoken to him personally, as she said she would. Alicia felt sick.

"What's wrong? Please don't tell me you're surprised by this. I knew something was going on. He's been in too much of a good mood lately. Old Mr. Grant and Ms. Buchanon. Hot damn! This is too much," Lyric said with a laugh.

She saw that Alicia was really bothered by their discovery. "Alicia, what's the deal? Come on, this is funny. I know you don't want me to be right, but Mr. Grant is a man, just like any other one. And believe it or not, men cheat. They are all just waiting for the right window to open for them to jump in. Look at you, moping behind Omar. I told you that you gotta get out before you get hurt."

"My issues with Omar ain't got nothing to do with you, so stay out of it, okay? You think I wanna be walking around here like you? So hardcore, using men to get what you can and then becoming so coldhearted that you no longer even desire a real relationship. Fuck that. You think I'm moping? Well, guess what? I can see right through you, and I know that you're lonely and miserable. That's not me, and it never will be." Alicia snatched her papers off the desk, stuffed them into her bag, and grabbed her purse. "Tell Mr. Grant I won't be back. I can't take being around either one of you."

"Alicia, wait! Don't leave like this. I'm sorry," Lyric told her.

"I know you are," Alicia said as she stormed out.

Lyric couldn't believe she left like that. She didn't mean to set the girl off. She was staring at Alicia's empty chair when she heard a faint ringing. She knew it couldn't be her phone because it was hanging on the waistband of her jeans and it was on vibrate. She opened the desk drawer to see Alicia's cell phone. Omar's name flashed across the caller ID. Lyric paused for a moment then decided to answer it.

"Hello," she said.

"Alicia?" Omar sounded confused, but his deep voice still caused the hairs on Lyric's neck to stand up.

"Yeah, she left her phone in her desk and I answered it. This is Lyric, Omar."

"Oh, I was wondering if I had the right number for a minute," he said with a laugh. Even his laugh was sexy. Alicia was a lucky girl if he looked anything like he sounded, Lyric thought.

"Alicia left work already. Um, when you talk to her, can you let her know that I got her phone for her? I don't have her home number."

"Sure, I'll tell her. Just leave it in her desk and she can get it tomorrow."

"I don't think she'll be coming to work tomorrow."

"Why not? She took the day off?"

"She kinda sorta quit," Lyric confessed. She told Omar about what happened.

"She's probably mad as hell. Well, she's actually supposed to be coming over here later. You wanna meet somewhere and I'll get it from you?"

Lyric thought for a moment then asked, "Where do you live? I can drop it off. I kinda wanna talk to her anyway." Omar lived not far from her house. She agreed to drop off the phone on her way home.

She cut the phone off and went back to work. Now she had the responsibility of two cashiers, and she was swamped with customers. How she was going to explain Alicia's quitting to Mr. Grant? Somehow, she felt that it was all her fault, and she didn't look forward to explaining to the old grouch. She did feel bad about upsetting Alicia, though. They might have had very different opinions, but she really did like the girl. The rest of her shift went by quickly as she thought about what she would say to apologize to Alicia.

Lyric approached the front of the building and checked the paper where she had written the address to be sure this was the right place. She walked up the steps and stopped in front of apartment 306. The thought of the conversation she was about to have with Alicia made her nervous. Lyric was not used to apologizing for her actions or her words.

When she knocked on the door and it opened, she could not help gasping. Before her stood the finest chocolate man she had ever laid eyes on. Lyric had been with some fine men before, but this brother had it going on. And from the way he carried himself, he had no clue. He stood in front of her, wrapped in only a towel and a pair of shower shoes. He was using another towel to wipe the water dripping from his hair. His arms were cut, and his body was diesel.

Damn, damn, damn! No wonder Alicia's ass never invited him to the office. I wouldn't trust his fine ass around me either.

"Hi, Omar?" She asked to make sure this wasn't just his brother or something. Then again, if this was his brother, maybe he was single, Lyric thought.

"Yeah. Lyric?" He smiled at her. His eyes were as black as coal, but they had a spark in them that drew her in.

"Yeah, you said you'd be downstairs waiting," she said, though she wasn't complaining that he was up here answering the door half-naked.

"My bad. Time got away from me. You wanna come in? You can wait for Alicia in here."

"Uh, I'd better wait out front if you don't mind."

Thinking again about how much she didn't want to deal with an apology, she said, "Better yet, how about you just give her the phone and have her call me? I'll give you my number." She hoped that if Alicia had some time to think about it before they talked, maybe she'd feel better and Lyric wouldn't even have to apologize. She took out a piece of paper and wrote her number on it.

"Here, why don't you just put it in her phone?" Omar suggested.

"That's a good idea." She took Alicia's phone out of her purse and programmed her number into the phone book. "Look, can you give a message to her? Tell her if she doesn't call, I understand, and just so she knows, she's already won the grand prize."

"Huh?" He frowned, taking the phone from her.

"She'll know what you're talking about. And it was nice to finally meet you."

"Same here," he said. "You know, I made some quick judgments about you without even meeting you. I'm sorry about that. You really aren't that bad."

213

"That's okay. I made some judgments about you too. But we're all guilty of that, I guess." Lyric smiled. "I better be going."

She reached up and gave Omar a quick hug then left, trying not to think about how smooth his skin felt. That Alicia was one lucky girl. Omar was different. Lyric was happy that Alicia had been right about having a good man. Any other Negro would have been trying to press up on her, girlfriend or not, but he was a complete gentleman. He was a true prize.

Caught up in her thoughts, she never noticed Alicia watching as she turned the corner in the hallway. Neither did she realize that the telephone number she wrote down for Omar was laying in front of his doorstep. Alicia picked it up just as she was about to knock on his door.

Every man cheats, and what women don't realize is that there's a woman like me waiting for that opportunity to step in and take advantage. Lyric's words echoed in Alicia's head, and she could picture Lyric's cynical smirk. *I just get them before I get got.*

"So, you think you can win the game, Lyric?" Alicia spoke out loud to herself. "Well, meet your fierce competition. And before it's over with, you won't know what hit you. Believe that." She rushed into Omar's apartment as soon as he opened the door.

Whack! Alicia didn't even let Omar get a word out. She palmed his face so hard that he was stunned.

"You triflin' bastard. You got a cunt like that all up in here and don't think I would know about it? What? You had to take a shower right quick so I wouldn't smell the fresh funk on your two-timing ass!" she screamed.

Omar looked like he wanted to swing on her as he rubbed his face. "I don't know what the hell your problem is, but you need to go, regroup and come back."

"I saw that ho Lyric coming up out of here, Omar. Oh, and by the way, here's her number she left for your ass to call her." She thrust the paper in his face.

"You're tripping. Shit, Lyric came over her to bring your cell phone that you left at work. And she wasn't even in here. She stood in the hallway. See, this is why I'm beginning to think this shit ain't gon' work. You tripping over something that ain't even happen." Omar turned away from her and tried to leave the room. Alicia followed behind him, still screaming that he was low-down dog who screwed around on her.

Omar sat down on the sofa and told her calmly, "I'm not even gonna argue with you about some bullshit. If you don't believe me, here's your cell phone to prove it."

Alicia snatched the cell phone out of his hand and threw it against the wall, smashing it into pieces. "I don't give a fuck about no cell phone! That's not the issue here."

Omar was through being calm. "Get the fuck out, Alicia. I told you I wasn't for all this. I refuse to be with someone that don't trust me. I told you I ain't fucking around, and you still don't believe me. That's it. It's over."

Alicia began grabbing things and smashing them in a fit of anger. Here she was this entire time, giving him everything she had within, and just as simple as that, he was ready for it to be over with. It was the exact same way Lyric said it was. She was right all along. Omar was just using her until he was finished and was ready to move on. She wanted to break everything in sight, and tried to.

Omar finally grabbed her and pushed her out of his apartment. She was heaving and crying in the hallway, and several people came out to witness the commotion. Not wanting to look like a crazy woman, she got herself together and left the building, her heart battered and her ego bruised.

Alicia didn't sit and feel sorry for herself for too long, though. By morning, she had come up with a plan and started putting it in motion. She went to Cash and More to tell Mr. Grant she was quitting. He was confused about her sudden urgency to leave, but she purposely remained vague, planting the seeds of doubt in his mind about Lyric.

"Well, I just don't feel comfortable working with her anymore," she explained.

He offered to move her to another shift, but she politely thanked him and refused. She didn't bother to tell him that he was a part of the reason she wanted out. Besides, that didn't really matter anymore. The only thing she was interested in was revenge.

"By the way," she told him, "you might want to keep your eye on Lyric."

"Really? Why?" he asked, eyebrows raised.

"Well, I'm not saying she's stealing or anything, but she has had some financial problems lately, and it just seems like a check-cashing place would be the perfect place to work when you need a little extra money to pay on your car note that's overdue."

"I don't know about that, Alicia. Are you sure she would do something like that? She might have an attitude, but she seems okay to me."

"Really?" she questioned. She wasn't worried about it if Mr. Grant didn't want to believe Lyric was stealing. She had something else that would definitely get his attention. "Well, you do what you feel you have to, but just watch your back. She did mention something about reporting Ms. Buchanon's mysterious paid-in-full account to the downtown office."

That was all Alicia needed to say. Mr. Grant's eyes got small, and Alicia knew it was only a matter of time before Lyric's ass would be sitting at the unemployment office watching the repo man tow her car out of the parking lot.

"I'll mail you your last check, Alicia," Mr. Grant managed to say, his mind obviously on other things now.

Alicia walked out of the office, satisfied that Lyric would suffer behind this.

4

"Okay, this is getting to be too hard." The man smiled at Lyric.

She knew he had been checking her out from the first day she started working at NY Fitness Club. Mr. Grant had fired her from the check-cashing place, claiming she had been stealing money out of petty cash. Lyric knew that was a lie. He probably didn't want her to squeal about him fucking with Ms. Buchanon. She figured one of the morning cashiers set her up, but Lyric didn't care. She didn't want to work there anymore anyway. It was boring without Alicia. She was glad when she spotted the *Help Wanted* sign in the window of the fitness center. She applied, wowed the owner and got the job.

"What's that?" She asked, trying to be polite. He was way too old for her taste, and since her reality check from Alicia and Omar, she had begun to look at life and relationships in a new light. She still didn't believe in the true love thing, but she figured there had to be a few more decent guys out there, and if she was a little more selective, she might just find one.

"It's getting harder coming in here day after day and not at least offering to take you to dinner," he told her.

"Aww, that's so sweet. But I'm sorry, I don't think that's a good idea."

"Why not? I'm one of the most powerful black men on Wall Street. I can give you your heart's desire, take you wherever you want to go and show you things you've only imagined. Come on, one date. What do you say?" He waited with anticipation, and for a brief moment, Lyric thought about his offer. Not long ago, she would have been salivating at the idea of getting with a man with that much to offer.

"I don't think your wife would appreciate it, for one. But if you like, I can ask her. She has a Pilates class this afternoon at three. What do you say?" she asked, still using that polite tone.

"I say I think we should keep this between you and me," he answered sheepishly.

"No problem. See you tomorrow, Mr. Davis." Lyric waved, amused by how easy it was to crush that fool's ego. He was not the first member to hit on her, and certainly not the only one to try to play like he wasn't a married man. How stupid did these men think she was? Lyric worked at the front desk with the computer, which listed the personal information for each gym member every time they scanned their cards, including whether the membership was a single or family. Most of them didn't even bother to look her in the face when they talked to her. Their attention stayed focused on her C-cup breasts jammed into her NY Fitness Club sports bra that management swore was a uniform shirt. She didn't complain, though. Working here most days was fun, and the money was great.

She began folding the towels that Conner, one of the aerobics instructors, placed on the counter. He was another reason she loved working at the gym. He kept her in stitches, often pointing out who was in the closet, out of the closet, on the DL, and/or otherwise. He was quite in the open about his own sexuality, sometimes too much, but in spite of his flamboyance and the fact that he broadcast their sexual info, the members loved him. His class was often booked weeks in advance, full of both women and men.

"You handled that one like a pro, baby doll. I thought he was going to piss in his pants when you asked if you should ask his wife." Conner giggled.

"Did he honestly think I would say yes?"

"Hmm, let him make that offer to me. You can bet your ass it would be an affirmative." He snapped his finger in the air and she shook her head.

"Wanna hear something funny? If he would have made that offer to me about nine months ago, it would've been affirmative for me too."

"We all have a price, honey. Don't feel bad."

They went back to folding towels and greeting members. Conner announced, "Look at what Mack done drug in. He is fine. Check it out."

Lyric looked up, expecting to see some scantily clad body builder, which was the usual cause of Conner's outbursts. She was, however, pleasantly surprised. One of the regulars, Mack, was standing in front of the desk with a handsome gentleman. They were both dressed in shorts and tank tops, carrying gym bags.

"Good afternoon, Ms. Lyric. How are you today?" Mack greeted her.

Lyric smiled smugly back at him. This was totally unlike him. Most of the time he didn't even stop and talk, barely grunting "hi" and "bye" as he entered and exited. She knew there must be a catch.

"I'm fine, Mack. And to what do I owe the pleasure of your unusual politeness today?"

"Yes, do tell," Conner added, "because I have never heard you address Lyric as Miss. Shoot, I didn't even know you knew her name the way you blaze in and out past her every day." He leaned on the counter, waiting for Mack to answer.

Lyric could see that Mack was not amused, although she noticed his friend trying not to smile. There was something familiar about this man that made her instantly like him without even knowing who he was.

"Uh, I was wondering if I could get one of those temporary guest passes for my friend. You know, so he can check out the club and see if he'd like to join." Mack tilted his head.

"Sure, no problem," Lyric answered, reaching into the drawer and taking out a card. "What's your friend's name?"

"Remy."

"Like the liquor?" Conner asked with a smile. Lyric elbowed him. She didn't want the first-time guest to be frightened off by his obvious flirtation. It usually took new members a while to get used to Conner's way-out-the-closet personality.

"Yeah, actually it's short for Jeremiah. Jeremiah Woods," he explained, leaning in and watching Lyric write his name on the card. She looked up and gave it to him. "Nice shirt," he complimented. This time, Lyric didn't mind when his eyes lingered a second too long on her chest.

"Thanks. This card gives you access to the gym, all the classes, equipment and activities for thirty days. Feel free to take advantage of all it has to offer." She was surprised to hear this last line come out of her mouth, wondering if he understood her double meaning.

"I'll do that," he replied, his eyes locked on hers.

"Why was my trial only good for two weeks?" Mack asked, interrupting their moment.

219

"Because we knew it wouldn't take you that long to make up your mind. You're a smart man, we could tell," Conner quipped.

Mack cut his eyes at Conner. "Come on, Rem. Let's go hoop."

"If you need any more balls, just let me know," Conner called after them. Lyric elbowed him in the stomach, causing him to double over.

"Will you stop? You just don't know when to quit, do you?" she asked, hands on her hips.

"Whoo, baby doll. You almost made me lose my breath. And why do I have to stop, Miss Take-advantage-of-all-we-have-to-offer?" He batted his eyelashes dramatically and lay across the counter as if he was swooning.

"I say that to all our guests, thank you," she insisted.

"You're a damn lie. You tell them bastards enjoy their stay. You ain't never invited nobody to take advantage except for Mr. Jeremiah Woods, mystery man. I ain't mad at you, though. Make your move, baby doll, and go for yours. But make it fast or I'm gonna have to step up, and he'll be taking advantage of me."

"Don't you have a class to teach?"

"I'm teaching my prize pupil right now. It's called the art of flirting. Pass this class and you may be promoted to Lovemaking 101—now that's a classic. You don't wanna miss that one. Ta-ta, love. I have to go attempt to make these flabby asses beautiful." Conner grabbed a towel and his water bottle then spoke into the microphone, announcing that his class was about to begin. Women came from everywhere, all following him into the aerobics room.

Lyric looked around the crowded gym, trying to catch a glimpse of Jeremiah. She knew that if they were shooting basketball, she wouldn't see him. The courts were located on the second floor, and she couldn't leave her post. She tried to think of a reason to go upstairs, but there was none that wouldn't be too obvious. She would just have to wait until they were leaving until she saw him again.

Time seemed to drag on, and Lyric found herself looking up at the clock every two minutes. She could hear Conner yelling "Pick it up!" at his class over the blaring Janet Jackson music. Lyric restocked the energy bars then the fitness magazines, trying to do anything to make time go pass faster.

She was on the phone talking to a woman whose watch was missing when she finally saw Remy approaching the desk. She interrupted the woman mid-sentence, put her on hold and walked over to him.

"Can I help you with anything?" she asked.

"Yes, you can. I was wondering if I could get a tour of the facility."

"Sure, that's no problem. Let me see if one of the trainers is available." Lyric began flipping through the appointment book.

"You can't give me a tour? I mean, if you're not busy."

"Well, I'm like the only one at the desk and I can't leave it unattended. I'm sorry." She shrugged. "I would love you to give you a tour if I could." That wasn't all she'd like to give him, she thought.

"Oh. Well, maybe we can schedule my tour during a time when you're not working the desk," he suggested, leaving Lyric to wonder if maybe he was thinking along the same lines as her. She decided to remain professional, though. If he was interested, he'd just have to come right out and say it.

"That would be fine. Let me look at my schedule. What day were you thinking?"

"What about Friday night? Around nine."

"I leave at seven on Friday."

"Perfect," he answered. Leaving no more questions about his real intentions, he said, "You can give me my tour and then we can go to dinner. So, I'll meet you at seven on Friday, right?"

"Uh, okay," she responded with a nod.

They were staring at each other when Mack walked up. "You ready to go?" he asked Remy. As they headed to the door, Mack gave Lyric his standard goodbye grunt.

"Bye, Mack. See you tomorrow. You have a good night too!" she yelled, knowing he would be pissed.

Lyric danced along to the Caribbean beat coming from the Soca-aerobics class.

"My, my, my, aren't we in a festive mood?" Conner commented. "And what has us dancing like a Jamaican call girl?"

"We have date Friday night," she announced.

"With Jeremiah Woods?"

221

"With Jeremiah Woods."

Conner grabbed her hands and they gyrated in harmony like two Sean Paul video extras. All was well at the NY Fitness Center.

5

Alicia loved the kids she worked with at the Community Center, but she still left work each day feeling empty. She was lonely, something she wasn't used to. After catching Lyric with Omar, life no longer seemed vibrant to her. She had been a hopeless romantic, and now that reality had shown her that she was a fool for believing in true love, she didn't wake up each morning with the same sense of anticipation that she used to. It was as if she was going about her daily routine out of obligation, rather than with a purpose. She had no drive about her.

"What is going on with you?" her mother asked one evening. Alicia had come home after work and lay on the sofa, flipping channels, looking like a zombie.

"Nothing. I just had a long day, that's all," she answered.

"Long day, my foot. You come home every day and lay around. That's not like you at all, Alicia. I'm beginning to worry about you. I know that you and Omar decided to take a break, as you say, but you're beginning to act morbid. It's frightening."

"What's frightening?" Jeremiah asked on his way out the door.

"The way your sister is behaving. I think she's depressed."

"I'm not depressed, Mama. Those kids just take a lot out of me, that's all. I'm drained by the time I get in, and I just wanna relax. Now, if I was out running the streets, you'd have something to say about that too." Alicia rolled her eyes to the ceiling, wishing everyone would just leave her alone to wallow in her depression.

"You wanna come hang out with me, sis?" Jeremiah offered.

"No, I don't want to tag along with you. I just want to relax and watch some TV, and since I can't do that out here, I'll go in my room." She clicked the television off and went into her room, leaving her brother and mother to discuss her mental state without her.

She lay across her bed and closed her eyes, not only physically tired, but emotionally drained. The summer was dragging by, and she regretted not enrolling in summer school. At least then she would have had reading to do and papers to write to occupy some of her time.

She hated the fact that she missed Omar. It had been over a month since she had talked to him or even seen him, though it was still hard trying to convince herself that he was a lying cheat and she would never be able to trust him. She ignored his calls and treated him like shit the one day he showed up at her house. She refused to let him in, telling him that she no longer cared about him. To say he was upset was an understatement. Furious and hurt was more like it, the same way she felt when she saw him with that tramp, Lyric. Knowing he was hurt was some small consolation.

She reached for the remote, hoping to find something to take her mind off her own life. Hopefully, reruns of *Law and Order* would do the trick.

Until she heard the phone ringing, Alicia didn't even realize she had fallen asleep. She tried to ignore it, but rolled over and answered when it wouldn't stop.

"Hello," she groaned into the receiver.

"Alicia, are you 'sleep?"

"Huh? No, I was just laying down. Raven, is this you?"

"Yeah, it's me. How've you been?"

"I've been good. How are you?" She and Raven had gotten close when she was dating Jeremiah, but since the breakup, they really hadn't talked much.

"Okay. Would your fine-ass brother happen to be home?"

"No, he's not here, Raven. I don't know where he is." Alicia was about to volunteer his cell phone number but remembered the warning he gave her.

"Well, just let him know that I called, okay?"

"I will. He'll be glad to hear it," Alicia said before she could stop herself. She always liked Raven, and was surprised when Jeremiah told them that the engagement was off. He said it had something to do with Raven not being ready for marriage, but somehow Alicia knew there was much more to the story. Deep down, she hoped that she could somehow lead them back to each other and they would fall in love again.

"Has he asked about me? Well, has he at least mentioned me?" Raven asked, her voice full of hope.

Alicia didn't want to disappoint her, so she said, "Yes, as a matter of fact, we were talking about you the night he came home. I'm surprised you haven't talked to him."

Well, that's not a lie, Alicia thought. *We did talk about her that night.*

"Well, please give him the message that I called and let him know I'm glad he's home."

"I will, Raven. Don't worry. He'll be calling you soon." Now, that was a lie.

"I hope so. Listen, maybe we can get together and hang out this week. Maybe go to dinner or something, catch up on old times."

"I'd like that, Raven. I haven't hung out in a while. Call me and let me know what's up," Alicia replied. Maybe hanging out with Raven, who was always so carefree, was just what she needed. And if she could help her and Jeremiah hook back up, that would just be a little icing on the cake.

6

"So, tell me about you," Jeremiah said after the waitress seated him and Lyric. They had decided to indulge in dinner and cheesecake at Junior's after they found out it was the one favorite restaurant they had in common.

"What do you wanna know?" Lyric shrugged.

"Everything," he answered with a smile.

Lyric could not believe she was actually blushing. Being coy had never been her nature, especially when it was unintentional. But somehow, Jeremiah made her feel as if being with her was like a reward of some sort.

"What is there to tell? Let's see. I'm twenty-three, an only child . . ."

"Oh no, not an only child. That means you're spoiled rotten."

"What? I don't think so. My parents don't play. Never have, never will. I am far from spoiled," she answered matter-of-factly. "I have a twelve o'clock curfew, by the way."

"Are you serious?" Jeremiah's eyes widened with surprise.

"No." Lyric laughed. She hadn't had a curfew since she was in high school.

"You still live at home?"

"Yep, I'm still at home with Mom and Dad."

"Mom *and* Dad?" Jeremiah asked, impressed. It seemed like everyone he knew lately came from a single-parent home.

"Yep, my parents have been married for nearly twenty-five years. Don't ask me how they've done it." This was true. Lyric really had no idea how their marriage survived when the marriages of her friends' parents often failed, mainly due to infidelity. She had seen so many broken families and the damage that resulted, and she counted herself lucky that her family didn't have to go through the turmoil. Her parents were strong, and the love they shared was special.

She doubted that she would ever find anyone to share a love like the one they shared. She had been dogged out by guys one too many times and learned that lesson early on in life. That was when she figured out how to play the game, and until she met Alicia, she thought she was winning.

"Wow, that's deep. I respect that. That's love, for sure." Jeremiah reached over and placed his hand on top of hers. "You're really blessed. You got the chance to grow up seeing firsthand how two people work together to make a marriage work. Think about it. You don't have the horror stories of a crack head mom or dope-dealing dad. And there's nothing wrong with that. For a while when I was hanging with my boys at work, I used to feel bad because they had all these crazy stories about growing up in the hood. They had to go through so much to get where they were, and there I was, the son of a hard-working widower who never got into any trouble.

"I felt less than, like I didn't deserve to be there with a decent job which I got fairly easy. But then I realized that I should just be thankful for the home that I grew up in. A lot of times, we create drama in our own lives just so we can feel a part of the crowd."

Lyric listened to what Jeremiah was saying. He was so right. The choices she made in men, all the times she acted like a bitch just so people would think she was hardcore, had all been an act. She never let her guard down because she didn't want to seem weak and make herself vulnerable. But in those rare moments when she really looked deep inside herself, she had to admit that tough chick wasn't who she really was. She wanted to feel safe and loved just as much as any other woman.

She relaxed and leaned her body against Jeremiah's, finally feeling like she no longer had to be whatever she thought he wanted. All he wanted was her, and it felt good for a change.

Jeremiah began toying with charms on her bracelet, and she opened up, telling him about each one and the story behind them. For once, she felt like a guy was listening to her because he really wanted to hear what she had to say, not because he thought it would make it easier to get in her pants later. She was starting to think that maybe Jeremiah really was one of the good ones.

7

"Well, according to my friend Traci, him and the girl looked pretty cozy in Junior's the other night. Are you sure you don't know who she is?" Raven asked, folding her arms and staring at Alicia. It was happy hour at Club Negril, and there was a nice crowd. They had found an empty table in the back of the club, and Raven was telling Alicia that a friend had spotted Jeremiah and some girl hugged up a few days before.

"I don't know who that could possibly be, Raven. Like I said, whoever it is must not be too important, because he hasn't mentioned her. Don't worry about it."

"I'm not trying to look like a fool, Alicia. If he has a girlfriend, I don't have a problem with that. I just need to know before I pursue this any further." Raven pursed her lips.

They placed their drink orders with the waitress and Alicia tried to figure out who Jeremiah could be going out with. As far as she knew, her brother went to work then to the gym with his friend, Mack. He hadn't even mentioned anything about taking anyone to Juniors or anywhere else. "Are you sure it was even Jeremiah, Raven?"

"It was him, Alicia. Traci even took a picture with her phone and showed me."

"What did the girl look like?"

"Typical girl, I guess. You know how those camera phones are. It was like a side view of them, so all I could really see was him."

"I don't know, Raven. But believe me, I will ask him when I get home tonight."

"Well, let me know. Because like I said, I don't want to be chasing after his ass and he's all caught up in someone else. I don't have no time to waste. Enough about that. What's up with you and Omar?" Raven asked as the drinks arrived at the table.

Alicia rolled her eyes. "Nothing's up. It's over. He cheated with my so-called friend, believe it or not." Alicia took a long swallow of her Blue Motorcycle and went on to tell Raven all about Lyric, her scheming ways and how she caught her coming out of Omar's place.

"Ewww, what a skank! See, that's why you can't tell your friends all your business. The entire time she was taking it all in so she could take your man, girl. You know that, right?"

"Now I do. But I thought Omar loved me enough not to fall for her stupid traps."

"Girl, Omar is a man. All of them are alike." Raven laughed.

"You sound like Lyric," Alicia told her and started laughing along with her. The alcohol was taking effect, and she began to mellow out and enjoy herself. She turned around and caught the eye of a nice looking guy seated at a nearby table. She was bouncing to the beat of Usher and Li'l Jon, so he gestured toward the dance floor. She nodded and joined him in the middle of the dance floor. Caught up in the music for a while, she forgot all about Omar, Lyric, Jeremiah, Raven and everything else.

"Damn, you got some moves, boo," her dance partner whispered into her ear. She could feel his arm tightening around her waist, pulling her closer. She quickly turned around with her back to him. The deejay began playing house music and she danced faster and faster to the beat. Her partner kept right up with her, so she decided to give him the once-over, seeing if he was worth any conversation.

She faced him again, noticing he was taller than she originally thought. He was handsome in a rugged way, dressed casually in jeans, a polo shirt and leather shoes. He had a nice smile, and his teeth were white and even, another plus. This time when he pulled her closer, she inhaled his cologne, recognizing the scent of Jean Paul Gautier. He looked good, smelled good and moved well, but she wondered, did he have sense enough to buy her a drink?

"Whew, I gotta stop," she said over the music.

"Let's go over to the bar. I'll buy you a drink," he replied.

Bingo, you may be on a roll.

They walked over to the bar, where she ordered another Blue Motorcycle for herself and an Incredible Hulk for him. He followed her back to her table where Raven was still sitting, talking to the guy who had been sitting with Alicia's new friend.

"Hey, Alicia, this is Marcus. Marcus, this is Alicia and— I'm sorry, I don't think we've been formally introduced." Raven extended her hand to Alicia's dance partner. "I'm Raven."

"Deacon, Deacon Carver." He graciously took Raven's hand into his and kissed it.

Alicia could not believe she had been dancing with and now drinking with Deacon Carver, the infamous thug she witnessed first hand getting played, big time.

"Oh, I know who *you* are. Nice to meet you," Raven told him and went back to talking to Marcus.

"Alicia, that's a pretty name," Deacon leaned over and whispered.

She didn't know whether to be flattered or annoyed, so she just smiled and said, "Thanks."

"That's the most fun I had on the dance floor in a while. I usually don't even dance when I come to the club."

That's because you're too busy dealing drugs out the back, was the first thought that came into her mind.

"It's been a while since I've been out myself," she told him. Though she knew about Deacon's reputation, she decided not to trip. It wasn't like she would have anything to do with him once they left the club that night, so what was the harm in letting him buy her a few drinks? Besides, he was a good dancer, and she definitely needed to enjoy herself a little after all she'd been through lately.

Get him before he can get you, girl. Lyric's words echoed in her mind as she enjoyed her evening with Deacon, Marcus and Raven. She continued making small talk and laughing in Deacon's face like he was the funniest thing since Chris Tucker in *Friday*. They hit the dance floor a few more times and before long, Deacon was buying drinks for the entire table. *Damn, this is easy as hell*, she thought.

Time flew by, and soon, the deejay announced last call. Marcus asked if they wanted anything. Raven told him that she had enough and was ready to leave. Deacon offered to give them a ride home.

"Hell yeah," Raven answered before Alicia could.

Alicia was enjoying her buzz as they walked out into the crowded parking lot and Deacon hit the lock on his truck. Just as he was opening the door for her, she heard someone calling her name. Immediately, she recognized the voice, and turned to see Omar. He muttered something to some hootchie-looking girl standing next to him and started walking toward her. She couldn't believe she had been so caught up hanging with Deacon that she hadn't even noticed Omar while they were in the club.

"I'll be right back," she told Deacon. She walked over to Omar, not trying to hide her annoyance. "What?"

"What's up?" he asked.

She tried not to notice how good he looked in his ivory linen pants suit. He had a fresh haircut and she fought the urge to hug him, just to feel his body close to hers.

"Nothing. We were just leaving, that's all."

"You think it's a good idea to be riding in the vehicle of a known drug dealer, Alicia? I don't think you should be leaving with him. Especially since you've been drinking."

"Excuse me? I don't think it's a good idea to be all up in my business like that. You ain't my man, and if I decide to ride shotgun with Charles Manson and Jeffery Dahmer's in the back seat, it's none of your concern. I ain't asking you about that hooker who's obviously with you," she snapped.

"Look, I'm just concerned, okay? Believe it or not, I still care about you." Omar took a step toward her. She stepped back, fearing that if he touched her, she would break down in his arms and admit that she missed him.

"Gee, thanks for the concern, but I'm grown, and I am capable of taking care of myself," she told him. Deacon pulled up next to her. She opened the door and climbed into the truck. "Goodbye, Omar."

"Bye, Omar," Raven called from the back seat then burst into a drunken laughter, falling into Marcus' lap. Alicia closed the door and Deacon pulled off. Watched Omar from the rearview mirror, Alicia cringed when the girl he was with walked up to him and put her arm around his waist. It hurt, but she had become good at denying her true feelings, and quickly told herself to get over it.

"Is that your man?" Deacon asked. "I ain't trying to fuck nobody up tonight."

"No, he *was* her man until she caught him with some trick-ass bitch that used to be her friend," Raven volunteered from the back seat where she was now laying down.

"Damn, that's fucked up. She wasn't much of a friend if she fucked your man, huh?" Deacon laughed. "Marcus, you know about friends, right? What one won't do, the other one always will."

Marcus reached over the seat and tapped Deacon's fist with his. "I know that's right."

Alicia cut her eyes at Deacon. The attraction that she had for him at first was gone, and the voice of reality swiftly took control. Something about his smugness turned her off. He acted as if he was all that, when here he was trying to get with her, knowing his baby mama was probably at home waiting for him. She was glad Lyric played him like she did. He was worthless, and she was sick of him already.

"You know what?" she said to Deacon. "You can let us off at the next block."

"What's wrong? I ain't mean to hurt your feelings. Look, I'm sorry, okay? Hey, why don't we go grab some breakfast and then get a room at the Clarion for the night and chill. Come on, what about it?"

"I'm game," Raven said, giggling.

"No, she's not. She's drunk. Just let us out and we'll be fine," Alicia told him.

"I can't believe your ass is tripping like this. I dropped damn near a hundred dollars buying drinks and shit for your ass, and now you gon' trip because you sweating your cheating-ass ex?" Deacon stopped the car, reaching over to open her door. "Get the fuck out. I thought you was cool as shit, but I see now you're one of those flaky-ass girls who's scared to have a good time."

Alicia got out of the truck and called out, "Come on, Raven."

Deacon looked at the back seat and asked, "What the fuck you gon' do? You partying or what?"

Raven looked at Deacon then Alicia then Marcus. "Fuck that. I'm partying."

"No, she's getting out." Alicia opened the back door and leaned in. "Raven, don't be stupid. There's no way in hell either one of us is going with them. Get your drunk ass out the truck before I pull you out."

Raven momentarily sobered and looked at Alicia. She sucked her teeth then slid out of the truck, nearly falling. Alicia caught her before she landed on the pavement.

"Let's roll, Marcus," Deacon said. "Close my door. And one day, when you grow the fuck up, maybe we can hang."

Alicia stood in silence, watching them drive away. She could not believe how much of an asshole Deacon Carver was. The two girls began walking toward the subway station, and Alicia thought of how six months ago, her life was damn near perfect. Now she wondered if it was even worth living.

8

Lyric was in love. That was the only explanation she could think of the changes in her mindset lately. Jeremiah was the first thing she thought of when she woke up, and the last thought on her mind when she went to bed at night. He was polite, well-spoken, informative, humorous, humble and outgoing. The thought of cheating on him hadn't even crossed he mind in the few weeks they had been seeing each other, which was a first for her. She had never been faithful to just one man.

They were standing in line at the movies, holding hands, and she couldn't think of any other place in the world that she wanted to be at that moment.

"What are you thinking about?" he asked, brushing a piece of hair from her face.

"How chill this is. I haven't gone out on this many dates since high school. It's like we're a real couple." She shrugged.

"We are a couple, aren't we? I mean, I thought that's what we were. Oh, you want me to formally ask you to go steady? Is that it?" he teased, kissing her neck. She couldn't help giggling.

"Yeah, that's it. Did you just assume that I was your girlfriend because I let you take me to dinner and the movies a few times? I don't think so."

"Okay, my bad. Lyric, will you be my girlfriend?" He tilted his head and pleaded.

"Uh, let me think about it. What do I get if I say yes?"

"Probable more than you can handle," he said with a smile.

"I think that's the other way around." She laughed. He began playing with the charms on her bracelet, a habit she noticed he had picked up.

"Pick one," she told him.

"Pick one what?" he asked.

"A charm."

"Why?"

"Just pick one. Jeez, can't follow simple instructions." She pretended to be frustrated.

"Hmmm, there's so many." He lifted her arm and began examining them one by one. He finally pointed to the musical note with the diamonds that Deacon had given her.

"Ummm, you don't want that one. Pick another one," Lyric told him.

"Nope, I want that one. It's my favorite."

"But—"

"Don't tell me, some knucklehead that you used to mess with gave it to you. Don't matter. That's why I want it. You told me to pick one, and that's my choice. It's not where it came from, but where it's going."

Lyric could not believe how wonderful this man was. Suddenly, where the charm came from didn't matter. It wasn't about looking at her past mistakes. She now had a future to look forward to. She slipped the charm off the bracelet, placing it in Jeremiah's hand, then reached behind her neck and unfastened the gold rope chain she was wearing. She slid the charm on it.

"Turn around," she told Jeremiah. Her hands were shaking with nervousness as she fastened the chain around his neck. "There."

He turned and looked at her, his face beaming with pride.

"What's up, Lyric?"

Lyric turned to see Curtis and his girlfriend standing in line behind them. For a moment, her heart began beating fast. *What the hell are you panicking for, fool?* She asked herself. *For once, you're with your own man and not anyone else's. Chill the hell out.*

"Hi, Curtis. Nice to see you," she said calmly, as if he was just any guy saying hello to her, not someone she'd messed around with.

"This is my girl, Renee. Renee, this is Lyric," Curtis said.

Lyric reached her hand out, but Renee didn't budge. The two women stared eye to eye, the tension thick and obvious.

"How you doing? I'm Jeremiah. You play basketball for NYU, right?" Jeremiah broke the tension and shook Curtis' hand.

"Yeah, man." Curtis smiled, obviously still uncomfortable.

"You guys had a nice squad this year."

"Excuse me. I'll be right back, sweetheart," Lyric told Jeremiah. She walked inside the theatre and located the restroom, entered the stall and tried to calm down. She could not believe that bitch tried to disrespect her.

Who the hell does she think she is? She better be glad I ain't swing on her.

She came out of the stall and found Renee standing near the sinks. Lyric's body tensed and she swallowed hard. She could feel Renee staring as she washed and dried her hands.

"Is there a problem?" Lyric asked, reaching into her Coach clutch and taking out her lipstick. Her eyes stayed on Renee's reflection in the mirror, making sure the girl wasn't about to jump her. Another girl walked out of the stall and paused, probably waiting to see if something was going to happen between these two.

"Actually, there is a problem. You."

"I beg your pardon?" Lyric turned to face Renee. She was taller than Lyric, but not as thick. Lyric figured she could flip this lightweight in less than ten seconds without a second thought.

"Look, I know all about you fucking Curtis and winding up pregnant. That shows how stupid and trifling both of you are for not being careful, but at least you were smart enough to get rid of it. I just want you to know that I know, and I'm still here. If that doesn't show how much I love him, I don't know what will. So, if you please stay the fuck away from him, I would appreciate it." She tossed her long hair over her shoulder and folded her arms.

"Bitch, please. I don't want his ass. If I did, I would take him. As you can see, I have my own man." Lyric put the lipstick back in her bag and placed it on the counter.

"Which *is* kind of strange for you. Usually you're sneaking around with everyone else's. Your reputation as the Cash and More whore is well known, Lyric."

Lyric took a step toward Renee, who didn't even flinch. Their silent observer gasped as Lyric reached for Renee's throat. The girl still didn't so much as blink as Lyric stared into her eyes, both women breathing hard.

"This is exactly what I expected from you. You think Curtis or anyone else would be surprised that you beat me up in the bathroom? I wonder how your so-called man would feel if I walked out all bloodied and bruised. He probably knows you don't have any class either."

236

"Shut up! Shut up! You don't know shit about me. You're just pissed because I gave Curtis what you wouldn't—some good pussy."

"You're absolutely right, but he's still with *me*, isn't he? I'm still the woman he came to, begging for forgiveness, because he loves me. Loved me enough to tell me the truth about you and him. You can sleep with every man you meet. I don't give a shit, because I can at least say I have one thing you'll never have."

Lyric dropped her grip. "What? Curtis's weak-dick, non-fucking ass?"

"Nope. Love. Something you'll never experience." Renee eased past and walked out the door, leaving Lyric standing silent. She felt the sting of Renee's words as she stared at her reflection in the mirror. The girl who had been watching them finally left, leaving Lyric alone in the bathroom. She reapplied her lipstick and was surprised to see tears forming in her eyes.

Don't you dare cry. You're stronger than that. She was just pissed that Curtis gave you some attention. Get your ass together, go back out there with Jeremiah and enjoy yourself.

She dabbed the corners of her eyes and took a deep breath. When she left the bathroom, she smiled at the sight of Jeremiah waiting for her by the door.

"Everything okay?" he asked.

"Everything's great," she answered as he took her hand in his. She saw her charm hanging around his neck and his smile made her warm inside.

That bitch doesn't know what she's talking about. I'm experiencing love right now, she thought as they entered the theatre.

237

9

Alicia was hung over. Her head hurt so badly that she could hardly lift it off the pillow. She opened her eyes and shut them tight, blinded by the sunlight coming through her window. Someone was moving in her room, but she couldn't open her eyes again to see who it was. She rolled on her back and covered her face with her pillow, moaning because her head was throbbing.

"Damn, you must've had a hellified night, girl," She heard Jeremiah laughing. She should have known it was him. Her mother always went grocery shopping first thing Saturday mornings.

"What are you doing in here? Get out," she groaned. She could hear him fumbling on her dresser and it was beginning to irritate her. "Jeremiah, please get out."

"I am. I just need to borrow your long rope. The one I gave you for your birthday. Where is it?"

"How are you gonna give me a gift and ask for it back?" She tried opening her eyes one at a time to see if that made a difference. It didn't.

"I'm not taking it back. I said I was borrowing it. There's a difference."

"Can you close those blinds for me?" she wimpered.

"You didn't say the magic word," he teased.

"Please, Jeremiah. Damn! Close the blinds. You play too much."

She could feel the brightness of the room dim and once again tried to see. This time, her eyes opened. "What time is it?"

"Almost one. Where's the chain?"

"It's in that silver box on the corner of the dresser. Since when do you wear jewelry anyway?"

"Don't worry about all that. I found it. Thanks," he told her then walked out of her room.

She slowly sat up, praying she didn't fall out. She couldn't believe she was hung over again. Until recently, she rarely drank at all. Her clothes were scattered all over the floor, and she was dressed in only her underwear. She grabbed a T-shirt from her drawer and slipped it over her head. Pulling herself together, she tried to remember what happened the night before. It was all coming back to her, and it was not a pretty picture.

She reached for her cell and dialed Raven's number. There was no answer. The house phone rang then stopped. Her brother's laughter drifted down the hall, and his obvious happiness added to her nausea. There was something up with him, but she was in no shape to be Inspector Gadget and find out what it was.

She lay back on her bed and was damn near startled to death when his voice boomed her name. "Alicia! What the hell were you doing last night?"

"What are you talking about? I went out. And why are you screaming?"

"I ain't screaming yet. That was Mack calling to check on you. He said you left the club, drunk, barely able to walk. What the hell is that all about?"

Suddenly, her anger gave her enough energy to sit up. "What? Oh, hell naw. First of all, my daddy is dead, so you and Mack need to step off. I think that's what everyone's problem around here is. You don't realize that I'm grown and I don't need anybody's permission to do shit." She knew he was surprised by her cursing, a habit she had picked up recently. Hanging out with Raven and her girls these past few weeks had added a little more flavor to her vocabulary. It had also resulted in her waking up with hangovers almost daily.

"You need to start acting like you grown then. You out with Raven acting like a bunch of chicken heads, getting drunk, and now your mouth is just foul!" he yelled.

"Jeremiah, please. My mouth ain't no worse than yours,"

"Whatever, Alicia. You'd better be glad that my friends care enough to check on your ass. And since when do you hang out with Raven?"

"Since when is who I hang out with your business?"

"It's a big deal when you start doing stupid stuff like being so drunk that you stumbling out the club. You ain't never been one to act like this. What's going on with you? Look, I know you're grown. All I'm saying is you gotta be careful. Raven is not the type of person you should be hanging out with."

239

"So, now you wanna choose my friends. Wasn't she good enough for you to marry?" Alicia questioned her brother. She hated when Jeremiah tried to pull this big brother role with her.

"But I didn't marry her. Doesn't that tell you something?" He shook his head at her. "You're right, you're grown. Do what you wanna do."

"Jeremiah, wait! What's that around your neck?"

"It's a charm, a music note. That's why I needed your chain. It's longer than the one it came on."

Alicia looked at the familiar charm and heat began to rise in her body. There was no way in hell her brother was dating Lyric Crenshaw. This could not be happening to her. It had to be a coincidence. But when she looked again, the charm sparkled almost like it was taunting her. It could've only come from Lyric.

"Where did you get the charm?" she asked, afraid of the answer.

"From Lyric," he told her, grinning, "That's the girl I've been kicking it with. She's cool as hell, and her body is off the chain."

Kicking it with . . . She repeated his words in her head, trying to convince herself it meant he wasn't all that serious, he was just fucking her.

"I know her. We used to work together until she got fired for stealing. I hope you don't get caught up with her. She's a tramp," Alicia told him.

"What are you talking about, Alicia?" He frowned.

She smiled, knowing that Lyric must be falling for her brother if she gave him her charm. She would show that heifer. She told Jeremiah all about Lyric and the guys she had been with and the tricks she pulled, then she threw in some embellished stories for good measure.

"So, you need to take that shit from around your neck before everyone knows you're with the Cash and More whore."

"Wow, that's deep," her brother replied. "I guess if you didn't tell me all of this, I never would've known, huh?"

"Aren't you glad I did?"

"Not really. That's how I know I must really like this girl. Even after you telling me all of that, I still wanna kick it with her."

"Don't be stupid, Jeremiah."

"I won't, Alicia. Thanks for the insight, though." He chuckled and walked out of her room. Alicia flopped back down on her bed. The thought of Jeremiah with Lyric made her head hurt even worse.

If that bitch thinks for one moment that I'm gonna let her be with my brother, she's mistaken. This shit has gone too far.

"Where the hell are you?" Alicia asked when Raven finally called her after 3 o'clock that afternoon.

"I'm home. Shit, I was so fucked up when I woke up, I thought I was dying."

"Yeah, I feel you. I woke up this morning and couldn't open my eyes. Then Mack had to call and give a full report to Jeremiah," Alicia told her.

"Shit, Mack told him you were high? What did he say? Was he mad?"

"Hell no! He told him I was drunk, and that was enough to piss him off. If he thought I had been smoking, you know he would've lost his mind!"

"He is so full of shit. He used to like for me to get high because that's when I would put it on him like no other." Raven laughed.

"That is definitely T.M.I., Raven," Alicia told her.

"Oh, sorry."

"You're not gonna believe this, though. You'll never guess who he's been seeing."

"Girl, who?"

"Lyric Crenshaw."

"The freak that used to work with you?"

"Hell yeah. Do you know of any other Lyric?"

"Oh my God. Did you tell him she was a ho?"

"Yep. And get this—he didn't even care. His stupid ass is still gonna go out with her."

"You sound funny when you cuss. I'm not used to hearing you talk like that."

"Fuck you, Raven. What are we going to do? I refuse to have that bitch dating my brother. You know she's gonna try and play him like everyone else. And he's acting like it's no big deal. Like he wants to be played."

241

"Okay, so what do you wanna do? You wanna go jump her?"

"No. True enough, I wanna beat her ass, but that's not what I'ma do."

"What are you gonna do then?"

Alicia thought for a moment and then asked, "Can you get me in touch with Deacon?"

"That asshole? Of course. Finding him is no problem. What do you need him for?"

"I need to put a bug in his ear, that's all." Alicia had a plan to teach Ms. Lyric a lesson.

Raven called back within twenty minutes with the number. Alicia picked up her cell phone and dialed, telling herself that what she was about to do was just the beginning.

"Yeah, who is this?" Deacon demanded without saying hello.

"Hey, it's me. Alicia," she answered.

"A—who?"

She rolled her eyes and repeated, "Alicia. You told me to call when I grew the fuck up, remember?"

"Oh yeah. Shorty from the club a while back. What's up?"

"I'm trying to see you. What's up with that?" Alicia said sexily into the phone. She was preparing for battle, and she knew that her game plan had to be tight if she planned on winning. If playing with the big dogs was what she had to do, then she was ready, willing and able to handle her business.

10

Lyric was shocked at what Jeremiah had just told her. She knew he looked familiar to her, but now she realized that it was because he and his sister looked alike. What were the chances that Alicia's brother would be the guy she met and fell for? However small those chances were, that was the reality of the situation, and it wasn't good. She knew from what Jeremiah was telling her that Alicia didn't want Lyric dating him, and she could understand why. She had actually bragged to the young girl about playing games with men. But she had changed. She really did care for Jeremiah.

Instead of thinking about how she was going to fuck Alicia up for lying on her, her mind was busy trying to think of how she was going to explain herself to Jeremiah in a way that he understood. As she tried to tell her side of the story, Musiq's voice bragged from the speakers, letting her know that the love he had would never change.

"I didn't know Alicia was your sister. She always talked about her brother being out to sea, but I thought he was in the Navy or something," she said, her voice barely above a whisper. They had driven to a secluded area near a lake and were sitting in his Montero. He told her he needed to talk to her, but this wasn't what she expected.

"So, I guess you don't wanna see me anymore, huh?"

"I didn't say that. I just told you what my sister said."

"And?"

"And what?"

"What the fuck do you mean 'and what'? You drove all the way out here, tell me this shit and then you're looking at me like I'm crazy. What? Do you want me to say she's lying? Well, guess what? I am the whore of the Cash and More. Well, I was, anyway. I used men the same way they use women. I did. I'll admit it. But now . . ." She stopped and turned away. Her eyes were burning and the tears threatening to fall.

Don't cry, don't cry, she told herself over and over, but her body disobeyed and she felt the wetness on her cheeks. She opened the door and jumped out of the SUV.

"Lyric, come on. We need to talk about this," he called to her. She kept walking, now wanting to get as far away from him as possible. She cursed herself for wearing four-inch heels, wishing she had on some Reeboks right about now.

She should have known this was going to happen. She knew karma was a bitch, and that was one reason she didn't get close to guys. Now she had fucked up and fallen in love, something she knew was dangerous.

She could hear Jeremiah getting closer, so she stopped and turned. "What do you want?"

"Why are you upset? Why the hell are you running?"

"Because I don't want to talk about this. There's no need. Alicia told you everything you need to know. I confessed. What more is there to talk about?"

"We can talk about us!"

"Us?"

"Look, I told you what Alicia told me because I wanted to be straight up with you. You told me a long time ago that you don't like to play games. Now, I didn't have to say shit to you about it, but I didn't feel like that was right. I came to you so we could talk and get it out in the open. But you're running away like a child. What for?"

Lyric didn't know why she was running. Maybe it was because for the first time in her life she was confronted face to face with the truth about herself. And what she saw wasn't pretty. Jeremiah was asking her to do something she never thought she would have to do—be honest.

"I'm not running away. It's just much to deal with right now, that's all. Look, can you just take me home?"

"Fine, let's go. You're right. I'm too much to deal with. Get in the truck," Jeremiah huffed. It was the first time she had seen him angry. He had a quiet demeanor, rather than an obvious furor.

They rode home in silence, which was exactly what Lyric wanted. She didn't want to talk because she knew the conversation could only lead to one conclusion: he didn't want to see her anymore.

He barely stopped the truck in front of her building before she got out and ran inside. She rushed into her bedroom and shut the door then peeked out the window. He was still sitting outside, his head leaning back on the headrest. She wanted to run back down and tell him that she was in love with him and despite what she had done in the past, it was him and only him that she wanted to be with now. But instead, she stared and cried and after a few moments, he pulled off.

For the first time in her life, Lyric felt lonely. She didn't have any girlfriends to talk to, and although she and her mom were cool, this just wasn't a conversation she could see them having. It was as if Alicia and Renee had both spoken a curse over her when they predicted she would never find love.

11

The next day, Lyric was sitting at the desk at the gym, talking with Conner about what took place the night before. His listening ears were just what she needed, and she found comfort as she poured out her heart. He didn't judge her at all. By the time she finished, she felt as if a load had been lifted, at least until she looked up and saw Deacon Carver, of all people, coming in with one of his boys. He was the last person in the world she ever thought would be walking through the doors of New York Fitness. Conner stopped mid-sentence to see what had drawn her attention.

"What's up, Lady Lyric?"

Lyric stood up and tried to conceal her true feelings about his presence. "Hey there, Deacon. What in the world are you doing here?"

"Alicia told me you were running things here at the gym. I came to shoot some hoops. I heard they be balling 'round here, and I wanted to show off my skills. I can't get no hug? I thought you'd be a little happier to see me."

Lyric laughed nervously. She was still trying to figure out how Alicia had talked to Deacon. Obviously, this girl was truly out to get her now.

"This is my job, Deacon. I can't be hugging you like that. I could get written up."

Conner came and stood next to her, his arms folded. "Do you gentlemen have a membership card?"

"Nope," Deacon said, walking closer, his six-foot-four body towering over Conner. "I don't think we need one, do we, Lady Lyric?"

"Uh, actually, you do," Lyric answered.

"What, you think we allow any riff-raff to come into our facility whenever they feel like it?" Conner asked. "This isn't the Y. We scrutinize our members closely."

"I'm quite sure Lyric will vouch for me and my boy here. She knows me very well. We're intimate friends from way back." Deacon smiled smugly. A chill went up her spine. She hadn't seen him since the day she got the money from him, and had hoped that would be the last. So much for keeping a low profile.

"I don't care how intimately you know her. She still can't make you a member," Conner said, looking Deacon up and down.

"Look here, you li'l faggot . . . "

"Deacon! Hold on now. You need to get up outta here with all that," Lyric interrupted.

The doors opened again, and Mack walked in. Lyric knew that Jeremiah wouldn't be far behind him. She knew she had better get control of the situation quickly before it erupted any further.

"I'm saying, all I wanted to do was shoot some ball. Now you're trying to get brand new on a brother cuz he ain't got a membership? That's some bullshit." Deacon was getting louder.

Mack, who had already passed the desk, paused then looked back at Lyric. She shook her head, hoping he would keep going. Her eyes followed his to the door, where Jeremiah was entering. She had decided that she would act like he was no big deal when she saw him today, but looking at him, her heart melted. She wanted to run over and kiss him, telling him how sorry she was for acting silly the night before. Instead, her attention was drawn back to Deacon, who had turned to see what she was looking at.

Deacon exclaimed, "I know that nigga ain't wearing the shit I bought for you, is he?"

Lyric glanced to see that indeed, her charm was hanging around Jeremiah's neck. Seeing it let her know that it wasn't over between them. She pleaded, "Deacon, please. This is my job. Don't do this."

"I ain't doing nothing. All I wanna do is shoot some ball. That's it." He grabbed her arm. "It's the least you could do to cover the four hundred dollars you didn't use for the intended purpose."

Conner told Jeremiah and Mack that he had everything under control and they should go on back. Jeremiah didn't obey. He went to step toward Lyric, but Deacon's boy stepped in front of him.

"That's their business, and you ain't got nothing to do with it," he said.

"That's my girl he got his hands on. If you think I'ma stand here and let him grab on her, you done lost your mind."

"Your girl? Yours, his and everybody else's. Hell, I coulda tapped that ass if I wanted to." The guy was laughing so hard he didn't see the fist that was about to connect with his face.

Lyric's heart began racing as Deacon released his hold on her and stepped to Jeremiah. She was afraid to think about what was about to go down.

"Oh, you think you're one of these tough motherfuckas, huh?" Deacon growled in Jeremiah's face.

"I know I can handle your bitch ass!" Jeremiah replied.

Lyric rushed between both men, warning Deacon to leave because Conner had already called the cops. She knew if there was one thing that would cause Deacon to flee, it was the thought of all his outstanding warrants.

"This is why we don't allow riff-raff in the club," Conner said, showing them the phone.

Deacon shoved past Lyric and grabbed his boy by the collar. "Let's get the fuck outta here!"

"Hell naw! I'ma fuck him up," the guy replied, glaring at Deacon as he wiped blood from the corner of his mouth.

"We'll deal with his ass later." Deacon continued yanking. He looked back at Jeremiah, telling him, "And hers too. You better beware and watch your back, ho!"

"Get out!" Lyric yelled before Jeremiah responded and things got heated again. She was relieved when they went out the door.

"It's okay, folks. Everything has been handled," she told the small crowd that had gathered.

"Go back to what you were doing, because it's nothing for your nosey asses to see," Conner called out, clapping his hands and guiding a few of the nosiest members over to the cardio workout area. Soon, the crowd dispersed, leaving Lyric and Jeremiah alone at the front desk.

"I'm sorry," she told him, unable to look in his eyes.

"It's cool," was his only reply. There was an uncomfortable silence then he mumbled that he would call her later.

She watched him go through the doors that led to the basketball court. She slumped down into her chair, no longer feeling any of the hope she'd had when she first saw the charm around his neck.

"Girl, you better perk up," Conner said when he came back to the desk.

"Why? My life is so fucked up right about now."

"What did he say?"

"He said he'd call me later."

"Then what's the problem? He said he would call you. But when he does call, you need to talk instead of brushing him off," Conner said. "Now is not the time for you to have a bitch attitude. It's time for you to be honest with both him and yourself."

"You're right," she said.

Later, Jeremiah walked by her desk as he was leaving. She called out, asking him to wait a minute.

He paused and looked at her. "What's up?"

She inhaled, willing herself to speak to him and deal with this mess. "I really need to talk to you."

"Okay, so talk."

"Not here. Alone."

He shrugged and replied, "What time do you get off tonight?"

"Nine."

"I'll pick you up out front," he said and walked away.

She began praying that she would say the right things to make him understand. She hoped he would give their relationship a second chance.

By the time the clock read 9 o'clock, her stomach was in a ball of knots. He had just pulled up when she walked outside. He got out and opened the door for her, a gesture that she had become accustomed to since she began dating him.

"Thank you," she said as she got in. She could smell his jasmine air freshener as she settled into the seat.

"So, where to? You hungry?" he asked as he pulled off.

She was, but knew she was too nervous to eat. "No, I'm not hungry."

He fumbled with his CD changer until the sound of jazz flowed through the speakers. "Well, is there anywhere in particular you wanna go?"

It was times like this that she wished she had her own place. "Not really. We can go back to where we were last night. That's cool."

He obliged, and soon they were back at the secluded area. He cut the engine and turned the radio down then turned to face her. "So, talk."

She stared at him, trying to remember the conversation she played out in her head, but none of it came to memory. "I guess I should start by apologizing for the drama this afternoon. I'm sorry that all that went down."

"You don't have to apologize for that. There's no need," he replied. She wanted to read something in his face, but it was blank. Was he angry or just didn't give a damn? She started to just say fuck it and ask him to take her home, but she refused to go out like a sucker twice in a row.

"Okay then, I also need to apologize for the way I acted last night . . . for running away."

"Yeah, that shit was foul. You do need to apologize for that."

"It's just that I'm really feeling you, Jeremiah, and I don't know, I got scared, I guess," she confessed.

"Scared of what?" He frowned.

"Scared of losing you. Scared of fucking up the one good thing I have going in my life right now. I've never been with anyone like you. You treat me like . . . like . . . "

"Like you deserve to be treated?"

"Better than I deserve to be treated, Jeremiah. That's what you don't understand. I've done a lot of messed up things without caring about anything or anyone but myself. I knew from the jump that I didn't deserve you, but for a moment, I thought that maybe I had been granted some sort of reprieve, and I was beginning to enjoy being a good girl for a change. Then you told me what Alicia said, and I knew that it was over."

Lyric didn't even try to hold the tears back this time. "I became a master at playing games and using men to get what I want. I've lied about being pregnant and suckered guys out of loot to 'get rid of the problem.' I've been the one to get the hush money so the girlfriends won't find out about the one-night stands. I've even been the mistress. I've been playing the game since high school."

"Oh, so that's when you decided to become hardcore, huh?" Jeremiah asked.

"Yeah, that's when I became a real bitch. Before then, no one even paid me any attention. But as soon as I started not caring, I became the most desired and popular girl in school. It worked for me. No one fucked with me, either. By senior year, I had my boyfriend eating out the palm of my hand, and when I publicly let him know at a party that I didn't want him because his dick was too small, it wasn't pretty."

"Damn, Lyric, you were vicious."

Yeah, I was. See, I've been out there for years. I'm not good enough for you. I'm not good enough for any good man. I don't know why I even thought I was." The tears began flowing again and she hung her head.

"Lyric, don't cry. It's a'ight. Look at me," he said, putting his hand under her chin and lifting her face. "It don't matter. I never said that any of the shit Alicia told me even mattered."

"What do you mean it don't matter, Jeremiah? You're the one that brought it up."

"That's because I needed to hear what you had to say about it. I wanted to know how you felt. What if I told you what she said wasn't anything I hadn't already heard about you?" he asked, placing his hand over the charm he was still wearing. "Out of all the twelve thousand charms you wore, I picked this one because it's you. Now, it's my best bet that the guy who gave it to you thought the same thing, but I don't care about him or why he gave it to you. All that matters is I'm wearing it now. We all have a past. You have one, I have one. You think I'm a virgin or I'm the perfect man?"

"I ain't saying all that." Lyric laughed lightly.

"I'm sayin', I've had some fuck-ups in my past too. I don't think you're playing games with me or trying to get into my head. For what? I don't give you a reason to have to do that. I trust you."

"I wouldn't be so trusting if I were you, Jeremiah," she told him.

Then he said something she never expected to come out of his mouth. "Why not? I love you."

Her eyes widened, and she looked at him like he was a stranger. "What?"

"I said I love you," he repeated.

Lyric couldn't speak. She was too overcome with emotion to say anything. She stared into his eyes to make sure he wasn't playing some cruel joke, and when she saw the sincerity, she kissed him with enough passion that he knew she felt the same way.

12

It was after 1:00 in the morning, and Alicia was on the phone with Raven when Jeremiah walked through the door. She wanted to ask him about Lyric, but she didn't want to seem obvious. She imagined Deacon had gone to the gym and caused a scene, resulting in Alicia being fired once again. She wished she could've been a fly on the wall to see Lyric's face when Deacon walked through the door.

"What are you doing coming home this late?" she asked him, trying to speak low so she didn't wake her mother.

Jeremiah looked at her like she had lost her mind. "I know you're joking, right?"

"No, I'm not. Where have you been?"

"I'm not even going to justify that question with an answer. What did you tell me the other night? Oh yeah, your daddy is dead. Well, so is mine."

"Where has he been? What happened?" Raven screeched through the phone.

"Let me call you back," Alicia said and hung up the phone. She followed her brother into his room, where he was sitting on the side of his bed, taking off his shoes.

"So, did you talk to Lyric today?"

"Why are you all in my business? Does it matter?"

Alicia leaned on his doorpost, her arms folded. "Hell yeah, it matters! Do you realize that she's just gonna use you to get what she wants and then kick your ass to the curb? Is that what you want?"

He still didn't answer. He just sat with a smug look on his face and she was becoming irritated. "Fine then. You know what? I don't give a damn what you do, Jeremiah."

"Good," he told her.

"You know what? You deserve each other. She's trifling and you're stupid as hell," she said and stormed out of his room. She didn't understand what type of hold Lyric had placed on her brother, but his nose was so damn open she could damn near see his brain.

As she sat her in her room fuming about her brother's stupidity, her cell phone began ringing. She was surprised to see Omar's number flashing on the caller ID. She hadn't heard from him in so long, and now he was calling in the middle of the night.

"What?" she asked without saying hello.

"You know, I was telling myself that I had to be a damn fool for calling your ass, but I did anyway. What's up?" he asked.

"Nothing. What do you want?" As much as she missed Omar and loved hearing his voice, he was the last person she wanted to talk to right now. His call reminded her of the power Lyric seemed to have over men, including him. Even he had fallen victim to the games she played, and it cost them their relationship.

"I was calling to check on you. You've been on my mind a lot lately."

"I'm cool. Believe it or not, I was just sitting here thinking about you too."

"Really?" She could hear the delight in Omar's voice and it irritated her.

"Yeah. Guess who Jeremiah's fucking? Lyric. You remember Lyric, don't you? You fucked her too. Now you and my brother have something else in common other than me. Neat, huh?" She laughed sarcastically. Alicia knew she was being evil, but she didn't give a damn.

"Alicia, you really got some issues going on in your life right now. It's like you're turning into someone I don't even know anymore."

"Why? Because I speak the truth?"

"This was a bad idea. I don't know why I even bothered." Omar hung up on her.

Cheatin' bastard. He makes me so sick. How dare he call me like he really gives a damn? If he cared that much, his ass wouldn't have been with Lyric.

She heard Jeremiah talking on the phone and slammed her door shut. There had to be another way to get rid of Lyric's ass, and she was going to find it.

13

The smell of garlic filled the house, and the clatter of pots and pans rang from the kitchen. Alicia knew her mother was making lasagna the moment she walked inside. Her stomach began to rumble instantly. Jeremiah was home. Music was blaring from his room.

"Ma!" she called, tossing her purse on the sofa. "I'm home."

"Oh hey, sweetie. I thought you were going out to the movies tonight." Mrs. Woods walked over and kissed her on the cheek.

"Raven got called in to work, so we couldn't go. It smells good in here," Alicia told her.

"I know it does. Oh, the bread. I gotta go take it out of the oven." Her mom hurried back into the kitchen.

The doorbell rang. Alicia walked over and opened the door, shocked by who stood on the other side. Their eyes met and her body stiffened. "Lyric."

"Alicia," Lyric said softly, a smile playing at the corner of her mouth.

"What the hell are you doing here?" Alicia asked as she held the door.

"I was invited to dinner." Lyric said without any hint of attitude in her voice. She was trying to keep the peace, but Alicia certainly wasn't.

"Not at this house," Alicia flared.

There is no way this is happening, she told herself. *No way in the world is this bitch standing at my door.*

"Alicia, did you answer the door?" Mrs. Woods asked as she entered the room.

"Alicia, what are you doing here? I thought you were going out tonight." Jeremiah pushed her aside and ushered Lyric into the room. He hugged her and kissed her forehead. "Hey, baby."

Alicia was so angry. She stood before her brother and demanded, "I know she's not coming into this house!"

"Alicia, you need to stop tripping," he told her. Then he turned to Lyric and said apologetically, "I didn't know she was gonna be home tonight."

"That's none of her trick-ass business!" Alicia exclaimed. "I live here, and I can come home when I feel like it."

"Alicia Danielle Woods! Apologize to your brother's guest right now," her mother demanded.

"No, I won't. And she'd better get the hell out of my house before I kick her ass!" Alicia shouted, taking a step toward Lyric.

Jeremiah stepped in front of her. "That ain't gon' happen. Calm down right now. And you need to stop disrespecting Mama like that. Have you lost your mind?"

"No, I haven't. Do you know who this is, Ma? This is the biggest whore in New York. Of all the women for you to get with, you have to fall for the most trifling, gold-digging, shiestiest tramp you could find?"

"You know what?" Lyric finally spoke up. "I don't know what's going on with you, Alicia, but I don't have to stand here and take this. I thought we were cool when we worked together—"

"Oh, is that why you took it upon yourself to step to my man, because we were so cool?" Alicia laughed sarcastically. "Oh no, maybe it was because Omar was just that—a man. And you were right, he was weak enough to fall for your little game. But my brother ain't that stupid. If you think for one second that you're gonna trick him out of some money with your little bullshit ploys, think again."

"Now you're really tripping because I haven't been anywhere near Omar." Lyric tried to keep her composure. "And as far as your brother is concerned, I love him."

"Oh God, don't go there. Please don't go there. You don't know shit about love."

"That's enough, Alicia! You need to go somewhere and get yourself together," her mother stated. By the sound of her voice, Alicia knew she was at her limit. Still, she knew if anyone could see Lyric for who she really was, it Mama.

"Fine, Mama." Alicia smirked and took a step back.

"Lyric, I would like to apologize for my daughter's behavior. I don't know what's going on between you two, but I do know that you are Jeremiah's guest and don't deserve to be verbally assaulted when you walk through the door."

Alicia's mouth fell open. She could not believe her mother was siding with Lyric.

"No apology needed, Mrs. Woods. I didn't know that Jeremiah was Alicia's sister, and I swear I don't know what she's talking about as far as Omar is concerned," Lyric replied.

Alicia couldn't take anymore. "I don't believe this shit," she said then stormed into her bedroom.

"I think I'd better leave," Lyric said.

"No, you don't have to leave," Jeremiah told her, grabbing her hand. "I can handle Alicia."

"He's right. We would still like you to stay for dinner," Mrs. Woods added.

"No, I'll take a rain check. It was nice meeting you, Mrs. Woods. You have a wonderful son and an awesome daughter. They are both remarkable people, and you should be commended. You did a great job raising them," she said, opening the door.

"Thank you, Lyric. I appreciate that." Mrs. Woods smiled. "Jeremiah, don't worry about the food. I'll put it away. You go ahead and try to enjoy the rest of your evening."

Jeremiah kissed her and followed Lyric out the door. Neither said anything as they walked down the street. After a while, he took his hand in hers and she looked at him.

"You don't have to walk me home. You should go back to talk to your sister."

"No, I should be right here with you. Her issues are not my issues," he told her.

"And what issues do you have? How to deal with dating the biggest whore in New York?" Lyric tried to smile, but the tears still formed in her eyes. "While we were working in the office, I shared a lot of things I did with Alicia. Things I'm not proud of. She pretty much knows all my dirty little secrets. I don't blame her for being pissed. Your past always comes back to haunt you."

"The only way it haunts you is if you didn't learn a lesson from it and you repeat the same mistakes over and over again." He hugged her close.

"There you go being the great philosopher again." She laughed and wiped her eyes.

"Did you mean what you said?"

"What?"

"You told my sister that you loved me, but you've never said it to me."

"Don't ask a crazy question like that, Jeremiah." Lyric posed with her hands on her hips. "You know I love you. I don't think that matters to your sister, though."

He swooped her up and swung her around. He kissed her softly on her lips and said, "If you love me, then that's all that matters."

She thought about all the things Alicia said to her. There was something about Alicia that had changed. She had a hardness about her that wasn't there before, and it bothered Lyric.

Back at the apartment, Mrs. Woods was yelling at Alicia. "How dare you disrespect my house like that?"

"What did you want me to do, Ma? Invite her in? She's a slut that uses men for money. That makes her a prostitute. You want someone like her in your house?"

"She's your brother's guest. He invited her here. He thought enough about her to introduce her to me. I don't care if she's the biggest pimp in New York. This is my house and you had no right to treat her that way. Do you realize the way you were talking to her? In front of me? You'd better get yourself together, young lady. I don't know where all this is coming from, but the road you're traveling down now is a dangerous one, and you're gonna find yourself one step away from being homeless. I mean that. You ain't as grown as you think you are!"

Alicia lay in her bed fuming. She was so mad that she wanted to vomit. Her mother had the audacity to scream at her about respecting guests in their home, but the last thing Lyric deserved was respect. Alicia was tempted to scream back at her mother, but her last bit of common sense stopped her.

Her brother had left with his whore, and she was glad. It gave her time to get her head together. She knew he would have a lot to say once he got home, and she wanted to be well rested for the argument that she knew would ensue. She promised herself that she wouldn't back down no matter what it took.

She heard the front door open and close, and listened as footsteps approached her door.

"It's open," she said and sat up when she heard a knock. Jeremiah walked in, closing the door behind him. "I'm warning you. Don't get loud, because Mama is not in the best of moods."

"I wonder why," he snarled, leaning against her dresser.

"Probably has something to do with the mess you left for her to clean up after you and your whore—I mean girlfriend left."

She watched as Jeremiah inhaled deeply. He told her, "You really are something, you know that? I can't believe how damn childish you acted tonight. I'll bet Mama's mood has something to do with your behaving like a fourth grader throwing a temper tantrum. You embarrassed all of us, including yourself."

"I didn't do shit but call your so-called girlfriend out. And for you to get mad at me for letting you know up front that she's a gold-digging whore, that's your problem. Let me ask you a question. If you found out I was dating a guy who was known as a womanizer, would you let me know? I mean honestly, would you tell me, or would you let me find out after I walked in on him and another woman in bed together?"

"I would tell you, but I think I would be a little more discreet about it, and I damn sure wouldn't do it in front of Mama. I don't have a problem with you telling me about Lyric's past indiscretions, which, by the way, she told me about a long time ago. I don't have a problem about you warning me or expressing anything you felt about her. It's not what you did, but the way you did it."

"I'm sorry, but when the woman that I caught Omar cheating with was standing on my doorstep, proper etiquette techniques were the furthest from my mind," she huffed.

"And you're sure about that, Alicia? Where is this whole idea coming from?"

"You think I'm lying? Forget it. You really are stupid," she told him. Her eyes fell on the necklace he was wearing. "You're still wearing her charm. Isn't that sweet? Letting all the world know that your whore has you on a leash. Do you even know who gave her that? I bet she didn't tell you it was a gift some nigga gave her for

259

having an imaginary abortion, huh? And you're around here wearing it with pride for all the world to see."

"You know what? I'm about to end this conversation now before I end up putting my hands on you. I will tell you this much—I love Lyric and she loves me. She makes me happy. You are my sister, and I love you too, but don't think for a minute that I'm gonna let you keep disrespecting her. So, you'd better get that shit under control right now."

Without a moment's hesitation, Alicia stood up and snatched the chain off her brother's neck. She slid the charm off and threw it at him. He caught it before it hit the floor, then he lurched at her. She flinched, but he stopped himself.

Staring him dead in the eyes, she told him, "You deserve everything you get. And when she plays you like she plays all the other ones, I'm going to be laughing just as hard as she is. Get the hell out of my room."

Jeremiah cut his eyes at her and left without responding. She looked at the broken chain in the palm of her hand then looked into the mirror. She was surprised to see that she was crying. She and her brother had never fought before.

This is all her fault. She thinks she got him like that . . . fine. But I can fight fire with fire. Lyric Crenshaw better get ready, because this time, it really is war. I don't play when it comes to my blood.

14

As she walked down the street, Lyric tried calling Jeremiah. His voicemail picked up immediately. She called his house, but there was no answer. They were supposed to get together later that night, so she was surprised that she couldn't reach him. She debated whether she should go over and see for herself if he was okay, but the thought of running into Alicia and beating her ass discouraged her from doing so. After taking a long hot shower and climbing into bed, Lyric tried to call again. She thought that the third time was a charm when she heard the phone pick up.

There was a brief silence and then a raspy, female voice said, "Hello."

Lyric looked at her phone to make sure she dialed the right number. After verifying that she had, she placed the phone back to her ear and said, "Hello. May I speak to Jeremiah, please?"

"He's asleep right now. Let me see if I can roll over and wake him up," the woman told her. Lyric could hear movement in the background and then, "Jeremiah, sweetie, the phone's for you."

She heard Jeremiah moaning, "Come on, Raven. I'm tired. Get off me."

Lyric told herself to remain calm as she continued to listen.

"But baby, your cell phone," the girl sang. "Jeremiah . . . Jeremiah . . . I'm sorry, girl, he's not waking up. You know how they get after you put it on 'em," she said, giggling.

Lyric was far from being amused, but she wasn't going to take it out on this girl. It was Jeremiah who would feel her wrath. "Okay, thanks," she told Raven.

"Wait! Who should I tell him called?"

"This is Lyric."

"Oh, the girl from the gym. Well, did you want to leave a message?"

"No, no message," Lyric answered then hung up, steaming with anger. She didn't know who to be angrier at, Jeremiah, for being a typical male and running to another woman, or herself, for caring that he did so. Either way, she was going to give him a piece of her

261

mind. She jumped out of bed and threw on some jeans and a tank top. She was on a mission to find his ass.

When she turned the block, Lyric spotted Alicia leaving her building with another girl. She waited until they were far enough down the street before she continued. She spotted Jeremiah's grey Montero Sport parked in front and knew that he had made it home.

The first thought that came to her mind was to wonder if the woman was still there with Jeremiah. As if broken out of a trance that she had been in for the last few months, the old Lyric jumped into her head.

I don't give a damn if she's in there going down on him in front of his mama. I got some words for Jeremiah's ass and that trick. No one else is going to stop me from speaking my peace about this bullshit.

She walked up to the door and knocked loudly. No one answered right away, but she wasn't giving up until someone came to the door. She started pounding.

She heard Jeremiah growl, "A'ight, a'ight. I'm coming. Who is it?"

"It's Lyric," she replied. There was a pause, and she wondered if he was going to open the door. If not, she planned on kicking the shit out of it until it fell off the hinges. Slowly, it opened and she found herself looking into his face. His lips were so sexy and her first reaction was to kiss him, but she told herself to focus. She still couldn't help admiring his chiseled body, wearing nothing but a pair of boxers and a wife-beater.

He took a step back, stretching, and said, "Come in. You can have a seat."

"I'll stand, thank you. I know you have company."

"Company? I was asleep until I heard you knock. Alicia and her friend were here for a while, but they dipped. Moms is working the night shift this week."

"I called your phone and some girl answered, Jeremiah. She tried to wake you up but you were too tired. She said she had just finished putting it on you. Personally, that's your business, and I—"

"Hold on, hold on before you even go any further, because I don't know what the hell you're talking about. I came home, took a shower, grabbed some aspirin because my damn head was hurting, and I laid the fuck down."

"I know I'm not crazy, Jeremiah. I called your phone and some Raven chick was in the bed with you."

"Raven? In bed with me? You got to be crazy if you think I'd be in bed with Raven. And my damn phone ain't rang all night." He stood up and walked out of the room, leaving her standing.

Oh, hell no. I know he ain't walk out while I'm talking to him! She went to follow him, but by the time she made it to the hallway, he was headed back, now wearing a shirt and some sneakers.

"Look, my phone ain't even on. Look at it!" He thrust the phone in her hand. She looked at the silver object and saw that there was nothing lit on the screen.

"Like you couldn't have just turned it off when you were in your room. Please, Jeremiah. You know what? This isn't worth the energy it's taking to talk about this."

Jeremiah took the phone from her hand and flipped it open. He pushed the power button then passed it back to her. "Check the history. I ain't got nothing to hide."

Lyric looked at the phone, which now displayed a red rose and the name Rae-Love. She shook her head. "You really are a piece of work. This is Raven's phone, asshole."

He took the phone from her hand and looked at it in amazement. "What the fuck? This ain't even my phone! Lyric, I don't know what the hell is going on around here, but I ain't got nothing to do with it."

"Whatever, Jeremiah. I can't believe I fell for your bullshit. I should've known you were just like every other man. It's all good, though."

"Lyric, I was gonna call you after I lay down for a minute, but I fell asleep." He sat back down. He began dialing numbers and suddenly they heard his distinct 50 Cent ring tone faintly ringing outside the door. He hopped up and opened the door.

"Boy, you scared me!" Alicia shrieked.

"Your ass needs to be scared. Where the fuck is my phone?" He brushed past her and stood before Raven, who was smiling wickedly.

"I don't know where your phone is, Jeremiah."

"She's lying. We heard it ring when we just called it." Lyric stepped forward.

"What the hell are you doing here?" Alicia hissed.

"Where the hell is my phone, Raven? And I ain't playing, either. Don't fuck with me, because I ain't in the mood." Jeremiah reached out and grabbed Raven's arm, reaching for the Baby Phat bag dangling from her shoulder.

"Ouch! Let me go!" Raven whined. He snatched the bag and stuffed his hand inside, removing a cell phone identical to the one that was now lying on the coffee table.

"Y'all play too damn much!" He shoved Raven out of his way and turned back to Alicia. "How the fuck you gon' take my phone? I can't believe you!"

"Get over it." Alicia shrugged, cutting her eyes at Lyric.

"And then you playing on my phone like you're in the damn eighth grade," he snapped at Raven. "I can't even deal with this shit."

Alicia's eyes widened. None of this was working out like she planned. When Jeremiah arrived home complaining about a headache, she felt bad. But then she realized that this could be to her advantage. She heard the shower running and called Raven to come over immediately.

When Jeremiah came out of the bathroom, Alicia gave him some Vicodin, telling him it was aspirin. She made sure he took the pills before he climbed into bed. When Raven arrived, they came up with the perfect scheme. Knowing Lyric would call Jeremiah, Raven waited in his room and answered the phone. Groggy from the narcotic he had taken earlier, he did just as they knew he would and refused to take the phone. After Lyric hung up, they switched the phones just in case she called back. What they didn't expect was for her to be waiting in the living room when they returned.

"Jeremiah, don't be stupid," Raven quipped.

"Don't go there with me. I'm getting ready to move out because I can't take being around you two immature broads anymore," Jeremiah spat. He grabbed his keys off the table and said, "Come on, Lyric. I'll drive you home."

Just as she was about to move, Alicia jumped in front of Lyric. "See what you're doing? Why don't you just leave him the fuck alone? Go play somebody else."

"No, why don't you just leave me the fuck alone? I keep telling you I'm not trying to play your brother. I wouldn't do him like that. Hell, I wouldn't do you like that. You're my friend and—"

"Puh-leeze! I am not your friend, and don't ever address me as that again."

"She has more people to choose from than a whore like you," Raven added.

"I know you ain't calling nobody a whore!" Jeremiah huffed. "Both of you need to just shut up. Let's roll."

He reached for Lyric and she placed her hand in his. She brushed by both women, who stood in angry silence. Jeremiah's behavior let them know there was nothing they could say that would change his mind about Lyric.

"That was a trip," Raven finally said after they were gone. "I can't believe Jeremiah said he's moving out. Do you think he's for real?"

"I don't know. But I see that Ms. Lyric is going harder than I thought. But that's okay. That's just how much harder she's gonna fall."

"Alicia, I really think she cares about him," Raven commented quietly.

"I don't give a damn how she feels. This ain't about her. It's about payback."

Outside, Lyric and Jeremiah decided to walk. All the way to her building, he kept apologizing for his sister's and Raven's behavior, but she told him there was no need. The sky was clear, and the world seemed lit up by the stars. She prayed that the roof of her building would be vacant and they would be able to be alone there to talk. She led him up the steps and opened the door leading outside, glad there was no one in sight. Jeremiah walked over to a lawn chair and sat down, pulling her into his lap.

To say that Lyric was horny would be an understatement. She wanted Jeremiah so bad at times, she thought she would die. She had no doubt in her mind that he wanted her. She could see the desire in his eyes when he looked at her, and felt his arousal when they became lost in their kisses. His touch caused a shiver to go up her spine.

"You cold?" he whispered. She shook her head. She knew she was ready and had been for awhile. But she was afraid. She had never felt this close to a man before, and although Jeremiah hadn't given her any indication that he would hurt her, she didn't know if ultimately, he was like the rest of them. She had always given her body first, but never her heart. This time, with Jeremiah, she had given her heart and had no clue what would happen if she gave him her body. The uncertainty was disturbing.

He placed his hand over Lyric's chest. She reached down and brought it to her lips, kissing it gently. She continued to his wrist, all the way up his arm until she was nibbling on his neck She felt his hand teasing the small of her back, and she felt the heat igniting within her body. She kissed him, taking his tongue into her mouth while maneuvering her body against his.

His hand slipped under her skirt and she felt his fingers brush against her inner thigh. She began sucking on his lower lip, her hands quickly reaching between their bodies until she felt his hardness. Without hesitation, she unfastened his khaki shorts and released his swollen manhood. His fingers had now made their way under the satin G-string she was wearing, and she rocked back and forth, enjoying the sensation. She looked deep into his eyes and quickly snatched his hand away.

"What's wrong?" he asked, frowning.

"Where's your friend?"

"What friend?"

She smiled, whispering into his ear, "The one you keep in your pocket for protection."

"Oh, that friend." He grinned. He leaned forward, fumbling in his pocket, and retrieved the small package.

She helped him put it on, then before he could make another move, she began riding him. His eyes widened and she couldn't tell if it was in ecstasy or surprise. She found her rhythm and stared as she moved back and forth, up and down, all at the same time.

"Damn, I been waiting for this a long time," she whispered as her tongue played with this earlobe. He sucked on her collarbone and she began grinding faster and faster.

"Wait. I want you to lay down," he told her.

She shook her head and continued, letting him know that she was in control. When he told her he was about to come, she told him, "No you're not. Not yet," and continued her journey. He felt so good inside her that she had to tell herself to calm down and enjoy the moment.

She tightened her muscles around him as she felt deep spasms coming from within. Neither one said a word as they climaxed simultaneously. When she knew it was over, she leaned into him and kissed his neck.

"I love you," she whispered.

"I love you too. This is definitely not what I pictured our first time together would be like, though."

"Me either." She laughed.

"But hell, this might have been better. I love spontaneity." He put his hands on her waist.

"I guess that means you enjoyed it?"

"Enjoyed is an understatement."

15

"Is your brother here?"

Alicia leaned against the door frame, smiling. "Nope, he's not. He and the tramp left about thirty minutes ago."

Mack laughed. "You're crazy."

"I think you've got that wrong. He's the crazy one, but I ain't going there. You wanna come in?"

"Naw. Just tell him to call me. I been trying to hit him on his cell, but I keep getting his voicemail. I saw his truck and thought he was here."

"Sorry, but I'll give him the message," she replied, as she checked him out and noticed he wasn't a bad-looking guy. He was about five-seven, and he was on the slim side. His skin was the color of sand, and he wore his dreads short and neat. He and Jeremiah had become really good friends over the past few years, but she had never looked at him that way.

"I'd appreciate it," he told her.

"You sure you don't wanna come in and wait?" she asked flirtatiously.

He gave her a look that told her if he did come in, it wouldn't be just to wait on Jeremiah. "Naw, I'll holla at him later."

At that moment, Alicia decided Mack would be the perfect practice dummy. He had a quiet, unassuming manner, and she figured using him wouldn't be that difficult. He was one of Jeremiah's closest friends, and he would never do anything to disrespect her. She reminded herself up front that this was all a part of the game, and her goal was to get what she could and get out. If her conscience started bothering her about using him, she would just pretend she was Lyric. She would act the way she thought Lyric would act, say the things she believed Lyric would say, and soon she would begin to feel the things she knew Lyric felt when she was in the game.

Alicia even began dressing the way Lyric dressed. In no time, she had Mack eating out of the palm of her hand. He wined and dined her. He would buy her things at the mere mention of her desires. She not only owned a new laptop, Palm Pilot and iPod, but she got all that before she even gave him any pussy.

Surprisingly, Jeremiah didn't even mind that they were seeing each other. If she hadn't had her sights set on higher ground, she could've easily played Mack until she had her own ride, but she could tell he was getting caught up, and it was time to move on.

"Oh, so it's like that?" he asked when she told him she didn't want to see him anymore. She had been dodging his calls all afternoon, and now he had shown up at the rec center where she worked. It was time to cut him loose.

"Like what, Mack? I'm saying, I'm young and I really don't wanna be in a committed relationship right now. You understand that, right?"

"Naw, I don't. But, it's all good. You know, I never figured you to be like that, yo. I mean, I thought we were cool."

"We are cool, Mack. I like you, really. But I need some space right now. Look, I gotta get these kids. I'll call you."

"Don't even worry about it," he said and walked off.

He didn't realize he was her guinea pig and she was only using him to rehearse for the real deal. She had a bigger fish to fry. Her game was now tight, and she knew that she was ready to make her move when she realized she didn't feel any guilt about how she treated Mack.

16

Alicia sat at the table, sipping her Long Island Iced Tea. She had only been waiting a few minutes, but she checked her watch to make sure Tony was indeed late.

They were supposed to meet at 9 o'clock, and it was now six minutes after. She smiled, thinking of the attitude she planned on having with him when he finally arrived. She really didn't mind that he was late, but she'd never let him know that or he might try it a little more often. One thing she recently discovered was that men had to be kept on a short leash or they would indeed attempt to stray. Her collar was so tight around Tony's neck that he could barely breathe, but he seemed to enjoy it. Alicia felt empowered for a change, and she was damn sure gonna use it to her advantage.

She glanced up and saw him heading over to the table, a bouquet of flowers in hand.

"You're late," she told him as he leaned over and kissed her cheek.

"I know. I got held up a few minutes, that's all," he said, placing the flowers in front of her. The bouquet was beautiful and obviously expensive. She decided that was good enough to make up for the fact that he kept her waiting, so she lost her attitude.

"Thank you. Anything wrong?" She raised her eyebrow at him. "You seem preoccupied."

"No, I'm fine."

"Tony, if you need to talk, I'm here." She reached across the table and touched his hand. His eyes met hers.

"I know you are, sweetheart, and I appreciate that. I'm glad that I finally have someone to talk to."

"She doesn't talk to you? You don't talk?"

"No, she's too caught up in the television. She's so complacent with her life. That's one thing I admire about my daughter. She's always on the go, making moves and getting things done with her life. She's the one good thing that came out of this marriage." Tony's eyes lit up and a smile spread across his face.

"I can see that you love her very much . . . your daughter. Are you close to her?"

"I try to be. She's older now, of course. But she knows she still means the world to me. She'll always be Daddy's little girl."

"Lucky her," Alicia said with a smirk, biting her tongue before she said anything else.

"No, lucky me." He shook his head. "So, tell me, how was your day? Did you get enrolled in all your classes?"

"Yes, that's all taken care of. I can't wait until school starts back. It keeps me occupied."

"Oh, I can think of a few more things to keep you occupied if you're that bored," he said with a wink.

She laughed flirtatiously. "I don't think I could earn a Psychology degree that way, do you?"

"Maybe not, but you'll make one hell of a therapist, that's for sure." He laughed, his baritone voice climbing an octave.

His laugh was one of the things she enjoyed about him. Being as attractive as he was didn't hurt either. He reminded her of Quincy Jones with his dark, mysterious eyes that lit up when he smiled. That actually made approaching him that much easier.

Alicia had been checking Tony out for days before "accidentally" bumping into him one evening as he was leaving his job. She knew his schedule so well that she was beginning to think she had stalker mentality. When she saw him coming toward her that humid July evening, she took a chance of brushing up against him, spilling the bottle of water she was holding all over both of them, hoping she made it look like his fault. She batted her eyelashes and flashed enough cleavage to make sure she could hook him.

"I am so sorry," he apologized over and over as he helped her up off the sidewalk.

"No, it's okay. I really wasn't looking," she smiled, wiping at her breasts.

"Oh, your dress. You're soaked," he commented.

She looked down, glad that the chill from the water caused her nipples to protrude through the thin rayon fabric. When she saw that he noticed, she knew that she had her foot in the door.

"I'm fine. It's just water. But your tie is a little damp."

He looked down and laughed. "I guess neither one of us has to wash clothes tonight, huh?"

She giggled. "I guess not. Too bad I wasn't drinking a burger. I could stand to miss a few meals."

"Ridiculous. You're perfect." He looked her up and down.

"I bet you give your wife compliments like that all the time." She sighed, pointing at the gold band he wore on his left hand.

"Huh? Oh, yeah. My wife," he said, suddenly looking uncomfortable.

"Lucky woman." Alicia didn't let up for fear that she would lose her nerve. This was new territory, and she knew it was do or die time. "And I was about to ask you to join me in the laundromat so we could dry these wet clothes together." She looked straight into his eyes and gave him the most enticing look she could have imagined.

Alicia read the spark in his eye as he asked, "Is that so?"

"That's so. Well, I have to be going. I can't be standing here dripping wet in the middle of the sidewalk all day. Have a good one." She gave a quick wave and walked away.

"Hold up," he called from behind her.

She stopped mid-stride, proud of her victory. She posed with a hand on her hip, and waited a few seconds before turning around. "Yes?"

"I, uh . . . The least I can do is buy you another water. Better yet, how about I buy you a drink?" he stood before her and asked.

She pretended to be deep in thought about his sudden invitation. "Well, it is only a drink, right?"

They exchanged numbers and made plans to meet the following evening at a small bar. She made it a point to be interesting, attentive, intelligent, and anything else she thought he wanted her to be. But most of all, she knew she had to be enchanting. And four hours later, when they walked out of the bar hand in hand, she knew this wouldn't be as hard as she thought it would be.

Tony was hers, hook, line and sinker. They had fallen into a routine of sorts, talking on the phone several times a day, meeting for dinner twice a week and now, they had their overnight rendezvous.

The first time she slept with Tony, she was petrified. She didn't know what to expect from an older man. The only people she had ever been with in her life were Omar and Mack. But Tony had proven to be a gentle lover, taking the time to make sure she was satisfied and comfortable. He was different than Omar, but he was still a good lover, and sex with him was pleasurable.

"So, are we eating or just having drinks?" she asked him, licking her lips.

"What are you asking?" he replied, his eyes wide with excitement.

She leaned over and whispered into his ear, "Are you hungry for food or for me?"

Tony motioned for the waiter so he could pay for their drinks. He grabbed Alicia to him, placing her hand on his crotch under the table. "Does this answer your question?"

Outside the restaurant, he hailed a cab and directed the driver to the hotel room she knew he had already reserved. The rest of the night was spent fulfilling his desires and satisfying a few of her own.

After they made love, she felt his body rise from the bed. She looked over at the clock, which read 2:12. She knew that Tony made it a point to be home by 3:00, so she didn't even question his actions. He quickly showered and got dressed as she remained in the comfortable bed.

Before he left, he leaned over and whispered, "I love you. Your cab fare is on the nightstand. I'll talk to you tomorrow."

"Okay," she whispered, glad that she could now enjoy the huge bed by herself.

17

"Girl, I can't believe you're dating a married man." Raven snickered. They were in the mall and Alicia was picking out a sexy surprise for Tony in Victoria's Secret. He had called and told her that he was taking her away for the weekend, so she was excited.

"It's no big deal, Raven. He's just a man like all the rest of them."

"Only this one has a wife. Girl, what if she finds out? What will you do then?"

Alicia held up a black, see-through nightie with a matching G-string. "So what if she does? If she was handling her business at home then he wouldn't have a need to be with me. All I'm doing is taking advantage of the opportunity that was presented before me. I'm not trying to make him leave his wife. Hell, I want him to stay with her. That makes it easier on me. She has to do all the hard stuff for his ass: the cooking, the cleaning, the caretaking. So, all in all, I'm helping her ass out. I'm doing all the freaking. That's one less thing she has to worry about." Alicia laughed so hard that tears came to her eyes. She remembered the first time Lyric told her those same words.

"I know that's right. And I'll bet wifey dear damn sure ain't rocking nothing like that when he gets into bed. That is fierce." Raven touched the negligee Alicia was holding.

"Yeah, I'ma go ahead and get this for old Tony boy. I would get the red, but his ass might have a heart attack while we're gone if he sees me in that. Then how would I explain our being together?"

"You were the one that said you ain't care if you get caught. Hell, I say get them both. One for when you go to bed, and one for the next morning," Raven teased.

"Girl, with Tony, if I get it at night, then ain't no way I'm getting anymore until damn near twenty-four hours later. But who knows? His ass might've hooked himself up with the Viagra since it's a special weekend for us."

"You are crazy. I never in a million years thought I would hear Alicia Woods talking like this. And dating an older, married man on top of that. I always thought you would be all up under Omar's ass, then y'all would get married and have a bunch of kids. The perfect family."

"I probably would be chasing his no-good ass if I wouldn't have got hip to the game," Alicia told her, thinking she had once had the same vision for her future.

They walked to the register and she paid for her items. She looked at her watch and said, "We better get outta here. I gotta go pack."

Alicia was putting her things in an overnight bag when Jeremiah knocked. Her door was open, but he still waited in the doorway. She looked up and asked, "What do you want?"

"I want to talk to you," he replied. It had been a minute since they had said more than two words to each other. She had been spending less and less time at home now that she was dating Tony, but she knew Jeremiah was still looking for his own place. She also knew that he was still with Lyric, but she would deal with that bitch soon enough.

"So talk. Or were you waiting for a special invitation to come in?"

Jeremiah walked in and leaned on her bed. "You going somewhere?"

"Is it any of your business? Do I ask about where you and your trick—I mean Lyric go?" She didn't want to hurt her brother, but she just couldn't resist talking bad about Lyric every chance she got.

"Why did you do Mack like that?"

"Like what?"

"You dogged him. That's my boy. I ain't bitch about you seeing him because of that. If I would've known you were gonna use him, I would've told him you weren't worth it."

"I didn't treat him any different than another certain female would, and I ain't calling no names." She rolled her eyes at Jeremiah. "Mack just wasn't my style, that's all. He'll get over it."

"I didn't come in here to argue. I just wanted to let you know that I found a spot. It's not far from here, and I plan on moving next weekend."

"Good for you. Hooray," she told him sarcastically and went back to packing. Beneath her new tough exterior, she missed the closeness she once had with her brother, and she was sorry he was moving out.

"I also found out the ship is going out again, so I'll be gone by Labor Day."

Alicia stopped packing and looked at her brother. Even as much as they seemed to dislike one another at this point, she still hated the fact that he spent most of his life halfway around the world.

"How long will you be gone this time?" she asked, suddenly saddened by his announcement.

"Four to six months, maybe longer."

"Then why are you moving out? I mean, what's the big deal?"

"It's time for me to leave the nest and get my own space. Like I said, it's not far from here. Don't worry. You can still see me when I'm docked." He smiled.

She walked over and hugged him. "I'll miss you."

"No you won't. You'll miss having my life to cause drama in, that's all."

Her cell phone rang and she picked it up. It was Tony. She flipped it open and answered. "Hey, babe."

"Hey, your cab's on the way to get you. It should be downstairs in a minute," he told her.

Before he could say anything else, she heard the horn blowing, "It's here. I'll see you in a minute." She closed the phone and grabbed the rest of her things.

"Where are you going? Who's taking you?"

"I need my own space too, Jeremiah. And I got my own life to cause drama in now. I'll see you when I get back," she said with a shrug. "Peace."

"Be safe, Alicia," he said as she walked by.

"Don't worry. I will."

La Jill Hunt

18

Lyric was helping Jeremiah pick out furniture for his new apartment. She still felt uneasy about his decision to move out, especially when she knew his ship was scheduled to leave in a few weeks. From his actions, she could tell there was still tension between him and his sister.

"Are you sure this is a good idea, Jeremiah? I mean, you won't even be in your place that long and then you'll be leaving again. That doesn't even make sense. You could be saving that money," she said as she admired a charcoal leather living room set. "This is nice."

"Yeah, I like that." He looked at the price. "It's time for me to get a place of my own. Why doesn't anyone see that except Mack?"

"Because Mack doesn't have anywhere else to go. His family lives in Baltimore. Your family is here, and I know your mom is sad to death that you're leaving."

"Nope, she's not all that sad. She came bragging to me about changing my room into a sewing room now that I'm finally getting out. She ain't that upset. Believe me," he said with a laugh.

A salesman walked over, and they negotiated the price of the set Lyric commented on. Once Jeremiah and the salesman reached an agreement, he gave the address for delivery. They did the same with furniture he bought for the dining room and bedroom and a nice-sized television. He never made a decision without consulting Lyric for her opinion.

"You act like I'm gonna be living there," she said, looking at a picture that she thought would go perfect with his new living room.

"I want you to. I mean, you are part of the reason I'm doing all of this."

"Yeah right." She laughed. Something told her to turn around because he didn't laugh with her. Her heart raced with the possibility that he was serious. She looked at him and murmured, "Huh?"

"We need our own space. Just you and me. I want to spend the time I have left before the ship leaves with you. I need to be with you. So, I want this to be our home." Jeremiah walked over and held her. She didn't say anything, so he kept talking, "It's not like we'll

277

be shacking up. I'll be gone most of the time. But when I'm here, I want to be with you in our home. I love you, Lyric."

"I . . . I don't—"

"Don't worry about the bills. I'll take care of all of that. They're all already set up to come out of my checking account anyway. So, what do you say? You wanna be my house sitter?" He grinned.

She kissed him full on the mouth, not a doubt in her mind that anywhere Jeremiah and she were together would be their home. She needed to be with him just as much as he needed her.

"Yes, Jeremiah, I would love to be your house sitter. Just as long as you promise me that you will never, ever cook in our kitchen."

"Oh, no doubt. You know I can do that! I promise."

"Well, we got one more thing to look at before we leave here," she told him.

"What's that? I thought we got everything."

"Mattresses!"

Lyric's parents took the news of her moving in with Jeremiah much better than she thought they would. She had prepared herself for the lecture that she knew her father would give and the tongue-thrashing/temper tantrum from her mother. Both of them gave them her blessing, though, which came as a total surprise to her. Her father had always been protective, but she figured he had just accepted the fact that she was growing up.

"Okay, you're going to have to leave some of these clothes here," Jeremiah warned as he looked at the boxes and bags she had started packing her belongings in. "We don't have that much closet space, and you're only getting three dresser drawers."

She walked over and kissed his neck. "Only three dresser drawers? Baby, I thought we were going to get the armoire and you were going to use those dressers for your stuff. Remember?"

He groaned and she rubbed her knee against his crotch. He grabbed her by the wrist and replied, "Your feminine ways ain't gonna work. Don't even try it."

Lyric pouted her lips. "Please, baby. I don't wanna leave my stuff. I wanna take it home."

She could see she had clearly won and wasn't surprised when he said, "Fine, I'm going to let you have your funky-tail dresser drawers, but only because I'm gonna be gone most of the time."

She hopped up and hugged him. "I love you."

"Yeah, whatever. I thought you had outgrown that manipulating men to get your way stuff."

"I did. Now I only manipulate *my* man to get my way. Now, hurry up so we can get home and I can really manipulate you."

By the time they had moved all of her stuff in, they were both too tired to manipulate anything. The sound of the doorbell woke them, and they both got off the floor where they had fallen asleep. They were pleased to see Jeremiah's mom standing outside the door.

"Mom. What a nice surprise. It's what, eight o'clock in the morning and you're here to visit." Jeremiah gave her a kiss on the cheek and took the bags she was carrying.

"Good morning to you too. I actually came to bring you two some groceries, something I know you all don't have. Am I right?"

Lyric hugged her and confirmed, "You're definitely right, and we appreciate you for it."

They went into the kitchen, where Lyric helped Jeremiah put away the food.

"Where's Alicia?" Jeremiah asked. Lyric kept her comments to herself, thinking that anywhere his psychotic sister was other than around her was the best place for her.

"I don't know where that girl is. She didn't come home again last night," Mrs. Woods said with a sigh.

"Okay, Mom. You act like she's never stayed out all night before. She was probably with Raven."

"No, that's the thing. Even Raven has been kind of worried and asking about her. There's something going on with your sister. I know it."

"I think you're just over-reacting, Ma. Alicia has always been the good apple, don't forget."

"Well, something about the way she's acting these days is telling me she's about to be rotten. I know she ain't perfect. I know about all those times I worked a double and she and Omar were screwing while I wasn't home. I ain't crazy." She walked out of the

279

kitchen. "Where is your kitchen table and chairs? I thought you said you had all your furniture."

"We bought it, but somehow they forgot the kitchen set and some more stuff."

"Like what?"

"The bed!" Lyric blurted.

Mrs. Woods began laughing. "I guess you all didn't get the chance to christen your bedroom last night, huh?"

Lyric and Jeremiah laughed and looked at each other as if to say, *Think again.*

19

The day Jeremiah's boat left, Lyric thought she would die. Her heart began aching that morning, and by the time they made the trip to the dock, she was a wreck.

"Lyric, baby, you gotta calm down or you're not gonna be able to drive. I love you and all, but if something happens to my truck because you can't see though them tears, I'm gonna have to hurt you. Now come on. We're still gonna talk every day and email."

She didn't know whether to be angry at his lack of emotion or her over emotion. This was all new to her. The night before, he asked her if she was sure she could handle it all. At first she was unsure of his question, but then she realized that for the first time in a very long time, not only did she have the challenge of being faithful, but being faithful to a man who would be gone for six months. She had to ask herself that very same question. But when she looked into his eyes and her heart nearly skipped a beat, she knew she wouldn't have a problem. Just the thought of Jeremiah Woods made her shudder with glee, and there was no way in hell she was going to lose him. She assured him that she would remain true to him, and he accepted her word.

"Okay, I'll call you tonight. Okay?" he said as he got out of the truck. She got out and helped him get his bags, unable to speak.

When he had unloaded, he took her into his arms and said, "I love you. You know that, right? I just want you to be safe and take care of yourself. If there's anything you need, you just let me know. You understand?"

The tears began falling once again, and he held her tight. She knew there was no way she could let him get on that boat without letting the words come from her mouth. "I love you too, Jeremiah. I love you. I need for you to be safe and know that I won't let you down."

"I know you won't." He hugged her one last time before grabbing his bags. Mack was standing nearby waiting for him. "Go ahead and get out of here," he told her. She tried to smile at him through her tears as she hopped back into the truck.

281

She had just gotten onto the Jersey Turnpike when her cell began to ring. She answered and was happy to hear Jeremiah's voice.

"I miss you already," he told her.

"Me too."

"You didn't even notice the gift I gave you," he told her.

"What gift?" she asked.

"Look at your arm," he said.

She looked down at her arm, glancing at her bracelet. At first, she didn't notice because of all the others, but then she saw a new charm there. It read: *#1 Wife.*

"Jeremiah . . . " was all she could say.

"Don't worry. I'm going to propose the right way. I just wanted you to get used to wearing it."

"I'll wear it with pride," she beamed.

"Sweetie, there's one more thing I need to ask before I go."

"What's up?"

"I know you and my sister got beef, and I accept that. But my moms is really worried about her. If you find out that she's into something that ain't her, then handle that for me."

Lyric knew that it had taken a lot for him to ask that. He had been worried about Alicia for a while now, she could tell. A part of her made believed that it was her fault by bragging to the younger girl about the men she used and the games she played with them.

She knew Alicia didn't have a reason to trust her. She had to change that. For that reason alone, she knew it was on her to try, no matter what, to make amends with her, for Jeremiah's sake.

"I got you, baby. Don't worry. I'll make sure that she's okay."

20

Alicia could not believe that her brother had left without talking to her. It was her own fault, though. Her mother told her that Jeremiah had been looking for her, but she already knew it. He left several messages on her cell phone, and she never returned his call. She was pissed at him because she found out that he and Lyric were living together. She had hoped that she would be able to use his place as a "spot" with Tony, but that tramp had spoiled that plan. Alicia didn't worry about it, though. Lyric would get her payback soon enough.

On the other hand, things with Tony were going well. She had expressed her need for a car, and he promised that by Christmas she would have one. Everything was looking good on that end, but something was still missing. *Love.* As hard as she tried to convince herself that love didn't matter, she knew that it wasn't working. She didn't love Tony and never would. She was using him.

Deep down, she knew that she still loved Omar. She often thought about the times they shared and was tempted to pick up the phone and call him, but her pride wouldn't allow her. If only she hadn't left her phone at work the day she quit, leaving an open window of opportunity for Lyric to get to her man, they might still be together. Sometimes she wondered if she had overreacted that day.

Hindsight is always twenty-twenty and there was no use looking back, she told herself as she grabbed her bag and headed out the door. She stopped dead in her tracks when she saw Lyric standing out front. She stopped and turned the other way, not having the mental energy to curse her out.

"Alicia, wait," Lyric called to her.

Alicia kept walking, hoping she wouldn't follow. She felt a hand on her shoulder and she snatched away. "Don't touch me!"

"I need to talk to you, seriously. Just give me two minutes. That's all I need to say what I have to say. Then I promise I'll leave you alone."

Alicia paused and looked at her. Lyric was as gorgeous as ever, but there something different about her. She seemed stress-free, and Alicia could see the happiness in her face. If she didn't know any better, she would have thought Lyric was in love.

"What?"

"Alicia, I know that you and I have our differences, but we're worried about you."

"Who the hell is we?"

"Your mom and your brother and hell, even me."

"You? Since when do you care about me? As far as my mother and brother are concerned, they know that I'm fine, so please don't add concern for me as part of your little act. Both of them may be fooled by it, but I'm not. I guess you really hit the jackpot when you got my brother. You got a new crib and a ride, all from a man that's hardly ever here. That gives you free reign to keep doing your thing since he ain't gonna be here."

"That's not true, Alicia. I will admit that I did some dirty deeds when it came to other men, but I don't have to play games with Jeremiah. There was no need to. He loved me for me. You were the one that warned me that I would never find my true love if I didn't stop treating men like toys. When I got to know Jeremiah, I didn't want to lose him, and I knew that it was time for me to stop."

"Somehow, I don't want to believe I had anything to do with the sad fact that you're with my brother. I don't trust you, and there's nothing you can do or say that will make me accept you, so you can stop trying. Your two minutes is up, and I have to go." Alicia walked away.

Lyric inhaled deeply, thinking that the conversation actually went better than she thought it would. She had pictured another screaming match between herself and her future sister-in-law. Suddenly, she was exhausted, and decided to go home and take a nap before going to work. She needed to revive herself before dealing with Conner.

21

"Well, what does it say?" Conner asked, standing over her. He had followed her out of the bathroom into the lounge. She scolded herself for telling him what was going on, knowing he would bug her to death until they knew for sure. She flopped down into the chair, her head leaning back against the wall. Conner stood directly in front of her.

"I can't look," she said, handing him the plastic stick wrapped in a paper towel. He hesitated but then took it from her. She closed her eyes, not wanting to see his reaction.

"Well," he said.

She opened her eyes and asked, "Well, what?"

"I'm going be an auntie!" Conner gushed and pulled her to her feet.

She stood, shocked by what he had just said. Numb with feear, dhe didn't return his hugs.

Never in a million years did Lyric think she would be having a baby. Being pregnant was the furthest thing from her mind. She had been on the pill since she was sixteen and had never missed one. There had to be a mistake. She had the flu, and that was all there was to it. She tried to tell Conner that when he first mentioned her continual tiredness. By the time she got to work, she could barely keep her eyes open. She told him it was because of Jeremiah leaving and a lack of sleep, but he insisted that she take a pregnancy test, and now things weren't looking good.

"What's wrong? Aren't you happy? This is a good thing."

"How? Jeremiah is gone for six months. I'm not ready for a child. I want to finish school and live my life. I don't want this. I can't do this."

"Wait a minute, Lyric. Don't make any rash decisions. A baby will not stop you from doing any of that. You're being ridiculous. He loves you, and this baby is a result of that love. Talk to him."

Lyric heard what Conner was saying, but her mind was telling her she needed to do what she had to do. She thought this was karma's way of getting her back.

She remained despondent for the remainder of the day, and didn't even get out of bed for the next two days. She tried to sound normal when Jeremiah called, but he sensed something was wrong.

"Are you sure everything's okay? You sound funny."

"I'm fine. I'm just worn out from working, and I'm still trying to get the house together."

"Well, try to get some rest, baby. I don't want you to be worn out when I get home."

"Don't worry. By the time you get here, I'll be fine. Jeremiah?"

"Yeah?"

"I . . . I . . . " She tried to gather the courage to tell him.

"What is it? What's wrong?"

"Nothing. I love you, that's all."

"I love you too. I'll call you tomorrow. Get some sleep."

She lay in bed and hovered under the covers. Her eyes were red and swollen from crying. Finally, she got up enough nerve to dial her parent's number.

"Hey, Mama," she said. Hearing her mother's voice seemed to bring some calm to her chaotic mind.

"Hey, sweetie. What's wrong?"

"How do you figure something's wrong, Mom?"

"It's after eleven o'clock at night, Lyric." Her mother laughed.

Lyric looked over at the clock. "I am so sorry, Mama. I didn't know it was that late."

"That's okay. I was up anyway."

"Where's Daddy?"

"Working late, as usual. Have you talked to Jeremiah?"

"Yes, I talked to him earlier. He's fine and sends his love."

"So, what's on your mind?"

"Mom, have you ever done anything that you thought would make Dad leave you?"

"Hmmm, that's a hard question. Let me think. I think that there are some bad decisions that both your father and I made that made us question our relationship. Neither one of us is perfect. But I think the love that we have for each other makes us overcome our faults. I've learned to know that love is tolerant."

"I don't ever remember you having to tolerate anything. I always thought you and Daddy had the perfect marriage. I never saw you all fight or disagree. To me it was all gravy."

"All gravy?" Her mother laughed. "That's because we were determined to not expose you to any of our drama. I didn't want you to grow up with a distorted view of relationships between men and women. Our common goal was your success and happiness. And judging by the way you turned out, we succeeded. Is there something going on with you and Jeremiah?"

Lyric was now feeling guiltier than when she called. "No, we're fine."

"Well, I hope I've given you some insight. I know it's hard being there by yourself, and I'm proud of you. You're already experiencing some of the tests of love. You're willing to tolerate solitude when you know it's the one thing in life you've always avoided. You always had to be with someone. Now the one person you want to be with is halfway around the world."

"You're right. I'm going to bed, Mom. I'll talk to you tomorrow."

"Okay, baby. I love you."

After tossing and turning for hours, Lyric finally fell asleep.

22

Alicia walked into her mother's room and quietly called her name. She knew her mother had been worried about her even before Lyric mentioned it. It was time for Alicia to have a talk with her mother.

"Mom?"

"Yeah." Her mother looked up from the television.

"I need to talk to you."

Her mother clicked off the TV and sat up in her bed. Alicia sat down beside her.

"What's going on, Alicia?"

"I went to the doctor." Alicia's voice was barely above a whisper.

"And?"

"And I'm pregnant."

Her mother just stared at her wordlessly. Alicia couldn't tell if she was hurt, angry, upset or just shocked. She looked down into her lap, waiting for some type of response. She heard her mother take a deep breath, and she prepared herself for whatever came next.

"I don't know what to say, Alicia. I would like to think that this wasn't something you planned on happening, since you're not married, don't have a decent job with benefits nor do you have a degree. It's not like you didn't know how to prevent this from happening, since we've had this talk several times. So, I guess I'll start with the basics. Who's the father? What is he saying?"

When she first found out she was carrying Tony's baby, Alicia was elated. Her plan had worked better than she could've imagined. The initial excitement wore off quickly, however, when she realized what it meant to be carrying his child. She was suddenly all alone and didn't know where to go. Jeremiah was gone, and her mother was the only person who could help her figure out this mess.

She told her mother about the married man she had been seeing for the past few months, and the child that was now the result.

"Are you mad?" Alicia asked.

Her mother paused and finally said, "No, there's no need to be mad. You made the decision to be with this man, now you have to deal with the consequences. But why would you sleep with a man you don't love? A married man, at that?"

"I didn't mean for it to turn out like this, I swear. I just wanted . . . I don't know what I wanted." Alicia's original plan for being with Tony really did seem pointless at this moment.

"Alicia, I warned you a while back that you were traveling down a dangerous road. Hanging out with Raven and getting drunk, the way you started dressing, your whole demeanor changed. I thought you were getting yourself back together when you started dating Mack, but then you kicked him to the curb. I just don't understand."

"I don't understand either. It's like I'm someone else sometimes, Mama. Someone I don't want to be." She thought about Lyric. "But then it became easier and easier to be her. I wanted to prove—"

"Prove what? Alicia, you don't have to prove anything to anybody. You don't have to be anyone else except you."

She could sense her mother's frustration. "You don't understand. No one will understand. I'm sorry, Mama." Alicia got up and left the house.

She walked down the street, trying to figure out what to do next. She was deep in thought when she felt a hand on her shoulder. When she turned around, she saw Omar standing there. He looked great. His held was bald, making him look sexier than ever. The smell of his cologne teased her, and it took everything she had not to reach out and touch his face. She would have done just about anything to have him hold her at that moment.

"Man, I been calling your name forever. You ain't hear me?" he asked.

"No, I'm sorry. I was thinking about something," she told him.

"Must be one hell of a thought. What's going on? You all right? You look funny."

"I fucked up, and I don't know what I'm going to do." She shrugged.

"What do you mean? What's going on, Alicia?"

289

His concern made her feel even worse. He had always been a comfort to her whenever she needed it, and now she needed him more than ever. But as she thought about the way she treated him during the past months, she knew she had no right to even think about leaning on him.

"I'm sorry, Omar. I am the stupidest woman in the world. I had a good man and I let you go, like a fool."

"Alicia, it's okay. You didn't let me go. I let you walk away. But I'm here now. Tell me what's going on. Talk to me." He put his hand on her shoulder.

"I can't right now. I messed my life up and I don't know what I'm gonna do."

"Let me help you then," he told her.

Alicia looked at him and saw the love in his eyes. *He still loves me. After all that's gone down, it's me that he still loves.*

A horn began blaring from a delivery truck across the street, and a guy yelled, "Hey, O. Nigga, come on. We gon' be late."

Omar waved at him then faced Alicia. "Look, I promised my man I would help him drop this furniture off in Philly. I wanna finish this. I'll be back in the morning. Can you meet me for breakfast?"

Alicia didn't know whether to agree. A part of her wanted to scream "yes!" while another part told her there was no point. *What? Are you going to discuss baby names over pancakes? Oh, I know. You all can discuss how you want to decorate the nursery.*

"I don't think so, Omar. You'd better go. Your boys are waiting."

23

Someone was in the apartment. Lyric could feel the presence when she walked in the door. There was something different from when she left this morning. She had been at the doctor, who confirmed that she was about to be a mother. Now, she had come home to call Jeremiah, but when she heard a noise coming from the bedroom, she was afraid.

She grabbed the wooden bat that she kept near the door and held it over her shoulder as she crept further into the living room. She heard the noise again, and her heart began pounding. She continued down the hallway, determined to protect her home and do some damage the invader. The bedroom door creaked and she prepared herself to knock the hell out of whoever was about to come out.

"Ahhhhh!" She screamed as she closed her eyes and swung the bat over her head. It made a loud noise as she missed her target and hit the wall instead, leaving a dent.

"What the hell?"

She opened her eyes and was almost floored when she saw Jeremiah standing in front of her. She ran and jumped into his arms.

"What are you doing here? I thought you were a burglar."

"And what were you going to do, strike me out? Your swing ain't shit," he said with a laugh then kissed her.

"I can't believe you're here. What happened? I don't care. I'm just glad to see you. I missed you so much." She hugged him tight.

"We were headed out and the electrical system started tripping, so we had to pull back in. The raggedy-ass ship still ain't fixed," he told her. "I was gonna surprise you at work, but they told me you had a doctor's appointment. You sick?"

She grabbed his hand and led him into the living room. They sat on the sofa and she said, "You know I've been tired these past few weeks."

"I thought it was due to stress with everything that was going on with school and the move," he questioned with a look of concern on his face.

"I did too, I swear. But I took a pregnancy test."

"A pregnancy test?" He frowned, and she became worried about his reaction.

"Yes. At first I took one out the store and it came back positive. So, I went to the doctor to make sure."

"And?"

"It came back positive too. I'm pregnant," she whispered.

He let her hand drop from his and stared at the floor. She knew he was not ready for this, and now she questioned whether she should have even told him.

"I'm sorry. I know neither one of us wanted this, and I swear I ain't plan it. I know we aren't ready for a baby. I don't have to go through with it."

"You don't want our baby?"

She looked into his face and tried to read his thoughts but couldn't. She didn't want to say the wrong thing. Out of all the times she had this conversation, this was the first time that there was some honesty to it, and she was scared. She wanted to say the right thing but didn't know what the right thing was.

"I don't . . . I can't . . . I don't know." She shrugged. "I never planned on ever having to deal with this. I never thought I would ever have a child. I mean, the thought never entered my mind."

"So, what do you want, Lyric?"

"I want you, Jeremiah. I want us to be together. I want us to be happy. We're just getting started in this relationship and I don't want anything that may break us apart before we really get together. I want to do what's best for us."

"How do you know this baby isn't what's best for us? This may be the thing that brings us closer than we can ever be. It's a part of both of us. I can't tell you what to do, Lyric. Whatever the decision is, I'll support you a hundred percent, and I'm going to love you no matter what."

"But you're gone six months out of the year, Jeremiah. Don't you want to be there when your son or daughter takes their first steps, says their first words? And what about me? I don't want to be stuck working a dead-end job at the gym forever. I can't go back to school with a child."

"You want me to get off the ship, I will. I can get another job. I'll work ten jobs if I have to. I can be on the ship *and* work ten jobs. Not just because of the baby, either. I'll do it for you, for us."

The phone rang and Lyric was relieved. She reached for the cordless and saw that it was his mother's number. "Does your mom know you're home?"

"No, I went straight to the gym then came straight here. I didn't even call anyone."

"Hello," Lyric answered on the third ring.

"Hello, Lyric. It's Mrs. Woods. Am I disturbing you?"

"No, Mrs. Woods. I'm not doing anything at all."

"I called because I need to talk to someone and well, I don't know why I called," she responded.

Lyric could hear the anxiety in her voice and knew she had been crying. She looked over at Jeremiah then said, "Don't worry. I'm on my way."

24

Lyric and Jeremiah sat silently as his mother told them everything Alicia told her. Lyric could not believe that Alicia was having an affair with a married man. She was so much better than that. She saw the anger building in Jeremiah as her mother continued, and when she told them that Alicia was pregnant, she felt his entire body tense. She began rubbing his back and leaned on his shoulder.

"Where is she now?" he demanded.

"She's asleep in her room. Pretty much what she's been doing the past few days."

Lyric gave Jeremiah a knowing look. "Is she okay physically? Has she been to the doctor?"

"Yes, I took her yesterday and everything is fine. I just can't believe this. Alicia has done a 180-degree turn over the past few months. I don't know what got into her." Mrs. Woods shook her head.

"Has the father been here? Have you talked to him? What is he saying?" Jeremiah stood up.

"She won't even tell me who he is. She said that it doesn't matter because she doesn't love him anyway."

There was a knock, and Jeremiah opened the door. Omar greeted him, but Jeremiah didn't respond.

"Is this a bad time? I came to see Alicia. Is she here?"

"She's here, but she's 'sleep." Jeremiah gazed angrily at Omar.

"Well, can I come in for a minute? I need to talk to you anyway," Omar replied.

"Yeah, we do need to talk. Come on in. Let's talk about you taking care of your responsibilities." Jeremiah stood back, allowing Omar to enter.

"What responsibility? What are you talking about?" Omar seemed confused, "How're you doing Ms. Woods? What's up, Lyric?"

"Hi, Omar. Jeremiah, now is not the time." Ms. Woods shook her head.

"When the hell is the right time then?" Jeremiah's voice got louder.

"Calm down, Jeremiah. Yelling is not going to help this situation," Lyric told him.

"She hasn't even decided if she's gonna have the baby," Lyric said.

"Baby, what baby?" Omar's eyes were as wide as saucers.

"It's not Omar's. I told you she said the father is married. I don't know what she's gonna do. It's like she doesn't care anymore." Mrs. Woods sighed. "I'm glad you're home. You just don't know how glad I was to see you standing there with Lyric when I opened that door."

"Don't worry, Ma. I'll take care of everything." He gave her a hug.

"Take care of what?" Alicia asked, entering the room wearing a tank top and some pajama bottoms. Her hair was pulled back in a ponytail, and she looked more like a 12-year-old than the pregnant 21-year-old that she was.

"The situation that you've gotten yourself into, young lady. I can't believe you could do this!" Jeremiah yelled.

"Who do you think you are coming in here trying to be my daddy? You'd better check yourself and come again," Alicia hissed at him.

"Girl, I will slap you into the middle of next week. How can you be stupid enough to get knocked up by a married man? Stupid, just stupid!"

"Jeremiah! That's enough. I told you yelling isn't gonna help," Lyric interjected.

"You need to shut the hell up. This ain't got nothing to do with you. I thought you were gonna be smart enough and be quiet, but you just have to put your two cents in, don't you?" Alicia flared. Jeremiah rushed toward her, but Omar jumped in front of him before he could get to her.

"Hold on, there, Jeremiah."

Alicia didn't even realize Omar was even there. "What the hell is this, an intervention? What are you doing here?"

"Alicia, we're only trying to help. I'm beginning to think your brother is right about you being stupid," Mrs. Woods told her daughter.

Alicia began laughing like she had lost her mind. "That's hilarious. I'm stupid! He's dating a woman that's been with more men than the ship's crew, not to mention she slept with my ex-boyfriend."

"That's a damn lie! I never slept with him. What is she talking about?" Lyric turned to Omar.

Alicia continued. "He's got her living in his house, driving his car, and I'm stupid. And Mama, you welcoming her all up in your house like she's Mother Theresa when she's playing your son like an accordion. You're the stupid ones!"

"Hold on, Alicia. I don't have a problem with you disrespecting me, but I refuse to stand here and allow you to disrespect your mother and brother. You're acting like a child, but when you were out there sleeping with a married man, you were as grown as any other woman. Your family is here to support you, and you're treating them like they've done something to you," Lyric berated her.

"They have. But you know that. They're loyalty no longer lies with me. It's all about you, Lyric. And since you are so great, I decided to become just like you. See, being with that married man wasn't that hard. I just played the game and got into his head. I got everything I could get from him before he got me or found someone else to replace me with when he got tired of me. I took advantage of that opportunity. Sound familiar?" Alicia smirked.

Lyric listened as Alicia threw her own words back in her face. She was appalled by what Alicia was saying. "Yeah, real familiar. That was me sounding ridiculous, thinking I was all that, and I'm ashamed that I ever spoke those words. But I don't have time for playing games anymore, and neither do you. We're both better than that. It's time for us to grow the hell up and face facts. I love your brother, and I'm about to be his wife and the mother of your niece or nephew." She reached back and grabbed Jeremiah's hand.

Alicia's eyes widened and she wore a wicked grin. "Oh, so it's like that? Game over?"

"Game over," Lyric said with conviction.

"Fine then, Ms. Lyric. And since we're all about facing facts and coming to terms, you need to accept that I am about to be the mother of your little brother or sister."

"What?" Lyric demanded, trying to understand.

"Let me break it down for you since you don't seem to get it. The father of my baby is Anthony Crenshaw. That's right, your perfect father who would never ever disrespect your mother or his marriage. The man that was too smart and strong to fall for a woman playing games. Guess what, honey? He fell, and he fell hard. Hmm, are you disappointed?"

Lyric stared at Alicia, unable to move.

She's lying. She's saying whatever she thinks she can to get to you. There's no way that can be true.

She looked at Jeremiah, who seemed just as stunned as she was.

"Alicia, tell me you're making this up," her mother pleaded.

"If she's not, then that's some foul shit," Omar said.

"No more foul than you sleeping with her," Alicia snapped. "Payback is a bitch, ain't it, Lyric? We're tit for tat now. You got my boyfriend, and I got your dad."

"I never slept with him. I don't know why you're even saying that." Lyric's heart was beating so fast that she thought she could hear it. It took all she could not to punch Alicia in the face.

"I've been telling her that for months, but she doesn't believe me," Omar said.

"So you planned all of this, Alicia? This was all some sort of revenge scheme you came up with? This is ridiculous." Mrs. Woods folded her arms and walked away.

"I've gotta go," Lyric announced. "I can't stand here with her anymore."

"Me either," Jeremiah agreed.

Alicia was left alone with Omar. She flopped down on the sofa. He continued staring at her silently.

"What? Can you stop staring and say something?"

"What do you want me to say, Alicia?"

She wanted him to say that he loved her, that he needed her. Her goal of devastating Lyric was complete, and now that she realized Omar still wanted to be in her life, she felt better about her situation. But she still needed him to tell her the truth.

"I want you to say you still love me. That you want us to move on. I want you to say we can get past all of this nonsense and everything's gonna be all right. I don't expect you to understand why I did what I did, but tell me you forgive me." She looked up at him.

Omar put his arms around Alicia. She leaned into his chest as he embraced her. "Payback's a bitch, huh?" he said.

She looked up at him, realizing he was finally about to tell her the truth regarding him and Lyric. "Omar, can you be honest and tell me the truth, please?"

"Yeah, I can. You know how you asked me to forgive you? I need to know that you'll be able to do the same for me. I ain't even gonna lie. I was cheating, Alicia."

She inhaled sharply and told him, "I know you were. But Lyric seduced you, Omar, and you fell for it. I forgive you, but I still can't believe you fucked her."

Omar stiffened. "Alicia, Lyric isn't the one I was fucking. It was Raven."

Alicia closed her eyes, feeling faint. She saw a vision of Lyric standing before her, smiling as the words came out of her mouth . . . *So you see, I learned a long time ago that you can't trust bitches or niggas.*